Lorna Windham

© Lorna Windham, 2019
Published by:
Tyne Bridge Publishing,
City Library, Newcastle upon Tyne, United Kingdom

www.tynebridgepublishing.org.uk

The right of Lorna Windham to be identified as the author of this work has been asserted by her in accordance with Sections 77 and 78 of the Copyright, Design and Patents Act 1988.

All rights reserved. No part of this publication may be reproduced, stored in a retrieval system or transmitted, in any form or by any means, electronic, mechanical, recording or otherwise, in any part of the world, without the prior written permission of the publisher.

This book is sold subject to the condition that it shall not, by way of trade or otherwise, be lent, resold, hired out, or otherwise circulated without the publisher's prior consent in any form of binding or cover other than that in which it is published and without a similar condition, including this condition, being imposed on the subsequent purchaser.

This book is a work of fiction.

I would like to thank my friends and family who have helped me not just write this novel, but to finish The Code of Honour Trilogy. Many thanks to my daughter Katherine for the overall title of the trilogy. It's nice to know she and Eleanor have enjoyed reading the novels. I must thank my husband David, for his critical eye and advice.

Also, a special thanks to the late Father John Ball MHM, who kindly gave me the correct Latin text which added to the authenticity and drama of several scenes

.

I owe a great deal of thanks to the vision and hard work of David Hepworth of Tyne Bridge Publishing, his team and Editor, Vanessa Histon.

CHAPTER One
Autumn 1732

Kirsty Lorne knew the moment she loved Johnnie Stewart. At four years old she sat barefoot in the dirt. An ant scrambled over the mountain of her knuckles. The weather-beaten sign of *The Salmon* creaked overhead and drunken songs seeped from the inn.

A repetitive tap on a window made Kirsty turn round. Father stood beside a large, grey-bearded man. Her brow creased. Father motioned with his chin and she smiled. The man nodded. Father slapped him on the back, fell into his seat and split a pack of cards. The drunken beast held Father in its claws and his laughter crashed over her in waves. *Wish I could make him happy.*

Then Father stopped, stared at his cards and hurled them on the table. He staggered to his feet, face crimson and eyes wild. Kirsty's hand covered her crumpled mouth. *I've nowhere to hide.* Father shook his head. She watched the big man raise his fist. Father's shoulders slumped. The ant burrowed itself under a grain of soil.

***

Six year old Johnnie Stewart whistled as he strolled along the muddy track towards the inn. He'd an ash pole over one shoulder and a wet gunny sack in his hand. It contained the largest salmon he'd ever caught. Proof for his brothers he could fish with the best of them. The Stewart household would eat well tonight. A child's wail and a low, gruff voice drifted towards him from beyond the bend in the track ahead.

A large, bearded man trudged into sight. He clasped the hand of a small, golden-haired girl. She shrieked and screamed as he dragged her along behind him. 'I want my mammy. Please sir, I want my mammy.'

The Jacobite Affair

Johnnie stood, arms on hips and legs apart and blocked the man's path. 'Why, it's wee Kirsty isn't it, Mrs. Lorne's bairn? What you doing, sir?'

The man blew out his weather-veined cheeks. 'Mind your own business, you little snot, or I'll be givin' you some of this.' He threatened Johnnie with the large knotted stick he carried in one hand.

'Let Kirsty go.'

'And if I dinna?'

Johnnie bunched his fingers into fists.

'You'd take me on would you, wee man? Well, let me tell you, I'm goin' about my lawful business. Won her in a game of cards from her daddy, didn't I?'

Won her? Johnnie's brain tried to work it out. In a game of cards? You didn't play for bairns. Well, he and his brothers didn't, they played for pebbles, but he'd not tell the man that.

Kirsty pleaded, 'I want to go home. I want my mammy.' Tears glistened, then drew lines of dirt down her face.

Johnnie studied the man and tried to remember what his oldest brother Rob always said: there's more ways to skin a cat.

The man held Kirsty in a tighter grip as she clawed at his fist. 'Let me go.'

'I'll trade you.' Johnnie's heart sank as he said it. His brothers would never see his fine catch.

'Will you now?'

'Yes, this salmon for her.' He held it up in front of him. 'It's fresh from the burn this morning.'

'That tiddler?' The man laughed and showed black stubs for teeth as Kirsty wriggled in his grasp.

Johnnie bunched his fists again.

'Jock Sinclair, return my daughter, this minute.' Leather-faced Mrs. Lorne bowled down the track towards them. She wielded a rolling pin in one fist and reminded Johnnie of an irate sporran.

Lorna Windham

'Now, Mrs. Lorne, I won her fair and square.' The man backed away with a wary look in his eyes. 'Your Fergus owes me money.'

The sporran drew back her arm and thwacked him across the forehead with her wooden weapon. He dropped like a felled tree.

Kirsty stared at Johnnie and her gaze never left his.

The sporran yanked at Kirsty's hand. 'Hmph. Your father wouldn't have done it if you'd been a son.' She hauled her daughter back along the track. Johnnie lost sight of Kirsty as she rounded the bend, headed towards her mother's farm.

The Jacobite Affair

CHAPTER Two
Winter 1742

At fourteen, that incident still burned in Kirsty's breast. *Why had Father done it?* The question remained unanswered even as his coffin was lowered into the grave.

The wind moaned down the farmhouse's chimney and rain drummed against the windows as Kirsty's mother, dressed in black, sat by the kitchen's meagre fire and eased off her worn boots. 'That churchyard's freezing, I'm wet through.'

Kirsty stood at the table. The damp shoulders of her patched, drab dress reminded her of the steady fall of rain throughout the funeral. *Don't think of Father in the cold ground.* Her hands gripped the table a she steadied herself. She took her coarse apron from its hook and tied it round her thin waist. A rabbit hung from an overhead beam. Her nose wrinkled, but she ignored its dead eyes and soft fur, placed it on the table and brought down a cleaver on the rabbit's leg joints. Thwack. Thwack. Thwack. Thwack.

Mother rubbed her stocking feet. 'When you've made the stew, you can clean these, they're covered in mud. I don't want it trailed round the house. Then fetch some peat.'

Kirsty set her teeth and pulled the rabbit's fur down its silver skin. She'd been fortunate to trap it. She stopped, wiped her eyes with her sleeve and took a deep breath before she gutted the carcase and cut the backbone away from the meat.

'I'm glad it's over.' Mother lifted the pile of bills from the table and waved them at Kirsty. 'He left us nought, but debt.'

'We'll manage, Mother,' Kirsty sniffed.

'How? There's just us to work the land and tend the cattle. If only I'd married better and had live sons. Not that anyone cares.'

Kirsty bit her lip. Three sons. They'd have been men now, worked with the black cattle, planted kale, onions and carrots, mended the farmhouse and done hundreds of jobs on their land. She glanced at the letters on the table. 'Aunt Lizzie cares and your friend… Mrs. Balfour and her daughter Peggie.'

'If only you were like her and an heiress.' Mother folded her arms. 'No one of substance came to his funeral. Just some of his cronies and that Johnnie Stewart.'

'Mother, Aunt Lizzie's in Inverness and the Balfours live in Edinburgh. Uncle Hughie and Aunty Mary came. You like Hughie.'

'Hmph. And they knew him for what he was, a spendthrift and drunk. The shame of it.'

'Mother.'

'Now you're older you should understand these things. You'll have to do more to earn your keep, my girl.'

'Course I will.'

'Of course.'

'Of course.' *No matter how hard I try, I'll never talk the way she does, the way a Tolbain does.* Kirsty looked at Mother. She'd grey hair scraped back into a bun, a long red nose, deep tracks between eyebrows and ploughed lines which dragged at her mouth. *She looks older than forty and if she's any love inside her, I've never seen it. No kind word ever passes her lips.*

Sometimes Kirsty longed for love. She'd watched the Stewart brothers and how their mother, the laird's wife, had a smile for each of her sons and smothered them in embraces and kisses. When they were younger, Rob fought to be free, Johnnie held onto her, Euan wrapped his arms round her and Duncan clung to her legs. *How I wanted one of her kisses.*

Once, when she'd been eight, she and Johnnie played in the Stewart's orchard. They'd collected windfalls and gave bruised apples to Johnnie's mother. Mrs. Stewart had stood arms akimbo and beamed. She'd kissed Johnnie whose face went bright pink and then Kirsty's cheek.

'Mother never does that.'

Mrs. Stewart gave her a puzzled look. 'You can have a hug from me whenever you want. It's nice to have another wee lassie close, there's too many men in this house.'

The Jacobite Affair

Johnnie grinned at Kirsty. 'See, you're in our gang.' He'd led her to his three brothers and Morag up to their knees in a peaty burn under a cloudless sky.

'Let's hunt for its source,' said Rob as Johnnie and Kirsty trailed along behind. The children wandered east until the roar of water made them stop at the bottom of a couple of hanging waterfalls. The water pooled and then raced west and south towards the loch. Euan stumbled on the rocks and plunged into a beck. Rob and Johnnie raced after him. Kirsty remembered her panic and shouted, 'Help. Help.' But no adult came as Euan disappeared and bobbed up again.

'Swim,' screamed Morag. She whirled her arms round in a frenzy.

'Keep your head up,' shouted Rob.

'Grab something,' yelled Johnnie.

When Euan's auburn head disappeared, Rob dived and in a few strong strokes grabbed his brother by the scruff of the neck. Euan coughed and spat all the way to the bank. By this time, Kirsty, convinced of the worst, bunched her fists in her eyes.

'Oh stop greetin',' Morag stood hands on her slight hips. 'You're such a cry baby, Kirsty Lorne.'

'No I'm not.'

'Yes you are. How does your mother put up with you?'

Each word cut into Kirsty's heart. *How can she say that? She doesn't even have a mother.* She stared open-mouthed at Morag.

'That's spiteful, Morag.' Johnnie squeezed Kirsty's hand.

'Right, no one tells, or the adults will stop us coming here.' Rob's hand swept his raven hair behind his ears. 'We'll swear a blood oath.' He took out his dirk. 'Euan, you're first.' The children lined up behind him with Kirsty last. She glanced away as a thin red line appeared on each palm.

'Look at me when he does it,' whispered Johnnie.

Her turn came and she stared into Johnnie's grey-blue eyes and lost herself in them.

'Well done.' Rob smiled at her. 'Stings, doesn't it?'

'That reminds me,' said Morag. 'Father says we can pet our foal as long as we're gentle. He's let me have my own calf and hen too. Suppose you'll have to get back to your farm, Kirsty?'

I hate you and your curly, brown hair.

'Morag.' Rob shook his head.

'She didna mean it like that.' Euan took Morag's hand in his.

Johnnie put his arm round Kirsty's shoulder.

That Morag's always so sure of herself and has a father who loves her.

'Let's go,' Johnnie said.

Morag and Kirsty wove daisy and clover crowns for Rob whilst Johnnie and Euan carried him on their shoulders. Then legs buckled and they all collapsed in a heap of laughter.

As his brothers and Morag continued their walk east, Johnnie, one finger over his lips, grabbed Kirsty's hand and pulled her up the hillside. 'Come on. I've a secret.'

'Won't they miss us?' Kirsty watched as the children disappeared round a crag.

Johnnie shrugged. 'They'll get bored, go and play at the den.'

The den had a waterfall and a pool. 'Can we go? I like the waterfall and pool.'

Johnnie stood beside a withered oak and shrugged. 'Maybe later. Look, I found a deserted croft. Used to be Tam Soutar's.' The crumbled walls and holed roof stood in front of them.

She ran to a stone trough surrounded by purple-crowned thistles in the cobbled yard. 'Bet you can't guess what's here?'

Johnnie grinned. Then gathered clumps of heather and laid them on the croft's dirt floor.

'What you doing?' asked Kirsty.

'You'll see. You gather grass.'

She bent her back to the task and watched him heap the green stalks on top of the heather and fling himself on it with a whoop. She joined him in the croft's cool interior. Johnnie pointed out hawks and eagles through the ruined gap in the roof's thatch whilst Kirsty counted clouds.

'We can meet here whenever we want.' He pointed at the oak. 'Put a pebble in yon tree, as a sign to each other. What shall we call this place?'

Kirsty touched the cold walls and wondered who'd lived here. A sense of peace and happiness flooded over her. '*Our Place.*'

'Ow.' Kirsty put a hand to her ear. Mother's slap brought her back to her senses.

'Stop the daydreams and get on with our dinner.' Mother's words cut the air like sharp blades. 'Couldn't even pick a nice day to be buried. Husband? Useless, useless man.'

A warm tear rolled down Kirsty's cheek and she brushed it away. *I should have been a lad.* She sliced the meat into chunks and swept it into the pot which bubbled over the fire.

A knock sounded at the back door and Kirsty turned from her task.

'You carry on, I'll get it.' Mother wrapped a shawl round her bony shoulders.

Kirsty peeled a carrot. She diced it as she heard voices. The door rattled and a draught circled her ankles. Several carrots later the door slammed shut.

Mother returned. 'It's that Johnnie Stewart, gave us his condolences, if you please, and asked if you'd walk with him.'

'Can I, Mother?' Joy leapt in her throat as she untied the ribbons of her apron.

'Certainly not. Have you no sense of propriety? We'll be in mourning for months. That's what I told Johnnie Stewart. Why you're interested in him, I don't know. He's only the laird's third son. The one to set your cap at is the oldest, Rob. Pity they've sent him north. It'll all pass to him you know, the title, land and all the wealth. That's why the laird sent him away, to be trained. We just have to wait, he'll come home one day.'

Kirsty hunched her shoulders. 'I like Johnnie and he likes me.'

Mother snorted. 'What do you know about men and the ways of the world? Nothing. You need to listen to me, or we'll both end our days in penury. Suppose I'd better get on with the bread.' She upended a bowl and pummelled the dough.

Kirsty sliced an onion. Her eyes watered and she sniffed. She threw the vegetables into the cook pot along with chunks of rabbit, adjusted the heavy chain over the fire and wiped her hands on her apron. Her mother's arms worked in unison as Kirsty slipped past the smoke-blackened wicker fence into the byre as if to answer a call of nature. The cow lowed as Kirsty patted the beast's neck. She paused. Her sharp ears picked out the repetitive beat of Mother's fists.

Kirsty headed for the storage room at the end of the croft, rummaged for her shawl on a hook and put her hand on the wooden latch. She listened, then opened the door. It rattled. A blast of icy air made her face tingle. She grimaced and waited for Mother to miss a beat. Nothing. Sunlight made Kirsty blink and she shaded her eyes with one hand as the other closed the door. Winter's tendrils wrapped round her and she shivered. *Mother will miss me, but it'll be worth the beating.*

Johnnie waved. He'd waited as she knew he would. His cheeky grin lightened her heart. His long, bony wrists stuck out of his shirt sleeves and his breeches seemed short. He held out his hand and she grasped it. She loved all the warmth and wiry strength it contained.

She looked back at the thatched farmhouse which squatted on a wide strip of flat, frosted land littered with granite boulders. Johnnie tugged her onwards across the snow-covered pasture towards Loch Linnhe, a rippled pewter sheet which lay a mile north.

His brothers and Morag sat huddled together whilst they fished. Morag cupped her hand to Euan's ear and mouthed something. Only eleven year old Duncan seemed pleased to see her and waved. She shared her worries about Euan and Morag with Johnnie.

'You're trying too hard,' he said. 'Give them another chance and pretend it doesna matter.'

Easy for him to say.

The Jacobite Affair

Euan's words dragged her into the present. 'What did you bring her for?' he asked as his line jerked.

Rob, his blue eyes full of concern, nudged Euan.

The breath caught in Kirsty's throat.

'Cos, she's my lassie.' Johnnie squeezed Kirsty's hand.

Rob gave Johnnie a wink.

My lassie. Kirsty sensed Johnnie had said something momentous. She raised her head and looked at Morag who'd turned away to help Euan reel in the fish.

'*Our Place*?' whispered Johnnie and squeezed Kirsty's hand.

'*Our Place*,' said Kirsty and raced away in front of him.

CHAPTER Three
Spring 1743

Johnnie's brow wrinkled in a frown. He shifted from one foot to the other as he stood in front of his Mother in her sunlit sewing room. The green silk curtains and seat covers made it a restful room to enter, but his mind whirled with a long list of misdeeds for which he could be beaten. He looked at her from under his lashes, clenched his fists and prepared for the worst.

His mother put down her linen and thread and took a deep breath. 'Johnnie, be a sweetheart, make up with your father, do it for me.'

Johnnie's brow furrowed even more. 'But Mother, he's wrong. There's more ways to judge a man than his sword arm. He doesna' listen, thinks he's always right and demands I agree with him. He sent Rob away for years with the Macdonalds and now he means to send him to France when he graduates. And why does he see such little value in books? Can he no' see what's in them?'

Flustered, she swept her brown hair from her brow. 'He sees it. Your father's a clever man and a fine warrior, but hasna' had your schooling.'

'He willna stop me going to university, will he?'

'You'll go to Glasgow like your brothers in due course. I want my sons to have a greater knowledge of the world than their tenants, so does your father.'

'He'll no' let me. Promise you'll talk to him.'

She took his hand in hers and unclenched his fist. Her palm smooth and warm. 'I will, if you promise to apologise and speak to him in a civil manner in future.'

'But Mother...'

'I mean it Johnnie.' He pulled away. 'You're only sixteen...'

'Seventeen in a couple of months.'

'Seventeen soon and think you know everything.' Her mouth curved into a smile. 'When you're older you'll realise you knew nothing. Your father's head of the household, Laird, and deserves our respect as Rob will when the time comes.' She sighed. 'Sometimes I think you and your father are like two stags locking horns. Aye, you're his son, alright, you have his eyes and temper, but you also have responsibilities.' Her arms wrapped round his shoulders and she kissed his cheek.

Johnnie breathed in her rose scent and everything he loved.

'You're stubborn like him and always have been. It'll stand you well in life once you've learned when to give an inch.'

'Oh Mother, it's no' fair.'

'Nought is, laddie, I thought you'd have known that by now. Think yourself fortunate you've a good home and parents who want the best for you, though you may not think it at the moment. Know, whatever you do and wherever you go in life, we'll always love you.' Johnnie started to interrupt, but she raised her hand and stopped him. 'Your father doesna always show it and he's hard on you and your brothers, but he kens the world out there, how short life can be... these rebellions... he's got a good heart. He means you to be men who fear no one and are respected by all. Now, I wish my sons to be lovers of wisdom and honour, men who'll make us both proud one day. Be a good lad and do what I ask.'

'I will, but it's difficult agreeing with Father all the time. If I bite my tongue any more, I'll have nought to talk with.'

'Oh, Johnnie.' Mother held him to her. 'I love you so.'

'I love you too, Mother.' He hugged her and enjoyed the warmth of her arms. A knock sounded at the door and he wriggled out of her grasp.

'Yes?' said Mother.

A maidservant curtsied. 'Kirsty Lorne's here and wants to know if the young master will see her.'

'Does she indeed?'

Kirsty. Johnnie looked at Mother, his body poised to run. She indicated with a movement of her head that he could go.

He raced to the door. Mother's voice made him turn. 'You'll remember to apologise?'

'Yes.' Impatient to see Kirsty, he made for the door again.

'Johnnie.'

Lorna Windham

'Yes?' Couldn't Mother see Kirsty would blame him for being kept on the doorstep?

'One day, lots of lassies will be interested in you. Make sure you pick the right one.'

'Oh, Mother.' He closed the door and ran towards the scullery. As if anyone, other than Kirsty, would ever be interested in him. His limbs never seemed to go in the direction he wanted and his voice squeaked or deepened at the most unexpected moments. He never knew what to say to lassies, apart from Kirsty. His brothers always laughed when he turned scarlet and stuttered in company. He had nothing to recommend him with his hair like bracken, eyes like cloudy weather and now the odd spot to add to his feeling of inadequacy. His mother viewed him with a loving eye, not an accurate one.

He paused at the study where his father poured over papers at his desk. Dougie, his grizzled tacksman, stood at his side. Better get it over with. 'Sorry, Father,' Johnnie shouted from the doorway and darted away.

'That laddie.' Father's gruff voice followed him outside.

Johnnie sped through the scullery, breathed in the scent of hot yeast and grabbed two small, loaves on his way.

'You little... I'll tell your mother,' yelled Una Galbraith, their apple-cheeked cook.

He evaded her hand, wrenched open the back door and juggled the loaves as they burnt his palms. The bright sunlight dazzled him and the air thrummed with dragonflies, butterflies and bees. His heart lifted even more. Kirsty sat on the far side of the meadow. Light glinted on her plaited wheat-coloured hair which shone like a halo.

'He loves me, he loves me not...' She pulled the petals off a daisy.

'Who loves you?' he said.

'No one, I'm just playing.' She tossed the ruined daisy on the grass.

He gave her a loaf as he planted himself beside her.

13

'Hot.' She took a deep breath and inhaled the scent of the warm golden crust. Her small white teeth bit into the dough. 'Mmmm. Lovely. Thank you.' Her green eyes stared at him from under long, black lashes.

The colour of jade. Why hadn't he realised it before? 'You're my lassie,' he squeaked. Damn.

'So you say.' Her white teeth took another bite.

'Kirsty?' He could see she was in one of those moods.

'What's it like to have parents who love you?' she asked in that open, frank way she had at times. She nibbled at the bread.

Her question took him unawares. He struggled to answer as it seemed incomprehensible to him that she felt unloved by those closest to her. 'Why it's… I'm sure your father tried his best and your mother loves you.'

'No' like yours. I've seen how your mother is with you, how she jokes and laughs. Her arms are full of hugs, her lips always ready to kiss and say sweet things.'

'Oh, Kirsty.'

He reached for her hand, so small, so delicate and inwardly cursed the Lornes.

Kirsty swept the crumbs from her skirt. She threw the ruined daisy away. 'It's alright. My mother loves me, for what I can do, cook, clean, milk, knit, sew, and… it's sons she needs to work the land. She's always comparing me to Peggie Balfour. You dinna know her, she's the daughter of Mother's rich friend. Apparently, the girl's graceful, beautiful and, oh yes, an heiress. It's taken me years to work it out, years of being miserable and blaming myself. I ken better now. No one will ever love me.'

'But I love you.' Johnnie held her waist. How could she not know this?

'You do?' Her brow creased as if she struggled to see why.

'Yes. You're my lassie and always will be.'

'Oh, Johnnie.' She clung to him. 'Do you mean it?'

'Course I mean it, I've always said it haven't I?' He drew himself up. 'I'm a man o' my word. Once I've been to university, we'll marry.'

'But that could take years.' Her eyes clouded. 'I'll be old and look like my mother then, working on the farm.'

'Tell your mother I'll help with the farm.'

'But you've your own chores.'

He ignored the growl of his stomach, unfurled her calloused palm and placed his loaf in it. He deepened his voice. 'I'll help with the farm.' He thanked God he didn't squeak.

The Jacobite Affair

CHAPTER Four

'So, that Johnnie Stewart's offered to help us?' Kirsty's mother sat in the kitchen. She squinted at the scarlet threads attached to her hand loom in the poor light from the cruisie lamp. The banked up fire at her feet sparked and spat. 'Sniffing round you.'

Kirsty's hand faltered and she dropped a stitch. 'Mother. He'll work hard.'

'Hmph. Hope he doesn't expect to be paid. I'm not weaving garters to pay him. To think I've sunk to this.' She held up strips of white felt and leather.

Kirsty rested her bone knitting needles on her lap. 'Mother, he's doing it out of kindness.'

'Kindness? If your father hadn't been a wastrel and a drunkard we wouldn't need Johnnie Stewart's help. Should have listened to my family. Cut me off without a penny.'

'The Tolbains did that? You never said.'

'You're old enough to know the truth of it now. Only your Aunt Lizzie, would speak to me. I should have had more sense. Grandfather Tolbain warned me. Said I didn't know what I was taking on. He knew. That's why he gifted me this farm and land. The rest of the family resented it of course.'

Kirsty wound a strand of thick yarn round her needle. 'That's dreadful.' She made a stitch. 'Johnnie said he'll come tomorrow after he's finished his chores.'

'Why would Johnnie Stewart feel kindness towards us?'

'Because…' Kirsty allowed herself a smile.

Her mother pointed a bent finger at her. 'Make sure you don't hand out any favours or he'll soon be off, got what he wanted on the cheap.'

'Johnnie's no' like that.'

'Not. How many times?'

'It's how I speak, how everyone speaks here. Stop correcting me.'

'You're descended from Tolbains, higher than the Stewarts. I'm only trying to guide you. Men. They're all like that. You mind my words, I'll not tolerate any bastards here.'

'Mother.'

'He must like you.'

'I suppose.'

'Pity he's not the heir.' Mother raised her arms, stretched and yawned.

'Mother,' snapped Kirsty.

'He'll do… for the moment.' Mother rose to her feet and tidied away the garters and loom. 'Hope he's a hard worker. The roof needs a new thatch, then there's the beasts to be looked after and fields to be tilled.' She paused. 'I'm away to my bed, don't be long. We've no oil to waste.' After a few minutes, the box bed creaked, the curtains swished and a grunt and whistle pierced the gloom.

Kirsty could have speared Mother with her needles, but continued to knit the stockings. *We've spare bulls for Murdo Leith to take south to the Drovers Tryst at Crieff. Pity they're not sturdier, but there'll be coins to spare when we sell them. Perhaps this year will be easier than the last. Might even be able to buy a second-hand dress at Maryburgh. At least Mother owns the farm and land, her greatest fear had always been Father gambling it away.*

Father had been forced to turn to leather work, attached silver and brass buckles to belts, made tassels and created studded patterns to make good his losses. Mother had wanted to sell the last of his wares: the seal, goat, otter, badger skins and sporrans. But Kirsty had exchanged some of her woollen garments with Mother for Father's fine otter skin sporran with a silver clasp. She took it from where it nestled on top of folded linen inside her pine chest. *Father's workmanship is every bit as good as I remember.* Her lips curved into a smile as she stroked the smooth leather. *Just right.* Then she put it back and closed the lid.

She turned to the ball of blue, worsted yarn and her hands moved at speed as she wound it round her knitting needles and

The Jacobite Affair

set them in motion with a clickety-clack. *If I can just finish this garter stitch, I'll have half a dozen stockings to sell at Maryburgh.*

Mother forbade her to sell such goods in Braedrumie, *beneath them* she said. With a triumphant sigh, Kirsty cast off, cut the yarn adrift with a knife and thought of Johnnie and his birthday. *He's always been taller than me, but now he's clumsy with long arms and legs. I don't care, he always smiles and says he loves me. Perhaps Mother will get to like him.*

Lorna Windham

CHAPTER Five

The first streaks of June's buttermilk light filtered through cracks and open stable doors at Braedrumie house, the air warm and pungent with the smell of fresh hay and manure.

'May I go now, Father?' Johnnie dusted himself down.

'Have you finished your chores?' His father scratched his beard.

'Aye, sir.'

Father's brow wrinkled. 'So, the stable's mucked out and ready to be inspected?'

'Aye, sir.' Johnnie stuck his fork in the dung heap behind him.

'You've laid fresh straw, filled the feed bags and given the ponies fresh water?'

'Aye, sir.'

'You've had no help from your brothers or my men?'

'No, sir.'

'He was up an hour early, Father.' Rob carried buckets of water from the trough. He threw their contents over the stable floor next door. 'Half-finished when Euan and I joined him. Got things to do on your seventeenth birthday haven't you, Johnnie?'

'Aye.' He'd missed Rob and Euan while they were at university and would have liked to have seen more of them during this break from academic life, but he burned to see Kirsty.

'Canna have a laird's son without a fine blade to see him into manhood.' Rob ruffled Johnnie's hair and handed him a silver sgian-dubh.

Johnnie's eyes lit up at the blade. 'Thanks Rob.'

'I'll inspect your work and you'll answer to me if it's no' up to standard. If you see Murdo tell him to call. I've cattle for him. Oh, and as you're now seventeen, I've cut a bullock out of the herd for you. He's in yon field.'

'Thank you, Father.' Johnnie grinned.

19

The Jacobite Affair

'You can have your pick of my cows.' Euan wiped his brow.

'Really?' Johnnie found it hard to contain his excitement. 'Thank you.'

'You'll soon have a herd almost as big as mine.' Euan set to work with a broom.

'Your mother wants to see you, mind,' said his father.

'Does she? Thank you.' Johnnie raced off to the house.

His mother lay in her bed, her long, dark hair plaited and her face drawn.

'Many happy returns.' She held out her arms.

'Thank you, Mother.' He ran to her and planted his lips on her flushed cheek. She smelt of roses. He sat on her counterpane. 'You're burnin' up.'

She coughed. 'Granny Mac's going to call in. I'll have to drink one of her potions no doubt and listen while she answers all of Morag's questions. It looks like she'll be a healer too, if Granny Mac doesna' have her kill one of us first. Anyway, never mind me. I'll be up and around in no time. What a braw laddie you are this morning. Seventeen, I canna' believe it and I declare you're so handsome. Dinna' let it turn your head, mind.'

'Oh, Mother.' His face burned.

'I want you to have my mare's foal. He should share her good nature. You've spent enough time with him.'

'Oh, Mother, thank you.' He stood. 'I'll call him Bucephalus, after Alexander the Great's warhorse.'

'It's a bit long.'

'Buc for short. What do you think?' He moved from one foot to another.

'Perfect. You want to be gone, I see. Are chores at the Lornes so inviting?'

'Mother.'

'Aye, well. Look after Buc and he'll look after you.'

'Yes, Mother.' He kissed her again, raced to the stables to pat the foal and admire his brown and white hocks. Then he sped into the field to see his bullock covered in black hair with wide shoulders, broad back and rump. The animal looked up at him, snorted and stampeded down to the bottom of the field. With Euan's cow and this bullock, Johnnie had the beginnings of a fine herd. He fingered Rob's sgian-dubh in his stocking

'Johnnie.' Duncan pumped his arms and legs as he raced towards him. A grass stalk stuck upright, like a feather in his dark hair. 'Many happy returns. I've something for you. It's no' much.' Duncan put a carved salmon made out of applewood in Johnnie's palm.

Johnnie turned it over and over. 'Thank you, Duncan, you're becoming quite a craftsman.'

Duncan's face lit up like a beacon. 'It took me weeks and weeks to make, Euan helped. I know you like fishing.'

'Thank you for making it for me. I bet no one has a finer salmon than this.'

Johnnie held the fish in his hand as he ran through the orchard and into the cool shadow of the wood. The sun higher in the sky than he'd thought. He imagined he'd become a deer as he sped towards the Lorne's smallholding. He'd hoped the help he gave Kirsty and her mother, would make the old woman like him, but she always looked at him with eyes like cold steel. He'd show her he'd be a good match for Kirsty. Deep in thought he tripped over a gnarled root and fell in a tangled heap. 'Ugh.' A rough hand covered his mouth.

Johnnie's heart beat as if it would burst. Murdo and his dog, Patch. The man pressed his lips to Johnnie's ear and hissed, 'Ssssh, laddie, dinna make a sound. Look.' He motioned with his bushy head. In between the thick tree trunks and lush foliage, Johnnie saw a redcoat patrol on the track below. If he'd stumbled into them he'd have been in trouble, blamed for anything from murder to theft from the British Crown. Murdo's hand released him.

'No' runnin' from an enemy are you?' The bear of a man had his dirk and sword drawn. His blue eyes pierced Johnnie's then scanned the trees.

'Sorry, Murdo. No. I was in a hurry.'

The Jacobite Affair

'A hurry? It's a wise man who looks before he leaps in these times. Thought your father taught you better.' His weathered face, surrounded by rust-coloured whiskers, creased in concern.

Johnnie hung his head. He'd let himself down in front of one of the most respected men in the area. Braedrumie paid Murdo to take their cattle to the markets in the south and every year he and his men returned with their profits from the sales. That profit, paid the Stewart tenants' rent or in the case of the Lorne's, kept them from starvation.

'I wasna thinking. I'm going to the Lorne's.'

'The Lorne's? Now, what would send you there in such a hurry? It wouldna be a bonny wee lassie, would it?' Murdo's whiskers wrapped themselves round a smile. He tousled Johnnie's hair.

How did he know? Johnnie clamped his lips together, aware his face had reddened.

Murdo surveyed the track till the tramp of marching feet disappeared into the distance. 'It's safe to move now.' He rose to his feet, and wrapped a tree-trunk arm round Johnnie's neck. 'I'm goin' the same way.'

Hope he doesn't mention Kirsty. 'Can I stroke Patch?'

'Aye. You ken where he likes to be tickled?'

'Aye.' Johnnie knelt beside the dog and rubbed the spot behind his black and white ear. Patch shoved his head towards Johnnie's fingers. 'The Lorne's have cattle for you and so has Father.'

'Let's hope they'll fetch a fine price.' Murdo strode across the rough pasture towards the croft as Patch plodded along at his side.

Johnnie followed them through the ferns and tangled undergrowth and onto the track. He had to trot to keep up with Murdo's long stride. 'What's it like at Crieff?'

Murdo scratched his bulbous nose. 'Like nothin' you've ever seen, laddie. There's herds of great snortin' beasts from all over the Highlands, so thick you canna' see the ground. Dust and dung from one end to the other all mixed in with the sour smell of ale, sweat and smoke. And people, why there's thousands, some who live there and market traders and others like me.'

Johnnie struggled to imagine it. 'Could I come with you, Murdo? I wouldna get in the way.'

'We could ask your father, I suppose. It's hard goin', even for me. Always lookin' after the herd, walkin' ten miles a day over hard country, ensurin' none gets thieved, lost, maimed or dies. No' mindin' floods or heavy snow on the passes. Knowin' where you're goin', the best tracks and grazin' for the cattle. You have to like your own company and no' miss your family too much.'

Johnnie's mind raced. An adventure beckoned. To be free of Father and the daily grind of chores. Then he remembered and looked at his leather boots. 'I'm thanking you for considering it, but I have to stay.'

'Have to?' Murdo stroked his whiskers.

'Aye. I gave a promise to help the Lorne's and canna break it.'

'So, you're an honest laddie, a man of his word. You'd make a good drover, lad. I hope the Lorne's appreciate your efforts. There's a lassie seems to.' He pointed at Kirsty who waved and ran across the fields towards them. Patch barked, looked at Murdo who signalled with his fingers and the dog bounded towards her. Johnnie leapt across the burn.

Kirsty stopped and patted Patch. 'You're a fine wee dog. Morning, Murdo. Mother's been waiting for you.'

'Thank you Miss Lorne, I'd best see her then as she's got cattle for market.'

Kirsty jigged up and down with her hands behind her back as Johnnie watched Murdo and Patch head across the pasture.

'I hope you've had a fine birthday.' Kirsty turned to Johnnie. 'You're late.'

He took in her bright eyes and flushed cheeks. 'I'm sorry, but I've a bullock and cow, a foal from mother and a sgian-dhu from Rob, see.' He pointed at the hilt in his hose. 'And a carved salmon from Duncan.' He opened his palm.

The Jacobite Affair

'I've a gift for you too. Here.' She handed the sporran to him.

'For me?'

'Aye.'

'It's finely crafted.' He turned it round in his hands. 'Silver and otter, you canna' afford it.'

'My father made it and now it's yours.'

'Johnnie slung it low over his slim hips. 'I'll put Duncan's salmon in it. I thank you for your gift. May I… may I kiss you?'

'Aye, but be quick, Mother may be watching.'

Johnnie brushed his lips against her warm cheek and felt his loins respond to Kirsty's closeness. A mournful low came from the farmhouse. He adjusted the sporran and coughed. 'You'd better milk yon cow.'

CHAPTER Six
April 1745

Kirsty didn't tell Johnnie, but she'd been up long before dawn every day to complete most of her chores, just so she could be with him.

The sun shone like a gold coin on a blue cloth as her brow clouded. *Will Johnnie receive a letter from Rob today?* The laird had sent his oldest son to France a year ago to learn about the family's merchant trading business.

She looked west in the direction Johnnie would come from. She closed her eyes, crossed her fingers and wished.

'Kirsty,' Johnnie shouted.

She opened her eyes.

'Father's heard from Uncle John.' Johnnie raced towards her past fields of oats and hurdled the burn. 'Rob's well and should be home, possibly this morning, if the weather stays fair.' He pointed at the farmhouse roof. 'I'll mend yon hole in the thatch and then we'll watch for him from a crag I ken overlooking Glen Briag and the mountains in the south.'

She hopped up and down as he scrambled up the roof. 'Hurry up.'

'Patience. You dinna want my shoddy work to let the rain in.' Johnnie used a bent blade attached to a wooden handle to tear off the ruined heather. 'I never spoke to you of it before, but I missed Rob when he was sent away at seven. Hardly recognised him when he returned at sixteen. Remember how tall and distant he'd become? Then he left again for university and Euan joined him a few years later.

I wanted to be with them, read and gain all that knowledge. Euan of course, canna it understand it, though Rob slapped me on the back and said my time would come. Wonder if he's changed?'

'You'll both have changed, but he's still your brother and the heir,' said Kirsty. 'Do hurry.'

'Aye. It'll be like old times.'

The Jacobite Affair

'Can you no' work any faster? Tell you what, I'll get us some bread, cheese and ale for the journey.' Kirsty disappeared indoors.

An hour later, satisfied with his handiwork, Johnnie took her hand and they crossed the moors and clambered up to Crag Briag, like an eagle's nest, strewn with rocks of all shapes and sizes. Kirsty and Johnnie sat side by side on a boulder and watched for Rob and his horse on the track which snaked north through Glen Briag. A herd of red deer grazed on a distant hillside and a golden eagle spread its wings and rode the wind. The sun blazed down as Kirsty quenched her thirst from the deerskin bag she'd brought and shared some cheese with Johnnie. He kept his eyes on the trail below as he chewed. Hours went by.

Johnnie's whoop of joy startled her. 'Look.' He pointed at a smudge on the horizon.

'It might not be him.'

Johnnie closed one eye and peered into the distance. The smudge became a blur, then a figure and pony. 'Told you, it's Rob.' Johnnie ran helter-skelter through rocks and left her to pick her own way behind.

She watched the brothers embrace. *Will I lose a piece of Johnnie now or will he remember me?* He turned, his eyes shone and he beckoned her towards them. She scrambled down beside the brothers and Johnnie's arms welcomed her as Rob's smile widened.

He towered over her. 'You were just a slip of a lassie when I saw you last, Kirsty Lorne. You've grown up, I see. Johnnie will have to fight others off.'

'I wouldn't want him hurt,' she said.

Johnnie's arm tightened round her waist and Rob's head went back as he roared with laughter.

Before she could stop herself the words were out of her mouth. 'Rob Stewart, if you grow any taller you'll only have the mountains to talk to.'

Rob's blue eyes flickered, then he laughed even more and patted Johnnie's back. 'She's a tongue on her. Let's away home. How's everyone?'

The brothers chatted all the way to Braedrumie House. As they entered the front door and hall the scent of fresh lavender wafted toward Kirsty. A grandfather clock stood against the opposite wall and a fine wooden staircase led to a balcony above.

The laird stopped mid-stride and shouted, 'Elizabeth. Elizabeth. He's home. Come and see.' He strode towards Rob and shook his hand.

Elizabeth, in nightgown and shawl, limped downstairs. Rob sped towards her, scooped her up in his arms and kissed her cheek. Kirsty hung back and watched how the family took him to their bosom and hung on his every word. Johnnie drew her close as they trooped behind.

'Put me down, silly boy.'

Rob placed his mother in a chair in the sitting room. 'You dinna look well. You need to look after yourself, Mother.'

'How's the business?' asked the laird.

'You've few worries there, sir.' Rob's brow furrowed. 'Though France seethes with rumours about Prince Charlie and an invasion.'

'Is that so? Interesting, I'll tell Dougie to open some of our best wine. This calls for a celebration.'

'But Father…' began Rob, his words forced between tight lips.

'Dinna worry, I can afford it, for my heir.' He patted his wife's hand and left the room.

Rob's dark brows lowered for a second or two, then he cast off his mood. 'Versailles takes your breath away. There are hundreds of rooms.'

'Hundreds?' Kirsty struggled to imagine such a grand place.

'Aye and the best craftsman in Europe have worked on them from ceiling to floor. There's gold leaf, marble, mirrors and lots of chandeliers. It's wonderful in daylight and always

The Jacobite Affair

crowded. You should see it, at night it sparkles with light from thousands of candles and the gardens are full of fountains, statues and…'

'And the ladies, how do they dress?' Kirsty leaned forward.

'They spend fortunes on wigs and gowns made of the finest silks and satins. They seem very proud, but also daring and very beautiful.'

'Oh.' Kirsty clapped her hands. 'It sounds so wonderful. One day I'd like to dress like that and be daring and very beautiful.' *Rob seems so knowledgeable, so worldly wise and talks of faraway people and places I can only dream about. How I long to see the world.*

'You mustn't have wanted to come home, Rob.'

'The family business isna that interesting, Johnnie. Uncle John kept my nose to his dusty accounts as much as he could, before he returned to Port Glasgow. But things are stirring in France. Too many Jacobites with The Cause eating at their innards.' Rob's face became grim.

'Rob.' His mother wagged her finger at him.

'My apologies.' He kissed her hand.

'They've right on their side.'

'Euan, in war both sides say they have right on their side. I canna see how the Jacobites can win, though Rome and Paris are full of their plots and schemes. Rebellion's in the air again, I could smell it.'

'Really, Rob?' asked Euan.

'Aye. Believe me, it's no' something in which this family should involve itself. Remember the 1715.'

'But, Father says we should,' said Duncan. 'There's men in Braedrumie itching to fight.'

'We've no chance, not against the might of the British army.' Johnnie set his jaw. 'Any fool can see that.'

Johnnie didna mean it.

Rob hissed in a breath.

Euan grabbed Johnnie's arm. 'Are you calling me a fool?'

Their mother paled. Duncan stared open-mouthed at his brothers. Kirsty flashed a worried glance at all of them as Rob stood between Johnnie and Euan.

'Your father.' Their mother motioned with her hand towards the door.

'What's this? What's this?' The laird glared at Johnnie. 'I'll have no fighting in my house.'

'Just a slight disagreement, Father.' Rob's face relaxed into a smile. 'Nothing to worry about, right lads?'

'I'll fight for the Jacobites.' A muscle twitched in Euan's cheek.

'Me too' Duncan plumped out his chest.

Rob's lips became a taut line and Johnnie stared out of the window.

The laird beamed at Euan and Duncan. 'Spoken like true Stewarts. The redcoats are too busy in Europe to worry about us. If I had my way, we'd strike now and when the French join us we'll be a force to be reckoned with. Isn't that right, Rob?'

'If,' said Johnnie.

Their mother went white, Kirsty's heart skipped a beat, Rob coughed, Euan looked at his boots and Duncan gaped. Purple veins stood out on the laird's neck and his face became mottled.

Rob put a hand on his father's arm. 'Johnnie means we've only a promise of support from the French.'

The laird's eyes glinted at Johnnie. 'Is that right, boy?'

'I meant that there's hardly a clan loves its neighbour, never mind joining together against the government and who knows what the French will do.'

Their mother closed her eyes, Rob groaned, Euan sighed and Duncan's forehead creased. Kirsty held her breath.

'Are you arguing with me, boy?' The laird glowered at his third son.

Johnnie glowered back at his father.

'I'm sure Johnnie doesna mean… began Rob.

Kirsty froze. *Surely they'll no' fight?*

'Johnnie was just putting forward a point of view.' Their mother put two hands on the arms of her chair and stood up. 'Rob's return seems to have given me new energy. Dinner's ready and I want no black looks on the first night of my eldest son's return. Kirsty, you must stay and eat with us, of course. Johnnie send a servant to inform her mother. Come, Rob, lead me in to dinner and sit beside me, I want to hear all about French fashions, food and of course all the delicious gossip.'

The laird's colour returned to normal as he beamed at his wife.

Thank goodness she's diverted her husband's attention from Johnnie. Kirsty's heart beat a little faster as she took Johnnie's arm. *What an honour to be invited to dine with the Stewarts. But why are Rob and Johnnie so against The Cause? Everyone in Braedrumie is a Jacobite, surely they can't all be wrong?*

Kirsty gasped as Johnnie led her into the fine oak-panelled dining room which danced with light thrown up from the fire. The silverware, crystal and pewter on the table, twinkled under the chandelier. Dougie, the Stewart's tacksman stood beside two serving maids.

Rob shook Dougie's hand. 'Good to see you,' said Rob.

'And you, young Master,' replied Dougie.

'Isabel?'

'She's well and will be pleased to hear, you're home at last.'

As Johnnie pulled out a chair for Kirsty she found it difficult to speak. *My home's rough and poor compared to this finery.* She flushed. *I should leave.* As she rose, Johnnie put a gentle hand on her shoulder. She sat.

Kirsty looked around the table, no one had noticed her moment of distress. The laird threw back his head as Rob told humorous tales about his travels. Euan grinned and Duncan clamped a hand to his ribs and begged for mercy. *Interesting how Rob's drawn the laird's anger from Johnnie.*

Johnnie quizzed an eyebrow at Kirsty and placed a snowy napkin on his lap. She followed his lead. *Perhaps this won't be such an ordeal. Mother talked of such dinners from her past, but I never imagined I'd be invited to one.*

Rob turned the conversation to the family business again and the profit made.

'And how's the *Elizabeth*?' asked the laird.

'Well named, sir.' Rob lifted a glass to his mother. 'Flies like a bird, I sailed home on her.'

The laird's mood lightened even more. 'Good. Good.'

'And how are those in Braedrumie? Granny Mac… Morag?' asked Rob.

*Why did his voice soften when he said **her** name?*

'Granny Mac's older if that's possible and Morag… Morag is beautiful,' said Euan.

Johnnie groaned and Duncan stuck a finger in his mouth and mimed being sick. A shadow flitted across Rob's face.

Kirsty wondered what it meant and then the dishes of jugged hare and a host of vegetables arrived and she forgot as Johnnie loaded her plate and told her to eat.

CHAPTER Seven

Next day, an ominous rumble rolled over Braedrumie House. Johnnie cast an anxious eye at the dark clouds outside and then turned to Kirsty as the wind moaned and circled the floor.

'It's cold,' she said as she shivered in the hallway.

'Here, borrow my cloak, it's going to rain before you get home.' Johnnie wrapped it round her.

The hallway darkened. 'Thank you.'

'There's been nothing but arguments since Rob's been home,' grumbled Johnnie. 'Rob and Father agree on most things, but no' the Jacobite cause and I find myself taking Rob's side.'

'Can you no' just listen?' Her fingers struggled with the cloak's ties.

Johnnie shrugged his shoulders. 'Not when I see no sense in what Father says. He's too set in his ways and wants us all to fight for the prince. I dinna think it wise, but he willna have it and I canna believe Euan agrees with him. It's Father's way or not at all. Rob bites his tongue and mine should be bleeding.'

'What about wee Duncan?'

'I'm sure he's no' expected to fight, he's still a bairn. I just wish Father hadna asked Rob about the failed French invasion. When Rob said, *Thank God for violent storms,* it went down like a soggy haggis. I thought Father would choke.'

Johnnie went quiet as footsteps approached the hall and he heard the laird's proud tones, 'Prince Charlie's twenty five, he'll no rest until he restores the Stuarts to the throne. By then you'll be married to the fine woman I've picked out for you.'

'Father…' Rob began.

The laird entered the hall with Rob a pace behind. 'You'll thank me when you see her.'

'But…'

'And perhaps you'll give me a grandson or two.'

Rob's brow darkened and he clenched his jaw as his father strode past Kirsty and Johnnie.

'Father.' Rob brought the laird to a halt in the sitting room doorway.

Kirsty's eyes widened and Johnnie's brow arched.

Rob, grim-faced spoke to his father in a low undertone which Johnnie couldn't hear. The laird's face flamed in response as he stabbed a forefinger at Rob's chest. 'You'll marry her or you're no son of mine.'

'Poor Rob,' hissed Johnnie between his teeth.

'Who's he marrying?' she whispered as Johnnie walked her to the front door.

'Lady Anne Kerr of Kerbilly, Mother told me.' Johnnie looked back at his father incandescent with rage and Rob's granite jaw and shook his head.

'A lady? Think he'd look happier about it.' Kirsty glanced through the doorway as the first drops of rain pattered on the ground. 'I'm away home, then. I've chores and Mother willna understand.' She slipped out the door.

'Right, well, I have to check on my mare.' Rob strode past Johnnie without a word.

The laird stared after him. 'He'll come round.'

Johnnie wanted to say he thought Rob should be free to marry whom he chose, but he didn't. It would just stir up more trouble.

'Have a look at the bull, the one in the top field, will you Johnnie? Looks lame to me,' said Father.

'Aye, sir.' He'd look for Rob afterwards, to see if he could help.

Thirty minutes later Johnnie searched the stables. No Rob. Johnnie walked the grounds and eventually found Euan and Morag arm in arm in the rose garden, oblivious of the fine rain. 'Morning, you seen, Rob?'

'Went on a ride I think.' Eua beamed at him. Morag, looked up at Euan under lowered lashes. Euan seemed unable to stand still. 'Guess what?'

'What?' asked Johnnie.

'We're betrothed.'

The Jacobite Affair

Johnnie whooped, hugged his brother, shook his hand and kissed Morag's cheek. 'This is good news.'

Rob didn't turn up for supper or the following day. The laird sent out search parties. As the weeks passed and turned into months they realised that Rob had done the unforgiveable and left them without a word and no one knew why.

'Johnnie, try and persuade your mother to take some air,' said the laird one evening. 'She's moping for Rob. I hope to God no ill's befallen him. If he's… you'd think he'd write.'

CHAPTER Eight

The afternoon sun cascaded over Kirsty's shoulder and onto the woollen bonnet she'd almost finished. She sat in the kitchen whilst Mother's head sagged in her rocking chair. Kirsty thought about the Stewarts and the note Johnnie had given her a few minutes before. Her right hand wrapped blue yarn round her needles. She finished the stitch and cast off. *Now, why does Johnnie's mother want to see me? Perhaps she thinks I'm not good enough for him.* She rose and left the bonnet and needles on her seat. *Without Johnnie, I'll be a ship without a sail, rudderless. He always said, 'you're my lassie', but does he mean it?* Kirsty braced herself to visit. She slipped out of the farmhouse and waved to Johnnie in the next field. 'I'll be back soon,' she yelled. He waved her on her way.

His mother had shrunk since the last time they'd met, her eyes dull, her skin sallow with bright spots on her cheeks and her gait slow. Kirsty put an arm round her. *She's lost weight.* Kirsty helped her sit on a low wooden bench which rested on two sawn logs in the herb garden. Mint, rosemary and sage perfumed the warm air as Kirsty sat beside her.

While his mother talked about the past, Kirsty listened.

'Ours was a love match,' the older woman said. 'I never thought it possible to love the laird more than the day we wed, but I do.' She looked at Kirsty. 'It probably seems odd to you, two elderly people still in love?'

Kirsty fumbled for words, 'No. It's… sweet.' *Wish I'd seen my parents in love.*

His mother clutched Kirsty's wrist, her hand cold but strong. 'I can see Johnnie… is very… fond of you. He's a clever lad, meant for university not… well… not war. He needs… someone who understands, believes in him… someone who loves him like I love the laird.'

Kirsty pulled her wrist from the older woman's grasp. 'What are you trying to say?'

The Jacobite Affair

'Dinna hurt him, dinna…' His mother's dark eyes pleaded with her. 'Be sure you love him as much as he loves you or you'll break his heart.'

Kirsty jerked upright. 'I will never break his heart, Mistress Stewart. I love him.'

A shudder gripped his mother's body as she coughed into a handkerchief. 'How much?'

'What?'

'How much do you love him?'

Kirsty looked at her hands and then out to the purple mountains. She searched for the words. Her mouth felt dry and her tongue thick. She needed this woman's approval, but she'd never shared her thoughts about Johnnie with anyone. Then the words tumbled out. 'It's difficult…I dinna ken… how can I…? Please dinna laugh, I'm no' as good as Johnnie with words. I can only tell you the sky's no' so blue, the heather loses its scent and the air's heavy when he's no' by my side. It's as though half of me is missing, the half that brings light and laughter and warmth. The better half.'

Beads of perspiration stood out on his mother's forehead as she took both of Kirsty's hands in hers. 'You're wrong. You're better than Johnnie at explaining. It was the same for me. You'll do. I may not… just steer a straight course. Now I'm very tired, lassie, if you'd help me to my bedchamber, I'd be grateful.'

***

Several days later Johnnie did his own chores as usual and then worked on the Lorne's farm until late afternoon. He leant on his shovel. He wondered why his mother had summoned Kirsty. Woman talk he supposed. Kirsty had just smiled and said nothing. He wiped the sweat from his brow and thought of the previous evening when his family had gathered round the great fireplace before dinner. His father whose black brows smothered his eyes, had one hand on a bottle. Euan, the new

Lorna Windham

heir, looked uncertain and his mother wan, as she rested her head on the back of her chair.

The Lorne's farm had become a refuge from the troubles at home, as long as Johnnie kept out of Mrs. Lorne's way. He remembered when Murdo had returned from Crieff a few years ago full of tales, such as one of a young English farmer, Robert Bakewell, who'd improved his livestock when he selected cattle with the traits he wanted and kept them in the same field. Johnnie followed suit. To his delight the weight of the Lorne's cattle almost doubled. When Mrs. Lorne sold her cattle, they should make a good profit.

Murdo had also spoken of another English farmer, Townsend, who didn't slaughter his sheep and cattle before winter, but planted turnips which he fed to his livestock. Apparently, the turnips made the soil more fertile as did the manure from more beasts. Johnnie decided to copy Townsend.

So, the Lorne's last few harvests had been larger and better quality. The land became more fertile and profitable as he'd worked on it. He knew every inch, each blade of grass and the best and worst pasture. Despite Mrs. Lorne's doubts, Johnnie cleared ditches, planted kale and oats and harvested what he planted.

Pity Father wouldn't let him do the same at home. He'd wanted to share his success with Euan, but he'd had only one thing on his mind: Morag. Rob would have listened, but where was he? They all missed him and poor Mother, who kept to her bed, most of all.

Kirsty's mother occasionally brought bread, cheese and milk out to the fields for him, dumped it on a flat stone and retired to her lair. She never asked about his family or Rob. Johnnie decided she'd never change. Today was no different. Even her pores oozed her dislike. He fingered his mother's brooch in his otter skin sporran. Kirsty would be back soon. She'd gone to Maryburgh market, so her mother said.

'Johnnie, Johnnie.' Kirsty waved to him as she called across the pasture.

The Jacobite Affair

He took a deep breath – courage. A light breeze caught Kirsty's hair. It reminded him of golden wheat as the wind rippled through it.

'See what I've bought.' She held up a green ribbon and a pair of boots as she ran towards him with a basket over one arm. 'Any news of Rob?'

'No. Mother's upset and Father's temper doesna improve. Father willna discuss it. Just said, *Rob's dead to us now.*'

'I'm sorry for you all.' Kirsty patted his bare arm. 'It's terrible him going, it's as if the silkies have spirited him away. Tell your mother, I'm praying for his safe return.'

Didn't she realise what her touch did to him? Each hair sat on end, each nerve poised, his skin tingled, expectant. He swallowed hard. 'Thank you, I'll do that.'

'Johnnie, is there something wrong? Your mother, how is she?'

He sighed. 'Father won't have it, but she's weaker every day.'

'Oh, Johnnie I'm so sorry.'

'Aye. Granny Mac's given her a new potion.'

'I'll pray it'll work.'

Kirsty's head reached his chest, her hair lay thick and long on her curvaceous breasts and her green eyes and long dark lashes made him struggle to breathe. He couldn't look on her without being aware of his inability to control the awkwardness of his body. His scythe would slip or ballock knife would fall at the sight of her. This time, he took a breath and held it. His heart stopped its race and his pulse slowed. Now, he'd do it now. Johnnie cleared his throat. 'You ken Morag and Euan are betrothed?'

'Wasn't I at their betrothal dinner?'

He got down on one knee in the peaty soil, looked up at her and took her hand. 'Kirsty Lorne, I have loved you since you were four and I was six. I'm no' much of a catch, I ken that as the laird's third son, but I swear I'll look after you and yours till I die if only you will marry me.' He held out a gold

38

luckenbooth brooch to her, two entwined hearts embellished with rubies.

His mother had given him the heirloom that morning for his future bride. He'd an image of his mother's pale face as she'd said, 'You're fortunate, Johnnie, to be able to choose whom you wed. Poor Rob and Lady Anne Kerr. Your father wouldna be swayed. God knows, I tried. Said Rob's the heir and would do as he's told. Now he's gone with no word, even to me his Mother. We've lost him, Johnnie. But when he comes home and I'm sure he will in time, tell him... No, he knows I love him, but treat him with kindness and understanding.'

'I'll try, Mother, but I'm sure he'll be back soon and then you can tell him yourself.'

She'd kissed his cheek. 'And Euan hasna been trained to be a laird, he'll need your advice and wee Duncan, keep him safe, he'll need you in the times to come. There's rebellion in the wind. Will you do that for me?' She'd held his hand.

'Aye.' Why did she talk as if she wouldn't be there? 'Mother...?'

'My trinket box, please.'

He'd given it to her. She'd rummaged in it, found a small object and held it out to him. 'This was my grandmother's. Dinna give it away lightly. Give it where your heart lies.'

'Why now, Mother?'

'Because it's time.' She coughed again.

'Oh.' Kirsty's eyes lit up and she clasped her hands. She took the brooch and held it to the light so it sparkled and glimmered in her fingers.

'Well? What have you to say?' said Johnnie. 'I'll ask for your answer, now if you please.'

She gave him a sideways look from under her lashes. 'You wish to marry me?'

'I've just said so haven't I? What's wrong with you lassie?'

She clasped the brooch in the palm of her hand. 'I thank you for asking, Mr. Stewart.' She curtsied. 'I'll think about it.' She turned from him.

The Jacobite Affair

'Mr. Stewart? You'll think about it? Kirsty…' He pulled her round to face him and lifted her chin with his fingers. Hadn't he taken courage in two hands and asked for his Father's black-browed blessing this morning?

His father had regarded him as if he dealt with a skewered animal. 'Have you been talking to Euan?'

'No. What's he to do with it?'

'Never mind. It's a pity your mother's so ill. Kirsty Lorne, the lassie that's always here? She's bonny I see that, but let's look at her dowry. There'll be none, I remember Lorne knew the inside of a tankard better than he knew his own home.'

'I love her.'

'There's the farm and land. You'll ken that and the poor soil very well as you've been working on it for years.'

'You knew? I've improved the yield and the stock. If you'd just listened to me…'

His father ignored him. 'The land, poor as it is, borders ours. You're a third son, there's no' many fine ladies will be after you. Always been on the scrawny side, but you're filling out. You've a look of me and I was regarded handsome in my prime.' He raised his chest. 'I'll put it to your mother, I'm sure she'll say yes to the match if it makes you happy.'

'I love Kirsty, Father. Thank you, thank you and can I go to university?'

'University? That'll cost money and there's The Cause to think about.'

'Father?'

'I'll think on it. Where's Euan?'

'In the garden with Morag.'

'Have you something useful to do or must I find you work?' asked Father.

Johnnie mounted his pony and rode to the Lorne's farmhouse, so he would be early. He'd found Kirsty's mother outside on her own, washing kale.

Her mouth turned down at the edges. 'If you're set on it,' she said, retraced her steps to her home and closed the door.

A joyless woman. When he and Kirsty married he swore he'd make it his life's work to ensure Kirsty felt loved and laughed every day.

'Hey, you,' said Kirsty as her mouth curved in a grin and relief flooded through Johnnie. She stood on tiptoe, reached up to put her arms round his neck and planted a kiss on his lips. A fire ignited in him. He drew her closer, his hands around her tiny waist. Plump and ripe, her mouth opened to his as they stood breast to breast and an urgent need coursed through him. He must not. Not until their wedding night. He hauled himself back from the brink.

She rested her head on his chest. 'Oh, Johnnie, you're so dear to me. I love you and the brooch. Of course I'll wed you.'

His heart settled and his breathing slowed. He pinned the brooch to her plaid. 'Sweetheart, I'll ask the laird to invite you both to Braedrumie House to celebrate.'

'To the house?' Kirsty hugged him, her body warm in his arms.

The hairs on his neck prickled. He looked out over the pasture towards the farmhouse. Kirsty's mother watched them. Her hand shielded her eyes from the sun. Then she turned, went in and closed the door.

The Jacobite Affair

CHAPTER Nine

That night, Johnnie stood beside Euan and Duncan as his mother took her last breath in her husband's arms. She'd been the laird's wife for forty three years. He sat with her lifeless body for hours before Johnnie and Euan prised him away. He raged liked a wounded bull whilst Euan sat pale and white-faced and Johnnie put an arm round Duncan as his brother's chest heaved. Waves of grief each greater than the last washed over him. Johnnie shook his head. Dear God, had his mother known, sensed something when she gave him the brooch? How had he not realised?

The following day, as clouds raced across the sky, the laird and his sons carried her pine coffin on their shoulders, up the hill, through the gate, past the rich loam scent of turned soil and into the old church. The clan waited in silence their heads bowed.

She should have had a priest. An ache coiled round Johnnie's heart.

The men laid the coffin on a wooden trestle in front of the altar. Wild, white roses cascaded over it and onto the flagstones. Johnnie sucked in a breath and smelt their sweet perfume. It almost undid him. His mother had loved them. Sunlight streamed through the coloured glass windows and dappled the coffin. All so unreal. Johnnie sat in the front pew with his arm round Duncan's shoulders as Euan and the laird stared at their feet.

Late that evening when the air grew still and warm, the Stewarts, shuffled with heads bowed, round her grave. The silent villagers encircled the sombre laird. Euan stalwart, stood beside tearful Morag and her stern-faced father. Johnnie stunned, had one arm round Duncan who bit his lip as tears fell and the other round Kirsty who sniffed into a handkerchief. Her mother stood grim-faced behind her.

'Elizabeth was everything to me', began the laird. He lifted his head and let his voice boom over their heads. 'A fine wife and mother, none better. She gave me…f… fine sons. May God keep her in his arms till we meet again.' He smothered a sob with the palm of his hand. 'I can say no more.' He shrugged off Euan and then Johnnie's hand and stomped out of the graveyard towards the mountains and left the villagers and his sons behind.

'I'll miss her.' Kirsty gripped Johnnie's hand as he hugged Duncan.

'We'll all miss her.' Morag used her fingers to wipe under her eyes.

'But we'll see her again in Heaven?' asked Duncan who sniffed and used his sleeve to dry his tears.

'Aye, lad. You can be sure of that.' Johnnie patted his shoulder.

Let's to the house. We've a wake to attend to.'

'In a minute, Euan. Would you look after Duncan?'

Euan nodded and led away Duncan, his face buried in his chest.

'Kirsty?' Mother tugged at her daughter's sleeve.

'I'll walk with Johnnie.'

'Hmph. I'll be close behind.'

'Mother…' said Kirsty.

Johnnie needed time to think. He took Kirsty's hand and they walked out of the churchyard and turned toward Braedrumie House. Rob. His disappearance worked like a dagger in Johnnie's breast. The family needed his eldest brother as they never had before. Johnnie remembered Mother's tear-stained face, the hideous cough and shortness of breath. Her voice a whisper as every word became an effort. The last word: 'Rob'.

As heir to the Stewart estates, Rob, had everything to look forward to. Could he have been taken by a rival clan or murdered? Johnnie thought back, Rob hadn't liked the idea of the arranged marriage. He remembered Rob and Euan's jests about loose women in Glasgow, but they'd shut up like clams whenever their mother entered the room. Johnnie looked out over the smooth waters of Loch Linnhe. No answer there. Rob's disappearance remained a mystery.

Kirsty tugged at his arm.

He gave her a wry smile. Life had to go on or the Stewart estates and tenants would suffer. 'It doesna feel right.'

Kirsty wrapped her arms round him. 'There's no joy in this for anyone. I'm so sorry about your mother and that Rob's still missing.'

He pressed his lips to her forehead and wished for the nightmare day to end.

'None of that.' Mother stood behind them.

Kirsty sighed and Johnnie raised his eyes to heaven.

CHAPTER Ten

Kirsty glanced out of the window in the spence, the best room in the farmhouse. Diamond clusters shimmered on the burn as midgies danced to their own tune in the early afternoon heat.

'I hope you're boasting about me and Johnnie to Aunt Lizzie and the Balfours,' said Kirsty as she dressed for her betrothal dinner. *If only Johnnie's mother had lived to see it.*

Mother looked up from the table, quill in hand. 'Pity he's not the heir, but at least he's one step closer.'

'Can you no' accept Johnnie for who he is?' Kirsty turned this way and that so Johnnie's brooch twinkled on her sapphire blue, silk dress. She'd never worn anything so grand and fastened up her hair with pins. One gold ringlet rested on her shoulder. 'What do you think?'

Mother gave her a resentful glance. 'That you'd never know it had a singed mark when you bought it. You're good with a needle, I'll give you that. Must have cost a pretty penny.' She felt the hem between forefinger and thumb. 'Reminds me of gowns I wore before I married.'

Kirsty thought of the hours she'd knitted so she could afford the dress. She knew she could unpick the seams and fashion herself a new gown. The previous owner had been a colonel's daughter, so the Maryburgh stall holder had told her.

'You'll need dainty shoes and silk stockings,' said Mother.

Of course her stout boots by the fire and darned woollen stockings which hung on the rickety clothes horse wouldn't do. *Why didn't I think of that?*

'No need to make a face like a creased sheet. Not if you want Johnnie Stewart's eyes on you all night. Here.' Mother thrust a small bundle at Kirsty.

'What's this?'

'Undo it and see.'

Kirsty sat on a stool with the bundle on her lap. Her heart surged. *Could it be, could it really be?* Out tumbled a pair of shiny leather shoes and white, silk stockings. 'These are for me? You bought them for me?' She leaned forward, her lips pursed.

'No kisses.' Mother waved her away.

'But it's so… kind of you and you're always saying we've no money.'

'Not a matter of kindness, an investment. Murdo sold our cattle for a good profit last year. Johnnie's the laird's second son now and you must look the part. What are you doing? Have you lost your senses?'

'I'm hugging you, Mother. Thank you.'

Her mother wriggled out of Kirsty's arms. 'Hmph. I've no wish for us to go to the Stewart's betrothal meal looking like paupers. You made a good job of my dress. That bolt of grey silk's the best thing your father ever won. Johnnie Stewart's got prospects and the family are wealthy. Granny Mac told me they've ships that sail to the Americas and France. Didn't know that did you?'

Kirsty shook her head.

'Ask him. When you marry we'll have a better life and people will look up to us.'

'I dinna care about money.'

'You'll care if the hunger-wolf comes knocking at your door, my girl.'

'Oh, Mother that'll never happen, we've always managed.'

'You know nothing. What it's like when your stomach aches to be filled, not to sleep for worry. Money keeps hunger at bay, girl, and don't forget it. '

'You've been hungry?' Kirsty stared at her.

'Yes when you were a babe and your father gambled our harvest away.'

Poor Mother. 'You've new shoes and stockings too?'

'Of course.'

'Oh, Mother this is going to be the best evening of my life.' She fingered Johnnie's brooch on her shoulder and thought of the good times to come.

***

Johnnie struggled to fasten his necktie. Duncan had already barged in and thrown wig powder over him. When he caught the little devil, he wouldn't be able to sit for a week. Johnnie looked at himself in the mirror. He'd have to dust himself down.

As he used a horse-hair brush, he thought of the night to come. He'd seal his betrothal to Kirsty and it would be the start of happier times. He grimaced as he thought of his father who'd been unsteady on his feet again this morning, avoided sleep and sought his own company at night. The empty brandy bottles told their own story.

Dougie, once he could prize Morag away, had taken Euan under his wing to train him in his responsibilities as the new heir. Duncan raced around the house and grounds like a wild animal, put nettles in beds, upset the cook and swore.

Mother's death affected them all. The house seemed dark, less full of laughter since she'd died. Squabbles became full blown arguments without her calm words. God, he missed her, they all missed her- and Rob. His eldest brother knew how to manage Father, most of the time. He wouldn't have tolerated him as a drunk or Duncan's foul tongue. Rob would have taken control until the black shadows rolled away and Mother lay safe in their memories.

He must stop thinking like this. Tonight would be a celebration when he and Kirsty thought about their future together as man and wife. If he could just steer Father away from the topic of a Jacobite rebellion, all would be well.

His image in the glass stared back at him. Two grey-blue eyes under strong brown brows assessed his long, straight nose, wide face and generous mouth. He gathered his light, brown hair and tied it with a black bow at the nape of his neck. The wig lay discarded at his feet - too prickly. He tucked his crisp white shirt inside black breeches which clung to his

The Jacobite Affair

muscular rump and long thighs. His broad shoulders made his waist and hips appear slimmer. He pulled on his black jacket. No sign of Duncan's schoolboy trick. He'd do. The handle of his bedchamber rattled.

'Johnnie?'

He turned to face another barrage of wig powder and Duncan's mischievous grin.

'You wee fiend, I'll tan your backside.'

Duncan disappeared and Johnnie sped after him. His younger brother slid down the bannister, gave a whoop and was out of the front door. Johnnie took the stairs three at a time as the grandfather clock chimed in the hall. He knew all the places his brother could hide.

'What the hell happened to you?' asked Euan as Johnnie dived past him.

'Duncan.' Johnnie didn't miss a stride.

The pungent scent of fresh manure and clean hay hit his nostrils as he cornered his young brother in the darkest corner of the stables.

'What did you do it for you wee devil?' asked Johnnie.

'You look like a ghostie.'

Johnnie wiped a hand across his face, another over his ruined jacket, then reached out and grabbed Duncan's collar.

'Ow. Let me bloody go,' yelled Duncan. The ponies pricked up their ears and whinnied.

'Dinna bloody swear.' Johnnie swiped Duncan's ear.

'Ow.'

'What did you do it for you little scut? You know it's my betrothal dinner.'

'You'll be leaving.'

'Leaving?'

'Aye. You'll leave just like Mother.'

Oh God. Johnnie's heart sank. 'I'll be getting married, but that's years off after university. It's no' like Mother at all.'

Duncan wiped angry tears away. 'Do you promise?'

'Aye.' Why hadn't he realised Duncan missed Mother so much, his world tossed upside down by her death? That Father had turned in on himself? Or that Euan was preoccupied as he learned how to run the estate and dreamt of his life with Morag? The family had left poor, wee Duncan to suffer the agony of grief alone. Johnnie ruffled Duncan's black hair. 'I was planning to ask if you'd like to go fishing with me tomorrow?'

Duncan's face lit up. 'Do you mean it, Johnnie?'

'Aye. There's a secret burn I know.'

'Oh, Johnnie, that would be grand.' Duncan reached out and brushed his brother's jacket with both hands. 'I'm sorry about the powder, but it'll come off. See.'

'Duncan, I want you to do one thing for me.' Johnnie held Duncan's shoulders and looked into his brown eyes, so like their mother's it pulled at his heart strings.

'Anything, Johnnie.'

'Come and find me when you feel... troubled. Will you do that?'

'Aye. Thanks, Johnnie.'

'Right, back to the house. I've got to get cleaned up and you, from the smell of you need a bath.' He lifted his brother over one shoulder. 'It's the loch for you.'

'Nooooo,' yelled Duncan.

CHAPTER Eleven

In the warmth of late afternoon, Johnnie watched a startled herd of deer bound across the moor. The Stewart's coach bowled along to the Lorne's so Kirsty and her mother would arrive in style at Braedrumie House. He paced up and down until he spotted the horses on their return journey and the wheels clattered to a stop at his feet.

Kirsty emerged first, like a beautiful topaz butterfly. She took Johnnie's hand and allowed him to help her down before he assisted her mother. 'Let me show you our rose garden,' he said. 'It's beautiful at this time in the afternoon. You can enjoy the air.'

Why so nervous? He saw Kirsty every day, but not how she looked this afternoon, dressed in a cloud of blue and her breasts high and pert. Her waist begged for his hand to pull her towards him. If only his mother had been there.

Bees buzzed and dragonflies fluttered in the warm sunshine as Kirsty picked a white rose, inhaled and held it to her nose. 'Such perfume.'

Her mother sat on the garden seat like a half-stuffed bolster between them, until her head nodded and she gave a grunt. Kirsty smothered a giggle and Johnnie stretched out his hand. 'A walk, Miss Lorne?'

She put her hand in his. 'Delighted, Mr. Stewart.'

Later, Johnnie remembered this precious time. He tried to forget the betrothal meal with Rob's empty chair, his father's angry outburst when Johnnie said he didn't want to join the rebellion and the awful bargain he'd made with Father.

No, Johnnie wanted to remember Kirsty's wide smile as they'd sauntered down the garden and found dappled shade under an apple tree. How her lips danced under his as he'd enjoyed her closeness. Every pore of him had wanted more. Most of all he wanted to remember when, at dinner, she'd dropped her napkin on the dining room floor. His hand brushed her foot and she allowed him to caress her dainty ankle. He returned, flushed, to his former upright position.

Lorna Windham

'My thanks, Mr. Stewart.' She accepted her napkin with a half-smile which revealed pearl teeth. She played with a ringlet as her eyes laughed at him. Then she whispered behind her fan, 'My garters are blue and embroidered with white rosebuds.'

Johnnie coughed and she patted his back as if his wine had gone down the wrong way. He looked round the table. Duncan's eyes never left his heaped plate. Morag and Euan didn't take their eyes off each other and Father started his second bottle of brandy.

Kirsty let her napkin slip a second time and Johnnie bent to pick it up. His hand wandered to her silk stocking. He stroked his way up to her knee, stretched a finger and felt her bare thigh. A jolt shot through him and gripped his loins. He hadn't realised her skin would feel so soft, so sensuous and he wanted, needed to explore further.

'So, Miss Lorne, Kirsty…' his father began.

Her knees shut like a trap and Johnnie just rescued his fingers. He resurfaced to hear his father say, '… of course, **all** my sons will fight for the Jacobites. I hope you are prepared for Johnnie's absence?'

'What?' Johnnie struggled to keep his temper and ensure wee Duncan stayed at home. Finally, Euan called an end to the evening and ushered out the startled ladies. Always the gentleman, he assisted Kirsty's Mother, who huffed and puffed her way into the carriage.

As Kirsty put her hand in Johnnie's she whispered, 'You may find this uplifting.'

He wrapped his fingers round the band of thin blue lace she'd given him as she mounted the coach steps. 'Good evening, ladies.' He waved as the coach and horses set off down the drive.

Kirsty's small hand appeared out of the coach window and waved something blue and feminine, the partner to that hidden in his fist.

The Jacobite Affair

Dougie poked his elbow in Johnnie's ribs which made him gasp for breath. The tacksman walked away as he shook his grey head.

Johnnie's heart drummed inside his chest as he stared at the garter in his hand. He and Kirsty would have a wonderful marriage. The wind moaned through the pines and the hair on the back of his neck prickled as he remembered Aristotle's warning: *The Gods are too fond of a joke.*

Lorna Windham

CHAPTER Twelve

Kirsty sat in the spense. She made a loop from the green yarn on her lap. Hens clucked in the dirt outside the farmhouse and grey clouds streamed across the sky.

Mother set her mouth in a grim line a she perched on a chair. The pale morning light cascaded over her round shoulders and onto her fingers which unfolded and re-folded a sheet of parchment.

'Something wrong?' asked Kirsty.

'Your cousin Michael's ill. Aunt Lizzie wants us to visit.'

'So, we'll go.'

'To Inverness? Just like that? What will we use for money?'

'Have we none to spare?'

Mother shook her head. 'Spent it on your betrothal and the harvest pays our debts. We need to wait until Murdo's back from Crieff. I'll think of something. I'm going to sew outside. Better light. Are you coming?' Mother tucked her sewing basket under her arm, and sat on a flat-topped boulder by the door whilst Kirsty sat opposite. She watched Mother's fingers search inside the froths of lace in the basket until she found an unfinished pink garter. Mother jabbed her needle in and out of a white rose she'd embroidered. 'He's not keen to fight for The Cause, this betrothed of yours, is he?'

Kirsty fingered the brooch pinned on her bodice. 'He's no' a coward, if that's what you mean?' Kirsty worked her needles into a fury as she jerked the green yarn and the ball raced across the grass. She scrambled to get it and sat back on her seat.

'Hmph. That's not what everyone will think.'

'I dinna ken what mean-minded people think. He'll fight and he's ensured Duncan stays at home.'

'Most reluctant. And according to Granny Mac the laird's drinking.'

'Mother.'

The Jacobite Affair

'Remember the dinner?' Mother pressed her lips together and stabbed the garter.

How could I forget? Kirsty turned her face away. *Does she suspect anything?*

'Have you thought what'll happen if your beloved doesn't return?'

Kirsty stared at her. *How can she make 'your beloved' sound like vinegar?* 'What do you mean?'

Mother leant towards her and tossed the lace into the basket at her feet. 'This rebellion will do us no good. How will we manage?'

'By God, you're heartless. He hasna even left yet.'

'The poor cannot afford to have a heart. Still don't understand do you? I shielded you from the worst. Your drunken sot of a father left us debts. We've nothing, but our wits and the sale of our cattle to keep us. We need to think ahead. Plan, just in case. You'll learn. Better to have a second fish to fry than none at all.'

'What do you mean by that?'

'Never you mind.' Mother got up and picked up her basket and went indoors. She returned wrapped in a shawl.

'Where you going?' asked Kirsty.

'Just ensure all the chores are done before I get back.'

Later that afternoon Kirsty sat beside the burn and scrubbed lye into a skirt as she let her mind wander. *He'll leave with the others. His hand on my thigh last night made my skin burn and I wanted him to go further...* She knew where that led: shame and want.

A few years ago Isla Kincaid's parents had thrown her out. Her large belly betrayed Isla as she begged from door to door. Kirsty remembered how Mother's face softened. She'd let Isla sleep with the cow for a night. *Judge not, lest ye be judged*, she'd said.

'Let me stay, Mrs. Lorne,' Isla begged, but Mother sent her on her away with bread and cheese in a kerchief.

Kirsty plunged the skirt into the water to get rid of suds. *Johnnie seems keen to learn about women and I want to know about men. I've been round animals all my life and hope it's more than just the act. When Johnnie holds me, I believe it has to be more. I'll miss him so much, but better he leaves to fight as a Jacobite than be regarded craven or a traitor by those in Braedrumie.*

If anyone had realised what I let him do under the table on our betrothal night… and I waved my garter at him. Worth it, though, to see his mouth drop open and the prim look on Morag's face change to wide-eyed shock.

Kirsty's mouth creased into a smile as she twisted the skirt, wrung it out and hung it over ragged balls of heather to dry. The sun hung high in a cloudless sky as she went into the gloomy byre. The old cow lifted her head and lowed. Kirsty patted the beast's neck and thought of the pitiful amount of milk she'd got from her that morning. 'You're no' much, are you?' *Where are we going to get money to visit Aunt Lizzie and Michael? And we need a young cow. I hope Murdo's back soon.*

***

That afternoon Johnnie's shadow arrived before he did as Kirsty gathered in her washing. He drew in lungfuls of air and enjoyed how her damp bodice clung to her breasts.

'You're late. Were you so eager to see me, you ran all the way?' Kirsty wagged her forefinger at him. 'Dinna' think you'll be taking any more liberties till we're wed.'

Johnnie heaved another breath. 'It's no' that at all. As if I'd…'

He looked at the upward curve of her mouth. 'You're teasing me.'

'Yes.' She left the washing and wrapped her arms round his waist.

'You seem sad, sweetheart.' His thumb swept her cheek.

'My cousin Michael's ill, he's in Inverness and my aunt's asked us to visit.'

'I'm sorry. It'll ease your mind when you see him.'

Her head drooped.

He held her shoulders. 'But, you've little money till the cattle are sold.'

'Aye.'

'I'll give you some.'

Her head jerked up. 'You will no'. I didna tell you so you'd offer me money.'

'Kirsty, we're betrothed.'

'But no wed. I willna do it.' She turned from him, but he lifted her and held her so his lips tantalised hers. She melted into his kiss and he savoured their closeness, all senses alert and aware of a fire in his groin. He put her down.

'I willna do it.'

'Very well, I can see you're determined, sweetheart. We'll speak no more of it for the moment.' He brushed her lips with his again. 'Sorry I'm late, Duncan's still no speaking to me and I've news. Father's just told me, Charlie's landed. They're raising the fiery cross tomorrow.'

'At last.' Kirsty's body poised as if to spring. 'We've waited so long.'

Johnnie grimaced. 'Father will have his wish. I'll never go to university and we... we canna wed till it's over.'

'Oh, Johnnie, but you'll be home soon, with the rightful king on the throne.'

'Is he... rightful?' He let her go.

'Everyone says...'

'Think for yourself, Kirsty.'

'I do.' She bundled the washing into a basket. 'I ken I dinna like Wade's roads or the forts or redcoats who watch our every move. What's England done for us? There's so many poor and we'll stay so as long as the Hanoverians cling to the throne.'

'We havena a hope of winning against them. Their army's...'

'In Europe, well, most of them. The French...' She hoisted the basket on one hip.

'Rob said their promises were worthless.'

'What did he know? Anyway, he's left.' Kirsty trudged towards the farmhouse.

Johnnie stared at her, outraged at her comments. But Rob with his black moods had cut himself off from his family. Rob, who they'd all looked up to. Rob, whose leaving, had probably hastened their mother's end. Rob, whose absence had caused their father to drink. Johnnie's voice cut the air like steel and halted her in her tracks. 'You know Rob may prove to be the most sensible amongst us.'

She whipped round. Hurt flickered in her eyes and he couldn't bear it. He took her basket off her and held her hands in his. 'Darling, I dinna want to quarrel with you. I've a field to plough and I want to ensure there's little for you and your mother to do when I'm away.' He turned to go and then stopped. 'You'll come with me to the Rising tomorrow?'

'Of course. I do love you, Johnnie.'

He strode towards her and clasped his lips to hers. She tasted of honey and a promise of sweeter things.

CHAPTER Thirteen

'Are you coming to the Rising, Mother?' Kirsty re-pinned her brooch so it would be in plain view on her threadbare shawl.

Mother sat beside the kitchen fire with assorted scraps of material and embroidery threads in her lap. 'No. I've these to put away and I want to read Aunt Lizzie's letter again.'

'Are you sure?'

Mother nodded. 'Take my shawl, it's warmer.'

'Thank you.' Kirsty eyed Mother, surprised at her warm tone.

Mother preened. 'Lizzie congratulated you, on the match.'

'That's nice.'

Mother waved her away. 'No kisses. Just dinna want you to freeze. Isabel said she'd be chaperone.'

Isabel? Oh, no, not Dougie's wife.

'Make sure you're back before I'm in bed and Stewart brings you home.'

'Course.' Kirsty hugged the shawl to her, grateful the soft, red wool hid her faded bodice and patched black skirt. The darkness would hide her from curious glances.

She waited and hopped from one foot to the next, in the spence, then turned out the cruisie lamp so she could spot Johnnie through the window before he knocked for her.

Two ponies trotted into sight. Kirsty ran to meet them whilst Mother stayed at the door.

'Good evening, Mrs. Lorne.' Isabel wore a blue bonnet.

'Isabel.'

'Evening, Mrs. Lorne, Miss Lorne,' Johnnie said.

'Hmph,' Mother retreated indoors.

Johnnie winked at Kirsty, put his hands round her waist and lifted her into her pony's saddle. They rode side by side with Isabel behind them, over the shrouded moor.

Times would become harder on the farm without Johnnie's help. Murdo. Where is he? We need the cattle money.

I'll not share the worry with Johnnie. He's been tight-lipped about leaving, his only consolation, a book he'd ordered months ago from Edinburgh, finally arrived. My heart aches for him. He's dosed the cow, cut the hay and checked the thatch.

Oh, God. He's done this because he thinks he won't return. I'll be strong, tell him how much I love him and not sob on his shoulder. He'll come home and we'll marry, I'm sure of that.

'Alright?' said Johnnie. Invererar Falls thrummed and gushed its peaty froth in front of them.

Kirsty nodded as her body quivered with excitement. Soon they'd light the Fiery Cross.

Johnnie hobbled the ponies and left them to graze at the foot of the Falls as he took Kirsty's hand and helped her up to the ridge.

'Wait for me.' Isabel scrambled up behind them.

Kirsty stood above the falls with Johnnie's arms wrapped round her. She rested her head against his chest and enjoyed the sound of his heartbeat until Granny Mac, Braedrumie's healer and midwife, let out a screech like a scalded cat. Johnnie's hand went to his dirk and Kirsty's hand to her throat. *What now?*

Morag and Euan melted into the darkness as red-faced Mary McBean shouted after them, 'She didn't mean anythin'' by it.' Then she hustled Granny Mac away.

Johnnie put an arm round Kirsty's waist when whoops sounded in her left ear and made her jump.

'It's that MacNab,' said Isabel. 'Granny Mac gave him some of her whisky to celebrate. Should have known better, look at him.'

Kirsty looked. MacNab, tall and thin, danced a reel with Mary's husband Hughie. MacNab held a jug in one hand and Hughie a claymore. Every now and then the men paused, drank their fill and staggered back in an attempt to join in.

Of course Uncle Hughie will have joined the rebellion. Mother willna be happy, he's the only relative she's something nice to say about.

The Jacobite Affair

'Men.' Isabel snorted with disgust. 'Rob would have…' Dougie's brow lowered and he led her away towards the wooden cross on the edge of the ridge facing north.

'Wonder where Rob is?' The words were out before Kirsty could pull them back.

'You're no' to mention his name.' Johnnie drew back from her. 'You ken what he did. Poor Mother.'

'But the other day… you've changed your mind.' Kirsty touched his arm.

'I've other brothers. We all feel the same.'

'And you canna forgive?'

'It's no' that easy. He had a duty, we all looked up to him… he's let us down. Look, they've fired the cross.'

Her gaze followed his finger. Flames leapt into the air twenty yards away and a string of gold lights responded across moonlit Loch Linnhe in the darkness miles to the north.

Johnnie put a hand on her shoulder and walked towards his father. Dougie took hold of a truculent Duncan. Johnnie bent, picked up a stone and set it on the cairn. Pride followed by a chill of foreboding rushed over her. She studied the faces of the men around her. *How many will return?*

Johnnie ruffled Duncan's hair, but his brother turned away.

Mrs. Stewart spoilt her youngest. Granny Mac said, Elizabeth almost died giving birth to him, so he was her last.

'Isabel's busy,' Johnnie whispered in Kirsty's ear. 'Sorting out a fight.' He jerked his thumb to where she stood, arms folded, between MacNab and Hughie McBean. 'Canna hold their drink, either of them.'

Kirsty smiled. 'Never could, but my uncle's a good man. Mother thinks a lot of him.'

Johnnie grabbed a drinking horn from Duncan and poured the ale on the ground.

Duncan's eyes narrowed. '**We'll** walk you home, shall we Miss Lorne?'

Both of them? No time to be alone with Johnnie.

Johnnie grabbed him by the scruff of his neck.

'Mother said you had to look after me.'

'You little scut. It's **you** we'll see home.'

Duncan squirmed in Johnnie's grasp. He flashed her and Johnnie surly glances. 'It's no' fair, I'm not allowed to do anything.'

Duncan. Kirsty set off at a pace and scrambled down to the ponies. She left behind Johnnie who dragged Duncan alongside him.

'Kirsty, slow down. What's the matter with you? Duncan will you stop wriggling or I'll kick your backside. Kirsty. Kirsty?'

She stopped and Johnnie, his head turned towards his brother, bumped into her. 'What's wrong?'

She swirled, hands on hips, to face the brothers.

Duncan's mouth creased upward.

'Look at the little devil, he kens what he's doing, stopping you and me going home together.'

'He's…' Johnnie began, then turned to Duncan and whispered in his ear. His brother nodded and skipped back the way they'd come. Johnnie took Kirsty's hand in his. 'Thought you'd understand. Rob left without a word, and Mother… he's lost the two people he loved most in the world.'

'It doesna mean he should behave like a…a…'

'What was it like for you when your father died?' asked Johnnie.

'It… that was different. He… wasna always himself… you ken what he tried to do…'

'But you loved him, aye?'

'Aye, but I couldna grieve. Mother, wouldna let me. Said life was hard enough without my tears adding to her burdens.'

'I'm helping him grieve, Kirsty. I'm giving him the time your mother wouldna give you.' He held her face in his hands.

'Oh, Johnnie you've so much love inside you.'

'Enough for all who are dear to me. Darling, promise me you'll keep an eye on Duncan when I'm gone.'

'Oh, Johnnie, I dinna think he likes me.'

'He doesna ken anything at the moment. You've seen how Father is since Mother's death. Duncan needs a friend, someone who'll listen.'

'I'll try. What did you say to him?'

I told him to find Dougie and promised he could see us off tomorrow and when I return we'd fish every burn running into Loch Linnhe.' He lifted her chin with his forefinger and thumb. 'It's a fair ride to your home. I think, as your betrothed, I need some practise in exactly what that word means.'

'Johnnie Stewart, if you think I'll…'

He pressed his warm mouth to her lips and silenced her outrage. Seconds later he raised his head. 'I'm no' sure I quite got it right. Let me try again.'

This time her lips closed on his. *To be so close.* He put his hands on her waist and pulled her against his hips. She nestled against him, aware of his arousal. His fingers stroked her neck, sought her collar bone and sent tendrils of need throughout her body.

He drew back. 'I think, Miss Lorne, I'd better take you home.'

'About time too, Johnnie Stewart.' A voice behind them made them spring apart. Isabel.

CHAPTER Fourteen

Johnnie gave up on sleep just before dawn. He dressed in the dark. His mind struggled with the fact he'd agreed to join the rebellion. He comforted himself with the thought, at least Duncan would be safe. He buckled his sword. A door banged somewhere in the bowels of the house. The servants would be awake and about their daily chores.

Dawn broke over the hills and the sky lightened in a peach haze. Johnnie turned this way and that in the mirror. He'd do, every inch a Highlander.

His door sprang open and the handle fell with a thud to the floor. 'Johnnie, Euan willna take me.' Duncan complained. 'Please let me go with you. I'll be no trouble. I'll look after your pony, keep your blades sharp and do as I'm told.'

'When will you learn to knock?' Johnnie's heart softened for a moment. He could take him, but heard his mother *Look after, Duncan. Promise me*.

'No.'

'But, Johnnie…'

He held Duncan's arms. 'I promised Mother. You ken what that means? It's a matter of honour, I canna go back on my word. Besides that I… dinna want any harm to befall you.'

'You dinna care, Euan doesna and Father doesna. I want to be a Jacobite and fight with you.' Duncan kicked the door.

'Listen to me, my wee man.' Johnnie held one of Duncan's arms. 'This is no way for a laird's son to behave. When Euan and I leave, you'll be Father's right-hand man. Euan and I trust you to look after him, Kirsty and her mother, Morag and her father **and** Braedrumie until we return. We wouldn't give this job to just anyone. Do you think you can do it?'

Duncan blinked at him. 'Yes.'

'Good,' said Johnnie. 'Spoken like a true Stewart.'

'You'll come back?'

Oh God, a huge fist squeezed Johnnie's heart and his throat was raw. He reached inside his sporran and found Duncan's

The Jacobite Affair

wooden salmon. 'Take this, it's my prized possession. When I see you again, you can return it.'

Duncan's fingers closed around the carving and he threw his arms round Johnnie. 'I'll look after it, but... come home soon, Johnnie. Promise?'

More promises. 'I promise.' Johnnie ruffled Duncan's dark hair. Dear God, why had Charlie landed? I want to read books, study, learn, not kill or be killed. Did Duncan understand my promise, just a word, a sop and I can't bring myself to tell him the truth.

Duncan pulled away from him and raced off. He just avoided his father and Euan.

'You're off then. I'll watch from the Falls.' The laird hugged Euan and extended his hand to Johnnie.

With a wry grin Johnnie shook it. 'Look after yourself.'

'Plenty of jobs to keep me busy. Dougie's left me a list, beginning with the handle of your door.'

'You're a bit late, it's just fallen off- Duncan's... upset.'

'Aye. He wouldna be if he'd been going with you.'

'Father.'

'It's maybe for the best. If it goes badly, at least I'll still have Duncan who's loyal to The Cause.'

'We'll win,' said Euan. 'You'll see, won't he Johnnie?'

'Aye.' Can't Euan see the futility of this?

'Dinna disgrace me. I want no wounds on your backs,' growled Father.

***

After Johnnie visited his mother's grave and left Euan and Morag together, he mounted his pony, but couldn't rid himself of the words, *Ye though I walk through the shadow of death...* They circled inside his head all the way to Kirsty's house.

Her mother made him wait on the front step. 'Think you could mend this hinge before you go?'

He dropped his knapsack and took the hammer and a strip of new leather from her. 'Aye, no bother.'

'The cow's off her feed again.'

'She's old. Make sure she drinks.' He wrestled the old nails out of the shreds which supported the door and tapped the new strip in place. He pushed the door forward and back. 'There you are, good as new.'

'So you say.'

Kirsty stood beside her mother. He'd eyes only for her and noted with a grin, she wore his brooch. She stood on tiptoe, put a blue bonnet with a white cockade on his head and gave him a knotted bundle. 'There's socks, a spare length of tartan and some cheese. No milk, the cow's…'

'Off her feed.' He patted a leather bag strung from his pony's saddle. 'I've water.'

'There's a bannock as well, baked fresh this morning.' She handed him the flat bread.

'Thank you.' Johnnie stuffed the gifts in his knapsack and hung it from the saddle. He didn't tell her he'd raided the laird's pantry. 'I'll eat like a king. We'd better be on our way. Goodbye to you, Mrs. Lorne.'

'And to you Johnnie Stewart and dinna forget to look after our Hughie.'

'I willna Mrs. Lorne.'

'And come home safe. That's what you mean to say to Johnnie, isn't it Mother?' said Kirsty.

'Yes. Come home safe.' Her mother regarded him with dead eyes and tight lips.

Johnnie took Kirsty's hand as the door closed behind them.

The Jacobite Affair

CHAPTER Fifteen

Some hours later, Kirsty tore the purple bells from a stalk of heather. *How could Morag defend Duncan's behaviour when the men left? It almost, but not quite, spoilt my day. She always thinks her opinion more important than anyone else's. Of course everyone understands Duncan doesn't want to be left behind, but Mrs. Stewart would have been shocked at his language.*

Kirsty had whispered in Johnnie's ear. 'I'll always keep a lamp lit for you. So you'll know I'm there, waiting for you to come home.'

'I havena forgotten about your sick cousin. Please stay with my Aunt Munro in Inverness'. Johnnie reached inside his knapsack, scribbled on a torn page from a book and handed it to her. 'Here's the address.'

'Maybe, once Murdo's back from Crieff.' Kirsty's fist tightened round the crumpled paper which held the precious information. *We've only to find the coach fare. Murdo's due any day, I'll write immediately. The visit will be wonderful. Johnnie's aunt will be delighted by his choice of bride and I, who've only ever visited Maryburgh, will see glorious Inverness.*

'It might be best to warn you no' to speak politics in her household,' said Johnnie. 'My uncle's a Whig and my aunt is... no' so fervent shall I say. Their son Jack calls them 'hammer and tongs'.'

'Form a column, lads.' Dougie's voice sounded above the excited chatter and tramp of feet.

Johnnie held her face in his hands as if he printed a copy of her on his memory. His lips seared hers and then he left. She watched his broad back disappear into the distance. An empty space opened up beneath her ribs and it ached. *Dear God, please bring him back to me.*

On her way home Kirsty decided not to divulge Mr. Munro's political persuasions to Mother who'd have hysterics about the Whig household. *Easier to inform her of this delicate fact once we arrive and can do little about it. The lure of Inverness and its social circle greater than being honest about our hosts.* Kirsty clutched Johnnie's note. *I'll tackle Mother at once.*

'It would save us money in the long run,' said Mother. 'Write and introduce yourself. If Mrs. Munro agrees, I'll see if I can sell some garters at Maryburgh. If not, we'll just have to wait for Murdo.' She picked up her wicker basket. 'Women will no' be buying much; they'll save their coin until the men return.' She twirled a blue garter embroidered with white roses around her crooked forefinger. 'But, patriotism always sells. I'll be back this afternoon. Make sure you finish your chores and no mooning over Johnnie Stewart.'

***

Several hours later Mother sped up the hill as if chased by the devil. In one hand she carried her basket and in the other she waved a piece of parchment. Her face reddened and bosom heaved as her twig-legs chased each other up the track. She paused, put her hand on her knees as her rib cage sought air and shouted, but the breeze chased her words away. Kirsty put a hand to her ear. Mother shook her head and set off again, her face set in the direction of home.

She sank onto a boulder beside Kirsty and sucked in breaths.

'Why are you back so soon?' asked Kirsty. She looked in Mother's basket. 'You've only sold half our goods. You almost killed yourself on that hill.'

Mother dangled the parchment under Kirsty's nose. 'I have it. Our way out of here… away from all this.'

'What have you got? You're making no sense.'

'Listen to this:

My dear Gilly,

Thank you for your letter. How could I forget my second cousin?'

'You wrote to a relative. Who?'

The Jacobite Affair

'Shush girl, listen.'

You are family, no matter how distant. If you can present yourselves at Toll House on Monday week, I should be able to spare you and your daughter a few minutes of my time.

I am, Madam, your obedient servant,

Tolbain

'Tolbain, daughter. See, he's signed it.'

'I didna think you close and he's a Whig. Why have you written? If the laird finds out he willna' be happy, nor will Johnnie. There's bad blood between him and the Stewarts, as well you know.'

'It's no one's business but ours, daughter. He's got power and money. Who knows what he can do for us. We're two women with no man. If your precious Johnny gets himself killed, we willna last long and we've an ailing cow. How long do you think we'll keep poverty from the door when we've no milk? He's family and he could help us.'

'I'd rather have asked Johnnie.'

'And how long do you think you'd stay betrothed? The Stewarts see you as a burden, daughter, not an asset. It's the land they're after because it borders theirs. They've seen how the harvests and cattle have improved. Dinna flatter yourself Johnny Stewart wants you for your pretty looks.'

'You misjudge him, Mother. Johnny loves me and I love him.'

'And how long do you think love lasts? Hmph. Not past the first child by my reckoning. Look at your father and me.'

Kirsty flinched. 'So it's my fault. You blame me for Father's behaviour towards you?'

'The duke's offered us his time…'

'A few minutes I bet. It will take hours to walk there and back.'

'Worth every step, mark my words, girl. Every step.'

'I'm no' going, he's our enemy.'

'Yes you are or you'll not stay in my house or set foot in it again. You'll leave with the clothes on your back and no more. You'll be dead to me.'

'Dinna say that. You wouldna throw me out, Mother, you wouldna. I'm your only child.'

Mother stood. 'He wrote *dear*. It's only polite to visit and wear the dress you wore at the betrothal dinner. I don't want you showing me up wearing rags. Leave the brooch here.'

Kirsty's hand went to it. 'We're no' going to beg?'

'No. We'll do business.'

'Business? Do you think he kens any wool merchants?'

'Perhaps.'

'You're no' thinking he'll be interested in anything you have to say?'

'Oh, yes I am. I think he'll be very interested.'

CHAPTER Sixteen

Kirsty and Mother walked through the iron gateway to Toll House. They'd set off at dawn, the sky streaked with magenta. Several hours later Kirsty spotted Toll House, a double-fronted building with a barmkin wall and defensive towers, on the edge of Loch Linnhe.

'Just as I remember it,' said Mother.

As the women approached the house, armed men sped backwards and forwards in front of them. Doors stood ajar. Chickens and geese ran amok as they clucked and honked on the lawn.

'Mother,' said Kirsty.

A white-faced maid hurried past as a young boy threw stones at her. 'Dinna, Bruce.' She wiped her tearful face in her apron.

'Get about your business.' A man with grey whiskers and wore moss-green, grabbed Bruce's collar.

'Aye, Mr. Campbell.' The girl spread her arms wide and guided the birds behind the house.

'I'll deal with this wee ruffian.' Campbell dragged the boy towards the stables.

'His tacksman,' said Mother.

Kirsty sniffed the air. *Gunpowder.* 'Something's happened here. Let's leave.'

'No,' hissed Mother, her face set. She strode up the steps and knocked on the oak door. A long-faced butler opened it. 'What do you want?'

Mother took a deep breath and raised herself to her full height. 'I'm Mrs. Lorne, His Grace's cousin and this is my daughter. Have the goodness to inform His Grace we've arrived.'

The butler's brow creased. 'Your carriage?'

'There's no carriage. My daughter and I felt in need of... exercise. Pray inform His Grace.'

The butler with a face like chiselled granite, closed the door and left them on the step. He returned a few minutes later. 'His

Grace is expecting you. You've come at a bad time, we've been raided.'

Kirsty glanced at Mother who'd gone pale.

'He's no' in a good temper. Come away in,' said the butler.

Kirsty and Mother followed him as he led them into an oak-panelled study. With a waft of his hand, he indicated two carved chairs in front of an oak desk and left the room.

Mother sat as the sun's rays moved from sash window to sash window. A light breeze came from one as time ticked by. Kirsty gazed out at the view of the placid loch below as Mother tapped her fingers on the wooden arm of her chair.

Then Kirsty paced up and down the room. 'He's kept us waiting hours. It'll be dark by the time we get back.'

'He'll see us. Remember what I said, we're Whigs.'

'He'll no' believe us.'

'He'll believe what he wants. Be agreeable and dinna offer any of your fine opinions. I know him well from when we were children. There's only one opinion, his, and we need him.' Mother studied the portraits of her Tolbain ancestors. 'It's much as it was in my grandfather's time.'

A door opened behind them and a dark, thick-set man, dressed in a green jacket and kilt stood there. A strip of bloody cloth covered his forehead and held his thick, black curls close to his rugged face 'Ladies,' he growled. He stroked his ebony beard.

Kirsty lowered her knees in an unsteady curtsey beside Mother. *So, this is Tolbain.*

He stepped forward. 'Gilly, it's been years. Hardly recognised you, to be expected I suppose. Your looks have gone.' Then he stared at Kirsty and his eyes worked their way from her head to her feet.

Kirsty waited for Mother's acid response.

Mother forced her mouth into the semblance of a smile. 'Your Grace, I hope we haven't called at an inopportune time.'

He brushed Mother's hand with his thick lips, whilst his eyes, hollows of blackness, stared at Kirsty.

'You're injured.' said Mother.

The Jacobite Affair

He untied the cloth from his head and revealed a livid gash which leaked blood. 'It's nothing. We men receive such scratches in battle.'

'Battle?' Mother's hand went to her throat.

'Jacobites raided my pantry and took ponies from the stables. No need to alarm yourself, we ran them off.' He turned to Kirsty. 'And this must be your daughter? Quite beautiful.' He circled her.

Kirsty's cheeks burned and she looked at the floor.

He put his forefinger under her chin and examined her face from every angle. 'Inherited her beauty from your husband's side, I suppose.'

Why does Mother accept his insults?

He took Kirsty's hand and pressed his cold lips to it. 'Amazing how a rose can grow amongst weeds. Hopefully, not a white rose.' His eyes pierced hers and he dropped her hand.

Everyone knows the white rose is a Jacobite symbol. What should I say?

'Please sit.'

Mother perched, whilst Kirsty sat upright with her back against the chair. *I won't be intimidated by him.*

Mother said, 'We're Whigs.'

Kirsty's stomach flipped as Mother's knee nudged hers.

He raised his head. 'Really?' He waved a hand towards a silver decanter and two goblets. 'Some wine?'

'Thank you.' The morning sunshine streamed through the window and puddled at Mother's feet.

'My apologies for keeping you waiting.' He handed a glass to Mother and then Kirsty. 'How's the farm?'

'We've had a better harvest than ever before and better cattle,' said Mother. 'We'll have made a good profit. We expect the drover any day.'

'The drover? Splendid, splendid. As the farm belonged to our mutual grandfather, I take an interest. Please excuse me a moment, ladies.' He left the room and Kirsty heard the sound of muffled orders. He reappeared moments later. 'Damned nuisance, we've just buried some of my men. I'll see those rebels hanged.' He slammed his fist on the desk. Black ink spilled from its pot and over some papers. He lifted a brass bell from the table. The tinkle of notes summoned a bald-headed servant.

'Clean it up,' said the duke.

The man knelt on the floor.

'Not the papers, fool, the ink.'

Mother will have her work cut out with him. A sudden thought came to Kirsty. *Could the raiders have been the Stewarts and Johnnie?* She'd a strange sensation of Johnnie in danger and close by.

Mother's hand went to her throat and fluttered there.

'My dear Gilly, you're quite safe.' The duke lounged back in his chair. 'I'll ensure my men escort you home.'

'You're too kind, Your Grace.'

'Alexander.'

Mother simpered. 'Alexander.'

'That's enough, man.' He waved the servant out and turned to Mother. 'They tell me that despite the Jacobite defeat in the '15 and other useless rebellions, Braedrumie and the Stewarts have again turned traitor and joined Charlie.'

'Yes,' said Mother.

Kirsty dug her nails into her palms.

The duke leant forward in his chair. 'Nest of rebels. Need burning out. Anyone who harbours, defends or hides them will meet rough justice, Gilly, when we win. A good thing you and your daughter are Whigs.'

'Yes.'

He paused and played with a gold signet ring on his finger.

'So, how is it she's betrothed to Johnnie Stewart?'

Kirsty took a quick breath. Her hand went to her bodice, where Johnnie's brooch should have been.

Mother's eyes flicked to the floor.

How much does this man know?

'Forced, Alexander. Our farm, we need... the Stewarts want my land.'

'Mother...'

The Jacobite Affair

'Quiet, daughter.'

Kirsty's thoughts swirled. *Johnnie loves me, no' the land. Why the lies?*

The duke stared from one to the other. 'I've heard this Stewart worked your land and improved the yield and stock. Must be difficult being the only Whigs in a nest of scorpions?'

'Yes.'

'You'll understand I'll no' take kindly if I'm lied to, Gilly?'

Kirsty regarded them both under lowered lids. *Oh, God.*

Mother looked straight at him. 'Yes.'

He clasped his hands together. 'So, your letter gave little detail of what this is about and I've much to do this morning.'

'I've been a widow for some years, Alexander. My husband…'

'A good for nothing. Well shot of him.'

Kirsty flinched at his words and clenched her fists, even though she knew tales of Father's drunkenness and gambling must be well known.

Mother warned her with a glance. 'Yes, you're right.'

She should defend him. Kirsty folded her arms.

'You were warned,' he said.

'Yes.'

'Made your bed… '

'Yes.'

Oh God. She's here to beg for money, so we can go to Inverness.

The duke pursed his mouth. 'So, why are you at Toll House?'

'Can we talk in private, your Grace- Alexander?' said Mother.

'Your letter mentioned a business proposition.'

'Aye.'

'It had better be good. I'm not used to doing business with women.'

'I'd like to talk to you on my own, if I may?' Mother nodded in Kirsty's direction.

'If you insist.' He rose from behind his desk and took Kirsty's hand in his. 'You can walk in the grounds.' His breath tickled her ear. 'Stay in sight of my men, no knowing if those raiders might return. It would be a shame if such beauty was sullied in any way.' He handed Kirsty out of a door and into the garden. 'Your business, Gilly?' The door closed behind him.

Kirsty pondered Mother's *business* as she stepped onto the sunlit cobbled path and breathed in the warm morning air. She stopped as voices came to her from the open window behind her.

'Alexander, use your eyes,' said Mother.

'And the Stewarts…?

The window banged shut. This subterfuge didn't sit easy with Kirsty. *What sort of Jacobite does business with a Whig?*

Gold rays shone between dark banner-clouds and dappled the northern hills with mauve and gold hues. She wandered further afield to the back of the house, towards the clock tower above the stables.

In the yard, flies buzzed round a ruined ham beside the water trough. She walked forwards. Wasps circled a broken jar and a trail of honey. Dark spots of what looked like blood splattered a muddy cart track which led to an open gate. A wicket creaked and strange moans came from the stables. She peered inside and jerked back. Wounded men lay side by side as servants pressed, dabbed and bound, anything to staunch the flow of blood which pumped from wounds, dripped onto the straw and congealed on the cobbles. She breathed in the metallic smell. Her stomach lurched and she couldn't stop the vomit which rose in her throat. After a time she wiped her mouth with her hand.

'Excuse me, Miss.' A dark-haired maid with a lopsided smile stood in front of Kirsty. The maid held a cloth in one hand and a basin of water on one hip.

Pretty apart from her jaw.

'I need to see to the men, Miss.'

'Yes. Sorry. You do that.' Kirsty stepped out of her way.

The Jacobite Affair

The sound of hooves made Kirsty peer into the distance and shield her eyes from the sun's glare. *Someone in a hurry.* The lathered pony had no rider or saddle. It slowed to a canter and then a trot as it entered the yard and walked into an open stable. *Has one pony escaped the raiders? Was Johnnie one of them? I miss his laugh, his always being around. He's the only one who's ever said he loves me. Everything he's done, he's done for me. When he comes home, we'll marry straight away. No waiting, I can't bear the idea of waiting. Mother doesn't understand about me and Johnnie.*

'Right daughter, I've finished my business.' Mother's voice came from behind Kirsty and made her whirl round.

'Will he help us?'

'He might,' said Mother.

'How?'

'My business.'

'What business? And why did you say you were a Whig?'

'Keep your voice down. Let's make our way home.'

Kirsty turned and saw the duke's cold eyes on her as he stood at the window.

CHAPTER Seventeen

A low mist covered the glen whilst bright blades of sunlight caressed the mountain peaks. Johnnie cocked his head at Hughie McBean as Euan strode towards him.

Blue-lipped McBean rested on one knee. His chest heaved in search of air. Johnnie stood over him. How to help? 'We'll rest here, shall we?'

McBean nodded as Johnnie waited for Euan.

The Jacobite army marched ahead of them over several miles of mountain track. This, reality after the euphoria at the raising of the standard at Glenfinnan and the Jacobite's successful raid at Toll House.

Johnnie never imagined Morag would join the baggage train or Euan would let her stay. Sometimes Morag only thought about herself. Why couldn't she see Euan needed to concentrate on the campaign? Women. He wished he understood them.

'Problem?' said a tight-lipped Euan.

'He canna keep up this pace. He'll be alright after a wee rest. That's right McBean, isn't it?'

Hughie nodded and wheezed at the same time.

Euan took Johnnie to one side and lowered his voice. 'We've orders from the prince. If we dinna reach Corrieyairack Pass before Cope, the rebellion's over.'

'He's sure?' Johnnie's brow furrowed.

'Aye. One of our spies in Edinburgh, God bless them. We've no' a minute to lose.'

Johnnie flicked a glance at McBean. 'Well, I dinna suppose two of us will make any difference.'

Euan put his hand on Johnnie's shoulder. 'You've done an honourable thing, keeping an eye on him for the Lornes. Just ensure he's no' the reason you're killed.'

Johnnie batted his brother's hand away and watched him set off at a run to catch his men in their march to the mountain pass. Alright for Euan, even if he hadn't wanted Morag to join them, she was here now and reminded Johnnie of home and

Kirsty. At least he'd left the Lorne's farm water-tight and once Murdo returned with the cattle money, she and her mother would be fine until he got back. That reminded him, he needed to finish Kirsty's letter. He settled himself down beside a flat rock. What to write? He took the crumpled parchment out of his leather pack and read the words he'd written so far:

August 1745
My Own One,
I hope you and your mother are well? I miss you very much. How are you managing with the harvest? It pains me not to be there to help. I hope the cow's health has improved. If she sickens again do not forget to ask Granny Mac for one of her potions.
I dare not write too much unless this ends in our enemy's hands. I wish you could have seen the Raising of the Standard at Glenfinnan and the prince. Everyone says he's a bonny lad. I only wish I had more confidence in him. He seems young and inexperienced next to General Murray. Euan says he does not know where I get my pessimism from.
Much to our surprise, Morag joined us and Euan has allowed her to stay. He and Morag send their regards to all, as does Hughie whose health is good and his fitness improves every day.

Johnnie glanced at Hughie who had a hand on his chest and whose breath whistled as he squeezed air in and out. A little lie would do no harm, he didn't want Kirsty worried. He continued to read.

We have been on a successful raid and are in good spirits and hope you are too. I hope we will gain victory soon and you will be in my arms again. Darling, you are in my prayers and dreams…

If truthful, she was in his loins as well. Like an itch he couldn't scratch. He knew he liked women, wondered about them, their minds, their bodies, but he'd never touched one, in an intimate way, until their betrothal dinner. God, if her mother knew what happened under the table, instead of being more interested in the talk above it. He couldn't get the thought of Kirsty's silken thigh and his arousal out of his mind. He'd thought his lower regions would burst as his fingers stole upwards, just past her garter. She'd savoured a grape and offered him one. His manhood throbbed at the thought. She'd awakened something, a beast which he wished to hide, but not bury. If he'd been home they could have married within a few weeks, though with no priest, it would have been difficult. But, he could have explored all of her and had his curiosity sated. Well, sated for the moment. He groaned as his balls tightened. He wished a certain part of his anatomy would behave itself.

He had swum in icy lochs and stood under waterfalls until numbness meant he doubted he had parts that worked. It helped for a time. When he listened to other men, his state at the thought of women sounded common amongst them all. The question, how to relieve the want and the lust? Would a letter from Kirsty help or make his balls ache even more?

He looked out to the far hills where the last of the Jacobite army disappeared over a ridge. Then he turned to Hughie whose wheeze had lessened.

Johnnie dipped his quill in ink, leant forward and wrote: *They tell me blue garters are in fashion.* That should make her think of him. He emptied the ink pot and packed it, the quill and the letter in his saddlebags. 'Come on Hughie, gather yourself, man. The pass is only over the next hill.'

'You said that before.' Hughie wheezed as he stood.

'Aye, well a man can be wrong, no'?'

'Five times?' Hughie grimaced.

CHAPTER Eighteen

Johnnie sat in the *Blind Beggar*, a half-timbered tavern in Edinburgh and drank another tankard of ale. The fug of tobacco smoke hung over its Jacobite customers who celebrated the capture of Auld Reekie, without firing a shot. Pity Guest and his redcoats still held the castle.

Kirsty's recent letter with its white ribbon tied round a sprig of purple heather made Johnnie miss her more than ever. He sniffed the parchment – roses? She'd called him *Dearest*, asked about the prince, mentioned her new gowns and planned visit to Aunt Munro. He read her last sentence several times. '*I send you my love.*' She seemed so distant. Perhaps he imagined things. Life would be hard without him on the farm. He'd write to her again.

He wanted this rebellion resolved so he could pick up his life where he'd left it. His boot tapped the table leg. University seemed a distant dream.

A familiar ache came from his loins. His body hungered for knowledge of women - carnal knowledge and a cardinal sin. Years ago he'd broached the subject with Euan and then Dougie, but had been brushed away like a persistent fly. Finally, his red-faced father took him to the stables. He could hear his rough voice now. 'You ken stallions cover mares, and that's how foals come into the world?'

'Aye, Father, I ken that alright.'

His father grinned and slapped him on the back. 'That's all you need to know till you're of an age to marry. Then you treat women with respect, all women. Marriage is an honourable state and you wait for the respectable woman who'll be your wife. You'll learn together.'

All very well for Father to say, he'd a wife and four sons. He'd no concerns about whether he could… perform. Johnnie couldn't imagine how women allowed a man to do such… shocking things. Then he thought of Kirsty who let his fingers explore her satin- thigh. She must have enjoyed it… he certainly did and he wanted more. He thought of their well-endowed stallions and doubt crept in. He shrugged it off. No need to be ashamed of himself, he'd seen naked men, but how did you compete with stallions? The thought re-wakened the part of him he wished would remain asleep. He'd say some Hail Marys.

He'd been expected to go to the prince's ball at Holyrood Palace along with Euan, Morag and Dougie. He'd said, with as much bravado as he could muster, 'I've an appointment with a friend. See you tomorrow at midday.'

A wry grin spread across Dougie's grizzled face and Euan cocked an eyebrow at him. 'A lady friend?'

'My business.' Johnnie strode away from them. In the back of his mind he pictured the army's victorious ride through the Nether Bow Port Gate. He'd enjoyed the sight of a lady in her night gown, who'd hung out of a tenement window, waved a handkerchief and revealed most of her bosom. And what bosoms, pale and rounded like dove's breasts. He'd known enough from the banter around him to recognise a whore, but reasoned who better to teach him the art of making love? The lesson over, he'd know how to be a fine husband for Kirsty. Not that he remembered the woman's face, he'd been too busy looking at her peach-mounds.

The sounds of an argument brought him back to the present. He finished his tankard of ale, held himself upright and lurched out of the tavern. A pale globe and a scatter of stars shone down on him. As he staggered, the cool air made him reel. He stopped and examined the long line of tall buildings ahead which swayed in front of him. Yellow light winked through shutters and open doorways as a low mist swirled round his boots.

Strange, but the tenement seemed dingier, than the last time he'd seen it. It stood at right angles to the Nether Bow Port. The screech of a fiddle and a woman's voice drifted down to him. He cupped a hand to his ear. She sang of a lost sweetheart, killed in the '15. His eyes searched the street from right to left. If Euan or Dougie found out, they'd never let him forget it.

The Jacobite Affair

A shaft of light, from a lantern above an open doorway, stretched across the cobbles and ended at his feet. He hesitated as his brain argued with itself. Should he go in? He could do penance. Back and forth the argument went until his feet seemed to command the rest of his body and he found himself in the dank hallway. The stained ceiling sagged and plaster hung off the walls. His nose wrinkled. Damp. To his right stood a closed, battered door. From behind it came the murmur of soft voices and then an explosion of laughter. Paradise? Or mortal sin and Hell? He aimed a quiet knock at the faded paintwork in front of him, but his fist beat a loud tattoo. The door swung open. The fetid stink of stale tobacco and tallow hit him, but beyond the murk - Paradise. Amongst the flicker of candles he made out women in different states of undress who decorated every chair in the room. One bared a shoulder, another a leg, the last a breast with a blackberry-nipple.

His jaw went slack.

'You took your time, 'andsome' said a middle-aged woman with a painted face. She patted her pepper-grey hair which cascaded in tangles from her lopsided bun. 'Watched you for some time.' She indicated the grimy window with her thumb. 'We'd a wager whether you'd summon the courage. Delilah won.' She pointed at a doll-like creature with a sunken face and long mousy hair to her waist. Delilah's winnings chinked in her grimy fist and her thin mouth widened into a toothless grin.

He tried not to stare in horror.

'They calls me Mrs. Leith. What's your fancy? Delilah's a goer. If you want her, it's sixpence'

Johnnie shook his head.

'How's about, Eve? She's younger, innocent and very shy.' Mrs. Leith took the girl's wrist. 'Come here, child.' She drew her forward and sniffed. 'Been on the gin again?' Mrs. Leith tutted. 'Show him what you've got.'

'Yes, Madam.'

'Er, no,' said Johnnie…' I'm sure…'

82

The girl swayed towards him with her head down. Straw-hair covered most of her face.

Johnnie blinked then stared at her. At least she's young and has a slim waist. At least, once I've paid her, she'll have enough for a good meal.

Eve let him feast his eyes on her naked breasts. Plump and round, just as he'd dreamed. And not shy. His loins stirred.

'May as well see everything you're getting.' A huge red-headed woman with beefy arms lifted a candle to Eve's face. The girl screamed, covered the purple craters in her cheeks with her hands and scuttled into the shadows.

His loins shrivelled.

Mrs. Leith shook her head and tutted. 'That was unkind, Jezebel. What will the gentleman think? Makes no difference in the dark.'

Oh, dear God, poor Eve. 'I dinna… perhaps…' Johnnie began.

'Choosy, are we? Should of come earlier, the rest of the Jacobite army 'ave.' Mrs. Leith lifted back her head, let out a raucous laugh and displayed black stubs for teeth. 'Listen.' From above his head Johnnie could hear the repetitive creak of his dreams. 'Better 'urry and decide. There's always Jezebel. Get more for your money. Taken a fancy to you already. 'Andy with a whip if you likes.'

Johnnie's privates curled up somewhere deep inside him.

Jezebel lumbered closer. She licked her lips, and her hands, like a boxer's, lifted the hem of her skirts to reveal huge dimpled thighs.

A whip? The fog in his brain cleared in an instant. He'd walked into Sodom and Gomorrah. Johnnie, reached into his sporran and his fingers fumbled with some coins.

'There you are 'andsome, thought you'd like a bargain.' Mrs. Leith put her hands on her wide hips.

'I like a bargain, Madam, but I dinna like being rooked.' Johnnie thrust the coins into her hands. 'This should tide you over before you find some blind, daft and desperate men willing to risk their manhood. As you can see, I'm no' one of them. I'll bid you good night.'

'Ere, 'andsome.' Mrs. Leith stopped him in his tracks. 'We like our customers to leave satisfied. Dinna want this high class establishment to get a bad name. 'ave this.' She threw him a well-thumbed book which he caught with both hands. 'You look like the readin' type. Once you've worked it out, come back.'

Raucous laughter followed him into the street. He rounded a corner, stood under the flame of a torch and read the words on the front cover, *The School of Venus, or the Ladies Delight, Reduced into Rules of Practice* by Michel Millot. Morag hadn't thought much of his last book and she'd have an apoplexy if she saw this, but then she didn't understand the importance of knowledge. He flicked a page. *Translated from French in 1680.* He flicked another. Good God. He didn't need to understand the words. He flicked a few more pages. He never dreamt. He turned the book upside down, then shoved it inside his breeches. He'd have to keep it hidden. What would Kirsty think? All he wanted to do was to not make a fool of himself on his wedding night. Well, he supposed the book would be helpful. He strode back to his quarters. He'd put it in his saddlebags and then go to Holyrood Palace. Jezebel came unbidden into his mind. All the way to the palace he tried to rid himself of her image.

CHAPTER Nineteen

A warm breeze caressed Kirsty's face as she stood at the door. She held Johnnie's letter to her breast, kissed his brooch and pinned it in its usual place. God bless postie, Jamie Moffat. Johnnie had written that he loved her, wanted her in his arms and couldn't wait to be home to wed her. In her other hand she held a letter from Inverness. Two letters in one day. She followed the scent of baked bread and ran into the kitchen.

'Mother, Johnnie's aunt has sent her sympathy about Michael's illness **and** invites us to stay with her and her son, Jack, in Inverness next week. Imagine, we'll be able to visit Aunt Lizzie and Michael and only pay the coachman.'

Mother stabbed her needle into an unfinished garter. 'If only Murdo were back.' Mother yanked at the white thread.

'Please listen.' Kirsty sat beside her. 'Johnnie's aunt could introduce us to wool merchants. We could sell what we make to them as well as at Maryburgh.'

'We can't rely on that. As if they'd be interested in anything we make.' Mother lifted the garter and peered at her stitches.

'You've asked Tolbain for money and he's a Whig.'

Mother flushed. 'He's... he's different.' She bent her head over her work.

'We shouldn't be beholden to him. I ken he's your cousin, but I dinna trust him.'

Mother bit her thin lip.

Oh, God. 'You haven't accepted Tolbain's money?'

Mother's needle worked faster. 'I had no choice.'

'Oh, Mother. What have you done?'

'Ensured we get to Inverness. Now who will we ask to look after the farm and livestock?'

Inverness. Somewhere different to Braedrumie. I'll travel on a coach and meet new people 'I know just the young laddie.'

The Jacobite Affair

***

The wind whipped white clouds across the sky as Kirsty walked to Braedrumie House. 'I'll pay you a penny a day, Duncan.' *I'll take it from my wool money.*

'A whole penny? But Johnnie asked me to look after you and I agreed. I'll take no payment.'

'Oh, Duncan, I insist.'

'No. Johnnie wouldna like it. I'll see what Fathers says. Come on, he's in the outfield.'

Duncan led her to where his father leant over a calf as he bound a mud poultice on its foreleg.

'I'm sorry to hear about your cousin, Miss Lorne,' he said. 'But Duncan will have to finish his daily chores, before he can come to your farm. Will that satisfy you?'

'More than satisfy me, thank you, sir. Though he willna accept payment.'

'He's a good lad. Any news?'

'I've just received a letter. They're all well.'

'Did Johnnie mention me?' asked Duncan as he hopped from one foot to another.

'He sends his love.'

'Yuk.' Duncan pulled a face and raced away.

The following week, Kirsty and her mother left for Maryburgh and boarded a coach to Inverness.

***

The coach arrived in Inverness on a dismal day and in the middle of a cloudburst. The sky lay like a vast, grey rug over the town.

Mother sat upright with Kirsty opposite as the coach bowled along and steam rose from their damp clothing.

'Mind how you speak and your manners.' Mother warned Kirsty before she stepped down from the coach.

Kirsty pursed her lips. 'Oh, Mother.'

Aunt Munro's home stood four square and upright in a street of higgledy-piggledy houses, taverns and inns. Kirsty glanced up and saw an imposing house with grand steps.

A long-faced butler opened the door.

'We're the Lorne's from Braedrumie, I believe we are expected,' said Mother.

Kirsty arched a brow. *Mother sounds like she has a mouthful of plums.*

Aunt Munro greeted them with a hug whilst Mother stood like a pillar of salt and Kirsty returned the gesture.

'My dear, Mrs. Lorne and Miss Kirsty.' Aunt Munro appeared unruffled. 'Do come in, such dreary weather. You look soaked. I'm so pleased to meet you, I'm Johnnie's aunt. Let me present my son, Jack.'

'Delighted ladies.' A pale, young man bowed and kissed their hands. 'Thomson.'

The butler stepped forward. 'Your cloaks, ladies.' He shook each cloak and diamond drops cascaded onto the carpeted floor before he draped the garments over his arm.

Kirsty touched her brooch as an image of Johnnie surfaced in her mind's eye. *I miss him.*

'Come, there's a fire in the sitting room.' Aunt Munro led the way.

Kirsty glanced at the crystal chandelier suspended from the ornate plaster rose on the hall ceiling and her eyes traced the sumptuous carpet up the stairs. *This house shouts: comfort, luxury and servants. Oh to be born into money.*

'We're so sorry to hear about your cousin… Michael isn't it?' said Aunt Munro.

'Thank you.' Mother placed a hand on her bosom. 'He's always had a weak constitution, Mrs. Munro.'

'Please be seated and get warm.' Jack pulled chairs to the fire. 'Have you heard from **my** cousins?'

'Johnnie and Euan joined the Jacobite army and are in good spirits.' Kirsty settled herself on a well-padded chair. 'Duncan stayed at home.'

The Jacobite Affair

'Bet **they're** having fine adventures.' Jack gave his mother a sideways glance.

'Hush, Jack.' Aunt Munro motioned him to be quiet. 'It's only right and proper you stay with me whilst your father is absent. And Rob?'

Kirsty blinked and realised the Stewarts hadn't told the Munro's about Rob. 'He … left Braedrumie some months ago.'

'He hasna written?' Aunt Munro's brow creased.

'I dinna ken.' Kirsty used a glove to fan herself.

'Oh.' Aunt Munro stared at Kirsty, then Mother. 'How odd.'

'Father should have let me join them, Mother.'

'Enough, Jack.' Aunt Munro pursed her lips. 'If it had been up to me… But what's done is done. At least I have no worries about you. Forgive us ladies, this rebellion has unsettled us all.'

'Mother.' Jack tapped her arm. 'Our guests need refreshment and to be shown to their rooms.'

'Of course. Thomson will see to the luggage.' Aunt Munro beckoned him with her fingers. When the butler left the room Kirsty heard the tramp of feet on the stairs.

One freckle-faced maid and another with a tousled head peeked at Kirsty from the door.

'Ina, the ladies will take refreshment in their room.' Aunt Munro's brow wrinkled. The freckled face disappeared. 'Mairi, come here. Tidy your hair please.'

The girl bobbed at her mistress and her fingers flew to her head. Mairi pulled her dark curls into a semblance of order.

Aunt Munro examined her efforts. 'You'll do. Now, show my guests to their bedchamber.' The brown-haired girl curtsied to Kirsty and Mother. 'Dinner is served at eight.' Aunt Munro's tone indicated late-comers wouldn't be tolerated.

'Starchy,' said Mother in their bedchamber. Her mouth curled in a downturn of disdain.

Kirsty put her forefinger finger to her lips. 'Ssssh, she'll hear you and Johnnie loves her. Be grateful Mrs. Munro has a son with a warmer personality.'

Kirsty lay back, hands behind head and feet crossed on the four-poster bed. She admired the gold counterpane and damask curtains which matched the shade of the carpet. 'I'm sure this is a feather mattress, you just sink into it and you can see the garden without even getting out of bed. This is going to be the most wonderful visit.'

'It cost enough,' hissed Mother. 'A pity we had to pay for Duncan as well as the coach and the gowns.'

'Duncan wouldna take my money, remember? This is what I want, a beautiful home, feather mattresses, servants.' Kirsty closed her eyes. 'Imagine lying in bed after the cock crow, breakfast in bed... even after I wed Johnnie my life will be the same. I'm tired of milking, manure, cattle...'

'Play your cards right and who knows.' Mother opened a glass jar on the dressing table and sniffed the creamy contents. She dug her forefinger into the mixture and rubbed it into her hands. She's only the one son, perhaps if you...'

'Mother, I'm betrothed to Johnnie.'

'What's done can be undone. You're going to meet society, my girl. It'll change you.'

'I'll always love, Johnnie.'

A slight tap sounded at the door.

'Come in,' said Kirsty.

'Would your ladyships like help dressin' for dinner?' asked Mairi.

Kirsty stared at her. *Ladyship?* Her face lit up. 'Well... er... yes... of course.' Kirsty sat up. 'Mairi, isn't it?'

'See.' Mother smirked. 'It's started already. Me first if you please.'

Kirsty's nails itched to scratch her.

***

The Jacobite Affair

Kirsty inwardly compared Aunt Lizzie's furnishings to the farmhouse's, byre, crude furniture and flagstone floor. *Why can't we live like this?*

Cousin Michael sat under a mound of blankets in his carpeted bedchamber. A cream silk-covered chair stood by the fire, a fine writing desk under the window and a wardrobe against one wall.

He coughed up green phlegm at every opportunity.

'Feel my forehead. I'm burning.' *Feels cool to me.*

'My heart's beating so fast… I'm sure I'm less well than I was yesterday.' The last statement, enough to send his Mother into a faint.

Kirsty did what she could, mopped his pale brow and fed him broth whilst she made him laugh with stories of her adventures as a child with the Stewart brothers. He then coughed until he became breathless.

'You see how very ill I am,' Michael said as the compresses and bowls of steaming water came and went. After a few days of the miasma in the sick room, Kirsty's toes tapped and she wriggled in her seat. She longed to laugh, hear music or dance, anything but this.

Michael must have sensed her restlessness as he took her hand. 'Thank you for your visit, coz. I'm dying, I know that, though I daren't say it to Mother.'

She made to disagree, but he squeezed her knuckles. 'This is no place for you. I remember you as a child, sparking with life. I've enjoyed your visits. Think of me in your prayers.'

She kissed his cheek. 'I will, Michael. I'll pray for you.' His cheeks had a healthy glow and there'd been strength in his grip. *Hard to believe he thinks death's near.*

He closed his eyes as she crept out of the room.

Her conscience writhed with guilt. *What a selfish creature I am. And yet… and yet… I want to meet Inverness society.*

***

Lorna Windham

Several evenings later, at the Munros, the red velvet curtains had been drawn and the dining room flickered with candlelight. The cut crystal twinkled, china sparkled and the silver shone on the dinner table.

'Your husband is away on business, Ma'am? Pray, what does he do?' asked Mother as she spiked a piece of chicken with her fork.

Aunt Munro replied tight lipped, 'He works for the government, Ma'am.'

'Admit it Mother, you wish he didn't.' Jack wagged his knife at her.

'Manners, Jack. I'll admit I love your father and that I'm a Jacobite.'

Mrs. Lorne's fork clattered onto her plate. 'A Jacobite.'

'A pity **he** doesn't have more sense.' Aunt Munro shook her head.

'Hammer and tongs.' Jack smiled. 'Hammer and tongs.'

'Jack, be agreeable, please. We will not talk politics at the dinner table even if I'm certain our company are of the same persuasion.' Aunt Munro leant towards Kirsty and Mother. 'My dear Mrs. Lorne, Miss Lorne, do tell us about the soirees and balls you've frequented?'

'Mother…' Jack spoke between tight lips.

'It's just, I thought Kirsty's cousin was ill?' Aunt Munro dabbed at the corner of her lips with her napkin. 'That is the case is it not?'

'It is of course.' Mother shifted in her seat. 'However, poor Michael is quite inundated with visitors, inundated. So, we've sacrificed our wish to be near him in his hour of need so that his friends may also visit.'

Kirsty thought of the previous social evening at the Abercromby's and how she'd been surrounded by several admirers, young men from Inverness, eager to make their mark in cities like Edinburgh and Glasgow. Then she thought of Mr. Sinclair.

'So, your cousin's health has improved?' asked Jack.

The Jacobite Affair

His words jerked Kirsty back to the present. 'Michael no longer coughs and has taken to getting dressed, much against his mother's wishes.'

'He has improved.' Mother looked at her lap, then at everyone at the table. 'My dear Mrs. Munro and Mr. Munro, you have been most convivial hosts, but we must return home. I've made arrangements for the day after tomorrow, if that is acceptable to you?'

'Of course.' Aunt Munro gave a gracious smile. 'You must do what you think fit.'

Once Kirsty and Mother retired to their bedchamber. Mother sank into the only chair. 'I know you're thinking about the last soiree and all those young men. The dark one's dependant on his parents, you can see they dote on him. And the tall, fair one with the long nose, not a penny to his name. You must have noted his frayed cuff? But that gentleman, grey-hair with sad eyes, Mr. Sinclair, now he's worth a penny or two.'

'He's a wool merchant and his friend is Mr. James Liddle of Glasgow who deals in leather.' Kirsty thought of how she'd crossed the room to a table which groaned with food and wandered backwards and forwards in indecision when a male voice made her turn.

'May I have the honour of presenting myself, dear lady? I'm James Sinclair.'

'Miss Kirsty Lorne.' She curtsied.

The goose looks particularly tempting.' He'd pointed at the carved meat with a podgy finger.

'Goose it is then.' She let him serve her a helping. Half an hour later Sinclair agreed, much to her surprise, that if she could supply him with woollens twice yearly, he promised to collect goods in Maryburgh and sell them to markets in the south. He pursed his thick lips. 'There's a rebellion, but I dinna think it will last long and certainly shouldn't interfere with business. Shall we say the first Monday of next month?'

'Yes, that will do very well.' Kirsty clapped her hands. *Can a heart burst from pure happiness?*

'We'll keep it to ourselves, if you dinna mind.' He tapped the side of his nose. 'Canna let it be known I'm dealing with a woman.'

'As you wish.' *Well!*

Kirsty shared her news with Mother in the coach on the way back to the Munro's.

Mother's eyes snapped open. 'He said that, did he?'

'Aye.'

'Let's hope this Mr. Sinclair is an honest gentleman. He must be quite taken with you to make such an offer.'

'I think he saw an opportunity for profit, that's all.'

'Such a pity to leave such luxury behind. I do so love syllabubs. Remind me of my youth. But, we've been on a fool's errand. Hmph. Spent good money on a coach and what do we find? Michael has a cough- a cough! Your Aunt Lizzie will kill that boy through a surfeit of kindness, mark my words. It will be good if something profitable comes from this visit.'

It wasn't until Kirsty started to undress with the help of Mairi, she realised she'd forgotten to wear Johnnie's brooch.

CHAPTER Twenty

Just before dusk, a light breeze wafted the marsh grass on Gladsmuir. Johnnie crept three abreast along Riggonhead Defile, a secret route, as he followed his brother and the Jacobite army.

He thought about James Kinross' actions in Edinburgh, he disliked the man and Euan loathed him. Dougie said you couldn't trust the father and the son made Johnnie uneasy. Kinross always seemed to be at the edges of conversation and had danced with Morag at Holyrood. He'd done it twice. Had she encouraged him? No, she hung on Euan's every word and the ballroom was too public. If Kinross' intention had been to infuriate Euan, he'd succeeded. Good thing he'd left Edinburgh, probably heard Euan wanted satisfaction.

Johnnie grimaced as he thought of his betrayal of Kirsty. He unfolded her letter, full of questions and her excitement at new gowns for her proposed visit to Inverness. She deserved to see some of the world away from the farm. He just wished he could be with her. Anyway, she sent her love whilst he'd almost shamed himself.

The Edinburgh stews. He'd been shocked. Hags painted to look like young girls. He wouldn't try that again, he'd rather die. What would Kirsty have thought? Weak and fit for nothing.

He'd act like a saint from this point, only think Godly thoughts and not about the sins of the flesh. Kirsty would be proud of him. He tried not to dwell on Miss Peggie Balfour or the beautiful Miss Betty Cochrane, two beauties at the Holyrood ball. He'd declined their offers having realised they were very free with their affections with every gentlemen they met.

Kirsty didn't deserve his disloyalty. He reasoned that he'd only betrayed her in his mind, though a black thought persisted that his body had risen to the occasion as well and if one of the girls had been young, looked innocent, he might have... He forced himself to remember how Kirsty's wheat-coloured hair curled in tendrils round her face and tumbled down her back. How her eyes were the colour of cornflowers, her skin fair and unblemished and in no need of artifice or paint. By the time he'd finished she was perfection and no other would do.

A marsh harrier flew out of the grass and startled him. Johnnie's thoughts snapped back to his present situation. General John Cope had picked a brilliant natural defensive position for his government troops. The redcoats faced south and his cannon lay ready behind a wagonway which formed an embankment protected by a marshy ditch. Preston House's park walls stood at the rear.

Thank God for Lieutenant Anderson, a local, who knew about the secret path east of Cope's position. No alarms sounded and as far as Johnnie knew the Jacobite flanking movement hadn't been spotted.

Euan's upraised hand stopped Johnnie before he bumped into him. Hundreds of yards away Johnnie could see a row of bonfires which lit up the government pickets. He sank to his knees, hugged the grass and kept low inside the ground mist as he crawled with the others towards the redcoat lines.

Kirsty's cousin, Hughie, couldn't have done this and kept his wheeze silent as he'd slithered forward. Johnnie had nudged Euan, who'd sent Hughie to guard the baggage train at Cockenzie, Hughie hadn't argued.

At dawn, on General Murray's signal, Johnnie rose from the mist like a wraith, beat on his shield and roared a blood-curdling war cry. The rest of the Jacobite army joined in. A redcoat opposite stood transfixed, an officer grabbed the man's collar and shouted orders at his startled face. A private grabbed his musket with hands which fumbled as he poured gunpowder into the pan, then the barrel and tamped it down with a ramrod. He aimed, discharged his musket at the attacking Jacobites and reloaded again.

Redcoats flew like flies to their cannon and manhandled them as their lines wheeled east to face the unexpected threat. In doing so, Johnnie saw the ditch to the south and the west walls of Preston House impeded any redcoat retreat.

A volley of government cannon roared and muskets fired at the Jacobites. Johnnie yelled and raced forward at Euan's side, until slowed down by the boggy ground. He pressed forward through the mire. The Jacobite line had formed a V because of the men's different speeds as they raced across the ground. The wings headed for the dragoons on either side of the government centre. As Johnnie and Euan emerged from the marsh, the dragoons broke and sped back towards the government lines. Horses reared and plunged at the redcoat picket line.

Johnnie's heart pounded as he fired on the run at the redcoat infantry, then threw his musket away. He swept his targe across a redcoat's bayonet, turned it aside and plunged his sword into the man's breast. A scream like a banshee erupted from the man's throat. Johnnie threw himself at the line of redcoats in front of him as he hacked, thrusted and cut. Ranks of redcoats stared at him as if at a demon and died where they stood.

Gunpowder and the acrid stink of cordite drifted across Gladsmuir. They mingled with the ground mist so figures appeared and disappeared in the swirl of it.

'Euan, look to your left.' Johnnie sprinted towards him, his sword raised at the redcoat private about to bayonet Euan in his side. A crimson mist descended in front of Johnnie's eyes.

Euan turned at his brother's shout and cursed as the bayonet sliced into his arm. Johnnie thrust his sword at the private's chest. The man slumped to his knees to fall sightless into some reeds.

'Thanks brother,' yelled Euan before he plunged into the fray again and disappeared amongst the tight knot of bodies who grappled with each other.

At the sound of hooves, Johnnie hurled himself at a young dragoon, ducked his sword stroke, grabbed the man's waist from behind and pulled him off his mare. The horse reared and both men rolled clear of the stamp of hooves. The dragoon launched himself at Johnnie and their swords clashed until a riderless horse with wild eyes parted them and stampeded away across the field. Johnnie lunged and the dragoon, his brown eyes startled and brow puzzled, grunted. Johnnie withdrew his sword and the man fell motionless on the ground.

The government soldiers panicked, caught between the ditch and the walls of Preston House. Those who threw down their arms were held as prisoners of war and the wounded tended. Any who fought on received an honourable death. The rest retreated at speed, lost in cannon smoke, the battle over.

The air rippled with groans and cries of the wounded and dying. Johnnie sat on a low rock, head in hands as Euan approached.

'It only took ten minutes. Can you believe it?' said Euan. 'We took on the redcoats and won.'

Johnnie didn't reply. He shivered, his head swam and black motes floated in front of his eyes.

'Are you wounded?' asked Euan.

'No' in the way you mean, brother. I like books, William Ellis' *Agriculture Improved or the Practice of Husbandry Displayed*, Defoe, Swift and his *Gulliver's Travels* - I should be in university.'

'If you hadna been here, I'd have received worse than this.' Euan showed him the bloody gash in his arm. 'You fought well, man. Take it from me, I went to university, it's a bit… dry for fighting men. No' as interesting as you might think - why the long face?'

Johnnie put two hands on the pommel of his broadsword and leant on it. 'I learned something about myself today and I dinna like it. I'm too good at this – killing.'

'Come on, Johnnie, it's what we've been taught since childhood.'

'I dinna like it, Euan. That's what I learned. I've an inner beast and I want to tear it out. Can you understand that?'

'You're no coward, Johnnie, I ken that.'

Johnnie grasped Euan's hand. 'I can see men's faces, hear their screams and long for absolution.'

The Jacobite Affair

Euan pressed his hand on Johnnie's shoulder. 'Be happy we won with few of our men lost. This black mood will pass, you'll see. You must think only of our victory.'

'I think of their families. Do you no' feel the same way?'

A muscle rippled in Euan's cheek. 'I do what needs to be done.'

Euan didn't understand. Johnnie spat in the grass and his vison cleared. 'You need to get that cut seen to.'

'Aye.' Euan glanced at his blood-soaked sleeve. 'I'll look to my men first.'

Johnnie watched him stroll away and unable to keep the bile down, vomited onto the blood-splattered ground.

Lorna Windham

CHAPTER Twenty-one

'Drat.' The late afternoon sun warmed Kirsty as she tugged her skirt free from the spiky fingers of gorse. She thought of Johnnie and home as she and mother traipsed up the hill towards the farmhouse, relieved to be out of the coach and back in Braedrumie.

Smoke curled from the farmhouse's thatch. *It looks so small and… humble after Aunt Munro's house.* Duncan, all arms and legs, scattered scraps for the hens by the burn.

'Duncan,' she yelled.

He whirled, a worried look creased his face.

'What is it laddie?' shouted Mother before Kirsty could stop her. 'Out with it, what have you done?'

'It's no' my fault the hens aren't laying.' Duncan glowered at her.

'Have you been chasing them or throwing stones?' quizzed Mother. She put down her bags and faced him.

'Mother. I'm sure Duncan's done no such thing, I'm right aren't I?' Kirsty placed a hand on his shoulder.

Duncan nodded. 'They went off their food after a few days, but I've been here every day and made sure the cow drank, and dosed her like you said.' His face brightened. 'She's given up a little more, see.' He showed her the creamy contents of the half full pail.

Better than nothing, but not enough and how would they manage with no eggs?

'Can I help with your bags?' Duncan stepped forward.

'You've done enough damage,' snapped Mother.

'Why don't you go in and rest? I'll see to Duncan.'

'Hmph.' Mother slammed the door on them.

Duncan drew down his brows and stubbed his toe in the dust.

Kirsty sighed and put her arm round him. 'Dinna mind her, she's weary from the journey. You're a good lad, Duncan. We're grateful to you for looking after our croft and the animals.'

The Jacobite Affair

He stood still. 'And your cousin's well?'

'Better, thank you.'

He looked up. 'And Johnnie? Have you heard from him?'

His words tugged at her heart. 'Only what I told you last time. Why, when they return, you'll soon be sick of your brothers bossing you about, you'll see.'

Duncan beamed at her and pushed out his chest like a bantam cock. 'They'll no' believe how grown up I am now, will they?'

She ruffled his hair. 'No. they won't.'

His face darkened. 'Morag's father called at our house. He blames Euan for her running off. There was a terrible argument. Father's no' happy.'

'I'm sorry to hear it, I'm sure it'll sort itself out.'

'Do you think so?' Duncan's face brightened.

'Aye, I do. You'd better be getting home or the laird will be wondering where you are. Here's your wages.' She held out her hand.

His eyes gleamed at the coins on her palm, but he fixed her with his gaze. 'I did it for Johnnie and you. I thank you for your kindness, but I'll no' take your money. I'll bid you good day.'

'Sure?'

He nodded. 'It's good to see you. I'll be back tomorrow.'

Stubborn and honourable. She watched him trot down to the beck, wave and leap over it. *Johnnie would be proud of him*. He ran round the gorse and hurdled the heather. She spotted a movement to her right on the ridge and shaded her eyes. A couple of men on horseback gazed down at the farmhouse. She checked behind her. Nothing moved on the loch. *What interest do they have in us?* She looked again, but the men had gone. Puzzled, she went inside.

Mother sat in a cloud of smoke as she fed peat onto the fire. 'I hope you didn't pay him. What are we going to do without eggs?'

'It was my money I offered, he refused it.' Kirsty went to the window. 'The hens are old, ready for the pot. We could use the rest of Tolbain's money and buy more.'

'And be paupers? What are you doing?'

'I saw riders on the ridge, seemed interested in the house.'

'We'll get all sorts, with this rebellion. Make sure you lock up tonight. We don't want to be murdered in our beds. Do you hear?'

'I hear. Duncan says Morag's father blames Euan, and the laird isna happy.'

'Joining the baggage train. The village is full of it. She's always been headstrong. No mother, and the father dotes on her. More fool him.'

Johnnie. Kirsty went to the spence and sat at the table. A single sheet of parchment lay in front of her. She dipped her quill in the ink well.

Mother's voice came through the wall, 'If you're writing to that Johnnie Stewart again, ask about Hughie.'

'Yes, Mother.' She sighed. Her head had been turned by her visit to Inverness. She must write Johnnie another letter, but she'd not mention the hens, he'd worry.

Braedrumie
September1745
Dearest Johnnie,

I thought I would write to inform you about our visit to your Aunt Munro's in Inverness. She and your cousin Jack were very gracious hosts and both look well. Your aunt asked after you all and hopes to see you again when these troubled times are over. She said your uncle is in London on government business.

So, how are you and Uncle Hughie? I miss you so much and wish you here by my side. Duncan comes to see us and helps most days. He is quite the little man and grows taller every day. He asks about you all the time and says your father is well. He looked after our farm whilst we visited my cousin, Michael.

I think we raised Michael's spirits. My Aunt Lizzie fusses over him so. If only she would open some windows or allow him to walk in the fresh air, but any suggestion of this gave her the vapours. Anyway, he appeared much improved when we left.

I am intrigued about Prince Charlie. Is he as handsome as they say? Also, what is Edinburgh like and the Palace of Holyrood House? I envy you seeing these wonderful places.

I forgot to mention that Morag's disappearance and your news she had joined Euan caused a furore here. Her father is not happy. I do not envy her when she returns.

The cow still gives us milk.

I cannot wait until you come home to me and I am in your arms again.

God keep you safe.

My love always,

Kirsty

CHAPTER Twenty-Two

Johnnie made several unsuccessful attempts to write to Kirsty

'What's wrong?' asked Morag. 'Is it so difficult to write to those you love?'

She sat beside him at a low wooden bench outside the stables in Edinburgh, whilst Euan disappeared inside to discuss a lame mare with one of the grooms. The scent of horse sweat and sweet hay permeated the air.

'You dinna understand.' Johnnie stuck his quill behind his ear. 'Kirsty seems so far away. It's as if I dinna ken her anymore.' He tried to conjure her features and gave up.

Morag said, 'Would you like some help?'

'If you can spare the time, I'd be grateful.'

'Aye. The sooner Kirsty receives word from you, the sooner you'll get her next letter. Come on, now what would she like to hear?'

Johnnie dealt with the facts and Morag made some suggestions. He sent a silent prayer that Kirsty or anyone else would never find out about his visit to the Edinburgh stews.

September 1745
My Own One,
I thank you for your letters. I miss you very much and long to see you again. I am pleased that you stayed with the Munro's and that your cousin, Michael, has recovered from his illness. Your Uncle Hughie, is well and sends his regards to you and your mother.

You will be pleased to know we are all in good health. We frightened off Cope from Corrieyairack Pass, have entered Edinburgh without a shot fired and just won a great battle against him at Gladsmuir. This has heartened us all as it was over in ten minutes. Jamie Moffat and Dougie will have told you all about it, no doubt. Have you heard about General Cope's coach? Dougie has driven it to Braedrumie.

You ask about the prince- he is not as tall or as handsome as people say and I have reservations about his ability as a

The Jacobite Affair

leader of men. He is too interested in the finer things in life and not the campaign.

We have been invited to several of the prince's balls at Holyrood Palace. I wish you had been with me. Holyrood is a wonder and has several splendid rooms full of mirrors and chandeliers.

We did the Stewarts proud, dressed in the height of fashion in silks and satins as was Morag.

You will be interested to hear I was introduced to numerous important ladies and gentlemen.

I am pleased you enjoyed your time with Aunt Munro. I send you my love, darling.

Johnnie

What do you think?' asked Johnnie.

'It will do,' said Morag. 'You didna have to mention me. Kirsty will welcome any news from you.' She stretched and clasped her hands above her head.

Should he tell Morag? Ever since he'd escorted her, at Euan's request, to the second ball, he'd been uneasy. The words burst out of him. 'Kirsty said your father's no' happy with you. You should go home.'

Morag's face reddened as she got up. 'And what would I do, sew? I've more important matters to attend to. Good day.'

Johnnie watched her slight figure disappear round the corner of the stable block. She'd changed, become more elusive and independent. He thought back to when he'd accompanied her to the last ball. Euan had been at the beck and call of their commanders and had begged this favour.

'She's been ill and deserves to enjoy the delights Edinburgh has to offer. Will you do this for me, Johnnie?'

He'd bitten his tongue. 'Ill?' He didn't want to share his knowledge of Morag's 'illness' with Euan until he'd talked to her. So, he'd taken her to the ball at Holyrood and struggled to formulate his question. He hadn't counted on being surrounded by a swarm of ladies and he'd lost sight of her. When he'd freed himself, he saw her dance with that bastard, Kinross. He

Lorna Windham

knew Euan would be furious. When the music finished he led her to an alcove. 'What did Kinross want?'

Morag turned to face him. 'To dance.'

'He seemed more interested in you than the bloody dance from where I stood.'

Morag stared at him with startled eyes. 'Johnnie. You can't possibly think that I'd...? Johnnie, I love Euan, I'd never do anything to hurt him. You must know that?'

'What I know is I saw you, out on the streets like a bloody doxy the night Captain O'Brien was killed, when you were supposed to be ill. Explain that.'

Her eyes widened. 'You were there. Oh Johnnie, I canna... I can't tell you.'

'Can you no'? And Euan? What about him?'

She blushed and looked at her slippered feet. 'You wouldna tell, promise me you'll say nothing. Johnnie...'

'My loyalty's to my brother.'

'And to The Cause?' she whispered.

He started. 'Why do you say that?'

'Not here. There are too many ears. Walk in the garden with me.'

He nodded his agreement, but she wouldn't speak until they were in the middle of the lawn, the music faint and they could look back at the palace illuminated by torches. 'You must believe me.' She wrung her hands. 'I've given my solemn promise not to divulge... what I've been asked to do. I'm asking you to trust me, Johnnie.' She put her hand on his arm. 'I'm... helping The Cause.'

He shook her off. 'You're embroiled in something dangerous. God damn it, Morag, you were out on your bloody own at night. Euan...'

'Doesna need to know,' she whispered.

'I dinna want to become entangled in your bloody intrigues. Euan thinks you'll be safe, but when we leave Edinburgh you'll be in more danger than ever. I should have known.'

'Johnnie, it's what I came for. I canna go back on my promise.' Her voice stayed low as she pleaded.

The Jacobite Affair

'And Kinross?'

'He knows something and tried to warn me...'

'Morag, you could be bloody killed and what for? A cause that... well, may be lost already.'

'We won at Gladsmuir. I couldna bear it if we lost, I couldna bear... Dinna say that, no' to me. '

'Morag, the French are full of promises, but they mean nought if they dinna send a bloody army. Without them, we're nothing against the might of the Crown. I fear we've gone too far this time.'

'And yet you stay?'

'I gave my word.'

'As I gave mine.'

'Aye. I see you canna be persuaded. Just warn me next time, I'll no' stop you, but I'll make sure the bloody enemy can't either. Will you do that Morag?'

'Aye, gladly.'

'Then we're friends again?'

'Friends.' She seemed pleased they'd cleared the air between them.

'Good, but you must tell Euan before we leave or I will.'

She blinked twice at that, then nodded her head.

CHAPTER Twenty-three

The wind blew in all directions as dark clouds scudded across the sky. 'Looks like rain.' Duncan settled his rump on the grass outside the Lorne's farmhouse. 'Did you hear Dougie drove General Cope's coach all the way back from Edinburgh? It's very fine.'

'So Johnnie said in this letter. Isabel will be pleased. Is it very grand?' Kirsty forced herself to sound cheerful.

'It's got leather seats and there was chocolate in a pocket in the door. Father let me have it. Mm-mm. Dougie says everyone's in good spirits and we won a fine battle at Gladsmuir. Oh and Murdo's back.' He checked the blade on a scythe and sharpened it with a whet stone.

'About time too.' Mother, with a dour look, pushed past Kirsty at the door. 'Where is he? He owes me for the herd.'

Duncan shrugged his shoulders. 'Said Patch died. Old age.'

'Oh, no,' said Kirsty. 'He'll miss him.'

'Looked out of sorts and wants a wife.' Duncan darted a glance at Mother.

'How would you know?' Mother gathered her shawl round her.

'We talked, said you'd…' Duncan searched for the words… '*weathered well*. That's what he said, *weathered well*.'

Mother clipped his ear.

'Ow. What did you do that for?'

'Hmph. He'll find no wife here. Best you tell Murdo he's an old fool and I'm waiting for my money. Got that?'

'Aye.' He rubbed his red ear. He turned to Kirsty. 'So you've heard from Johnnie?'

Kirsty nodded and her grip tightened on Johnnie's letter. 'They're just as Dougie says, in good spirits.'

'Wish I was with them. Tell him I'm asking after them all and we're all well at home.'

'I will.'

The Jacobite Affair

He turned to Mother and wiped his nose with his shirt cuff. 'Canna help any more today, Father needs me in our fields. And I'll just mention the money, if you dinna mind, Mrs. Lorne, Murdo's hand's bigger than yours.' Duncan raced away to the burn, let out a great yell and vaulted the beck.

'Do himself a serious injury, that laddie.' Mother sniffed, closed the door and then pointed at the creased parchment in Kirsty's hand. 'Is that Stewart's letter?'

Kirsty screwed up the parchment and threw it on the ground. 'As if you didn't know.'

Her mother's back creaked as she picked it up. 'Is parting not such sweet sorrow then? Is there news of Hughie?'

Kirsty went to grab it back, but Mother held her off with one hand, scanned the words and gave a sigh of satisfaction as she thrust it at her daughter. 'So, Hughie's fine.'

'I was going to tell you.'

Mother pressed her thin lips together. 'And Stewart?'

'As you can see enjoying himself dancing at Holyrood balls.' Kirsty snapped.

'Wastrel.' Mother walked into the kitchen and Kirsty trudged behind her into its warmth.

Unwelcome thoughts circled inside Kirsty's head. *I should have been there, in a fine gown, like Morag. What if Johnnie met a beautiful lady and forgets me? No. We love each other. He'll return and the farm will thrive. We'll grow even better crops and breed sturdier cattle.*

'Mrs. Balfour's last letter mentioned the Holyrood balls.' Mother stirred the broth in the kettle over the fire. 'According to her the prince looked very fine. Well, she would, her family have always been ardent Jacobites. They'll lose everything.'

Kirsty closed her eyes. *What if Johnnie… doesn't come home? A few more years on the farm and I'll look like an old woman. Who'll wed me then?* She walked back into the byre and turned left into the spence.

Mother's shrill voice followed Kirsty. 'You're no writing to him again? Ink, parchment and quills cost money you know?'

Kirsty ignored her, pleased she'd put space between herself and Mother. She unpinned Johnnie's brooch and put it in her applewood trinket box. Then, head bowed at the table, she dipped her pen into the black ink. *What to write? Not 'dearest' but dear.* She scratched words by the light which filtered in from the window in front of her.

Braedrumie
October, 1745
Dear Johnnie,
Thank you for your news about Uncle Hughie, also about the battle. Mother is very relieved. I am pleased to hear you are all well.

I hope you did not forget me when you met those fine ladies at Holyrood, nor think they were better company.

Duncan continues to visit and help us. You will be pleased to hear he and your father are well and asking after you.

When we were in Inverness, we also met society and went to soirees and balls, though not perhaps, as fine as the ones you attended. Your aunt introduced me to several handsome young gentlemen and at times I did not know which way to turn.

I think of you in my prayers and wish you were all home and Uncle Hughie of course.

All my love,
Kirsty

Kirsty put the quill in her mouth. Her lips curved into a satisfied smile. *Johnnie will long to be back with me in Braedrumie. And once I meet Sinclair and Murdo arrives with Mother's cattle money, we'll repay Tolbain's loan.* A firm knock sounded at the door. She sprang up to answer it.

Murdo stood bonnet in hand. 'Good day, Miss Lorne.'

'I was just thinking of you, Murdo. Come away in. You must have had a hard time of it. Sorry about Patch.'

'Aye, a sad business, just went to sleep, never woke up.' He took off his bonnet and followed her through the byre and stopped. 'Yon cow doesna look too good.'

The Jacobite Affair

The animal's head drooped as it leant against the wicker fence.

'No. She hasna been grand for some time. But now you're here, we've no need to worry. Come through to the kitchen.'

He glanced at her, then his eyes flicked away.

'Hmph. You're late. Mother pointed at him with her wooden spoon.

'Will you sit by the fire?' Kirsty pulled out a stool. 'Some whisky?'

'I thank you.'

'So you should.' Mother scowled at him.

'Here's your money.' He took gold coins from his sporran and put them on the table. He sniffed the air like a hunting dog. 'You've broth I see.' He sat and warmed his huge hands at the fire.

Mother stared at the coins and him. 'Why, there's only a few pounds.'

'Aye. We were attacked by thieves in the English borders. Curse them. I'm sorry… they took your cattle, cut them out of the herd.'

Her mother sat down with a thump on a low stool. 'I cannot believe it. We trusted you. We're ruined, ruined.'

'You've the farm and I've given you more than I should, out of my own pocket.'

'Your own pocket? You planned it,' Mother shrieked. 'Want us poor and beholden to you. Take your money, I don't want it.'' She threw it at him. 'And take your conniving carcase out of here. How do we know you aren't hand in hand with those thieves?'

Horrified, Kirsty sank to her knees. Her fingers sought the coins as they rolled on the flagstones and under the dresser, whilst their voices raged above her head.

Murdo drew himself up. 'Will you listen, woman? You insult me, stain my honour. Ask young Alastair, one-eyed Peadar and old Frazier, they'll all tell you the same. We were attacked and your cattle taken. They were the best beasts we were driving. Whoever took them, picked them out- Now, I'd like a word… in private.'

Kirsty struggled to take it all in. *No cattle and no money. Did he really say that? The cow ails and the hens won't lay. Will our bad luck never end?*

Mother got up from her stool. 'Didn't we pay you enough?'

'It's no money I'm after. We had an agreement and I'll abide by it. Just give me a moment of your time, if you will?' He stared at Kirsty.

'I'll get on with my knitting in the spence.' The cow sagged against the fence as she passed. 'Poor old girl.' Kirsty patted the beast's neck. She found her knitting basket on the table, pulled a chair close to the fire and picked up her needles. *I need to have as many woollen goods as possible for Sinclair.*

Low voices came from the kitchen. She wrapped a strand of crimson yarn round a needle to turn a sock.

Thwack.

Kirsty froze.

Murdo's voice raised in anger came to her from the other side of the wall. 'Are you mad woman?'

Thwack. Thwack.

'Never been more right in the head.' Mother sounded forceful.

Thwack. Then a crash and rattle as if something landed and rolled across the flagstones. *What on earth?* Kirsty sprang out of her chair and peered through the wooden partition. Murdo, with lowered brows and set lip, ignored her and strode past the cow which had sunk closer to the ground. A draught of cold air signalled the door being opened and a slam, as it closed. Kirsty retreated to the warmth of the kitchen. *What's been said?*

Mother flushed, patted her hair in place and then warmed her hands at the fire. 'He wanted me to wed him.'

Kirsty stared open mouthed. 'Really?'

'I'm not that old, it's an.... interesting proposition. He thought it would make up for our lost cattle money. Imagine me married to a common drover? Set his sights on my farm

The Jacobite Affair

and land. I made him skedaddle, laid about him with my broom. As if I hadn't enough of men.'

'He might love you.'

Mother turned on her. 'Love? Don't talk to me about love. Your precious Johnnie Stewart produced quality cattle that no reiver could resist. I knew his new-fangled ideas on breeding wouldn't work. Look where they've got us.'

'You never let it drop, do you? It's no' his fault thieves took our cattle. Blame them. Johnnie reads and he's bright and thinks ahead. He's worked like a slave on this farm. Where would we have been without him?'

'I'd have my cattle.'

'You dinna ken that.' Kirsty put a protective hand over her brooch.

'I know this, we're going to starve,' said Mother.

CHAPTER Twenty-four

Evening fell, candles sputtered and the succulent smell of roast lamb hung in the air. It had followed Johhnie to the small study where he sat at a desk in Mrs. Perkin's town house in Carlisle. Her servants had slammed the meat, plates and cutlery on the dining table alongside the worst wine he'd ever tasted. Dougie, with a disgruntled look on his face, raided the cellar. He returned with ale and fine brandy which made the Stewarts happy men.

The memory of young Rory Graham's useless death hung over them all day. Damn the McIntryres. The laddie had been careless with his musket. Johnnie saw no sense in more blood spilt, neither did Euan. But the McIntyres insisted on their rights or they'd leave. That poor laddie and his father.

After the evening meal, Dougie told rude jokes, Johnnie laughed and Euan became morose.

Dougie put his arm round Euan. 'Its no' your fault. You did what you had to do.' His grizzled head moved closer to Euan's auburn locks as he reasoned with him in front of the fire. The flames cast long shadows on the floor.

'I should have saved him, Dougie.' Euan downed the last of his tankard and slammed it on the table. 'The decision was mine. I'll see his face all the days of my life.'

Johnnic shook his head. 'You couldna save him, none of us could. Talk sense, man.'

'Listen Euan, I ken you didna expect to be heir and havena been trained as Rob was, but you had to be strong in front of the others. My Isabel would say, *a great leader looks beyond an individual.* That's what you did today, held the army together.'

'Dougie's right.' Johnnie added a log to the fire. 'We're losing men the further south we go. We canna afford any more. Think on that and perhaps you'll sleep well tonight.'

'Think.' Euan grimaced. 'I do nought but think. Say a prayer for Rory Graham and me, no matter what you say, the lad didna deserve his fate.' Euan got up and strode away.

The Jacobite Affair

Johnnie went to follow him, but Dougie put a hand on his arm. 'He needs time, Johnnie. Being a leader, making decisions like this, comes hard to good, honest men. The Grahams will no' be happy and the McIntyres will be cock-a-hoop. He needs both clans to bury this and fight alongside each other. You ken that?'

'Aye, but he's no' the only man that canna sleep.'

Dougie glanced at him. 'Aye, well.' Dougie stood up and stretched. 'I'm away to my bed. I doubt I'll enjoy another night on a feather mattress. You?'

'I'll follow you in a wee while. I've a letter to read and another to write.'

He followed Dougie out of the door, but headed for the study and sat to the tick of the clock on the mantelpiece as the candlelight waned.

He'd saved Kirsty's letter until he was on his own. He read it and didn't like the sound of Inverness soirees, balls or Kirsty meeting *young, handsome gentlemen.* Why had she written that?

Half an hour later he rocked back in his chair, quill behind ear, and read the letter he'd composed in reply.

Carlisle
November, 1745
My Own One,

I miss you and wish you were beside me now. Darling, I long to hear your voice. Do you think of me as I do you? Once this is over, I intend to stay on the farm and never leave your side.

I am pleased you were able to see your cousin and enjoyed your stay at Aunt Munro's. Though, if I had known you would be meeting young gentleman, I may not have proposed the visit.

We are all well and full of good spirits. Hughie sends his regards. I have read parts of your letters to him and he says it warms his heart. He asks about Mary and the bairns and sends his love to them.

I hope you sold the cattle for a good price at market. They were fine looking beasts, the best I've seen. A pity Father didn't listen to my ideas. Keep an eye on the cow, I fear she's coming to the end of her days.

How is everyone in Braedrumie? I hope the women and bairns have not had too hard a time of it. It's good to hear Duncan is so helpful.

I must confess the army has achieved more than I thought we could. General Murray shows real guile. He sent some of us to show ourselves near Newcastle's walls, so the town thought we would attack them. We deceived them and the good news is that we have taken Carlisle.

I can say no more.
All my love,

That should do. He yawned and wrote his name with a flourish of his quill, sure Kirsty would be his for ever.

The Jacobite Affair

CHAPTER Twenty-five

Kirsty's fist crumpled the letter. *Sinclair. How could he? Him and all his fine promises in Inverness.*

'Well?' said Mother. 'Whose it from? What does it say?'

A knock on the door of the Lorne's farmhouse, made Mother scurry towards it. She passed Kirsty and Duncan who knelt beside the cow. The beast lay on its haunches. Kirsty sighed. It had been off its feed and given them no milk for days. She patted its scrawny neck. *Too weak to bleed. No more blood pudding, a staple through the winter months. So much bad luck.*

Duncan lowered his voice. 'It's good Morag's back. She looks- different. More grown up.'

'Aye.' *Of course she's back, her father's ill. At least she said Uncle Hughie's alright, apart from a heavy cold.*

'And Lachie Ross and Ian Skene. It's good they'd been allowed to leave the army to help their families, isn't it?'

'Aye.' *I wish... No point.*

'Murdo left with them to join our men in the south. He didna seem happy, offered to deliver our letters. He wouldna take me with him.'

'Oh, Duncan.' Kirsty sighed. 'Johnnie went to keep you safe.' *Hope my note reaches Johnnie soon.*

'I didna ask…'

Kirsty turned at the rattle of the bolt as light flooded over Mother as she opened the door.

'My God, Gilly, you fell low, living here, but it's amazing how a rose can grow in a dung heap. Where's Kirsty, coz?'

Tolbain's voice.

Duncan's brow creased.

'Sssh.' Kirsty put her finger to her lips. 'Stay here.'

Mother squinted into the light as Kirsty joined her.

Tolbain had two of his men on either side of him and raised his bonnet at Kirsty. 'Good morning, Miss Lorne, and what a lovely morning it is, not a cloud in the sky.' He looked up and then out over the burn. 'Though I must say your land looks neglected. A pity after all Johnnie Stewart's work and I heard your cattle were thieved? Lawless times. This is what happens when men seek to overturn the rightful government, don't you think? Makes beggars of some?'

Her mother went rigid. Kirsty could see it in her neck and spine. *How Mother hates being poor and even worse him knowing.*

'I… '. The hair on the back of Kirsty's neck stood upright. *How does he know so much?* She curtsied. *Better play the simpleton.* 'I know little of politics.'

'Of course, need a man to guide you. I've come to see your mother.'

Kirsty twisted a stray strand of hair behind her ear and hoped Mother wouldn't invite him inside.

'We didn't expect you, Your Grace,' said Mother.

'Alexander.'

'Alexander. Get on with your chores, daughter whilst I talk to my cousin.' Mother opened the door wider to let him in.

He brought a silk handkerchief out of his lace cuff, so it hid his nose. 'I prefer, if you don't mind, to talk out here, Gilly.'

Tolbain led Mother away from the farmhouse and towards the burn.

Duncan's finger prodded Kirsty's back. 'Tolbain's your cousin?'

'Second cousin. He's of no account.'

'He's ill-mannered for a gentleman and you never said your cattle had been stolen.' Duncan wide-eyed, stared at her.

'We have other sources of income.' *Drat Sinclair. What 'pressing business elsewhere'?* 'I think you'd better go home now, Duncan, and stay out of the way of Tolbain and his men.'

His eyes assessed her as he struggled with what he'd overheard, then he left her alone in the byre with the cow.

She folded her arms and walked into the warmth of the kitchen. *Hope Duncan keeps Tolbain's visit to himself. The village willna like it.*

The Jacobite Affair

Sometime later the sound of hooves announced Tolbain's departure.

'What did he want?' Kirsty's knife cut a carrot into chunks. *Broth again.*

'He's taking his men to join the redcoats.' Mother sniffed. 'Says it's his duty to stop the rebels. Poor Hughie, he'll be fortunate to come out of this alive.'

'All the more reason to despise Tolbain.'

'Don't be silly, daughter. He's a Whig, wise to keep him close and then there's the loan. Says he expects our first payment as soon as he returns. It's business. I trust that Duncan knows to keep his mouth shut. I dinna want everyone knowing our business. – So, what was in your letter?'

Drat. 'Sinclair canna meet. I've to wait till next month.'

'Hmph. Told you. Don't trust a man.'

Kirsty needed fresh air and took herself outside with her writing materials and sat on a tree stump with her makeshift desk, a thin pine board, on her knees. She placed the ink on the ground beside her. *Johnnie's brooch.* She felt the outline of intertwined hearts pinned to her breast and thought of him. His last letter made her love him even more. *I must make up for my note.*

Her quill dripped ink as she thought about what she wouldn't write. She wouldn't mention the hens, sick cow or the cattle money and definitely not the loan from Tolbain. But Granny Mac and Dougie's wife, Isabel, had asked after the Stewarts.

Braedrumie 1745
Dearest Johnnie,

I am so sorry about my short note. Lachie Ross was in a hurry to be on the road.

It was so good to receive your letter about Carlisle. So, you are in England and I miss you so.

Duncan and your father are well and as always ask after you. You will be pleased to hear your brother continues to be a great help to us and we are extremely grateful to him.

Life is not the same without you here. Every day seems longer than the next.

Please stay safe.

Mary and the bairns are fine, please send their love and ours to Uncle Hughie.

How is my Uncle Hughie? Morag said he had a heavy cold and Ian Skene mentioned a cough? Mother is so worried. It will surprise you to hear she received an offer of marriage from Murdo the other day. She refused him and now we hear he's joined you in the rebellion.

Granny Mac and Isabel send their regards and hope you are all well.

I send you my love.

Kirsty

The Jacobite Affair

CHAPTER Twenty-six

Clouds hung like a grey canopy above Johnnie. Snow. He could smell it. He scanned the frost-covered track behind him. No sign of the redcoats. He dismounted and leant on his saddle. Had he time to write? He took his quill, ink and a sheet of parchment out of his saddlebags. He hungered for sight of Kirsty, his father and Duncan, to see Braedrumie, Loch Linnhe's silver waters and the mountains of home. Home. His nib scratched the grainy surface in front of him as he coaxed his pony to stand still.

England
December, 1745
 My Own one,
 I thought it better you heard the news straight away. I hope you understand when I say I should be nearer you soon and I miss you so much.
 Do not concern yourself about the note. Any news from you, no matter how short is welcome.
 Darling, I long for the feel of your hand, your lips so I can drink you in like fine wine, your eyes so I can see your soul's fire, your breast so I can hear the beat of your heart in tune with mine and your voice so I can hear the sweet inner core of you.
 I want you so much and wish all the evils of the world would fall away so we can be together at last.
 Please tell Father and Duncan and everyone in Braedrumie, we're all fit and healthy, including Hughie, despite his cough, and there is no need to worry.
 All my love, darling.

Johnnie

'Have you mail, Johnnie?' Jamie Moffat reined-in his pony.
'Aye.' He thrust his letter into Jamie's outstretched hand.
Johnnie blew on his cold hands and watched Jamie spur north with the Jacobite's post, through a curtain of snow.

Johnnie wished he and the Jacobite army could take wings and fly as he turned his face to brave the icy wind and snow flurries which followed Jamie. This would end as he thought: in disaster. The retreat signalled it. Prince Charles had wanted them to march on to London, but he'd been outnumbered by Murray and the rest. What had it all been for?

Euan had pinned his hopes on the French and their fine promises and ignored Rob's warnings. Euan had been left dismayed by Lord Drummond's letter which suggested the French would lend their support in Scotland, but not England.

Johnnie felt sure the French had used the rebellion to concentrate British minds on events in their own country and away from North America's rich pickings. Now he marched north with the rear guard. Every day a different town, their only respite a troubled sleep. When Prince Charlie had originally led them into Preston, Johnnie remembered the cheers, church bells and cannons fired as a salute. Now the streets remained empty, the town silent. He ached for Scotland.

Johnnie glanced behind him and expected to see the redcoat horsemen who'd trailed them for about three miles on the way to Kendal. A flash of red. Damn. Johnnie's jaw tightened. Along the route Johnnie had spotted more and more groups of government horse, sometimes stationary, often on a parallel course some miles distant. All done to disconcert, but none attacked.

A woman from the baggage train staggered in front of Johnnie and fainted by the wayside. Her bare feet bloody. Another vomited, a third keeled over and lay still. Their condition tore strips off his heart. He left food and water, but the army had no carts to transport those who couldn't keep up. The priority to cross the Esk and get back into Scotland. Thank God, Kirsty and Morag hadn't come on this journey. A child wailed behind him. Some of the baggage train would never see home again. All of his being wanted to help and he couldn't because of his orders. Damn them.

The Duke of Perth had been attacked in Penrith and advised them to sleep overnight at Shap. The tired army marched on in

The Jacobite Affair

darkness until they reached that place. The Stewarts arrived and found shelter in a hedge, whilst some slept in stables, outhouses and homes. Next day the Jacobite rear guard marched towards the village of Clifton.

On December 18th Euan scanned the blue hills behind him, Johnnie and Dougie. English light horse dotted the slopes. Euan galloped off to warn Murray.

Euan returned several minutes later. 'Not to worry, he'll send a message to the prince. Thinks they're just militia.'

'Oh, yes?' Johnnie pointed half a mile down the road behind them where 200-300 horse formed as if to attack.

'Look over there.' Euan jerked his thumb to the east.

Johnnie watched as redcoats, two abreast, marched up a hill and disappeared to the sound of trumpets and rat-a-tat-tat of kettle drum. 'They're not militia. Could be the whole bloody redcoat army. What the hell is Colonel Brown doing?'

Euan and Johnnie watched in consternation as four companies of the Jacobite army raced up the hill.

'Bet Murray hasn't ordered this. Look at McDonnell of Glengarry and his men... Johnnie? Dougie?'

Johnnie ignored Euan's shouts, his lungs wanted to burst as he raced across an enclosure and followed Dougie. Brown needed support. Madness.

Johnnie reached the top of the hill, one step behind Dougie, his claymore raised above his head. Johnnie expected to see the whole British army. Instead he saw several redcoats whose steeds reared and plunged. Their panicked riders yanked at reins in an attempt to spur their mounts away.

One, a poor horseman, by Johnnie's standards, fell on his back and fumbled for his sword. Dougie ran towards him and put his boot on the man's right wrist which clutched his weapon. The redcoat's left hand scrabbled for a pistol on the ground. His fingers found it and raised it just as Johnnie's sword swept across his neck. A red stream spouted and he lay still.

'Thanks, lad.' Dougie thumped Johnnie on the back, then bounded away to re-join the fight.

Johnnie glanced at the splatter of blood at his feet and turned away. A captain, about thirty. Johnnie wrestled with the dead men on his conscience. He didn't want to see their faces, not when their wraiths came at night and he needed sleep.

He turned his attention to the fray and blocked out the clang of steel as it met steel, the jangle of bit and bridle, the squeak of leather, the screams and cries. He'd become used to the single focus, kill or be killed, when muscles, tendons and sinews tightened and his ears became deaf. Then, when his sword had done its work, he waited for his body to collapse. He spat to clear his throat. He loathed himself and the deeds he'd done.

Johnnie's hands shook as he wiped them on his plaid. At least he didn't taste bile this time. A good or bad sign? He didn't know. He wiped the blood off his sword on a dead man's tunic. The Jacobites roared their victory as the last light horse disappeared down the hill and into the distance.

The Jacobite Affair

CHAPTER Twenty-seven

Winter. Kirsty pushed open the farmhouse door and drew in a frosted breath. Under an overcast sky, jewelled-icicles hung from the thatch. She pulled her shawl around her. The world lay muffled as if a white blanket had been flung over the moors. Snowflakes fluttered onto her head. Her breath shimmered in the air and she blew on her hands and stamped her feet. She folded the letter. *How will I tell Mother, Sinclair's let us down again?*

Her eyes shifted to a figure who ran and slid down the far slope towards her. *Duncan.*

He slewed to a halt at the snowdrifts on the far side of the ice-covered burn, then leapt the frozen gap. His kilt flew up and revealed two blue knees.

I daren't share my worries about the Jacobite's retreat with him. 'I've news from Johnnie.' She forced a smile.

'Does he mention me?' Duncan blew into his cupped hands.

'Yes and says they're all well and you and your father mustn't worry.'

Duncan beamed at her. 'Anything else?' He stamped his boots on the soft white ground.

'No. How's the laird?'

Duncan's brow creased. 'He misses my brothers and Dougie, I think that's why he drinks. He misses Mother too.' He rubbed his blue hands together and his lower lip trembled. 'I do as well.'

His words sliced into her heart. 'Of course you do. You look cold, laddie. Here.' She offered him her shawl, but he refused it as he hopped up and down on the door step.

'They'll come home soon, won't they, Kirsty?' He blew on his hands again and his cheeks reddened with the effort.

What should I say? She managed, 'If they can, Duncan, they will. You Stewart men are so stubborn.'

'Yes. They willna let redcoats stop them. Have you jobs for me?'

Lorna Windham

'You could fetch water from the burn.'

She watched as he dashed off bucket in hand, broke the ice with his boot and returned. He ignored the splash of water over his bare legs. 'Anything else? How's Clover?'

'Clover? You mean our cow?' Kirsty shrugged her shoulders. 'See for yourself. Bring the water inside will you?'

Her mother peered round the wooden slats which divided the kitchen from the byre. 'Is that Duncan Stewart? Look at the state of our beast.'

Duncan patted the beast's scrawny neck. 'It's no' my fault. Clover's old and on her last legs.'

'Clover. Hmph.' Mother snatched the bucket out of his hand and retired to the kitchen.

'Kirsty ruffled his hair. 'She doesna mean it. Johnnie will be so proud of how you've helped us.'

Duncan nodded. 'Thanks, Kirsty.' He grimaced. 'I dinna think Clover will last much longer.'

'I know.' *More worries.* She stroked the cow's withered flanks. *No cow, no milk- we'll starve unless Sinclair buys our goods.*

'Going the same way as my poor hens,' shouted Mother from the kitchen.

We miss those eggs.

Duncan's face fell.

'We dinna blame you for them either.' Kirsty tried to sound cheerful. 'We'll manage.'

'You need more men. The lower field will flood when it thaws.'

'Men, he says.' Mother stepped past both of them. 'And where are we supposed to find them? Will nothing go right? I'll clear the path.'

'Can I help?' said Duncan.

'No.' She shut the door behind her.

An icy blast circled Kirsty as she patted Duncan's shoulder. 'You've tried your best, Duncan. We thank you for your offer.'

'That's alright, Kirsty, I promised Johnnie.'

The Jacobite Affair

'Best be getting home, then. No knowing how bad this storm's going to be.' Kirsty led him outside.

Mother's shovel hardly made a start on the path when a curtain of snow fell round her. 'Hmph. Can't do any more today.' She dragged the shovel, scraped the mud off her boots and stamped back into the house. The door slammed behind her. Snow slid down the thatch and landed in a heap on the ground.

'I'm away home then.' Duncan gave a wave.

Kirsty covered her head with her shawl as he cleared the burn and her heart leapt with him.

He stopped and turned. Snowflakes covered his bonnet and brows. 'I forgot. There's tracks where men dismounted on the other side of the ridge. Someone's spying on you.'

'Spying?' Kirsty caught a breath. 'Why do you say that?'

'They came from the west, lay behind that gorse and looked this way.'

Her eyes followed his finger to the high ground and she shivered in the icy wind. The sky lowered and a whirlwind of hailstones spattered into her face. 'You'd better go home. You shouldna have come on a day like this. Promise you'll hide if you see more men.'

He raised his chest. 'I can look after myself.'

'Duncan.'

'I promise.'

She watched as he struggled through the deep snow and up the hill. *Who are these men?* She continued to brave the cold and the hail until Duncan, with another wave, disappeared over the edge of the escarpment. *Johnnie where are you?*

She retreated into the warmth of the house and went into the spence. Her palm stroked the smooth surface of her applewood box. She closed her eyes and tried to dispel the prickle of worry. Her fingers opened the lid and she untied the white ribbon which held Johnnie's letters. She settled herself in a chair, unfolded the parchment of one and whispered his words aloud. He felt close, in the air all around her and joy rose in her throat.

Johnnie would be home soon, but the Jacobites hadn't taken London. Why? Her fingers worked at her apron. She glanced up as the wind rose to a howl outside and hailstones beat at the shutters. *I hope Duncan gets home soon.* Kirsty lost herself in Johnnie's letters as she savoured every word.

Sometime later she folded his last letter and slipped it inside the slit in her dress and into her pocket. *I'll read it again and again, tonight.*

Easy to imagine him there beside her, in bed together. She flushed. *Such shameless, wanton thoughts. What would Mother think? What would people think and what would Johnnie think?* Her lips kissed the brooch and tried to imagine his warm flesh instead of cold metal.

She looked in on the cow which lowed at her from the byre and sank down beside it. 'Poor thing, you're not well are you? Wish I could do something to help.' She tried to forget its doeful eyes as she went into the kitchen where her mother sat and speared a garter. *Warmth.*

'Light's bad.' Mother squinted, but didn't look up.

'Yes.' Kirsty folded a plaid.

'He should have cleared that ditch.'

'Duncan's only a laddie, Mother. He doesn't have to come here and help. Says he saw men on the ridge and we're being spied on.'

Mother tugged at her thread. 'Bound to be scoundrels roaming around when Braedrumie's men are away fighting. Tolbain's got influence, he'll see us all right. Keep close to the farm. Do you hear?'

'Yes.'

'And Sinclair?' asked Mother.

Drat. 'He wrote, says he's ill, should be in Maryburgh in a couple of weeks.'

'Hmph.'

'Pray the weather's no' bad.'

'Pray he's a man of his word.'

'Oh, Mother. We should be paid a fine amount for all these.' Kirsty lifted handfuls of garters, socks, bonnets and

The Jacobite Affair

plaids from a wicker basket in the corner. *It'll be quite a trek, especially through snow. Perhaps I can persuade one of the fishermen on Loch Linnhe to take me.*

'So, what news from Stewart?'

Kirsty's hand went to where Johnnie's precious letter lay hidden. *Mother must have heard Jamie Moffat's been seen in the village.* Her lips became a straight line of resentment. 'I think they're heading back.' *Her heart sang. Closer, he's closer to me. He's probably in Scotland now. Maybe it's good news after all.*

'Retreating you mean?'

'Suppose so. Johnnie didna say why.'

'That changes everything.' Mother stuck her needle in her pin cushion. 'The government won't be so forgiving this time, there's been too many rebellions.'

Mother's words seemed to echo Johnnie's from a long time ago. 'Surely we're safe here?'

'Best forget Johnnie Stewart.'

'What do you mean?'

'I mean our army's outnumbered. There'll be a battle and when the redcoats win, and they will, there'll be no men left to defend us. Jacobite families and those close to them will be singled out.'

'Mother. You talk as if it's a foregone conclusion. What if we win?'

'Hmph.'

Kirsty's mind raced. Was Mother right to say the unthinkable? *Would the Jacobites lose? Will I see Johnnie again?* Her heart couldn't bear it, but her head told her: all things are possible.

'Good thing I've bound my Whig cousin closer to us.'

'If the village knew we were close they wouldna like it.'

'Wouldna like it?' Mother snapped her thumb and a finger together. 'That's what I think of their opinion. If the government win, they'll take a dim view of his loan to a Jacobite. He may even be persuaded to forgo it.'

'You'd blackmail Tolbain?'

Lorna Windham

Mother raised her chin a little higher.

The Jacobite Affair

CHAPTER Twenty-Eight
January 1746

Johnnie tucked Kirsty's letters into his saddlebags. Ever since the Jacobites crossed the Esk he'd longed to hear about his family and Braedrumie.

An ocean of sullen faces, rude gestures and anti-Jacobite cries had greeted the army as they trudged north. The French, with all their promises had never come to their aid. Johnnie knew there had to be a decisive battle with government troops. He crossed himself. God help us if we lose.

On January 4th the Jacobites left Glasgow behind and marched north east to Stirling. Four days later the town surrendered. Troops lay siege to the castle whilst the rest followed the prince as he left on January 17th and marched to meet the redcoats on Falkirk Muir.

Johnnie stared into the campfire flames as bagpipes played and men danced victory reels. 'My God, I canna believe how easy that was.'

'Aye.' Euan looked troubled. 'But we still head north.'

'Damn the prince.' Johnnie dug his dirk into the wet earth. He looked across at the campfire 15 yards away where the prince finished a bottle of brandy and threw it over his shoulder to shatter on top of a pile of broken glass. Murray approached the drunken man, only to be dismissed with a flick of the prince's wrist. 'Look at Charlie, the man's a sot, incapable of taking any advice.' Johnnie gave the prince a rueful glance. 'If we'd only taken advantage of our victory, but no, we retreat instead of consolidating what we've won. I dinna think it good tactics. I have a really bad feeling about all this.'

Lorna Windham

CHAPTER Twenty-nine

The first pit-pat of rain and then sleet made Kirsty dash outside to her washing strewn over the heather. She gathered the skirts and bodices to her breast just before the blizzard started in earnest. The smell of damp wool assailed her nostrils as she closed the door. *And I thought the morning sunshine would dry them.* The cow sank on its haunches and lowed at her. 'Poor old, Clover.' She patted the animal's head. *Oh, dear.* 'The cow's in a bad way,' she said as she entered the kitchen.

'Useless animal.' Mother leant back in her chair and fanned herself with a letter.

'From Aunt Lizzie or the Balfours?' asked Kirsty. She hung the damp sheets on a wooden clothes-horse round the fire.

'The Balfours. Not so full of boasts now.'

Kirsty forced her lips together. 'I'll see if I can get the cow to eat, shall I?' The cow lay on its side, its caved-in ribs still. *No. Oh, no. We'll have no milk, butter or cheese now.* She sucked in a deep breath and called out, 'It's dead.'

'Can't be.' Mother elbowed Kirsty to one side and then wrung her hands. 'Why now? I'd thought she'd get better. We daren't eat the meat. Could have been disease killed her.' Her voice rose to a shriek. 'What are we going to do?'

'What about Tolbain's loan?'

Mother shook her head. 'We need what's left to plant seed this spring.'

'There's always Sinclair. Let's get the cow outside.' Kirsty tied a rope under its belly while Mother did the same with its front legs. 'One, two, three, pull.' The animal didn't move. 'And again. Pull.' Inch by inch they hauled the cow outside.

'We'll have to burn the beast.' Mother sucked in a breath. 'Over in that that dip.' They dragged the carcase to a point where gravity took over and the cow slid into a circular hollow. 'Typical it happened when Johnnie Stewart's playing at war.' She took an axe and hacked at the bracken and gorse.

The Jacobite Affair

'Playing?' Kirsty heaved the branches to the pyre. 'You wanted him to go. He kept us fed and warm. There's nothing he could do would please you.'

'Nor will it,' spat her mother. 'Not unless he's the heir. Who knows, his brother mightn't return.'

'Mother, dinna say that.' Kirsty crossed herself. 'Euan's betrothed to Morag McColl as well you know and I love Johnnie.'

'Johnnie. One of us has to plan ahead. You could ask the laird to lend us a cow. He'd not tell the neighbours for the shame it would bring on him, as you're marrying into the family. If you'd only been a boy.'

'Well, I'm not.' Kirsty bit back tears of frustration. 'And I'll do no such thing. We're not beggars and I'll no' have the Stewarts think we are. There has to be a way.'

'Well, find it. We'll starve without a cow.' Mother stamped off.

She watched Mother return and hurl a crimson brand on the damp wood. Grey tendrils rose, then flames crackled as their main source of food burned. Kirsty's nose twitched with the scent of roast beef and her mouth salivated.

That evening she sat opposite Mother by the kitchen hearth. Kirsty stared at the embers as smoke curled up the chimney. Mother put the last wad of peat Johnnie had cut, on the fire and the fierce glow dimmed.

'Thought of something?' asked Mother.

'Only my meeting with Sinclair tomorrow.'

'Hmph.'

Hailstones beat a tattoo on the window pane.

'Weather's bad. Good thing you've got me, girl.' Mother held up a folded piece of parchment.

'Another letter?'

'Forgot to open it earlier, with this business about the cow. Prepare yourself, it's awful news. Your Aunt Lizzie says poor Michael's dying and begs us to visit again.'

'Dying? But Mother, don't you think Aunt Lizzie makes more of illness than she should? He wasn't that ill last time.'

'He's very fond of you. You know that side of the family have all the money. My father… wasna a kind man, but Michael is and Lizzie hinted he'd remember us.'

'We'd be rich?'

'It doesna say.'

'Oh God, Mother, you dinna want poor Michael to die?'

'Of course not, but not to be poor, not to have to grub in the dirt, work the land, care whether a cow lives or dies, would be…' Mother sighed. 'Suppose you sold those fancy clothes?'

'You told me to.'

'Can't go in these rags. We could use the wool money you saved. You're good with a needle. We'll buy second hand again. No one would know.'

It's taken me years to save. That money's meant for Johnnie and me. What if Michael doesn't die? We'll have spent everything we have and still have to pay Tolbain. But I so enjoyed the Munro's and going to soirees and balls. 'Alright when I'm in Maryburgh I'll buy us some of the officers' wives dresses. Oh, Mother, it'll work out, you'll see and Johnnie will be home soon. I just hope Sinclair keeps his promise to buy these.' She lifted the small mountain of gloves, socks and bonnets.

'You might want to raise your sights above Johnnie Stewart.'

'I'd never do that, never. I love Johnnie.' Kirsty covered her brooch with her hand.

'We'll see,' said Mother.

***

The following day a burnished disk, rose in a lapis lazuli sky. Kirsty tramped through snow drifts to the fishing boat which would take her to Maryburgh.

By late afternoon Kirsty trudged home. There'd been a thaw, but the air had ice in it as the afternoon sun sank towards the top of the far mountains in the west. She'd been delayed by Granny Mac and Isabel who fished at the side of the loch.

The Jacobite Affair

They'd asked for news of the Stewarts and Dougie of course. Isabel said Dougie only wrote short letters and assured Kirsty she'd nothing to worry about. Kirsty had only half-listened, too full of her of worries.

Kirsty paused at the bottom of the hill, put down her basket and massaged the ache in her arms. *What will Mother say?* The farmhouse's windows twinkled as darkness fell and stars dusted the clear sky.

Kirsty grasped the basket handle and trudged on. The door opened as Kirsty arrived.

'Well?' Mother stood on the threshold. 'How did you fare?'

'Let me come in first, even my bones are frozen.' Kirsty followed Mother into the warmth of the kitchen. She flung her basket on the flagstones. 'I bought us a dress each, I had to before someone else saw them. Real bargains. See.' She held up one. 'Thought you'd suit the green.'

'And Sinclair?'

'Didna show, I waited ages.'

'Hmph. Thought as much, the wretch.'

'Even tried selling our goods myself, no one was interested and the officers' wives wouldna take the dresses back.' Her mouth trembled. 'I've no money left. We canna go to Inverness now.'

'You stupid girl.'

'But they were so lovely.' Kirsty burst into tears. *Why did I do it? False pride and covetousness, that's why.*

Lorna Windham

CHAPTER Thirty

Rain thundered on the farmhouse thatch and slid down the window panes. Snow covered the mountains like lace bonnets, but Braedrumie lay as if it waited for spring.

Mother pushed a piece of parchment into Kirsty's hand. 'Read this. Another letter from Lizzie. Your cousin Michael's worse. *Near death,* she says.'

'Oh, no. Mother, we canna afford it.'

'I know.' Mother put her head in her hands for a few moments and then looked up. 'We have to go- It's a risk, but we could use some of Tolbain's money. If Michael dies... Lizzie says... he's remembered **you** in particular in his will, **in particular**. Most insistent she said... called you... his *sweet coz.*' She took a deep breath.

Will. Kirsty's head ached. *To inherit money and not have to worry. But I don't want Michael to die.* She paced the floor. *Inverness, Aunt Munro's comfortable house, the luxury of being waited on, the wonderful social life and gentlemen's compliments.* She clapped her hands unable to suppress a sudden rush of excitement. *Inverness. But Aunt Munro seems judgemental and Michael's sick room makes my stomach churn and yet... don't my fingers throb from knitting? Don't I deserve some enjoyment instead of working on this farm from dawn till dusk?* Thoughts of being waited on by servants, hot water brought to her bedroom and meals prepared by servants made Kirsty more determined. *I just need to replace borders and flounces on the dresses I've bought.* She made up her mind. 'The sooner we visit Michael the better.'

'Quite, I'll make the arrangements. We've no choice. Write to Mrs. Munro, see if she'll offer us her hospitality again. I suppose you'll have to ask Duncan Stewart if he'll look after the farm. It comes hard, being beholden to others. I don't like it.'

'I'm sure they'll both understand, Mother. I'll go across this afternoon, Duncan will be pleased to get news of Johnnie and Euan.'

135

Mother nodded and rose to stir the contents of the blackened pot which hung over the fire.

'First, I'll write to Johnnie.'

'Hmph. Wish you'd forget him.'

'Mother.'

'Ask about poor Hughie.'

'I will.'

Kirsty sat down at the table in the spence, took off her brooch and brought it to her lips. She found the parchment, only a few sheets left. She sharpened the quill, dabbed it in the ink and began to write.

Braedrumie
January 1746
Dearest Johnnie,

I am sorry I have not written sooner. Forgive me, the price of parchment makes life difficult.

Christ Mass was strange without you. No skating, snowballs or making strange creatures from snow. I miss you so. I know you will not find my imaginings strange, but though we are miles apart, I feel you close to me, breathing the same air.

Your father and Duncan are well. I bumped into Granny Mac and Isabel by the loch. They seemed fine, though Granny Mac complained about her joints.

My mother asks about Uncle Hughie. Please tell him Mary and the children are well.

I have some bad news. Aunt Lizzie believes my cousin, Michael, is dying. I am sure you will understand that we feel duty bound to visit Inverness again and may have to stay at your aunt's for some time. Do not worry about us, we will try to travel in the best of weather.

All my love,
Kirsty

***

The weak February sun did its best to shine in Inverness. Aunt Munro's house looked the same and the servants just as numerous.

'It's so pleasant to see you again,' said Aunt Munro. 'A pity it's not in better circumstances. We were so sorry to hear about your cousin. Such awful news, but you must bear up.'

'Ladies.' Jack bowed and kissed their hands. 'If there's anything we can do to alleviate your distress at this time, please let us know.'

'Thank you, you're too kind.' Mother gave him a thin smile. 'You've done so much already. If you dinna mind, once we have rested, we'll visit my sister and poor Michael.'

'Of course, of course. Please come in. Jack will see to your bags.'

***

'So, you've come at last.' Aunt Lizzie showed them into her sitting room. Her sharp features seemed all planes and angles. 'I thought you'd changed your mind.'

The morning light streamed through the sash window onto the jade brocade sofa and silk cushions.

'We were delayed by the weather, another snowstorm.' Mother perched herself on a straight-backed chair. 'You look tired, Lizzie. How's Michael?'

Aunt Lizzie sniffed into her silk handkerchief. 'My poor, poor boy's not long for this world.' She sank onto the sofa in a deluge of tears.

'There, there, dinna upset yourself.' Kirsty sat beside her aunt and took her hand.

Her aunt's eyes lingered on Johnnie's brooch. 'I suppose… Johnnie Stewart's with those fool rebels?'

Kirsty straightened her shoulders. 'He joined them so his youngest brother could stay at home.'

The Jacobite Affair

'Very noble of him, I'm sure. I've been ill with worry, I don't expect you to understand, Gilly, you've only a daughter.'

Kirsty bit her lip and longed for her mother to say something in her defence. Nothing came.

Aunt Lizzie went on. 'Of course, the poor boy has always been frail, the slightest change in the weather goes to his chest, always has. The nights I've sat by his bed, the agony of waiting for his next breath… it's torture being a mother. You'd like to see my poor ill boy, I suppose?' She didn't wait for their reply and led them out of the room and up the stairs.

The heat from the fire in Michael's bedchamber made Kirsty wish she'd worn something cooler. A startled maid, jerked herself upright beside Michael's rumpled bed. Her pinched features flushed.

'Praying for him again, MacPherson?' Aunt Lizzie asked.

'Ma'am.' MacPherson stared at the rug as she bobbed a curtsey.

Aunt Lizzie's eyes swept to a pair of breeches over a chair, shoes on the carpet and a waistcoat which hung from a wardrobe door.

'That's all very well, but you're off task again, MacPherson.'

Michael groaned, though his eyes remained closed.

Aunt Lizzie whispered, 'It will not do, it will not do at all.'

'Sorry Madam, it willna happen again.' MacPherson looked at the floor.

'I should think not.' Aunt Lizzie's voice rose. 'There's many on the streets would like your job. Well, girl?'

MacPherson, tidied the clothing and shoes away, bobbed a curtsey at her mistress and sped out.

'Servants.' Aunt Lizzie turned to Michael. Sweat beaded his brow and his nose shone like an ember above the blankets heaped up to his neck.

'Here's my poor, invalid boy. He looks so peaceful when he's asleep.'

It seemed to Kirsty that Michael lay trapped in a cocoon. *A smaller fire and an open window might mean he'd survive my aunt's administrations.* 'Perhaps… if he had fewer blankets?'

Her aunt gave her a frozen look. 'And kill him sooner?'

'No. All I meant was…'

'Please allow me, his mother, to know what's best for her own dear son.' Her hand went to her heart and beat a rhythm. 'Really… some respect for one's elders would not go amiss.'

'Now, sister, Kirsty only thought to help.'

Kirsty gaped at Mother.

'Thought?' Aunt Lizzie snapped. 'That she did not do. She has no idea what I have I gone through for my son. His birth… what has she to know of such things? The indignities… the pain.'

'You forget yourself, Lizzie. Such talk is not for a young girl's ears.'

'She lives on a farm, Gilly. Dinna pretend she's of our c…'

'Class? It's in her blood, sister as it in in ours, no matter what befalls us.'

Kirsty blinked. *Mother's defending me.*

'If you say so,' said Aunt Lizzie. 'Then I've had worries over every fall, ache and cough. Oh, yes. Parenthood is not to be taken lightly, nor is a poor mother's care.' She hiccupped and sniffed into her handkerchief.

Michael sighed.

Mother stared at Kirsty. 'You'll apologise, won't you, daughter?'

Kirsty bit her lip. 'I'm sorry, aunt, if I've upset you, it wasna my wish.'

Her aunt sniffed again. 'Accepted. I'm sure.' She patted her son's hand and kissed his cheek. 'We'd better leave him. He'll be pleased you visited. His trials are almost over, it won't be long now, I fear.'

***

The Jacobite Affair

Kirsty determined not to be plunged into a depression about Michael's health. She and Mother visited him every day, but also accepted several invitations to soirees, balls and social visits.

In the next few days Kirsty received the attentions of several handsome gentlemen whilst her mother watched from the side of the ballroom. Kirsty wondered if she'd meet Sinclair, but Mr. Liddle informed her he'd gone to the borders. 'Owed money, they say,' he said. 'Got out one step ahead of his creditors. Do tell me you're not one, dear lady?'

Kirsty forced a smile. 'Of course not.' *So, he's a rogue. I've been fortunate. At least I've still goods to sell.* She moved on and stood on the outskirts of a rowdy crowd who discussed the rebellion. *This talk all of retreat.* When wagers had been laid on who would be the victors, she struggled to conceal her anger. *Don't they realise their bets rely on men's deaths?* She thought of Johnnie and his smile. She couldn't, wouldn't bear it if he died. She found her mother and they left the ball.

That night, Kirsty woke with a start in the nightmare of a battle where she'd seen Johnnie struck down. Then she realised her head lay on a fine, silk pillow. She yawned and stretched as the sun and warmth streamed through the window.

'You've woken late.' Mother sat at the dressing table. She patted the bags under her eyes with a forefinger. 'Hurry or we won't eat anything this morning.'

The bustle of the household on the floor below encouraged Kirsty to throw back her bed clothes.

Aunt Munro pressed her lips together in a line of disapproval when Kirsty arrived late as Mother breakfasted on bread, honey and several cups of hot chocolate.

'Breakfast is at eight; that is my rule, Miss Lorne. Any later and it disrupts my maids' routines.'

'Please accept my apologies. I did no' sleep well last night.'

'Perhaps longer visits to your sick cousin, might alleviate any concerns you have on his behalf. And how is he?' asked Aunt Munro

Kirsty took an unladylike bite from a crust and savoured the sweet taste. She started to wipe her mouth with her sleeve, but with a nudge from Mother, used her damask napkin to dab at the crumbs and stickiness at the corners of her mouth. 'Bearing up, wouldn't you say, Mother?'

'Yes. Bearing up, but he is, alas, worse. My sister thinks he hasn't long.'

'Oh dear, please give her my best wishes for his recovery when you visit today.' Aunt Munro swept out.

'These Inverness gentlemen are moneyed,' hissed Mother. 'They're Whig dandies. You just need to catch the eye of one and we could live like this.'

Aunt Munro swept in once more. She held several cards in one hand and a small posy in another. She sniffed at the flowers. 'I declare, Miss Lorne, several invitations and a posy from Mr. Liddle for you. At a time like this. What would Johnnie think? Well, it's not as if Liddle's a young buck, he's fifty if he's a day. Shall we retire to the sitting room so my maids can clear the table?'

'I love Johnnie.' A flicker of anger flared in Kirsty. 'We dinna have soirees or balls in Braedrumie and Mother thinks they cheer me. I am inconsolable about my cousin's present state of health.'

'We are both beyond grief, Mrs. Munroe, beyond grief.' Mother dabbed her nose with her handkerchief. 'But must keep our spirits up or we will be of no support to my sister when her darkest hour comes. My daughter's young and in these times, she might never have the opportunity to partake of such social occasions again.'

'Indeed.' Aunt Munro lifted her chin. 'A pity she has to break so many hearts whilst taking this 'opportunity'. She is betrothed.'

'She hasn't forgotten that,' snapped Mother. 'It's not her fault if she draws foolish admirers.'

'Mother, please. Mrs. Munro is quite right to remind us of our duties.' Kirsty clenched her teeth. *What business is it of*

The Jacobite Affair

Johnnie's aunt? 'We will, of course, continue to call on Michael and my aunt every day before we leave Inverness.'

'Good morning, ladies.' Jack entered the room and bowed. 'How are you both? It seems… uncommonly close … for this time of the year. If you'll… excuse, I thought… to walk on the hills. I should… be back … within the… hour.' Sweat beaded his brow.

'Jack, are you well?' asked Aunt Munro.

He looks the same colour as the milk pudding we ate last night.

He tugged at his cravat. 'I feel… unlike… myself, if… you'll… excuse me, ladies.' He put a hand to his brow, staggered a few steps and crumpled to the floor.

'Jack,' screamed Aunt Munro and rushed forward.

Kirsty's hand went to her mouth. Mother took a step back.

'Fetch Doctor Jakes,' shrieked Aunt Munro as she knelt beside Jack and cradled his head. She stared at the stunned Lornes. 'I do hope you haven't brought contagion into my home.'

'You blame us?' Kirsty took a deep breath.

Kirsty's mother left the room in a flurry.

'Darling, boy.' Aunt Munro cradled Jack's head in her lap. 'We'll soon have you well. What will your father say? London's so far. What will he say?'

Kirsty's mother returned with a couple of manservants. 'I've sent one of the maids for your physician. Perhaps if you'd allow your servants to put him to bed?'

'Yes. Of course.' Aunt Munro put a plump hand on the arm of a chair and heaved herself from the ground. 'Mind his head, be gentle with him.' She followed the servants and Jack out of the door.

Kirsty and Mother waited for the arrival of Doctor Jakes, a young, cadaverous man who checked his watch. 'My patient?'

'In bed.' I'll show you the way.' Aunt Munro led him upstairs.

'The message said he fainted.'

'It's so unlike him.' Aunt Munro's voice faded as she and the physician reached the top of the stairs.

***

Kirsty and Mother visited Aunt Lizzie and Michael. The cobbles glistened with fallen rain as the coach stopped outside the town house.

'Don't tell your Aunt Lizzie about Jack or she won't let us near Michael.'

'I hope Jack will be alright.' Kirsty got down from the coach.

'I'm sure he will.' Mother's limbs refused to move. 'Give me a hand. That's it. You concentrate on Michael.'

Aunt Lizzie ushered Mother and then Kirsty into Michael's bedroom.

He coughed and spluttered under numerous blankets. 'Thank you for coming, Aunt Gilly and coz Kirsty, I'm fit to die. Aaatishoo.'

'You see, I told you. My poor, poor boy.' Aunt Lizzie rushed to his side with a handkerchief.

He blew his nose several times. 'It's the very devil having a cold.'

'A cold?' Kirsty blinked.

'The very devil.' Mother gave her sister a sharp look.

'I was sure it was much worse.' Aunt Lizzie stared at the ceiling.

'Dear, dear.' Mother flicked a sour look at Kirsty. 'We've come all this way for a common cold.

The Jacobite Affair

CHAPTER Thirty-one

Twenty-four hours later a black drape covered Jack Munro's coffin. Aunt Munro lost her voice and Kirsty comforted her.

'Close the curtains.' Mother ordered the servants. 'No talking and prepare some light refreshment for your poor mistress.' She drew Kirsty to one side and spoke between clenched teeth. 'More expense. We'll have to wear black.'

That afternoon, Aunt Munro spoke as if her throat had been clenched in a fist. 'I must write to my poor husband. How will he bear it? And so far away in London…' She smothered a sob in her lace handkerchief. Her head went up and her back stiffened. 'It's my duty, he'll expect it of me and I must do it at once. If you'll excuse me.' She took herself off to the study and closed the door.

Poor Aunt Munro, who'd have thought it?

Later that week, Kirsty and Mother, dressed like crows, propped up Aunt Munro, her crumpled face awash with tears. They stood amongst a host of mourners in the churchyard which overlooked the River Ness. The headstones leaned at all angles as if tired in their grassy beds. As the words 'Dust to dust…' swept over Kirsty, a breeze made the river's grey surface swirl and ripple. Aunt Munro sagged at the knees as Kirsty and Mother bore her weight. Kirsty imagined Jack's soul borne over the waves and up and over the azure mountains in the north.

Kirsty thought back to how Johnnie's aunt had slept for a few hours whilst she'd sat by Jack's bed as his fever heightened and he struggled to breathe. *Taken too young and only a few years older than Johnnie. This could happen to him.*

A crack of thunder and the first drops of rain made the mourners scurry out of the churchyard gate.

'So unseemly. Oh dear, oh dear. And I haven't informed the Stewarts.' Aunt Munro's muffled tone came from behind her handkerchief.

'We'll do that, dinna concern yourself.' *How can I tell them?*

The following morning Kirsty closed her eyes and tried to sweep Jack's final days from her mind. The coach lurched, swayed and rattled and allowed its two passengers no rest on its way to Marybugh.

Mother stayed silent until she dumped her baggage in her kitchen and Kirsty closed the farmhouse door behind them.

'First our cattle, the hens, our cow and now a healthy young man dies and Michael, who we thought at death's door, lingers on with a cold.' Mother sat on a low stool and threw peat onto the fire. Smoke billowed in the room.

'Mother, how can you say that? You love him.'

'I do, it's just that… Lizzie's fortunate she married with the Tolbains' approval and a generous dowry. The family warned me. I'd have had nothing if your grandfather hadn't given me this farm and land. I was young, thought your father and I could live on love alone. I've lived to regret my waywardness, by God I have. Did you move that lamp?'

'No.'

'Strange.'

'Why don't you ask Aunt Lizzie for help?'

'And have her laugh at my fall. No. I'll not do it. I'd rather die.' She rested her head and arms on the table. Sobs racked her body

'Mother, dinna take on so. We'll work something out. You'll see. At least we've the rest of Tolbain's loan and you should be happy Michael's well again.' She patted her mother's back. 'Look.' She went over to a wooden kist, opened the lid and rummaged inside in search of the leather bag which contained the last of Tolbain's coins. She searched amongst clothing, took everything out and became more and more frantic in her efforts. Her mother wiped her eyes and knelt beside Kirsty.

'Are you sure you put it in here?' Kirsty creased her brow.

'Yes.'

Kirsty lifted plaids, felt inside pillows and sheets. 'Sure you haven't moved it?'

'Yes. Did you take them?'

The Jacobite Affair

'No. My God, has it come to this?' Kirsty stared wide-eyed at her. 'How can you ask?'

'Perhaps you wanted to play a joke on your old Mother?'

'No.'

'Well, who would do such a thing?' Mother spat out the words with venom. 'Duncan Stewart?'

'No. He's an honest laddie, and has no need for money. He's worked for nothing, looked after the farm twice and ensured the fire stayed lit both times. He's honest. He couldn't be here all the time.'

'I knew that lamp had moved.' Mother wrapped her arms round herself and rocked back and forwards on her knees. 'What are we going to do? It's all we had. How can we plant seed? We'll starve. Oh God, and Tolbain will want his loan back. We're ruined. Even Johnnie Stewart won't be interested in you now.'

I don't want to become old and have never lain with Johnnie or had his bairns. If the rebellion hadn't happened, we'd have been wed. Johnnie would have bred even better quality cattle on land more fertile and prosperous than it's ever been. Instead I have to go to bed a spinster and spin dreams of heaven to come and I know, life in Johnnie Stewart's bed wouldn't be dull.

Kirsty unpacked and smoothed one of the patched silk skirts she'd worn in Inverness. 'I can always sell this.' *One day I'll have new, beautiful dresses, eat rich food and live in luxury with Johnnie.*

A cry burst from her mother, 'What's to become of us? What's to become of us?'

Kirsty kissed her mother's sunken cheek. 'We'll get by, you'll see.' *Strange how Mother doesn't shrug me off and places her hot, wet cheek on mine.*

CHAPTER Thirty-two

The morning began with a damson-streaked sky as Kirsty pinned Johnnie's brooch on her bodice to remind the laird of her betrothal. Her conscience pricked. *I should have visited.* Her stomach cramped on her way to Braedrumie House. Only oats left. *We need money and food, but I can't tell him. Oh, the shame of it.*

A young maid with bright eyes and copper-coloured hair showed her into the sitting room. Sunlight played on paintings of Stewart ancestors. The laird stood with his back to her as he stared out of an east facing window. The smell of horses and hay wafted towards her.

'Miss Lorne, sir.' The maid dipped him a quick curtsey, tidied a stray strand of behind her ear and left.

Kirsty glanced around her. *Looks tidy, the rug's been swept, the oak desk polished and a fire's lit. Why do some people live such protected lives? No thought of where the next meal comes from or whether they'd have a roof over their heads next morning. Money bought all this, no worries and all the fine things in life, just like the Munros.*

The laird turned to greet her. He'd straw in his hair and streaks of mud on his shirt 'Kirsty, my dear how are you and your mother?'

Oh, dear. 'Well sir, thank you. I'm sorry I havena come to see you. We've been in Inverness visiting my ill cousin who's happily recovered. We stayed with your wife's sister, Mrs. Munro? The weather's been so bad.' Her mouth went dry. 'I'm afraid I've sad news. Her son, Jack, passed away, a fever. In her grief, she asked me to tell you.'

The laird stared at her for a moment. 'Just a lad. No. It's difficult to believe. Poor Ciara and Ian. I'll send my condolences at once. Euan's the same age you ken? I thank you for coming. Will you drink to the laddie?'

The Jacobite Affair

She nodded. As she sipped the amber liquid, it set her throat on fire. 'I'm sorry for your loss,' she spluttered.

'A wee bit strong?' He patted her between her shoulder blades. 'Can't beat Stewart whisky.'

He finished his drink in one swallow and smacked his lips. 'As you can see I've a lot to occupy me here.' He waved at the scattered papers. 'Have you heard from Euan and er... er... Johnnie?'

'They're both well. You know they're probably in Scotland by now?'

'Aye. Lured Cumberland into a trap. But they'll be home soon.'

'Aye.' *I must cling to that thought. Johnnie will be home soon.* Her stomach gnawed.

'You look pale. Dinna tell me you're no' eating? Must be missing that rascal son of mine? May I offer you some refreshment?'

Thank God.

'Some tea perhaps? It's Indian, brought over on our ships. Only the best.'

'Thank you, sir.' Her nails bit into the palm of one hand. 'I came to see if you need help of any kind.'

He rang a small brass bell on his desk and the copper-haired maid returned. 'Refreshments for Miss Lorne and myself.'

The maid closed the door behind her.

'Help? That's thoughtful of you, but I've all the help I need, thank you. Come, sit. I won't, been up since dawn in the stables.' He sniffed the air around him. 'Sorry my dear, I've no wife to remind me not to traipse indoors looking like this, not now Elizabeth's gone. Just as well, she'd have hated this cursed wait for news. Can't settle, somehow. Miss my sons.'

'Aye,' said Kirsty.

The laird took her hands in his. 'Now, you're not to worry, I know what you women are like. They'll be back, mark my words.'

The maid returned carrying a silver salver loaded with shortbread, fruit cake, a huge silver teapot and two china cups and saucers. The air filled with a moist, richness. Kirsty could hardly wait for the tea to be poured and the milk added. She tried her best to sip, not gulp and eyed the food.

'If you dinna mind, I'll have a wee nip in mine.' He took a bottle from his desk drawer and poured a dram of whisky into his tea and gulped it down.

'A biscuit or some cake, my dear?'

It took iron discipline not to grab the plate from his hand. 'Perhaps one slice.'

'You women and your figures.'

Heaven. Exquisite, heaven. Sweet sultanas and raisins burst on her tongue and the creaminess of butter and milk melted in her mouth. *I'd almost forgotten what cake tastes like.*

'Another slice, my dear? And more tea?'

'If you insist.' *Oh, God.* She forced herself to take small bites.

'I'll just have another wee nip.' He tossed the whisky down his throat and followed it with a piece of shortbread. 'Mmm. Must congratulate Cook, think she's outdone herself today.'

Everything in her craved more. 'I must go.' She stood. 'Mother will be expecting me.'

He kissed her on both cheeks and almost overpowered her with the smoky scent of whisky overshadowed by the rank stench of stables. 'Now, promise me you won't worry.'

'I promise.'

His eyes glazed over as his hand reached for the whisky bottle.

He's drinking a lot. A good thing he doesn't know about our situation. I wouldn't be able to bear his pity or charity. We'll get over this, somehow.

She managed to say, 'Goodbye then.'

'Good bye, my dear.' He turned once more to the window.

Kirsty breathed in. *Baking bread.* She followed the warm, yeasty scent to the scullery. The heat hit her like a furnace. *I mustn't drool.* Una Galbraith had one plump arm wrapped

The Jacobite Affair

round a bowl whilst she beat a mixture into submission. Rows of small, golden loaves sat on a long pine table and gave off swirls of warmth. Kirsty's taste buds danced a jig and her mouth swam with saliva. *Should I?* Her fingers reached out to the crusty tops, then she whipped her hand away. *What sort of creature have I become? The shame of it. What would Johnnie think?*

Una looked up.

Did she see?

Una regarded her with open eyes.

No.

'You've been visitin' the laird, I suppose, Miss?' Una dug the wooden spoon into the creamy mixture. 'What brings you here?'

'The wonderful smell.'

'Would you like some wee loaves and a jar of my best raspberry jam to take home?' Una put her meaty hands on her broad hips.

Thank God for a generous woman. 'That's… very kind.' *At least the laird knows nothing of our plight and we'll have something to eat tonight.* Kirsty sped home with her precious gifts held tight to her bosom. *Mother will be pleased.*

'Just one loaf. Pity there's no butter,' Mother licked her sticky fingertips with her tongue. Her portion of bread and jam disappeared in a few mouthfuls.

Kirsty broke her bread in to small pieces in a vain attempt to make it last. 'I'd almost forgotten the taste,' Kirsty said. Her stomach cramped.

***

The next morning Mother's mouth drooped. 'My, we've come down in the world. Mother shovelled the porridge into her mouth, scraped the bowl clean, licked the spoon and placed it on the table. 'Nicer made with milk.'

Kirsty lifted the empty wooden pail.

Mother's eyes narrowed. 'Where are you going?'

'Better no' ask.'

'Better not get caught, then.'

'I canna conjure our cow back to life, Mother.'

Mother stacked the dirty dishes. 'No. But folk are no' stupid.'

'I'll milk a cow from different owners once a week. We'll starve if I don't. I'll be back soon.' Kirsty took the pail and marched out.

Kirsty's breath frosted in the clear air. *No Duncan.* She almost dropped her bucket when she heard the faint boom of cannon which came from Fort William.

A few miles later, Isabel stopped her on the moor. 'Well, Kirsty Lorne. Good to see you. That noise? It's our men. No wonder I've more white hair amongst the grey. They're attacking the fort. God help them and Maryburgh.'

Johnnie. Kirsty's hand went to her brooch. *Can he be so close and yet not come to see me?*

Isabel squeezed her arm. 'They'll be home soon, just give them time. Have you talked to Morag? You'll be pleased she's back. Well, I'm on my way to see if Granny Mac's alright. She's struggling this winter. And you and your mother?'

'Well. Thank you. I'm just out for a wee walk before I start my chores.'

Isabel stared at the pail and her mouth opened as if to ask a question, then she seemed to think better of it. 'You be careful on the moor on your own. You're just a lassie. There's talk of strange men hereabouts.'

Men? Kirsty's eyes searched the hills around her. *Not the first time strangers have been mentioned.* 'I will. I must be going.' *If I can just get away before she asks about the pail.*

'Give my best to your mother, mind. Be careful.'

'I will.' Kirsty grateful to escape, scrambled through crisp and icy undergrowth and over the hillside. *No sign of strange tracks.*

Half an hour later, her breath came in gasps. She sank to the ground so she couldn't be seen. *If only it had been Michael who'd died and not Jack. No I mustn't think that, but, if we'd*

The Jacobite Affair

money I wouldn't be skulking like a cattle thief behind a gorse brush. A thorn caught her stocking and scratched her leg. She rubbed at the livid mark. *God forgive me for wicked thoughts. I don't want Michael dead. If only my aunt had asked after us or offered something.* She kept her head low whilst Old Grant beat the gorse with his walking stick as he limped from cluster to cluster.

She'd heard the tap-tap of his stick on the flagstones move towards the byre on the other side of the wicker screen in his croft. Her head had been buried in the cow's bulging side as she'd worked the teats and milk splashed into her pail. She'd relied on Old Grant's poor sight, deafness and inability to walk fast, but he'd almost caught her as she'd grabbed the bucket and overturned the stool in her race to get out.

'A curse on you, you thievin' devil,' he'd shrieked and tugged his silver beard 'My cow's milked dry. May God, strike you down. May you never know happiness or live to see your grandchildren. May burnin' pains shoot through your body, so you know no rest.' He paused, gasped for breath as a distant explosion sounded and used his dirty sleeve to mop his brow before he continued. 'Damn those cannon. May worms gnaw your innards and maggots…'

Kirsty clutched the half-full pail to her breast as the old man turned his back to attack another cluster of gorse. Her heart thudded against her ribcage. *At least Old Grant still has his cow and we've enough to keep us going for another day.*

She crawled through the bracken and over the brow of the hill. *Hope his curses have no power.* A shiver ran through her. She pulled her shawl over her head. *More snow.* She could see it in the clear blue sky, taste it on the icy breeze and sense it in the stillness of the undergrowth. The wild creatures knew and she imagined them snug in their burrows, dens and nests. She increased her pace and headed home.

Loch Linnhe lay like a silver necklace below her and she knew she wouldn't be safe from Old Grant until she reached the shelter of the canopy of oak trees below. If caught, she'd be shamed and whipped. Her mother would never forgive her. The whole of Braedrumie would know she'd thieved.

I hate hunger. The way it takes over, so you think of nought else except the empty gripe of your stomach. Such ill luck – our stolen cattle, useless hens all eaten long ago and a dead cow. What have we done to deserve such bad fortune? Mother, too proud to ask neighbours or relatives for help. She'd be happy to die with no one aware of our poverty. And I can't bring myself to beg from the Stewarts. Our pride will be the death of us. If only Johnnie was here, then everything would be back to normal. Not that he'd approve of my stealing milk. I'll make sure he never finds out. Today will be the last. Spring's always late in the Highlands. What to do? Kirsty considered their options. *We've still goods to sell.* She looked at the sky again, it had changed from blue to steel-grey, the clouds pendulous. *We've few oats left.*

That night Kirsty sipped hot milk huddled next to Mother, who'd downed hers. The fire gave out some heat as the wind howled outside and its fingers curled under doors, round windows and settled over the women's backs.

'Haven't seen much of that Duncan Stewart.' Mother darned a hole in a shawl. She squinted. 'I can't see, move that lamp closer.'

Kirsty did as asked. 'The laird's probably given him some extra chores. Anyway we dinna pay him, he's his own wee man.' She paused. 'Mother, we've little to eat. It's Braedrumie Market tomorrow. I 'm going to try to sell these.' She held up her woollen goods. 'And I thought the garters.'

'You can't.' Mother's needle paused in flight. 'What will people think?'

'That we have honest means to make money.'

'But they'll know we're in need. At least no one in Maryburgh knew us.' Mother dropped her sewing on her lap and put her face in her hands. 'The shame of it.'

'Mother, the whole village is in need. They won't think any the less of us.'

The Jacobite Affair

'Hmph. So you say.' Mother's stomach growled. 'I suppose I'll have to come with you, we don't want a repeat of Maryburgh, but you can act as a tradeswoman, I won't, not in front of our neighbours.'

***

Next day the first drifts of downy-white fell as Kirsty and Mother picked their way along the banks of the wind-lashed loch towards Braedrumie.

A vague hum of many voices drifted through the pines as well as the earthy tang of peat. Ahead, crofts stood in a higgledy-piggledy fashion. Crowds milled in a circular area covered with carts and eager stallholders who yelled, 'Come and buy,' 'Finest leather' and 'Eggs for sale.' Mother and Kirsty wound their way past a rosy-cheeked woman who sold ale, a man, like an ancient oak, who offered to mend shoes and a dirty child who sold rags.

'Ow.' Kirsty rubbed at the red wheal on her foot and looked up. *Morag McColl. Trust it to be her of all people.*

'Sorry,' Morag said.

Does she mean it? They say she still won't talk about her time away. Goodness knows what she got up to. I bet Euan sent her home, worried about her reputation. Though Granny Mac says she behaves with authority, as if she's given orders.

Oh, no. Why is Mother boasting about my wedding to Johnnie? She hates him and it means little to Morag, I can see it in her face. Let's see what she makes of this. 'Euan's cousin Jack has died. A fever, whilst we were in Inverness.'

Morag went pale. 'This is sad news. Thank you, but you must excuse me. I have things I must do.' She moved away.

Kirsty watched her pause and finger some fine lace. She stood behind her and couldn't resist a mean remark about Morag's chapped fingers, then regretted her unkindness. *Why do I take such pleasure in Morag's discomfort? Why do I dislike her so much?* The answer came to Kirsty in a flash: *because she has a father who loves her.* The thought wormed

Lorna Windham

itself deep inside Kirsty's brain and she didn't like it. *Johnnie loves me, his love should be enough for anyone. I must try to be kinder in future.* She looked for Morag, wanted to apologise, but she'd disappeared in the throng.

Kirsty sold a woollen bonnet, stockings and pair of woollen gloves, whilst Mother pretended to shop at other stalls. She scurried to Kirsty's side when she saw the few coins in her daughter's hand.

'We'll buy a few vegetables and have soup tonight.' Mother's eyes glowed.

'Coz Gilly… and Kirsty.' Tolbain loomed over them as he signalled his men with a sweep of his arm to spread out and mingle with villagers.

'Your Grace.' Mother curtsied, Kirsty bobbed up and down.

'Alexander.'

'Perhaps you can help?' His eyes lingered on Kirsty. 'I seek a notorious young woman: the Jacobite Jade. Quite a beauty, long brown, curly hair, hazel eyes, temper like a spitting cat. Involved in the rebellion, one of the Pretender's lovers, do you know her?'

Kirsty froze, shocked. *One of the Pretender's lovers? He's just described Morag McColl and Morag loves Euan.* She scanned the market. *No sign of her.*

'There's no one here like that that,' lied Mother. 'Is there Kirsty?'

Kirsty shook her head. *I mightn't like Morag, but I'll never betray her.*

'Now, are you sure she's from these parts?' asked Mother.

'Rumour has it she is.' Tolbain's black eyes studied them. 'You're both thin. Short of food are we?'

'Isn't everyone?' asked Mother and wrapped her cloak round her. 'Thought you'd joined the redcoats?'

'I've returned… for a while. I'll get Campbell to send men over with… some provisions and I'm sure you could do with their protection? There's a lawless band of men in the vicinity.'

The Jacobite Affair

Lawless men. 'There's no need…' began Kirsty.

Mother interrupted. 'Thank you, cousin.'

He picked over Kirsty's woollen goods in her basket and lifted up a purple shawl. 'Did you make this?'

'Aye.'

'I'll take it in lieu of money owed. I assume you forgot your first interest payment, coz?''

Kirsty made to snatch back the shawl, but Mother elbowed her out of the way. 'We were robbed of your loan.'

'Not my problem.' His eyes flicked to Kirsty and back to Mother. 'You'll stick to your side of the bargain?'

'Yes.' Mother's lips formed a line. She glanced at Kirsty, then away.

'I'll leave it to you, shall I?'

Mother nodded.

'Very well, I've matters to settle first.'

'Mother?' Kirsty looked at her and then stared at Tolbain with his ox-shoulders, black hair and beard.

'I'll send word… mid-April, I'll be a tad busy 'til then.' Tolbain bowed, pecked at Mother's hand and worked his lips up to Kirsty's wrist. He strode away.

Kirsty wiped her hand on her skirt. 'He's disgusting and we'll never be able to pay him back.' She watched in dismay as he cuffed one of his men who leapt into action and overturned a stall. 'What bargain have you made, Mother?'

A scream rent the air as a woman lay trampled underfoot.

'What's happening? We must do something to help.' Kirsty clutched Mother's arm. 'Can you no' stop him?'

'Sssh…' Mother grabbed Kirsty's wrist and pulled her into the trees which crowded the loch and stopped once they'd rounded an outcrop of rock and could no longer see Braedrumie. 'Are you mad to speak so?' Mother flung the words at her. 'You know he's a Whig and this a Jacobite village. What he wants, he takes. You must have recognised the description of the woman he's after?'

Kirsty nodded. 'Morag?'

'Yes… God knows how he got wind of her and her doings.'

'She isn't the prince's lover, she loves Euan too much.'

'That may well be, daughter, but **we** know nothing, understand?'

'Course. I wouldn't give her away even though I dinna like her and her high-handed ways. Now let me go, you're hurting me.'

Mother released her. 'We'd best get home. Didn't I warn you about the rebellion?' She walked on. 'This is only the beginning. We need to make sure we're seen to be on the winning side.'

'What do you mean?' Morag massaged her wrist.

'Forget Johnnie Stewart.'

'Oh, Mother, I'll love him until I die.'

CHAPTER Thirty-three

A blizzard found the laird on the Lorne's doorstep, his beard, eyelashes and plaid encrusted with snow. He tipped his head back and drank from a brandy bottle then threw it aside. It landed with a crash. 'Have you seen wee Duncan?'

Kirsty used the door as a shield against the bitter wind, but drew it open for him. 'No, but come away in.' She led him through the empty byre to the kitchen.

'Little fiend hasna come home.' He swayed on his feet. 'I ken he's often here, helps out.'

'Not been nigh for a couple of days, that's right isn't it, Mother?'

'Yes.' Mother tossed more peat on the fire. A cloud of smoke erupted around them.

The laird coughed.

'Have you tried Morag?' asked Kirsty.

'Aye and the rest of the village. Probably joined the Jacobites.'

'But, you'll bring him back?' said Kirsty.

'And why would I do that, woman?' The laird glowered at her.

'Well, you promised Johnnie you'd keep him safe.' Kirsty stood arms akimbo. 'It's the only reason Johnnie joined the rebellion.'

'Johnnie, that... at least I'll have two sons **keen** to fight for The Cause.'

'But, you'll bring Duncan back?' Kirsty persisted. 'You agreed.'

He leaned into Kirsty's face. 'Dinna think you're betrothal means you've the right to tell me what to do. No one, least of all you does that. I'll bid you good day ladies, I'll see myself out.'

Kirsty stared after him.

A few seconds later an icy blast swept through the kitchen and the door slammed.

'Always was hot-headed,' said Mother. 'Fortunate to have Elizabeth, she knew how to handle him. Now he's missing her and their sons. Thinks he'll find comfort in drink.'

'Poor Johnnie.' Kirsty unpinned her brooch and turned it over and over in her hand.

'Look at your father and that Sinclair. Never trust a man.' Mother spat into the fire.

CHAPTER Thirty-four

The grey-faced sky glowered at the exhausted Stewarts. Ordered to make a futile night raid on Cumberland's army at Nairn the night before, the men sat in a disconsolate circle on Drumossie Moor near Culloden.

Johnnie clenched his fists in frustration. He'd a bad feeling in his gut as he looked across to Beinn Bhuidhe and Beinn Bheag, the Yellow Hills in the distance. Their Highlanders would be unable to launch an attack from crags above their enemy as the prince had chosen to fight on moorland. Johnnie weighed up their chances. Scouts had reported the redcoats outnumbered and out gunned them. How had it come to this?

Disgruntled, Johnnie wore the ears off Euan and Dougie with his list of complaints. 'If I had to be in this rebellion. I'd rather we'd risked all and marched to London, than turned tail like frightened deer at Derby'

Euan stabbed his sword into a tussock of grass. 'Dinna forget Prestonpans and Falkirk Moor. But, you're right, the decision at Derby was key. If we'd moved fast, London and the Crown would have been Charlie's. I blame Murray and his supporters.'

Johnnie pointed at the tattered figures stretched out and seated over the moor. 'How can we fight on just meal and water?'

Raucous laughter came from the prince's followers as he drank from a leather flask.

'We'll never win with him pissed out of his head,' said Johnnie.

Dougie threw his dirk into the ground and Duncan collected it.

Duncan. He should have been safe at home. Johnnie rubbed his forehead to stop the throb inside his skull. 'And the damned weather's turned against us.' He thought of how the Jacobite army had struggled north through snow drifts as high as his shoulders. At least they'd arrived in Scotland with few casualties, though the redcoats had caught them by surprise at

Lorna Windham

the River Spey. He and Euan had spurred back to guard the ford only to find the government troops had arrived early and crossed elsewhere. Damn them.

The grey sky released a curtain of sleet which the wind blew into the Johnnie's eyes. The Jacobites had fewer men now because of deserters and foragers. Stomachs touched backbones as men sat or slept as they waited for Cumberland and his army to arrive.

A cough behind Johnnie alerted him to McBean's presence. Johnnie's conscience pricked. A few useful sword strokes later, McBean waved his sword like a broken branch till his cough and concave chest forced him to stop to catch his breath.

At least he tried. 'Sit down for a while, man,' Johnnie said. 'Have some water.' McBean gulped it down. Not a fighter, but he was here.

'Thank you kindly,' wheezed McBean.

How McBean had made it this far defeated all reason. His thin frame and wan complexion should have made him the butt of jokes, but the Stewarts defended their own. He'd earned his right to be treated as one of them now.

'Here, whose side you on?' asked Murdo and shifted his backside away from McBean's sharp, pointed blade.

'Sorry.' McBean looked forlorn.

Johnnie set his jaw. 'Just like droving, needs a bit of practise.' He pointed to a spot several yards to the rear. McBean dragged his sword as he plodded towards the flat ground.

'His chances?' asked Johnnie in hope Dougie had spotted some fighting potential.

Dougie squinted and assessed McBean's prowess. 'He'll die.'

Johnnie's stomach churned. He liked to think he'd escape the ignominy of being the only Jacobite cut into collops by his own side.

Haggard Jamie Moffat shoved a battered letter into Johnnie's hand. 'Sorry it's so late, the army's been hard to find and redcoat patrols like fleas. You'll be fightin' soon?'

The Jacobite Affair

Johnnie put his hand on Jamie's thin shoulder. 'You've done well, rest a while, laddie.'

Jamie accepted water and a handful of oatmeal from Euan. Johnnie wandered away and examined his letter. Kirsty's handwriting. He tore it open and read it twice. Bloody hell. She could be so close and in so much danger. Surely she and her mother hadn't travelled to Inverness? His insides twisted at the thought she could have been there for months, now trapped too terrified to leave.

'Johnnie, have you something you want me to take?' asked Jamie and patted a weathered leather bag hung over his shoulder.

'Aye. Can you wait a few minutes?'

Jamie cocked his ear. 'You'll have to be quick. Hear the drums? The redcoats will be here soon.'

Johnnie scanned the moor. He hoped Kirsty had stayed in Braedrumie. He rested a crumpled sheet of watermarked parchment on his saddlebags and scribbled.

Scotland
April, 1746
My Own One,
Please excuse this scribbled note, but have only just received your letter. I warn against a visit to Inverness, sweetheart. The country is seething with unrest and I would not have any harm befall you or your mother. Stay close to the farm. Ensure the doors and shutters are sound and hide the cattle as soon as the weather permits.

If this letter arrives too late, know I will come for you wherever you are.

All my love, darling,

Johnnie

No time to write to his father, perhaps Euan had done that. Johnnie flung the letter at Jamie. 'Go with God.'

'Rather stay here. But my duty's to get news home. I could take Duncan with me.'

Steel rung on steel. Johnnie glanced across at his young brother and Euan as they circled each other with swords raised.

'No. He'll never forgive us, but thank you for the thought.'

The stamp of marching feet drifted towards Johnnie.

Jamie raised his voice. 'Let no man say I'm coward because I left the field.'

Johnnie grasped his hand. 'No one thinks that, Jamie lad. Without you, we'd have had no word from those we love. We all serve in different ways. God speed.' He watched Jamie mount, spur his pony west and wished Duncan rode beside him.

The first redcoats swirled flags which heralded Cumberland's arrival. The Stewarts scrambled to their feet.

'Damn the deserters and those foraging food,' said Johnnie.

The Jacobites stood fast and their cannon boomed first. The Hanoverian field guns then replied. The air echoed with the sound of shot and cries of anguish.

Euan's eyes gleamed in anticipation. Johnnie knew his brother had longed for this battle. And Dougie? He clamped his lips together and gave nothing away. McBean shuffled from foot to foot. Johnnie, put an arm round Duncan's shoulders to pull him close, but his brother shied away as if too old for a show of affection. Johnnie looked at Dougie who gave an imperceptible nod, grabbed Duncan by the scruff of his neck and hauled the lad behind him. Johnnie faced the redcoats, closed his eyes and whispered the Lord's Prayer to himself, then thought of Kirsty.

The Stewarts stood in line with the rest of the Jacobites for what seemed hours. Men tried not to flinch at the whistle of shot and sting of burnt wadding. Cannons roared. Johnnie watched in horror as mortars pounded and cannon balls cut bloody paths of gore through their ranks.

The Stewarts beat on their targes with their broadswords. Blood lust surfaced and overpowered terror as a low animal growl spread from clan to clan. An impatient ripple of movement started in the Jacobite centre and moved to the right.

The Jacobite Affair

Stewart throats joined over 5000 others as they sprinted like unleashed madmen at the redcoats and screamed, 'Claymore!' Round shot and mortar bombs exploded overhead. More cries and shrieks. Johnnie sped forward, confident that Dougie had kept Duncan and McBean to the rear of the Stewarts in the first wave.

Johnnie yelled a war cry at the red lines in front of him. He aimed, fired and hurled his musket away. Grape shot, scrap iron, nails and musket balls rained down and scythed men like wheat. The Jacobite charge slowed as wounded men slumped to the ground.

Johnnie plunged up to his knees in boggy ground and hoped to God Dougie had kept Duncan well behind him. The Stewarts faltered – men fell. More bloody spaces as mortar rounds fragmented heads.

No time to think, he needed to press on. Johnnie shifted to the right. The Stewart clan followed him, squeezed as if in a funnel towards the redcoat left and their musket balls. Strange how he registered the spouted smoke from cannons and mortars, but not their roar. How men fell in slow motion either side and in front of him. How blood spurted from wounds and men died without a sound or so it seemed.

The redcoats loomed closer and closer. He made out the distorted faces of a pasty-faced private, a spotty lieutenant and a third, a bulldog sergeant who growled at his men to, 'Stand and fight, you whores' sons.'

Johnnie heard that. He used his shield to knock the private's bayonet to one side, but found himself thwarted by another soldier's blade aimed under his right arm. It missed. At three yards from the enemy the Jacobite line charged full pelt at the red lines. Hughie's contorted face reeled away as he fell, his neck a red slash of blood.

The yells and high-pitched screams of men in their death agonies filled Johnnie's head. Confusion. He slashed at the private who dropped like a wet fish. Chopped at a lieutenant who retreated as blood dripped from his useless arm and smashed his shield on the sergeant's hooked nose. Shattered bone disappeared in crimson mist as the man keeled over.

'Cover the enclosure, men. They'll outflank us.' Euan's voice.

On the Jacobite right, redcoats got behind the walls of the enclosure and fired at them. Johnnie swivelled to help Euan as the redcoat ranks pressed forward. No sign of Duncan and Dougie.

Dragoons spurred their mounts as redcoats tore down the walls and fired volley upon volley.

'They've outflanked us. Follow me!' Euan yelled.

Johnnie raced across the battlefield towards his brother. A cacophony of men's shrieks, groans and guns boomed in his ears. To Johnnie's horror the Jacobite line wavered and broke. A mortar exploded overhead. His brain clouded as he fell. He knew no more.

***

Sometime later he woke. He struggled to free a hand and put it to his cheek. Blood. His lungs fought to suck in air. A great weight pressed down on him. A hand flopped in front of his face and a leg sprawled over his waist. Hell. He groped around in the darkness and realised he lay under a pile of wounded and dead from both sides.

The battle had passed over him and moved on when the Jacobites ran. Desperate for air, he heaved himself out of the tangle of blood-soaked bodies towards a chink of light. His lungs ached as he crawled. He clawed his way out into a ground mist and took a deep breath. His senses cleared. Drumossie Moor.

The metallic click of a cocked trigger came from his left. Johnnie froze.

'Well, well, what have I found?' said a cultivated English voice. A young redcoat captain sat on horseback with his pistol pointed at Johnnie's heart.

The Jacobite Affair

'Damn.' Johnnie measured the distance between them. He'd be shot before he made a yard. So, this is how it would end. He'd not beg. 'Shoot and be done with it.' He bared his chest.

The officer and Johnnie stared at each other for several seconds. A contest of wills?

The captain un-cocked and lowered his pistol. 'Piss off!' he said.

'What?'

'Piss off!' the officer repeated. He slipped the weapon into its leather saddle holster. 'I've had enough of killing this day.' He leaned forward in his saddle. 'Get back to your hovel and family if you can. Warn them. Cumberland's giving no quarter, not on this battlefield and not to any Jacobite. But, I'll not have a defenceless man's blood on my hands. A point of honour don't you see?'

Had he really weighed duty against humanity and decided on the latter? Johnnie's heart stopped its thud against his rib cage. 'Thank you. What's your name?'

The captain tapped his nose, then wheeled his horse. 'Not all redcoat officers are cut from the same cloth as Cumberland.'

Harsh voices sounded through the thin streaks of fog which revealed a group of redcoats headed towards them about a hundred yards away.

The captain fumbled for his pistol. 'Run you bloody fool!' he hissed at Johnnie. 'They'll expect to hear a shot.'

Johnnie ran. He heard a crack and felt a hot wind as a ball whistled by his ear.

CHAPTER Thirty-five

Duncan, Euan and Dougie? Johnnie's head thumped in time with their names as he vomited into the heather. His limbs shook as he tried to see through the grey sheet of mist which crept over the battlefield. Behind him, in the distance, came muffled orders, intermittent musket shots and screams.

Johnnie wiped his forehead with the back of his bloodsmeared hand. He knelt on the damp earth. His chest heaved. They'd lost. The realisation hit him like a blow. What about Duncan? He bit back the sour taste in his mouth. By God, if he made it back- **when** he got back- he'd have words with his father, but without a weapon he'd little chance.

He hugged the ground, knuckles white with tension. Then he slithered between tussocks of grass, hid behind gorse and buried himself in heather to evade groups of redcoats in their hunt for survivors.

He had to get off Drumossie Moor, but what about the Stewarts, his brother and Dougie? And Kirsty and her mother? He needed to get to Inverness before the redcoats.

He surveyed the area around him and rested in a hollow surrounded by marsh grass some miles from the battle. The mist thickened and wavered. He cocked his ear. The voices and shots grew more distant. Safe – for a time. He hunkered down by a beck and caught his breath. Then he scooped up a handful of brackish water which eased his dry throat and dashed two handfuls in his face to clear his sluggish brain. After all they'd been through, they'd lost. Damn the bloody prince and the French, their promises like leaves in the wind.

He stiffened as harsh, foreign voices came to him on the breeze, difficult to know how close or from what direction. Gorse lay like a thorny crown round the rim of the dip. He crawled to the top, crouched and tried to scan the grey haze beyond the thorn branches. Hopeless. He retreated and set off at a lope towards Inverness.

The Jacobite Affair

CHAPTER Thirty-six

To the east, hung banks of grey clouds, but a sapphire sky lay overhead. Kirsty looked up from the codling she gutted on a flat stone outside the farmhouse. *Thank goodness I caught several in the loch. We'll eat today.* She let the sun's rays warm her face. There'd been a terrible storm the night before and it had been difficult to sleep through the mournful sound of the wind and the creaks of the farmhouse's timbers.

Last time she'd visited Braedrumie villagers had whispered behind hands. *Assumptions will be made about our talk with Tolbain. And what about Johnnie? And I haven't heard the repetitive boom of cannon at Fort William for weeks. What did Isabel say? The Jacobites had slipped off to Inverness and left the fort to the redcoats. Was Johnnie there, had Duncan joined him and the Stewarts? And what about those two ships which plied backwards and forwards along the loch? And Granny Mac said French ships had been seen off the coast. An invasion?*

The slap of leather, rattle of harness and gruff voices caught her attention and brought her back to the present. Two bearded men in Tolbain's moss-green colours rode towards her from the west. They dismounted and tied the ponies' reins to an iron ring set in a boulder for that purpose.

She wiped her hands on her grubby apron and tutted at the bloody streaks and silver scales. The men walked towards her. The young one favoured his right leg and the other looked like Methuselah. *Unusual to see men, as most have joined the rising. What now?*

'Mother, we've visitors,' she called and then addressed the men. 'Can I help you?'

The young man rubbed his thigh and grimaced as if in pain.

'You'll be Miss Lorne?' Methuselah, his whiskers stained yellow, hawked and spat.

'Aye.'

'The duke's orders: we've to guard you. Said he'd mentioned it at the market.'

Lorna Windham

'Are we in danger? Has something happened?'

'Not as far as we ken.' He stroked his whiskers. 'While he's away, he doesna want you to come to any harm.'

'Harm?'

'A nice lass like you, wouldna want rogues to attack her.' Methuselah scanned the ridge behind him.

Kirsty blinked. 'Nothing ever happens here.'

'Let us be the best judge of that, Miss. We'll make sure you're alright.' The young man rubbed his thigh.

'And who are you?' Mother stood in the doorway, besom in hand. 'What right have you to come on my land and give such an assurance?'

The young man took a step back and his right leg buckled under him. The older man put an arm round his waist. 'Careful, lad.'

'Mother, they say Tolbain sent them.'

'Your names, if you please?'

'Angus Boid. He's my son Finlay.' He jerked his thumb at the young man. 'We'd have been with the duke, 'cept Finlay here had a fall.'

'He wouldna have let you go anyway, Father. You're too old.'

'I don't know either of you,' said Mother. 'You're not from these parts from your accents. Could be robbers for all I know.'

'Not wearing these colours. We're from the borders, Mistress, and been ordered here till His Grace returns from battle.'

'Battle?' Kirsty couldn't swallow.

'Aye. Near Inverness, His Grace said, and Cumberland's trained his troops in a new tactic. Few safe in the Highlands if they're on the wrong side.'

Kirsty's hand went to her brooch. *A new tactic? Johnnie.* She wanted to scream his name out loud, but dared not. *He could be wounded or worse. Please God, not dead, I couldn't bear it.*

The Jacobite Affair

A breeze raced the heather and gorse and played with her hair and apron. *If we lose and the redcoats come, how can this old man and lame boy guard us?* Panic rose in her breast. *I must not lose control. We'll get through this somehow and so will Johnnie and he'll come home to me. I have to believe this, I've nothing else.*

Her mother smiled. 'So, my cousin thinks us worthy of his protection. And so we are. You'll have to fend for yourselves, mind and you're not coming in my home, not with those filthy boots. Did you bring any food for us?'

'No.' Methuselah's jaw tightened.

'Hmph'. Mother made to snap at him, snatched the fish from Kirsty and slammed the door shut.

'I'm sorry. We thought… Mother can be… abrupt at times. We canna feed you, we've hardly enough for ourselves.'

'We'll bed down out by those rocks.' Methuselah pointed to a spot about 50 yards to the right of the farmhouse.

'Do you really think, if the redcoats win, it'll go badly for us here?'

'You're a stone's throw from a Jacobite village, Miss Lorne. What do you think?' said Methuselah. 'There's been too many rebellions. If you ask me the King's had enough of them.'

She walked to the burn and washed her hands in the icy water. Methuselah unsaddled the horses whilst Finlay cut branches, she supposed to build a crude hide in the huddle of rocks. She dried her hands on her skirt and jumped over the burn.

'You're to stay close to the farm,' shouted Methuselah. 'Those are our orders.'

What? She swirled to face him. 'I'm visiting Laird Stewart,' said Kirsty. 'It's no far.'

Finlay went red in the face. 'He's a Jacobite and so are his sons. It's our duty to see you stay safe. I need to rest this damn leg. It'll mean my father will have to go with you. There'll just be me on guard here. The duke willna like it.'

170

Won't he? And why the sudden interest in us? 'I'm no' one of his men.' She stalked away.

Finlay didn't answer.

***

Kirsty's stomach growled as she and Methuselah tramped to Braedrumie House. He'd insisted he'd accompany her, despite her protests. *Men.* Cattle lowed and sheep grazed as they walked on the Stewarts' land.

As they turned into the laird's cobbled yard, hens clucked at their feet. The warm smell of baking snaked out of the scullery's open window and made her drool again. *I will not beg for food. No, but you could steal it,* whispered a little devil on her shoulder.

Kirsty left Methuselah outside and stood aghast at the entrance to the study. Stale food and whisky fumes invaded her nostrils. Johnnie's father lounged at his desk surrounded by stacks of crumpled parchment, empty bottles and dirty plates.

He regarded her with red eyes below drooped lids. Comprehension took its time then his slack mouth spluttered, 'Miss Lorne isn't it?'

She looked around at the dust which covered every surface. 'Is your housekeeper no' well? Mrs. Sanderson isn't it?'

'Who? Her? Aye she's well enough. Nothing seems to matter since Elizabeth.' He waved at a pile of dirty linen thrown over a fireside chair.

'Shall I have a word with her? I dinna think Johnnie or Euan would be happy if they knew you lived like this.'

The laird took a half-empty bottle and slopped the amber liquid into a tumbler on his desk. 'Aye. You do that, lassie. You do that.' He took a swig.

Goodness, I've permission to deal with his housekeeper. Thought he'd have cut off my arm, before he allowed me this much leeway in his home.

The Jacobite Affair

'You must mish Duncan's help?' said the laird.

Oh God, he's drunk. 'We do, it was kind of him to offer. Johnnie shouldna have made him promise.'

'Nonsense. Gave the laddie something to do. Mished Rob - his brothers, you know. Found his poor mother's death... difficult. Johnnie helped him, made it bearable and now Duncan's left too.' The laird took another swig of his drink.

'There's talk of Cumberland with a new tactic and there's to be a battle. It could be happening as we speak.'

He gave a soft whistle. 'A battle? You know thish for a fact?' He leant forward over his desk and his elbow caught an empty bottle. It rolled and crashed to the floor in a shower of broken glass.

'Some... travellers called at the farm... they mentioned it.' *How can I tell him I'd heard it from Tolbain's men or that I'm related to the duke through Mother? He'd think us traitors and not let Johnnie marry me.*

'A battle you say? Wish I was younger. To hear the skirl of the pipes and see the banners wave. Enough to thrill the blood. Mind, it's Duncan I'm concerned about, I dinna mind admitting it. We've had no word since he left. At leasht his brothers wrote until a few months ago.' His hand trembled as he lifted some sheaves of well-worn parchment off a side table. 'Only a few lines from Euan, mind, and a few more from Johnnie.' The letters fluttered to the floor. 'A battle? They'll soon be home then and all will be well. We'll have fine times, fine times.'

Is he trying to convince himself as well as me?

The laird rose from behind his desk, swayed and took her hands in his. 'Dinna worry. I know what you women are like. They'll be back, mark my words. Euan's a braw fighter and so's Johnnie when he takesh his mind off blashted books.'

'But...' said Kirsty.

'Dinna defend him.' He snarled and let her hands drop.

His change of mood stirred her memory and made her take a step back. *Just like Father.* 'I must go. Mother's expecting me.'

Lorna Windham

He kissed her on both cheeks and almost overpowered her with the smoky scent of whisky and tang of ponies. 'Now, promish you won't worry.'

'I promise.'

His eyes glazed over as his hand reached for the whisky bottle.

He's got enough troubles. What to do?

Kirsty caught the housekeeper as she came downstairs into the hall. 'Mrs. Sanderson, I'd be grateful if you tidied the laird's study.'

'Would you now?' The housekeeper looked down her long nose at Kirsty and folded her arms against her flat bosom. 'Says he doesna want to be disturbed. I've tried.'

'Just a minute.' Kirsty marched into the study where the laird, glass in hand, stared out of the window at the distant mountains. She gathered up the wreckage of plates, marched into the hall and shoved them into the startled woman's hands. 'There you are. If you want to remain here, I'd remember his sons will be home soon. They'll expect you to do your job. Good day.'

The housekeeper looked as if she'd eaten a cherry and found the stone.

Kirsty's stomach, still empty, gnawed at her. She inhaled and followed her nose to the scullery. A tray of golden brown scones cooled on the open window sill.

Una, her back bent and up to her elbows in flour, kneaded dough on the table in the middle of the room. She looked up. 'So, you're back Miss Lorne? And how were my loaves and jam?'

'Delicious.' Saliva gathered in Kirsty's mouth 'The best we've ever tasted. Thank you again. I must go...' *Before I forget myself.*

Una beamed. 'I'm a dab hand at scones too. Here, you come in and try one and take one for your mother. Wasted on the laird. Hardly eats and doesna want folk fussin' round him, so Mrs. Sanderson says.'

The Jacobite Affair

Kirsty stepped into the warmth and inhaled the scullery's rich, fruity smells. 'Thank you.'

Una cut the scone in half. Kirsty watched the steam rise as the cook lathered butter on both halves, followed by a dollop of blackberry jam. She closed the scone and gave it to Kirsty. 'See if you don't enjoy that. You tell me if I dinna make the best scones and jam in the Highlands.'

Kirsty unable to resist, bit into the succulent sweetness in her hand. 'You do. Oh, you do.'

Una laughed, a gurgle which started in her plump throat and erupted from her mouth like a rush of water. 'Here, take some home. It's a pleasure to cook for someone who appreciates my bakin'.' She handed Kirsty some wrapped in a clean cloth.

Heaven. 'Thank you. I'm sure you realise the laird's missing his wife and sons. I've told Mrs. Sanderson... he needs looking after and I'm sure if you bake him treats like this, he'll be tempted to eat. Well, I'm away home now and thank you again.' She juggled the scones as her palms stung from their heat through the cloth. Methuselah came out from behind a garden wall and fell in step beside her.

'By, I miss home cooking.' He licked his lips.

Ravenous, she ate half a scone on the way home and ignored his expectant look.

Lorna Windham

CHAPTER Thirty-seven

A volley of shots and shouts sounded behind Johnnie. He grimaced and ducked behind a huge clump of heather.

The mist had covered his escape, but now clung to his ankles. His chest heaved. He had to put as many miles as he could between himself and the redcoats. He set off again.

A grizzled figure with raised dirk reared up from the gorse in front of him. Johnnie staggered back.

'Johnnie? Is it you, lad?'

'Course it's me.' Johnnie spoke in a hushed voice. 'Lower that damn toothpick of yours, Dougie.'

'Knew you'd turn up.' The tacksman clapped him on the shoulder. 'God help the wounded. Redcoats are killing everything that moves. Any sign of the murdering bastards?'

'Some way behind me. My God, I never thought to see you again. Euan and Duncan, are they here?'

Dougie grunted. 'Last I saw, Euan was clambering over dead redcoats to kill the next man.'

Johnnie grinned. 'Sounds like him. And the rest of the clan?'

'On guard in the heather.' Dougie gave a low whistle.

Murdo's gaunt and weary face peeked out from the gorse and strode towards them.

Bloody hell. 'Good to see you both.' Johnnie shook their hands.

'Saw Euan fall, sorry lad,' Murdo said. 'Didna like to say earlier.' He looked shame-faced at Dougie.

Johnnie's stomach twisted into a knot. 'And Duncan?'

'He's over here.' Dougie pointed to a still form in the bracken.

Johnnie started towards his brother.

Dougie put up a hand. 'He's in a bad way. Tried to keep him behind me, but I couldna stop the laddie.'

Johnnie hesitated for a second as he let Dougie's words sink in. A second knot tightened in Johnnie's stomach. Then he stiffened his spine and strode through the gorse towards

The Jacobite Affair

white-faced Duncan who lay, eyes closed, teeth clenched, on a green plaid-bed.

'Stumbled across him in a ditch.' Dougie's eyes glinted. 'Recognised his black pelt of hair. We managed to carry him this far. I'll stand guard with Murdo.'

Johnnie knelt on one knee and felt the slight pulse of life at Duncan's throat. He raised the plaid, saw the Stewart's ruined banner, blue with a yellow saltire, wrapped round his brother's middle and soaked in a crimson tide. Bloody hell. Johnnie forced a smile. 'I need to see your wound, Duncan, I'll try no' to hurt you.'

Duncan opened his eyes. 'Hello... Johnnie.' He bit down on his lower lip and blood dribbled down his chin.

Johnnie unwrapped the dressing and his insides twisted. The wound in Duncan's gut gaped and pumped blood. The stench made Johnnie want to gag. 'Well done laddie.' He forced out the words as he tore the sleeves from his shirt and tied them to his brother's torn flesh. 'We're all proud of you. Hope you got the bugger that did this.'

'I... got him... alright.' Duncan's eyes misted. 'Mother. Mother... where... are... you? It hurts so.'

Cries sounded close at hand, followed by a shot.

'Johnnie, we've got to go.' Dougie raced to Johnnie's side. Johnnie stood. 'Right, this way.'

'Inverness? Dougie whistled and Murdo came at a run.

'Aye.' Johnnie tried to ignore Duncan's cries, as he took up one end of the plaid with Dougie and Murdo in charge of a corner each. The men staggered as they carried the lad mile after bone weary mile. The crack of a musket sounded to one side of them. Johnnie ducked and signalled to the men to lower Duncan to the ground.

Duncan groaned.

'We're at the Inverness Road,' hissed Murdo from behind a patch of brambles. Some distance behind came the fusillade of shots.

Dougie raised his bushy eyebrows and stared at Johnnie. Murdo's eyes begged an order Johnnie struggled to give. More shots, closer now.

'We'll guard your backs.' Dougie stared at Johnnie then at Duncan, shook his head and put his weighty hand on Johnnie's shoulder.

Johnnie watched as Murdo followed Dougie and slunk into the undergrowth.

Johnnie knelt and brushed Duncan's hair with his hand. Like mother's. Silk.

Duncan's brown eyes held Johnnie's in a steadfast gaze. 'Home…' He gasped in a slow painful breath.

God. Johnnie whispered to him, 'Think of Braedrumie House and our land. Can you see them, Duncan?'

Duncan's eyelids flickered.

'And Braedrumie's green glen and the blue waters of Loch Linnhe? Mother's waiting for you, can you see her?'

Duncan sighed.

Johnnie nestled his brother in his arms. Home meant peace and tranquillity, not this nightmarish Hell. He wrapped the green and brown plaid tight round Duncan's body.

Random shots sounded close by.

'Mother…' Duncan's eyes pleaded. He shook as pain racked his body.

Johnnie held him tighter. He wanted to shriek to the skies, *He's too young and doesn't deserve this.* Johnnie softened his voice and smiled at Duncan. 'She's waiting for you. Just let her come.' He slipped into Latin, 'Indulgeat tibi Dominus quidquid deliquisite.' *May the Lord forgive you for any wrong you've done.* And me, he thought and me.

He kissed Duncan's cold forehead and cradled him with one arm.

A grimace. A tremor. 'Agh… Johnnie? Cold… so cold… Mother.' Duncan's eyes flickered once or twice in seeming recognition as he exhaled his last breath. He looked much younger than fourteen. Johnnie gathered Duncan to him and pressed him closer to his chest. His brother became heavier

The Jacobite Affair

and as the fingers of one hand relaxed, they released a small, wooden object which tumbled to the ground. The salmon carving. Johnnie fumbled to put it inside his sporran. He kissed Duncan's cheek. Johnnie's soul died as he pulled the plaid over his brother's face.

A sudden rush of bodies surrounded him. 'Redcoats over that hill, hundreds of the devils.' Dougie jerked his thumb backwards. 'We've got to go.' He looked at the still body, the pool of blood. 'Sweet Jesu.... he's dead.' He crossed himself and Murdo followed suit.

'Aye,' said Johnnie.

'How ...?' asked Murdo. His grey eyes searched Johnnie's, then the drover nodded.

'The end came fast.' Pray for him.' And me he thought, dear God, pray for me. He whispered, 'Requiescat in pace' *May he rest in peace.* He eased himself from his knees and stood as if made from granite. A muscle twitched in his cheek. No time for burial. They shouldn't have stopped.

'Your orders?' asked Dougie.

'Orders?' Johnnie stared through him. His head full of Duncan.

'You're the laird's heir, if Euan's… What would you have us do, man?'

Heir? Johnnie tried to clear his head. He'd lost two brothers in one day. Think.

'Quickly, man.' Dougie risked a glance behind them.

'Bastards are on that crest,' snarled Murdo.

Johnnie's mind cleared. 'Get home as fast as you can. Warn them.' He stared at the faces of the desperate men.

'And you?' asked Dougie.

'I'm for Inverness, need to be sure Kirsty's not at my Aunt's.'

'Have you no sense, man. Cumberland's troops havena quenched their thirst for blood yet. You'll never get out of that bottle-neck. They'll seal it tighter than a drum.'

'Do as I say. I need you to warn the Glen. Give Isabel a kiss from me.'

Dougie grinned at that, then started at the rattle of harness, tramp of boots and curses.

'We need to move,' hissed Murdo.

'I'll see Kirsty safe and then head for Ruthven.'

'Ah! No, Johnnie.' Dougie's face creased. 'It's over can you no' see, man? The Cause is finished. I was in the '15, I've seen it all before.'

'They killed Euan… and Duncan. The prince will be there.'

'You damn fool, the prince left the battlefield with nary a scratch. Didn't you see him run?'

'You taught me to fight and I'm grateful, though not for the bruises and cuts that came with it.' Johnnie remembered when Dougie had tied him to his older brothers with strips of leather round their wrists. The winner cut himself free with the only dirk. Johnnie had learned not to lose, for a savage beating from Father would follow that. 'Without you I wouldna have survived this day. I know it's me you think of. But I'm a grown man and must tread the path I choose and I choose to fight on.'

Dougie nodded. His sinewy arm stretched out and he shook Johnnie's hand.

Johnnie took the flag from Duncan's body whilst he covered him once again with the plaid. 'Take this, Dougie. Give it to the laird. Tell him it has the bravest blood on it - Duncan's. And that he paid for it with his life.'

'I can see their ugly faces, we have to leave now,' raged Murdo.

'Go with God.' Johnnie extended his hand. Dougie grasped it and then Murdo.

Dougie tucked the precious parcel inside his plaid and signalled to Murdo who followed him at a run towards the west and home.

Johnnie set his face towards Inverness and made his limbs spring into action. He sprinted along the track, ached for his brothers and hungered for a priest. The Moray Firth stretched in a silver line below him. Gorse tore at his bare legs, but fear drove him on. The Jacobites had beaten the redcoats several

The Jacobite Affair

times and dared to get within 120 miles of London. Cumberland wouldn't forgive that. He had to get to Kirsty and Inverness.

Silken strands of cold mist floated around him and shrouded the moor on either side. Then it lifted to reveal the walking-dead, or so it seemed to him. He became part of a tide of Jacobites, fearful of being left behind at the mercy of Cumberland's troops who pressed at their backs. The shrieks and shouts of the redcoats' victims rose and fell. Panic drove the throng on.

Johnnie looked back to see what caused the furore hundreds of yards behind him. An exhausted Jacobite lay by the wayside, unable to go any further. A dragoon motioned him, with a prick of his sword, to run for his life. The man staggered a 100 yards into the heather. 'Haloo!'cried the redcoat as he gathered companions around him. The chase began with sabres brandished high. Hooves pounded as the leader cut downwards with a brutal stroke. The man let out a scream which died away to nothing. Johnnie surged on to Inverness as this hunt played out time and again behind him.

Johnnie joined a group of ghost runners. One staggered as part of a mass of heart-sick, weary men, boys and camp followers with wild faces. Some leant on others, one ran alone. All fled in one direction towards safety and Inverness.

On the outskirts of the town, people eager to help the wounded, crowded forward and others just stared. Johnnie didn't stop, eager to get to his aunt's house before the arrival of Cumberland's troops. More shrieks and cries followed him as he ran on. He looked back. Several redcoats wiped their swords on the clothes of those who'd been alive on the road moments before.

CHAPTER Thirty-eight

An icy wind blew through the streets of Inverness. Packed coaches and stacked carts careered past Johnnie as drivers whipped wild-eyed horses. Doors and shutters remained closed. The huddled houses and inns looked under siege.

Where the hell did his aunt live? Johnnie ran on and ignored the hullaballoo in the distance. He'd only visited her once when a laddie. Damn it. What was the bloody address? He'd written it for Kirsty. Not that lane, nor that. Think... Church Street. He glanced back. No redcoats yet. He glimpsed the dour River Ness over a low wall. He must be close. Think. Georgian, stone built and grand. Not that house or that. There. Several steps led up to a stout, black door and on either side shuttered windows.

He raced down the dingy wynd by the side of the house. Thank God, she'd a first floor window open. 'Aunt,' he hissed as he scanned the wynd. Where was the woman? 'Aunt... Aunt...' He gathered several small stones at his feet and threw them so they pinged against the pane. 'Aunt... Aunt... Aunt Munro.'

'Who's that making such a noise?' His aunt's head peered down at him. Her grey hair streamed round her face.

'Aunt.'

'Johnnie? Johnnie Stewart?' Her eyes searched up and down the wynd.

He turned at the distant sound of voices raised in fear and saw figures race across the wynd's junction with the main street.

He called up to her, 'Let me in for the sake of God. If I'm caught...'

'The garden gate, I'll unbolt it.'

'Quick.'

She put her hands on the sash window and pushed downwards. It rattled as it closed. Johnnie stood with his back to the iron-gate and wished she'd wings as the hubbub from the street grew closer.

The Jacobite Affair

The gate squeaked open behind him. His aunt's hand grabbed his shirt collar, hauled him inside, then shot the bolt. The same hand bundled him through the back door and into the scullery.

Johnnie stared at Aunt Munro. Not quite the mirror image of Mother, but just enough likeness round her eyes and mouth to make Johnnie feel at home. Mother's older sister, well into middle age and usually immaculate in her dress, had buttons undone and apron strings which hung loose.

'Johnnie, you alright?' she spoke in a hushed whisper.

'I'm well Aunt, just a few scratches.'

She sprang forward and put her head on his chest. 'Oh, Johnnie. You remind me so of Jack and I'm so sorry about your poor mother. If we hadn't been in London… '

Nonplussed he wrapped his arms round her. 'Aunt, there's been a battle and we lost.'

'I ken that and now you're in danger. The battle… 'What to do? What to do? '

He held her at arm's length. 'Aunt, is Kirsty here? I need to get her away before the redcoats arrive.' He wiped sweat from his brow with his sleeve.

'Kirsty? She and her mother left after... she left some time ago for Braedrumie.'

'Thank God.' The tight band of worry round his head relaxed. He'd never been so pleased to hear his aunt's voice.

'I've been watching for you and your brothers ever since news of our defeat. The servants have taken fright and fled, of course. It's a bad day for both countries. Did anyone see you come to the house?'

'I dinna think so. My uncle and Jack?'

'Your uncle's in London and Jack... I asked Kirsty to inform your family about poor Jack. He's dead, Johnnie.'

Johnnie put a hand to his head as it swirled. 'Jack's dead? How?' Johnnie stared at her in shock. He reached for the settle for support. His limbs shook

She put her hand on his shoulder. 'What am I thinking? You're done in. Sit by the fire. You need to get out of those

182

clothes.' She handed him a cloth and poured hot water into a bowl. 'Clean yourself. The redcoats will search every house. What will I tell them? How explain?'' She thought for a moment. 'I know, you're a friend... Alan Brown... a solicitor's clerk... visiting me from Edinburgh. You work for... *Kinkardine and Sons* in Castle Street. But you must look the part. You're about Jack's size.' She sniffed. 'I'll get you some of his clothes, I hadna' the heart to throw them out.' She paused and wiped away a tear. 'I nursed him to his last breath, me who gave him his first. Fair broke my heart. Just faded away at the last. A fever, the physician said.' She filled a porcelain bowl with water.

'I'm sad to hear it Aunt.' Hard to think of his tall, genial cousin in a grave. So many deaths in such a short time. Time to tell her about Euan and poor Duncan, but the words wouldn't come. Johnnie shrugged off what was left of his shirt. His teeth chattered.

'Aye. Take this.'

'May God have mercy on his soul.' Johnnie pressed the wet cloth to his head and winced. The water turned red in the bowl.

She tutted. 'You're hurt. Let me.' She examined the cut. 'You've got a fine lump the size of a goose egg on your head. Your hair will cover it.'

'Duncan's dead.' The words spurted out like blood from an open wound. He ached to say more, but couldn't meet her eyes.

She paused in shock. 'Duncan was with you in the battle?'

'He ran away to join us. I tried to... it was no use.'

'Your poor father. And Euan?'

'I dinna ken about Euan.'

'And Rob?'

'We dinna speak his name Aunt. He left with no word, before the rising, it killed Mother. He's dead to us now.'

'Oh Johnnie.' She sighed and shook her head. 'He's still your brother. Your mother wouldna have wanted...' A shout in the street and distant shots made her spring into action. 'Hurry

The Jacobite Affair

lad, we've no time to waste. Here's some nice warm broth. Get it down you. I can only help the living now.'

He didn't bother with the fine silver spoon his aunt placed before him, nor the linen napkin. The earthenware bowl didn't leave his lips until he'd finished and pushed it towards her. She re-filled it three times and each time he drank in its steamy goodness. Warmth returned to his numb limbs.

He fought the tiredness in his bones. 'I need soap and a razor, Aunt... and some privacy if you please.'

'I held you naked in my arms the day you were born Johnnie Stewart, as I did your poor brothers and I dinna suppose ...'

'Yes, yes, Aunt, my clothes.'

'But you need help.'

Johnnie bundled her out of the room and let his plaid slide to the floor. The water did its job. It soothed, refreshed and stung.

Johnnie made a quick assessment of the damage: upper torso covered in livid bruises with cuts which varied in proportion from nothing to bloody serious. Everything ached from the broad, muscles of his shoulders down the long, lean rib cage forming the shape of a taut 'V' at his hips. He sat and then sprang up. How could he have a deep gouge, the shape of a horse shoe, on his backside and only feel it hours later? Welts and scrapes crisscrossed his arms and legs. At least he was whole and alive, unlike so many. Shouts sounded in the street.

His aunt knocked on the door and eyes averted handed him the clothes he needed.

Johnnie thought of Kirsty. At least she wasn't near this blood bath. Duncan.

Johnnie shook his head to clear Duncan's last minutes from his brain. He could only guess what the redcoats would make of his aunt, the wife of Ian Munro, one of Scotland's most senior law officers and a known Hanoverian sympathiser. She just happened to be an outspoken Jacobite.

By the time he'd dressed, the streets had cleared and the town became eerie and silent as night descended. He peered out through a knot in the shutter. Not so much as a stray dog. He had to get out of Inverness. He paced the floor whilst his aunt took his place.

'What will you do now?' she asked.

'Go home.'

'It willna be safe.'

Johnnie shrugged, his only thought to see Kirsty. He yawned. His eyes heavy, desperate for sleep.

'Get your head down laddie. I'll stand sentry whilst you sleep. I'll wake you if I hear anything.'

'But I need to get away,' Johnnie protested. 'If I'm caught here…' His mind dulled and body sagged.

'You need to rest, body and mind.' His aunt led him back to the stairs.

Just before his eyes closed in Jack's feather bed, Johnnie realised he hadn't had a good night's sleep since Derby.

The Jacobite Affair

CHAPTER Thirty-nine

Dawn shouldered its way through the cracks and crevices in the oak shutters and stole across Johnnie's pillow. He woke and stretched. Strength had returned to his limbs and he'd a clear head. Good to be alive- then he remembered- but still hunted. He shuddered at the thought of the bodies he'd been buried under and- Duncan. His brother's face appeared in front of him as an urgent drum beat sounded in the distance.

Damn. He sprang out of bed, shivered as he stood on the cold floorboards and put his right eye to a crack between the shutters. Nothing stirred in the street below. Perhaps the bastards had tired of killing. To give no quarter- it had been murder.

A slight knock at his bedroom door made him leap back into bed and under the woollen blankets.

'Come in.' His breath misted in the cold air.

'Morning. See the redcoats are stirring.' His aunt's eyes looked heavy and her face lined. 'Stayed awake all night. Thought you'd want to sleep as long as possible. Just brought you these.' Steam rose from a jug as his aunt put a china bowl on the dressing table. She placed a folded towel over a chair and fresh clothes on top of the oak chest.

'Bless you, Aunt.' He wished he'd woken before dawn. He had to escape.

'There's breakfast in the scullery when you're ready.' She looked round the room as if she searched for its original occupant, Jack.

Johnnie gave her a weak smile. She closed the door behind her. As he pissed into the chamber pot he thought of Kirsty and his father. God knows what Father would be like once he knew about Euan and Duncan. And what about bloody Rob? Perhaps he'd done the right thing and cleared off before the rebellion.

Johnnie lifted the jug and poured water into the bowl. He used lye soap and water to clean his hands, then daubed his

Lorna Windham

face and applied Jack's cut throat razor to his face. He looked in the mirror, a new man appeared, older, wiser.

He put on Jack's clean clothes and studied himself in the mirror. His bony wrists stuck out of his sleeves. Why couldn't his cousin have had longer arms? He tugged at the sleeves, to no avail. Oh, well.

Glorious smells from the scullery invaded his nostrils and beckoned him downstairs. He followed his nose and hobbled. Jack's shoes pinched. Damn.

Aunt Munro had made them a breakfast of crusty bread, butter and cheese. He sat beside her at the scullery table and ate his fill. God, it tasted good. A jug of ale washed it all down.

'You'll head straight home?' she asked.

'Aye.'

'Take this.' She thrust a bundle of food at him. It's no' much, but should see you on your way.'

She started at the tramp of boots outside, then darted to the spy hole in the front door. Johnnie peered through the shutters. Damn.

'Redcoats, lined up in the street. God help us.' His aunt wrung her hands. 'We've no' so much as a priest's hole. Your uncle wouldna have it, said he'd no one to hide from.'

She pulled Johnnie onto the wooden seat beside her. 'Johnnie, you know how much I care for you and your brothers?'

'Yes, but is this the time…?' He searched the scullery with his eyes, he'd be found in seconds.

'I think you should know something.' She took his hand in hers.

'Aunt?' He needed to think.

'Kirsty and her mother...'

'Yes?' Why mention Kirsty? A vision of her sweet face came to him.

'They... I dinna think she, Kirsty, is... right for you.'

He sighed. 'Aunt... we love each other and you know yourself, love grows in a marriage.'

The Jacobite Affair

'Or not, Johnnie, it can wither and die on a green branch. I dinna want you to live the rest of your life regretting....'

He withdrew his hand. 'Aunt, I just wish you knew her better.'

'She hardly mentioned your name. Enjoyed more soirees than visits to her sick cousin. I think she's a self-serving little madam.'

He stood. 'Aunt. I canna have you talk like that about my betrothed.'

She folded her arms. 'I'm only thinking of you.'

'I've never heard you speak ill of anyone. Mother liked her.'

Boots drummed and guttural orders came from outside. Damn. His aunt's hand went to her mouth. Johnnie put his forefinger to his lips to quieten her and squinted through the shutters. Redcoat rifle butts hammered on their neighbour's door.

One lieutenant brayed on the window until glass shards sprayed onto the ground. The door opened to a ragged chorus of screams. Soldiers bundled their way inside and hurled furniture and china through the holed and jagged glass so it splintered and crashed onto the flagstones.

'The poor Fergusons.' His aunt brushed away a tear.

A muscle worked in Johnnie's cheek. He signalled his aunt to stay back. A redcoat mounted Aunt Munro's steps and used his rifle butt on her front door. 'Open up in the name of the King.'

'How dare they.' His aunt's face paled. 'Don't they know whose house this is?'

'Aunt,' hissed Johnnie. 'It'll go worse for you if you resist.'

She clenched her fists. 'We'll brazen this out. Remember, you're Alan Brown, an Edinburgh clerk who lodges with me.'

Bloody hell.

Several rifle butts rapped on the door and rang through the house.

Aunt?' whispered Johnnie.

'Yes?'

'Thank you. I'm sorry I've put you in danger.'

'Whisht, laddie.' She placed a hand on his cheek. 'Now let me open the door whilst I've still got one.' She took a deep breath, stiffened her shoulders and turned the key. The door burst open and she staggered backwards into Johnnie.

A pimple-faced private, charged into the hall with bayonet raised. A surly sergeant followed close behind them. 'Hande hoch. Hands up.'

A bloody Hessian.

Johnnie and his aunt raised their hands.

'I'm Mr. Munro's wife, he works for the government. Please leave.'

'We know who you are, bitch.' The sergeant growled. 'Husband should have taught you better. And this fine man?'

Johnnie bowed. 'Alan Brown at your service, sir, solicitor's clerk for *Kinkardine and Sons*, Castle Street, Edinburgh. I'm lodging with this dear lady whilst I have business in the town.'

The sergeant looked Johnnie up and down. 'Too big to work behind desk, Alan Brown. Look at size of hands and shoulders. Bet if we stripped him, Private, we'd find... how you say?'

'Interestin' scratches, sergeant.' The private smirked.

Johnnie groaned inside. Why did his aunt suggest he be a damned clerk?

The pimpled private strode past Johnnie and his aunt and entered the sitting room. Silence. Then crashes.

'You've no right.' Aunt Munro stood ashen-faced.

The sergeant's eyes mocked her as he pocketed a silver jug from a side table.

'Thief.' The word out before Johnnie could stop his aunt.

The sergeant held his meaty fist to her chin. 'You are a known Jacobite sympathiser and will go to gaol till we decide what's done with you.'

'But my husband...' she began.

'No!' Johnnie just too late to stop the sergeant's thwack across her face with his open hand. She staggered back. Blood streamed from her cheek which reddened and began to swell.

The Jacobite Affair

'You bloody coward.' Johnnie lunged at the sergeant, but received a rifle butt to his stomach for his pains. Johnnie heaved and retched.

The sergeant snarled at his aunt, 'Your husband cannot help you. Women should know place. Do as told, not meddle in politics. Take her.' The private grabbed an arm and bundled her out of the house.

'And you.' The sergeant's eyes narrowed. 'You might be clerk, might not.' He shouted through the open doorway, 'Two men in here at the double.'

Two privates burst in.

'Hold him,' he ordered. The sergeant's fists pounded Johnnie's face into pulp.

Through the pain and bloody haze Johnnie thought Dougie and Father had taught him well. The sergeant didn't get a groan from him, not even when his nose broke in a spray of blood.

The privates dragged Johnnie outside and left him, sprawled on the ground beside a group of prisoners guarded by redcoat bayonets.

Johnnie lifted his head as two soldiers hoisted his aunt on to a donkey, so she faced its tail. One private jeered and a drummer tapped out the deadbeat. She straightened her back and looked. Like a queen going to her coronation.

Pride for his aunt surged through Johnnie. As all eyes centred on the spectacle, he got to his feet and punched his guard's chin. The man keeled over and Johnnie ran.

If he could just get round the next corner, he would double back and somehow spirit his aunt away. Then muskets fired and red hot pain seared his arm. Damn. If meant to slow him down, it had the opposite effect. He raced towards the market square to the cheers of those prisoners he'd left shackled behind him.

'Bloody hell!' A wall of sound hit him as he juddered to a halt. Shrieks, cries, yells and orders moulded into one. Had he run into Hades itself? In front of him, a ragged man raced off as gold coins spilled from a box he carried under one arm. A wild-eyed woman tussled with a bearded man over a bale of blue satin and a young girl shared a bottle of brandy with a crone. The packed square heaved to and fro as groups of redcoats wrestled to keep order. In the centre, a ring of men and women jigged round a bonfire whilst soldiers threw chairs and broken shutters onto it. Smoke swirled and flames crackled and roared.

Johnnie kept his head down and shouldered his way through the crowd which surged round him. Dear God. In front of him a man in executioner's garb waved Jacobite flags above his head, then set them alight. Johnnie glanced behind him as a group of soldiers broke from the shadows of a street to his rear.

'That's 'im,' a private shouted.

Damn. Johnnie elbowed his way through the waves of people in his haste to get to the other side of the square, but he spied redcoats lined up there too.

'Johnnie!'

Johnnie wheeled. He knew that voice. Saw a soldier aim his musket and an officer knock the weapon away. Redcoats raced towards him with bayonets drawn. Before he could act, the soldiers closed in and surrounded him, their steel blades aimed at his chest.

'Dinna fire.' The officer shouted above the melee. 'Dinna fire. I'll deal with this.'

Good God in heaven. It couldn't be. Johnnie blinked twice. Rob, dressed up as a redcoat lieutenant. It couldn't be. His eldest brother a bloody redcoat. A mist formed in front of Johnnie's eyes. Duncan dead, Euan missing, and their older brother could have fired the shots that killed them.

'Take him,' ordered an officer with a lantern jaw.

'Bastard,' Johnnie snarled. Two burly soldiers grasped an arm each and dragged him away.

The Jacobite Affair

CHAPTER Forty

The morning light played on a dead fly caught in a spider's web outside the scullery window. Kirsty thought of Johnnie and the battle. *Has it happened and have we won? Or is Johnnie wounded with no one to care for him? Or is he dead? No. Don't think that.*

A series of clatters brought her back to reality as Mother opened and shut cupboard doors and peered inside. 'I thought we might have a little flour. Why don't you call on the laird?'

'Oh, Mother. That's not why I go.' *I can't take food from Una again, but stealing is worse. I mustn't think of it. But I'm so hungry. What would a priest say? Not that I've seen one for years. Who'd want to be burnt to death? Still, I sinned with the milk. Perhaps a good deed would cancel the bad one? Two good deeds.*

With a firm sense of purpose, Kirsty closed the farmhouse door. The overcast sky held the promise of rain. *Better hurry.*

'Where you off?' asked Methuselah. He cleared his throat and sent a spume of green phlegm onto the grass.

She wrinkled her nose. 'My business.' *The sooner these men leave our farm, the better.*

'The duke's made it his business too. Make it easy for an old man.'

She could have sneaked away, but took pity on his lined face. 'Braedrumie House,' she said.

'Again?'

'Aye. Again.' She allowed him to accompany her. *The first good deed?* She jumped across the burn whilst he landed with one boot in the water.

'You're kind to visit the old laird so regularly or is it food you're after?' asked Methuselah.

She bristled and increased her pace up the hill.

'It's alright I willna tell.'

'Nothing to tell,' said Kirsty and quickened her pace again.

'I hope to go home soon.'

Lorna Windham

'Where's that?' She crested the ridge and the moor stretched in front of her.

'Hawick. Wife's gettin' on, canna see much. Her sister helps.'

She trudged on, with him beside her, over the purple moor to Braedrumie House. The sweet smell of moist yeast came from the scullery.

'Stay here.' Her stomach rumbled. 'I willna be long.'

She entered the house by the front door. *Oh, no.* The laird, his head on his chest, sprawled in an armchair in his study. He cradled an empty claret bottle. Books lay open on his desk beside a pool of ink. Kirsty inspected the mantelpiece and wrote her name in the dust. *I'll give that housekeeper a piece of my mind.*

Kirsty followed the sound of snores and found her in the sitting room. She shook her. 'Mrs. Sanderson, you're no' paid to sleep, the study needs to be tidied and dusted.'

The woman jerked upright. 'Canna have eyes in the back of my head,' she snapped. 'Takes two women to do the heavy work now there's no men. There's no one spare to dust.'

'You're spare. Dinna think the laird has no kin here to look after him. I'll help you make a start on the study if you do the sitting room.'

The woman's surly expression remained unchanged, but she found two cloths and gave one to Kirsty.

My second good deed. Kirsty set about the study, cleaned up the ink, put books in the bookcase, dusted everywhere and set peat aflame in the fireplace. The laird didn't stir.

She popped in on the housekeeper and watched her rinse out a cloth and use it on a windowpane.

'It looks so much better. I wouldna disturb the laird, but if you tell him I called, I'd be grateful. I'll see myself out.'

Mrs. Sanderson gave her a sour smile.

Kirsty left the sitting room and strode towards the scullery and the scent of cooked food. Saliva gathered in her mouth and her stomach griped.

'Good day, Una.'

The Jacobite Affair

'Good day.' The cook stopped as she pounded dough, her arms dusted in flour to the elbow.

Kirsty tried not to look at the pink, cooked ham and rows of loaves. 'I just came to say the scones were lovely. Thank you.' Kirsty's stomach rumbled. 'Sorry.'

'Visitin' again?'

'Aye. I gave Mrs. Sanderson a wee hand. You've been baking I see.'

'Every day, but the laird's still no' got much of an appetite.' She lowered her voice. 'The drink, you ken?'

Oh, dear. I can't stop him. 'His sons would be grateful if you'd try to ensure he ate.'

Una reminded Kirsty of a fluffed up hen. 'I'm sure I do my best.'

Oh, no. 'You do. Just… well… He's old, his sons are in danger and with Duncan missing…'

Una's hand went to her throat. 'Of course. That poor, wee laddie and our poor men. May the Lord have mercy.'

All this food, while we starve. 'Is that a mouse in the corner?'

'No' in my, scullery.' Una grabbed a besom.

I could take just enough food not to be missed. Kirsty clasped her hands behind her back. *I mustn't.*

Una leant on her besom. 'Canna see the wee beastie. I'll lay some traps. Hot in here.' Her plump forearm left a trace of white powder on her forehead. 'Daren't open the window 'cos of thieves. Stole my last batch of scones just as they cooled. Had to start all over again.'

Guilt pricked at Kirsty. *That could have been me.* 'I'm sorry to hear it. I'm sure the laird appreciates your labours.'

'Oh, my bannocks.' Una rushed to a pan which sizzled over the fire. 'Caught them just in time. It's no good, open that window.'

Kirsty did so and a cool breeze wafted over her as Angus, outside, beckoned towards home with his thumb. She ignored him and thought of Johnnie.

That's better.' Una placed the tray on the window sill.

Lorna Windham

'You'll have some bread and ham to take home?' Una wrapped slices of each in a small cloth. 'And some bannocks?'

'Thank you,' said Kirsty. *Food.*

'You know…' Una used her forefinger to count. 'I'm sure I made more bannocks than that.'

Kirsty looked out of the open window to see Methuselah give her a smug smile as he leant against the garden wall.

***

Kirsty burst into the farmhouse kitchen with her hoard.

'Give it here.' Mother snatched the meat. 'Ham.' She held it to her nose and sniffed. 'We used to have ham at Toll House. Smells just like I remember.' She tore it in half, savoured it on her tongue and then swallowed. 'Tastes so good. Bread and bannocks too? You did well.' Her head jerked up. 'Dinna expect to see Johnnie Stewart again or any of the rest.'

'Mother.'

'At least Tolbain's left his men to protect us. Thoughtful of him. Why don't you be nice to him?'

'Because I dinna like him.'

Kirsty turned from her mother and thought of the battle and Johnnie. She closed her eyes, but found it difficult it imagine his face. *Has he changed? Does he still feel the same about me?* She unclipped her brooch and pressed it to her cheek, unaware the rubies looked like fresh beads of blood.

The Jacobite Affair

CHAPTER Forty-one

Kirsty lifted her head from her knitting and breathed in fresh air through the open window. The mountains and moors glistened, washed by rain the night before.

'I've news, Kirsty,' shouted Jamie Moffat as he led his pony up the hill towards her.

Dear God, the lad's plaid hangs on him.

Methuselah unsheathed his sword and Finlay whipped out a knife.

'It's alright, he's a friend.' Kirsty called out, flung her kitting aside and raced out of the door. She placed herself between Jamie and the Boids and breathed a sigh of relief when Methuselah signalled Finlay to return to their seats round their campfire.

Tolbain's men, here?' hissed Jamie. 'Never did like moss-green.'

'So?' said Mother. 'What news?'

He lowered his voice, 'There's been a battle on Drumossie Moor.'

Kirsty sprang towards him. 'Who won? How's Johnnie?'

'And Hughie?' asked Mother.

'I dinna ken. They looked well enough when I left them.' He looked at the ground.

'You left the battle?' Mother's eyebrow shot skywards.

'I was ordered to come home with these.' He opened the flap of his worn leather bag to reveal several letters.

'God have mercy on them all.' Kirsty put out her hand. Jamie glanced across at the Boids and slipped her a letter. She clutched the parchment to her breast. *Johnnie.* 'We've water, but…'

'I canna stop, I've others to deliver. Dinna fash, they'll all be home soon.' His brow creased as he stared at Tolbain's men.

God, please protect Johnnie. The scent of cooked meat wafted towards Kirsty. Her mouth filled with saliva. *The*

Lorna Windham

Boid's. 'Thank you.' She waved at Jamie as he guided his pony down the hill.

'You didn't tell me Jamie Moffat was here?' Mother leant against the doorpost and sniffed the air. 'Any letters?'

'Just for me.'

'When I was young at Toll House, cook used to make a cherry cake, so moist and sweet, like eating air.' Mother closed her eyes as if she smelt it.

'I've told you before, dinna talk about food.' Kirsty watched as the Boids cut slices of succulent meat from a chicken. She could almost taste it. *I must read Johnnie's letter.*

'Hmph. Tolbain feeds them well.' Mother pulled her darning needle through a stocking. 'Think they'd offer us some. It's a long time since I tasted chicken.'

'Wish the Boids would leave. Thought Tolbain promised us food. I feel we're being watched all the time.' *I hope Johnnie's alright.* She clutched the letter closer.

'Why don't you share your news? I don't suppose Hughie will have eaten much.'

'Kirsty put the letter in her pocket. 'Later.' *Johnnie's last letter before the battle. So precious. If I don't open it, he's still alive.*

'Poor Hughie's out in all weathers, fighting for his life and you don't care. I'll never forget the time he lent your father money for one of his grandiose schemes when no one else would. Of course the addle-brain gambled it away. Beggared Hughie, but he never complained. Said it was God's will. Open your letter.'

'I said later.' *I can't.* 'Anyway, Hughie probably has a fuller belly than us. Bet he misses Mary, she must be due any day. We should visit, see if she needs any help.' *Johnnie.*

'Hmph. With those ragamuffins? You go, I'll stay here.' Mother jabbed her needle into the yarn. 'Can't see why you won't share that letter. Tolbain's got a lot to offer, you know.'

'What do you mean?'

'He's taken a fancy to you. Offered a handfast marriage.'

The Jacobite Affair

'What? When?' Kirsty's brain reeled.

'Never you mind.'

'I'm betrothed to Johnnie, he knows that.' Kirsty set her chin.

'Think about it.'

Kirsty turned from her. 'I dinna want to think about it.'

Mother stood. 'We're starving. Think of his house, lands and our position.'

'No. I've reading to do.' Kirsty stalked off.

'Please yourself. But when the Jacobites lose, Johnnie Stewart will not have much to offer... if he's survived.'

Kirsty spun round. 'Mother. As long as I live, I'll love Johnnie. I'll no' take another in his place.' She pointed at her brooch. 'We're betrothed and I'll never forsake him.' The rubies winked at her.

Lorna Windham

CHAPTER Forty-two

A few days later, when the first touches of spring showed as green amongst the brown bracken, Kirsty crept out of the farmhouse. She kept low behind the gorse to avoid the Boids and tasted freedom again. She wandered onto Braedrumie Moor, thought of the battle and Johnnie's letter. *Such scribbled words and he thinks I'm in Inverness. Have we won? Is he safe?* She closed her eyes and willed him home.

'Miss Lorne.'

She whirled and staggered back as a number of wolfish men scrambled from behind tumbled boulders. 'What do you want?' She held her shawl to her breast. Blood-smeared, lean and desperate, they could do anything. She cursed the ridge which hid her from where Methuselah shoed a pony and Finlay mended a stirrup leather at the farm.

Her senses returned. *Wait a minute. They're from Braedrumie.* Dougie stood like a fierce statue and Murdo's anxious eyes scoured the moor behind them.

'Jamie said there'd been a battle? Did we win?' She scanned their haggard faces for an answer.

Dougie looked at the ground and Murdo squinted at the horizon.

Oh, God. Where's the rest? And Johnnie? She clutched her brooch and strained her neck to look for him. She stared at Dougie. Her heart pounded as she set her chin. 'Tell me.'

'We've come about Johnnie and your Uncle Hughie.' Dougie's head dropped. 'We lost.'

An icy premonition enveloped her. 'They're no... dead?' She held her breath.

'Johnnie survived the battle, lassie.'

'Thank God, I prayed and prayed.' Waves of relief flowed over her.

'But Hughie didna.' Dougie stared into the distance. 'He died a brave man, fighting for what he believed in.'

Kirsty's world crashed around her. 'Poor Uncle Hughie, we thought a lot of him.' Her eyes pricked.

The Jacobite Affair

Dougie didn't look at her and Murdo leant on his sword.

'There's more. Dougie's face hardened. 'Duncan's dead and we've no news of Euan.'

'Duncan? What was he doing with you?'

'The laddie wanted to fight.' Dougie's lips tightened.

'And where's Johnnie?' Tears formed and her throat burned as she fought for control.

'Thing is, he thought you were in Inverness.'

'Oh God. Of course, he's put himself in danger for me. She wiped her eyes with her sleeve. 'Will he be safe?'

'No one's safe. No' anymore. Look, Johnnie was fine last time we saw him. He should be home soon.'

'You've told the laird and Morag?'

'Aye.'

'Dougie, what's going to happen to us?' she begged.

'Redcoats are in charge now. No one to stop them. Gave us no quarter. Butchered the wounded. We're all that's left of the Stewarts, as far as I ken. You and your mother need to look to yourselves.'

'Will they…' she wet her lips… 'will the redcoats come to Braedrumie?'

He nodded. 'Aye, they will. They've burnt crofts behind us. Saw the smoke on the horizon.'

Kirsty stared at him wide-eyed.

'Be strong, lassie.' Dougie's hand pressed her shoulder. 'There's many will have more to bear than you this day.' He signalled to Murdo and the Stewart survivors with a wave of his hand. 'We need to go. We've bad news to give to some in Braedrumie and have to see to our own families, you ken?'

'Aye. Of course. Thank you. Johnnie **will** come home, won't he?' She pleaded.

'Aye. He'll do everything he can, lassie. You can be sure of that. I see you've Tolbain's men at your farm. Canna mistake the moss-green.' Dougie's eyes narrowed.

Her hand went to her breast. *Does he think we're traitors?*

'He… is a… distant relative and thinks to keep us safe.'

200

Lorna Windham

Dougie's eyes narrowed. 'Oh, aye? Thought the Tolbain's disowned your mother when she married?'

'That wasna his doing.'

Dougie spat in the grass.

So, now they knew. *Oh, God. Poor Hughie and Duncan. And where's Johnnie?*

She watched the exhausted men jog away towards Braedrumie. She drew herself up. She had to get home and tell Mother.

***

Kirsty kept to dips in the ground and shadows of the farmhouse as she slid past the Boids. Excitement mixed with fear pulsed through her as she entered the house. She found Mother, back bent over the kitchen table with her scrubbing brush.

Kirsty hissed, 'I've news from Dougie and Murdo.'

Mother froze and stared at her with bleak eyes until Kirsty mentioned Hughie.

'I don't believe it.' Mother flung her scrubbing brush into the bucket and ignored the splash of soapy suds which streamed across the flagstones. 'Hughie will come back. You'll see. Many a man's been thought dead in battle and come home. This is all that Johnnie Stewart's fault. He promised to keep poor Hughie safe.'

'For God's sake, Mother, no' again.' Kirsty gripped Mother's arm. 'Johnnie will have done all he could.'

Mother pulled away. 'Hmph. He'll return playing the hero whilst poor Hughie…' Mother's eyes lit up. 'No. Hughie will come back.'

'Mother, Dougie said the redcoats gave no quarter.'

'I'll not believe he's lying in a ditch on some windswept moor and neither should you.'

Can Uncle Hughie be alive? Kirsty chewed her lip. 'We need to think of poor Aunty Mary and the bairns. We must visit now.'

The Jacobite Affair

'You go. You're good at sympathy.'

'Mother, you haven't visited once.' Kirsty folded her arms. 'We need to prepare ourselves. Dougie said the redcoats will come here. Oh God, Mother, we're an easy target. There's so few of our men left. Soldiers will come and kill, burn crofts and take what they want.'

'Not here and not this farm, Tolbain's men will see to that.' Mother looked at Kirsty. 'See how wise I was to remind him of our kinship? And you'd be wise to tie the knot tight.'

Kirsty's fingers rubbed her neck as if a rope had just tightened. *Can Tolbain protect us from redcoats? But what about Braedrumie? I have to think.*

'Where are you going?'

Kirsty paused. 'The sconce.'

'You've chores you know.' Mother put one hand on her back. 'I'm not getting any younger. Can't do what I used to.' She plumped down on a stool. 'Never been so weary or hungry.'

'You rest, I'll be back in a minute.' *I shouldn't have left her to do all the work this morning.*

The sconce lay in shadow as Kirsty unpinned her brooch, kissed it and placed it in her trinket box. She stared out of the window at the mountains in the east. A shiver ran through her. *Dearest, darling Johnnie. Please come home.*

Lorna Windham

CHAPTER Forty-three

The Inverness sun passed its zenith. A redcoat's rusty key grated in the Old Church's lock. The door's hinges squeaked. Two burly redcoats, a corporal and private, hurled Johnnie into the gloom and he stumbled on an outstretched limb.

'Aaagh!' cried its owner.

'Sorry,' said Johnnie. He'd rolled away onto the dank earth floor and pain seared his injured arm. He set his jaw, at least he'd only been winged. 'Bastards.'

The sunken-faced private showed him two fingers.

'Gallows meat.' The snaggle-toothed corporal smirked as he slammed the door and shut out the light. The key jangled in the lock.

Johnnie struggled to breathe as a fetid stink filled his nostrils. His eyes couldn't penetrate the dark. He sensed movement as bodies stirred. His sight adjusted and he made out vague shapes and naked limbs wrapped in makeshift bandages.

Damn. Johnnie could have kicked himself. If only he hadn't stopped when he'd heard his name called. He'd been dragged from the market square and thrown into the church near Aunt Munro's house.

His poor aunt. What would become of her? And Rob dressed as a bloody redcoat? Had he dreamed it? Then Johnnie remembered Rob's arguments with Father. Bloody traitor. If Rob's voice hadn't distracted him, perhaps he'd have escaped. A black worm squirmed deep inside Johnnie's head. Perhaps this imprisonment was God's judgement for Duncan's death.

A gruff voice came out of the darkness, 'Which... Clan, laddie? I'm... Chattan... myself.'

A thin figure limped towards Johnnie.

'Stewart.'

'They fought well I'm thinkin'. Christy Chattan at your service.' A gnarled hand sought Johnnie's.

'Pleased to meet you, though I can think of better places.' Johnnie shook Christy's hand. 'I'm Johnnie.'

The Jacobite Affair

'Where were you caught?' Christy's eyebrows lifted in unison like grey brambles in a furrowed field.

'Inverness. You?'

'On the outskirts.' The man's hand fingered Johnnie's coat. 'Wearin' a good set of clothes. Had help then?'

'No.'

Christy let out a hoarse laugh. 'Have it your way. Doesna matter, most of us will be dead by mornin'. You havena water or bread?'

'I'm sorry, no.'

'No matter.' Christy sighed. 'Would only lengthen the end.' He patted his blood-soaked thigh. 'Better sit.'

'What do… you think… they'll do with… us?' A young voice spoke between gritted teeth from the deepest shadows. Its owner crawled nearer until Johnnie could make out his pale face, freckled nose and fiery hair. A boy, no more than sixteen. Blood trickled from the corner of his mouth and seeped from a chest wound through the fingers of one hand. 'Will they… send us… to… trial?'

'Perhaps.' Johnnie had no wish to share his deepest fears.

'I'm… Malcolm Fletcher.' The lad extended his hand.

Johnnie stared at it. He didn't want to know the laddie's name because then he'd care. And he didn't want to feel anything when Malcolm Fletcher died. Johnnie fought his demons and shook the lad's hand. 'Johnnie Stewart.'

Malcolm sank back to the ground. 'Mother.' A cough racked the lad's body and blood streamed from his lips. He wiped it away with his dirty sleeve.

Like Duncan.

The old man stared at Johnnie, shook his head and held Malcolm's hands in his twisted fingers. 'It's alright laddie, she's here,' he lied.

Unable to bear it, Johnnie shrugged off his coat and laid it over Malcolm. He had to get out of this place or he'd go mad. He left the lad to Christy's ministrations and squinted into the darkness. There must be over thirty souls entombed here. He tried the door: locked from the outside. He looked upwards, but couldn't see the rafters, then felt the damp stone walls of the tower. Solid, with one way in and out.

'Lookin' to escape are you?' asked Christy, his voice fainter. 'We've had nothin' to eat or drink since yesterday. Are you sure you've nothin', laddie?'

Expectant faces turned towards Johnnie who shook his head, embarrassed. He'd had a good breakfast whilst they starved.

Malcolm's chest rose once, twice and then ceased.

'He's gone.' Christy and crossed himself.

Johnnie followed suit. 'May God keep him in his tender care.' Would this never end? He sat beside Christy and leaned against the icy wall. Thoughts of Kirsty's sweet face and home tiptoed into his brain. When he closed his eyes he could hear Invererar Falls as it pummelled the rock face; smell the peaty heather and see Kirsty's home and the silver salver of Loch Linnhe. His mind clanged shut like the door of his prison.

He must have drifted off to sleep. His body trembled. Cold. So cold. He jerked upright as the stink of human waste, putrid flesh and the metallic tang of blood made his nose wrinkle. The darkness had deepened, men groaned or snored. He had to escape.

Johnnie circled the prison's interior again and stepped over and around bodies as he searched for a way out. The two sentries' mumbled complaints came to him through the door. His eager fingers examined the oak planks. Solid. He searched the earth floor and stone walls again. Nothing. This couldn't be the end, he'd too much life in him.

He sank down and an icy draft circled as he remembered the night of the Rising, Glenfinnan and all their victories. By God, the Jacobites had treated the redcoat wounded in an honourable fashion at Prestonpans, not like this. He needed to get out, get home and find Kirsty.

The Jacobite Affair

CHAPTER Forty-four

Dawn. A curl of grey smoke rose from the Boids' campfire. Kirsty let go of the empty fishing lines and baited hooks so they dropped back into the burn. *Oh, dear.* Her stomach growled at her as she lifted two buckets which slopped over her stockings and boots. *Where's Johnnie?* The gold disk which hovered in the east gave her no answer. Kirsty trailed back towards the farmhouse. Her skirt hung on her hips, not her waist. *We need food.* She swivelled as rooks cawed in the trees and she heard the canter of hooves.

Mother opened the farm's door and stood on the threshold. Her gaunt face scanned the newcomers. 'More of Tolbain's men. My coz must think a lot of us.' She sniffed the air. 'Someone's cooking fish.'

Fish?

The group dismounted by the Boid's campfire and shook hands.

'Why's he sent more?' Kirsty stared at their brutal faces. She lifted her nose and breathed in. *Fish.* Her hand went to her empty stomach. 'Wish it was ours.'

'Mother kneaded her spine with the knuckles of her hand. 'I'm getting old. You've checked the lines in the burn and the loch?'

'Nothing.'

'Snares?'

Kirsty shook her head. 'Check them again.' Mother's thin lips snapped together.

'Mother.'

'My back aches, joints ache, everything aches.' Mother stretched her arms. 'When I was a child there was plenty of food and fine meals. The Tolbain's always had a good table. Finest silver and linen. It could all be ours.'

Kisty shared a thought. 'Mother. The empty lines and snares. That fish, could be ours. I wish Johnnie was here.'

'Daughter, I married the wrong man, don't make the same mistake with Stewart.'

Lorna Windham

CHAPTER Forty-five

Cold days and ice-cold nights went by in the gaol as groans, movement and conversation died to almost nothing. Johnnie judged time by the light under the door, the church a mortuary. Good to see old Christy Chattan still clung to life, though his blackened leg stank. The redcoats met Johnnie's demands for a physician with rifle butts. The prisoners had been left a bucket of brackish water, but no food.

Night. Johnnie jammed his ear to the lock. He listened for the change of guard, the stamp of boots and the grumble of voices outside which carried on the icy wind funnelled off the Ness. This time another voice. 'Have a drink with John Rob, lads.' A drunk? Laughter. Who the hell was John Rob? The clatter of a rifle. Another. A muffled drag of feet. Johnnie's dull wits puzzled over the names. John… Rob.

'Johnnie, Johnnie are you there?' Rob's voice. Johnnie leapt to his feet. It couldn't be his brother?

A key turned in the lock and the door swung open to let in moonlight, an icy draft and a white world where snowflakes swirled. None of the prisoners moved except Johnnie who sprang to the door. Rob. The two guards lay tied up and in the shadow of the church tower. Rob.

Later, Johnnie tried to make sense of the situation. Did he call Rob a bastard? Did Rob ignore his outburst and tell him he'd little time to escape? Did he accept Rob's cloak and provisions? Yes he did, even though Rob wore the redcoat's uniform. Johnnie couldn't go back inside that wretched prison.

Johnnie had stared at Rob and fought back the bitterness inside him. 'Mother, Cousin Jack and… Duncan are… dead and your bloody redcoats have Aunt Munro.'

Rob's eyes had flickered, then steadied. He'd fixed Johnnie with a cold stare. 'Euan's alive, should be on his way home.'

Johnnie almost sagged with relief at the news as his breath frosted and mingled with Rob's. Thank God. No time to ask questions. Johnnie couldn't bring himself to thank him.

The Jacobite Affair

'Mother…' began Rob.

'Dinna. No excuses.'

'What about those in the church?' said Rob.

Christy Chattan's voice rang out in the darkness, 'God… speed, lad. None of… us has… the strength. Get home, get… home… for… all… of… us.'

'Take this.' Rob took off his cloak.

Johnnie wanted nothing from him, but he needed a disguise and it would keep him warm. He took it, turned his back on Rob and headed for the River Ness. A hoarse shout, then a bawdy song from a tavern made him dive into the shadows. Johnnie didn't look back and raced through a maze of wynds. He paused in a doorway that smelt of urine. Drunken men staggered past and into an inn, opposite. His breath exhaled in ghostly wraiths as he slid past water butts, strung with ice-tears and ran. He skidded to a halt, dealt with a nosey redcoat then spied the guarded bridge over the grey ribbon of the river. His chances - slim. The weather and tide against him, he forced himself to wait.

Footsteps. In the distance, a pistol shot followed seconds later by the report of a musket. His heart raced. The feel of a dead man's uniform alien against his skin. His senses alert, he kept his nerve, crossed the bridge and strolled past the sentries. Shouts and a fusillade of musket shots behind him spurred him on.

Johnnie headed west, scrambled up rocks, cliff faces, through heather, round gorse and evaded redcoat patrols. He travelled at night, hid through the day and on the third night stumbled over the body of a red-bearded man, slumped against the trunk of a rowan tree. The wounds that killed him spread like crimson stars on his chest.

Johnnie crossed himself and said a silent prayer for the man's soul as he wondered about the man's family and all those who waited for news of loved ones. Like his father and Kirsty. How could he tell them about Duncan or Rob? He had to get home.

Lorna Windham

He grimaced as he stripped off and replaced the uniform with the dead man's plaid. The bracken colours would act as camouflage until he got to Braedrumie. He took the man's dirk from his hose and the meal from his sporran. At least he had food and the means to defend himself. Johnnie left the corpse behind and walked on.

He made his way west over the hills to Glen Conith and Loch Glorm. He slept in fits and starts in caves, holes in the ground and sheilings. Duncan's face pursued him wherever he went.

He ate little, drank spring water and saved the last piece of Rob's bread until hunger drove him to gnaw at it. His mind wondered to Ruthven. The Jacobites had agreed to rally there if they lost. Should he go?

The call of home too strong, he ran on with the first glimmer of dawn behind him. He scanned the wild horizon and slate sky ahead. Curled mist circled hills topped with snow and covered the bleak moor. He plunged thigh deep into a burn and cursed. He struggled out of its icy grip and used his plaid to mop himself dry as he wondered at the group of strange stone mounds in front of him. The hairs on the back of his neck prickled. He sped on as if his life depended on it in an attempt to shake off the ghosts who guarded the place.

He looked behind him to the east. Crimson and blue light streaked in a fan-shape over a knuckle-mountain range. He should have found a place to hide long before now.

A clatter of hooves. Damn. A redcoat officer on horseback came from behind an outcrop of rock to his left and blocked the track ahead. Johnnie slewed to a halt. He glanced round, there had to be other soldiers close by.

'Captain Forster, of the Argyles' The young redcoat looked down his hooked nose at Johnnie and swept off his hat to reveal strands of straw-coloured hair topped by a wig. He held his sabre over one shoulder as if in rest from bloody work. 'I suggest you ...'

Johnnie noticed the loose hand on the rein.

The Jacobite Affair

'Yaaah!' Johnnie leapt from the ground, used all his six foot two inches and wind-milled his arms like a mad man.

The black stallion's nostrils flared. Its eyes rolled back in its head as it reared. Johnnie stepped back as the hooves lashed out and he noted the captain lost a rein, then a stirrup. As the redcoat fell, his horse skittered to one side.

Johnnie buried his dirk up to its hilt in the captain and watched blood spurt from his mouth until he lay still. Johnnie's stomach heaved and he tasted bile. He crossed himself and longed for a priest. Think. He had to get away. The horse.

He had to be quick, but if he rushed, the stallion would take fright. The horse cropped at the rough grass at the foot of several boulders. Johnnie walked towards the stallion.

'There's a bonny lad.' He let the animal sniff his outstretched fingers. 'You'll be alright with me.' He took the reins and calmed the horse with slow, gentle movements, blew into its nostrils and whispered in its ear. He let the animal get as much of his scent as possible. It whinnied as if offended, but knew Johnnie now and nuzzled him.

Johnnie climbed up on the fine leather saddle and put the sabre in its rightful place. With a light touch of spurs to the horse, he rode off.

The stallion had a glossy coat, a nose that would fit in a wine glass and ran for hours like Pegasus. The wind caught at Johnnie's hair and plaid. He forgot about the daylight, lost in the animal's speed.

Scarecrow figures rose from the mist in front of him. Johnnie hauled on the reins, the horse reared and he found himself surrounded.

Lorna Windham

CHAPTER Forty-six

The Lornes stood under a crimson and lemon sky in front of Toll House. Mother looked drawn. 'It's cold for April.' She rubbed her hands together. 'We need food.'

'I wish you'd come on your own.' Kirsty shivered inside her cloak.

'It's **you** he wants to see.'

'But, I dinna want to see him.' Kirsty crossed her arms.

'I've told you, forget Stewart and his brooch. We can't carry on the way we've been doing.'

Kirsty shrugged her off. 'Tell him to send his poxy guards away.'

'We wouldn't be safe.'

'Ladies.' Tolbain stood behind them.

Mother whirled with a fixed smile and Kirsty's shoulders sagged.

'Miss Lorne.'

'Your Grace.' Kirsty flushed and gave him the slightest of curtsies.

'Gilly.'

Her mother bent her knees. Kirsty put a hand under her arm and helped her up.

'Have I intruded on a quarrel?' Tolbain ran a hand through his beard. 'I hope not. I wanted Miss Lorne to admire a new mare I've purchased.'

'A mare? You brought us all this way for a mare?' Kirsty stared at him.

'And for afternoon tea. Cake and little fancies you women seem to like.'

Mother's tongue played on her lips.

Kirsty's stomach answered of its own accord. She pressed her hand to suppress the ache. She hadn't dared to think of such food.

'Didn't my men say? Most forgetful of them. Couldn't help overhearing that you find their presence, difficult, shall we say? I apologise if their behaviour has been not of the best.

The Jacobite Affair

Ladies have no idea of the world of men. After our glorious victory, I'm afraid the Highlands is a dangerous place, especially for women. My only concern: your welfare.'

'How kind, Your Grace,' simpered Mother.

How dare he crow. Our welfare, indeed.

'I thought the mare first? Give us an appetite. Ladies, after you.'

Kirsty's stomach rumbled and Mother ground her teeth.

He led both of them to the clock tower and the stables. The stink of the dung heap and fresh hay pervaded the area. A chestnut mare stood in the end stall.

'I'll stay outside, within call.' Mother's hand went to her forehead. 'I feel the need for fresh air.'

No she doesn't. Oh, dear. Tolbain walked behind Kirsty, too close, which made her increase her pace to meet the mare. The horse whinnied.

Kirsty patted its glossy neck. 'She's beautiful. What's her name?'

'Lady. She's graceful, obeys my commands and…'

'Acts like a lady?'

'Yes.' He laughed and the sound rolled around the stable.

She smiled and he moved closer. So close she could smell his lemon scented cologne.

'She's yours if you agree to our handfasting.'

What? Is he mad? Her hand went to the empty space where Johnnie's brooch had been pinned. 'I canna, I mean I'm betrothed.'

'To Johnnie Stewart? A traitor? A Jacobite who's probably dead or hunted like a deer with a price on his head.'

'Dinna say that.' She put a hand on his arm, but he winced and pulled away. 'You're wounded? I'm sorry.'

'A scratch. You'll find the Stewarts, like so many, will not be so grand any more. The clans are finished. Our victory at Culloden has ensured it. Let me show you what fighting for the right side means.' He led her out of the stables, round his extensive grounds, into the house and his study. Mother trotted behind to keep up. He unlocked three large oak chests and let her see the silks, silver plate and jewels. Paintings stood stacked against a wall, fine china sat on a table, rolled carpets lay in heaps and rich curtains had been strewn across his desk. 'All this and more will you be yours if you agree to be handfasted to me.'

Her mother gasped.

Kirsty stared at him open mouthed. *I've dreamed of luxuries like these, but they're plunder, surely?*

Mother spoke first. 'My daughter is young, overcome by the favour you show her, Your Grace. A handfasting is all very well, but a wedding would be more agreeable to me.'

'Mother.'

'Would it now? You aim too high, Gilly. A handfasting gives us both time to consider our choice of partner. I suggest this as I can see Miss Lorne is… hesitant. She'd be free in a year if she wished and so would I. Don't you agree this would be the best course of action?'

'Of course, Your Grace, knows best.' Mother curtsied.

Does he? What about Johnnie? Kirsty's brow wrinkled. 'But…'

'Good. I wouldn't want to withdraw my offer.'

Mother threw a malicious glance at Kirsty.

'Tea?' said Tolbain.

Fruit cake, farls, shortbread, butter, blackcurrant jam and honey marched along a table of fine linen. Kirsty sat like a wooden doll. She craved to eat everything offered to them by the maid with the lopsided smile. *Should she?*

'I declare the fresh air has given me quite an appetite.' Mother stacked her plate and added huge dollops of honey.

Kirsty's nose twitched. *The jam smells of mellow autumn days. How can I resist?* Kirsty took tiny bites out of a buttery scented farl and fifteen minutes later accepted a thin slice of fruit cake. Sultanas, raisins and brandy released their rich flavours in sweet bursts as she tried to hold the last crumb on her tongue. She relished it, rolled it round, squeezed the last juice out of a sultana then relinquished it with the last sip of tea. Her stomach begged for more. *We're such weak creatures. What would Johnnie and the Stewarts think if they knew?*

Whilst she and Mother ate off dainty plates and dabbed at the corner of their mouths with linen napkins, Tolbain boasted of pillaged Jacobite homes whose inhabitants he'd turned out and how his pantry held their spices, tea, coffee and chocolate.

From the poor homeless families you've robbed. Her stomach gurgled. *We're just as bad, we've eaten some of the spoils.*

His deep growl pierced her thoughts. 'Your mother and I agree, we would make a good match, Miss Lorne. Of course she owns ancestral lands which are worth a lot to me, not financially, but in terms of them returning... home. Consider this also, I offer you both security, in an increasingly violent world.'

'I... I...' Kirsty's throat had been clenched by a fist. *Johnnie.*

'She needs time.' Mother glared at her.

'To think?'

'Yes.'

'I'll give her time, but not too long.' Tolbain wagged a finger at Kirsty. 'My men will guard you, night and day. It's more dangerous now than before. There are traitors to be caught, men who'd stop at nothing and I want you to be safe.' He stood. 'I believe that is all, ladies.'

Lorna Windham

CHAPTER Forty-seven

The sky darkened as charcoal clouds gathered and covered the watery sun. Swirls of icy mist crept down the mountain sides. Johnnie's hand went to the hilt of his sword. The Highlanders surrounded him and raised their claymores. Which side did they fight for? Johnnie lowered his brows. 'Good day to you.' The men looked fresh, untouched by war.

'And you'll be...?' asked a man with the look of a blacksmith. He gripped the rein of Johnnie's horse with a muscular arm and held a claymore in the other. One fellow with shaggy, brown hair hawked and spat, another showed his yellow teeth and a third with one ear glowered.

'Johnnie Stewart. And yourself?' Johnnie's finger trembled on the rein. Delayed shock, fatigue or hunger? He didn't want these men to think it fear. The horse sensed the movement and jigged to one side.

The blacksmith tightened his grip on the rein. 'A Stewart? I'm MacNair, Steenie MacNair. By the look of you, Johnnie, you've been in a wee fight with Cumberland's army, if I'm no mistaken?'

'Aye and you'll have heard we lost.'

'MacNair sucked his teeth. 'We walked for days tryin' to join you, didn't we boys?'

'Aye,' nodded Shaggy Head.

'Bastards are hunting and killing our wounded. You could have been one those poor beggars lying on Drumossie Moor.' Like Duncan. A bitter taste came into Johnnie's mouth. 'Have you water and something to eat? I've had nought but bloody meal for days.' The wind picked up, numbed his skin and made him long for a fire.

'You'll make do with some whisky I'm thinkin'.' MacNair handed him a battered leather saddle flask.

Johnnie unscrewed the stopper and breathed in heady, peaty fumes. He couldn't stop himself. The fiery liquid burnt its way down his throat. On an empty stomach it wasn't a wise thing to

The Jacobite Affair

do. His head reeled, but the heat gathered in his gut and gave him his first warmth for days.

Shaggy Head nudged One Ear.

MacNair patted the horse's neck. 'A redcoat's from the brand and saddle.' He turned to his men. 'Mind me, Johnnie's a friend.'

A friend? He didn't make 'friends' that easily.

Shaggy Head sheathed his dirk, and One Ear lowered his sword. The others followed.

'My thanks for the whisky, I'll be on my way.' Johnnie kneed his mount.

MacNair held onto the rein and patted the brand on the animal's rump. 'A fine redcoat horse.' MaNair's mud-eyes squinted at Johnnie.

'Aye.' Damn. Yellow Teeth had moved up to one stirrup and One Ear the other. Johnnie's neck prickled.

'Could break a leg in this mist… You'll no' be interested in roast venison I suppose? We killed a stag this afternoon.' MacNair indicated behind him.

Johnnie's eyes took in the string of ponies. Each carried packs and one, the carcase of an adult stag. Saliva gathered in this mouth.

'In exchange for a hot meal, perhaps you'd tell us of this battle we lost and how you came by such a fine horse and saddle?' MacNair looked at his men for approval.

Johnnie's stomach twisted and cramped in an ecstasy of half-forgotten memories. He hadn't had fresh meat for a very long time. He threw caution to the wind. 'I'd be delighted.'

'Look.' Yellow Teeth pointed behind them as ominous swirls of smoke rose over the hills.

Redcoats?

'Follow us.' MacNair and his men galloped up the hillside. A pack slipped on one of the ponies' backs. 'Damnation.' MacNair cursed and stopped to tighten the girth.

A shout made Johnnie rein in his mount. He turned to look behind him. Fifty yards away a bald-headed man and grey-

Lorna Windham

haired woman hauled a cart east, towards the line of MacNair's ponies.

The bald man cupped his hand to his mouth. 'Run. Get away from here.'

A family group. The mother and father hauled a cart piled with their meagre possessions: a couple of stools, an iron kettle and a bed. A young, red-haired man had his shoulder to the load.

Behind him a white-faced girl, carried a cloth bundle over her shoulder. She tugged at the hand of a small, dark boy who waved a wooden dirk in the other. 'You must walk faster, Cormick.' She glanced behind her. 'Faster.'

'Is it redcoats?' shouted Johnnie.

'Run! Run! They're behind us, just a few miles back.' The bald man had a mad look in his eyes.

'They're killin' everyone, burnin' people out,' cried the woman, her voice high with panic. She pointed a thumb at the red-haired man. 'We're lucky, our Tam was in the top field, saw the smoke and what they did to the Macpherson's. They're no' far behind us. Oh God. Oh God.'

The cart trundled past Johnnie who spurred his horse and caught the bald man's arm. The cart stopped.

'Leave us alone.' Tam's wife looked back.

'How many?'

The bald man looked behind him. 'About six ahead of the main party. Thirty in all.'

'We've got to go. Tell him, Father.' Tam's eyes never left the horizon.

'How long have we got?' asked Johnnie.

'I...I...' The bald man stared at him and he mouthed words he couldn't speak.

'Father?' The girl's voice trembled.

'Steady man, steady,' said Johnnie.

The bald man spat twice. 'Depends how long they stay at the last croft.' He paused. 'Tam said they had some lassies. Perhaps ten, fifteen minutes.' A fusillade of shots sounded in the distance.

The Jacobite Affair

The girl screamed and hugged Tam.

'Perhaps sooner.' The bald man threw off Johnnie's hand, bent his back and set the cart in motion again.

Johnnie galloped back to MacNair. 'You heard him. I'd send a man to warn when they're near. We need to get off this road, now.'

Yellow Teeth snarled. 'And let the bastards stroll past us?'

Johnnie surveyed the ground around them. 'We'll ambush the bastards, that's if the MacNairs are up for it?'

Yellow Teeth's hand went to his claymore.

MacNair pushed Yellow Teeth away and gave a wolfish grin. 'Hamish, hide the horse and ponies.'

Shaggy Head did as ordered.

'Dand,' said MacNair.

One Ear trotted to his leader's side.

MacNair jerked his thumb at a crinkled sugar-loaf mountain in the distance. 'Tell the men to get down here.'

Dand galloped off to the east.

Johnnie drew in his breath. More men?

'Steenie…' began a man with a tangled beard

'Shut your trap.' MacNair snarled. 'Scout behind us. Make sure you're no' seen. Come back when you see their red coats.'

Tangled Beard turned his pony and set off.

'No one moves until my signal and the last redcoat is surrounded. Then we kill the swine.' MacNair's lips formed a smile and revealed two sharp, canine teeth.

Way up above Johnnie's head, an eagle hunted in an ice-blue sky and birds called to each other. A few feet away a spider waited on its lace-frosted web for its next victim. MacNair spread out his men, then lay in the marshy ground beside Johnnie and hid.

Tangled Beard returned, but brought his pony to a walk as he peered at the marsh grass and gorse. He broke into a wide grin when MacNair and his men rose out of the heather. The scout slunk down beside MacNair. 'They're about a half a mile away and coming fast. Counted thirty.'

'Well done. Now we wait some more.' Johnnie swivelled as children's voices rang out from the drovers' track to the south. *'So, we'll tramp and we'll stamp and we'll fight for Charlie.'*

'What the...?' said MacNair. 'Bloody hell.' A pair of barefoot, ragged children rounded a rock face and marched as they sang. The boy carried something on his back. The girl had a stick over one thin shoulder from which she'd suspended a small knotted piece of plaid.

Johnnie searched the brow of the hill to the east. No sign of redcoats yet. He signalled for everyone to stay down while he and MacNair crawled towards the children. Johnnie got behind the girl and MacNair, the boy, put a hand over each mouth and raced with them into the heather. The children were left with two of MacNairs' surprised men, whilst Johnnie and MacNair crept back to their former positions.

Johnnie scanned the ridge to the east. Nothing. Then the first redcoat strolled over the crest followed by groups of soldiers and the sound of raucous laughter, course jests and boasts. The soldiers straddled the road. This should be easy.

***

When the last redcoat took his final breath, Johnnie wiped the vomit from his mouth.

'No stomach for killin', lad?' MacNair sneered.

Johnnie ignored him.'Put the bodies in the bog.' He indicated a lake of black murk to one side of them.

'Not till we've got our pickin's,' snarled MacNair.

Johnnie watched as lookouts sped off in different directions as the rest of the MacNairs stripped the bodies of weapons and searched pockets. Dand and Hamish admired each other's plunder, but Johnnie knew they risked discovery the longer they stayed. He hissed, 'Let's get the hell out of here, before the main force arrives.'

Hamish kicked the last body into the black depths and padded after him.

The Jacobite Affair

'Sir?' The boy's pale face peeped up at Johnnie from behind the marsh grass.

Duncan. Johnnie knelt in front of the boy who'd shaped his mouth in a straight line and the little girl curled her fists.

'You could have hurt Jeannie, earlier.' The boy pointed at the tiny pack on his back.

The little girl pulled back a thin, grey blanket and revealed a thin, pale face with closed eyes.

A baby. God in heaven. Johnnie stared at it.

The boy swept his brown fringe out of his brown eyes. 'If you'd asked we'd have helped you kill redcoats too.'

Dand and Hamish mounted their ponies eager to be gone.

'I'm sure you would.' The boy couldn't have been more than eight, the girl no more than six. Johnnie fought back a vision of Duncan at the same age. He coughed. 'I'm Mr. Stewart, what're your names?'

The boy answered, 'I'm Neill Douglas, called after our Dadda and she's my sister Comrie.'

'Do you know our Dadda?' The little girl pressed her cold hand into Johnnie's. Her large hazel eyes looked into his. 'He went to fight the redcoats in a great battle. Is he here?'

Johnnie shook his head. They had to leave, now. 'MacNair.'

MacNair strode across. 'Problem?'

'The bairns.'

MacNair studied Comrie and growled. 'Where's your mother? Why's she no' here looking after you?'

Comrie took two steps back and held onto her brother's grubby arm. 'We left her in Lochanhully, she's in Heaven, isn't she Neill? She'll be there some time. So, we decided to come and look for Dadda.' Her mouth opened in a wide yawn. 'I'm tired of walking. We've only got some crumbs of cheese left, but Neill says we've to wait and share them with Dadda.'

The boy snapped at her. 'Course we have Comrie. How would it look if we'd nothing and him always sharing with us?'

Lorna Windham

Droplets appeared in Comrie's eyes and she rubbed at them with tiny fists.

Johnnie patted her back. 'Hush, hush, now. And what about the baby? How did you feed her?'

MacNair's brows jumped to his hairline, then lowered when Johnnie shook his head.

'Women gave us milk, but we've only a little and it smells sour,' said Neill. 'When Jeannie's awake she screams a lot and won't do what she's told.'

'Can we rest for a while?' asked Comrie.

'Leave them.' MacNair hissed in Johnnie's ear.

'We'll never find Dadda if we rest all the time. She doesna understand.' Neill's face crumpled.

'Tell you what,' Johnnie knelt on one knee. 'We've too much food and you'd be helping us out if you'd join us. You can sit on Pegasus. MacNair, will fetch him, won't you?'

'Pegasus?' MacNair scowled.

'My horse.'

MacNair spat on the ground. 'I'll fetch him.'

Johnnie narrowed his eyes.

Neill took his sister's hand. 'Did you hear that Comrie?'

'Can I eat as much as I want and then ask for more?'

'Of course little one,' Johnnie said.

'I'm no' little.' She put her right thumb in her mouth.

Johnnie smiled. 'Give me Jeannie, Neill.'

'Mother said I was no' to let her out of my sight.'

Johnnie patted Neill's shoulder. 'You've done a grand job looking after her, but you and Comrie need to eat and rest. Will you trust me laddie? I willna harm her.' Johnnie held out his hands.

'You'll be careful with her,' said Neill.

'I'll be careful. It's alright, I'll treat her like my own. We need to hurry.' Johnnie took the bundle. How light. The baby's dirt encrusted face and cracked lips made him want to weep. He turned at the sound of horse's hooves. MacNair led Pegasus towards him.

221

The Jacobite Affair

'You're good at givin' orders. Think you were in charge. And who's lookin' after them?' MacNair jerked his thumb at the children who shrank from him.

'Me.' Johnnie spoke without thought.

MacNair stood, hand on hips then turned to the children. 'Aye. Right, you two, who's goin' to be first on Mr. Stewart's fine horse?'

'Me. Then I can hold Comrie so she doesna fall.'

MacNair lifted Neill onto the saddle then Comrie. 'You're a bright lad, hold onto them reins.' He raised his voice. 'Let's go.'

MacNair led the group west for hours over several hills as Johnnie walked beside Pegasus with Jeannie in his arms. A light drizzle fell as the sun sank and they reached a rocky outcrop and a cleft concealed by loose boulders, rough clumps of gorse and heather.

'Hamish, tell the men to bed down here.' MacNair brought his pony to a halt.

Neill slid down the saddle to the ground as Johnnie held Comrie.

'Hungry,' she said.

MacNair dismounted. 'You work for food here. Unpack the horses, laddie.'

'But I'm tired.' Neill's mouth opened in a yawn.

MacNair's calloused hand caught Neill on the side of his head. He reeled to the ground and Comrie shrieked.

'Better learn fast you little whelp. There's more where that came from. Mind me, unload the ponies or it'll be the worst for you and yours.' MacNair glared at Comrie who shrank back.

Johnnie let Comrie run to the shelter of Neill's arms.

'You'll no' raise your hand to the laddie again, nor threaten the lassie.' Johnnie stood grim-faced.

MacNair looked Johnnie up and down. 'I'm in charge here. I say the lad earns their keep.'

'I've no quarrel with that, but I'll no' see the bairns hurt.'

Lorna Windham

MacNair's lips curled into a semblance of a smile. 'As you wish, Stewart.' MacNair raised his voice, 'Dand, send out scouts and I want sentries.'

Neill fingered the red wheal across his cheek.

'We'll unload the ponies.' Johnnie hefted the stag to the ground.

'Thank you, Mr. Stewart,' whispered Neill.

Johnnie lowered his voice, 'It was nought, laddie, but listen to what I say. If you and your sister wish to eat, dinna anger the man. Smile and pretend all's forgiven.'

Neill's lips widened and showed white teeth.

He reminded Johnnie of Duncan. Guilt? It twisted his gut. And Euan, was he alive? What about Kirsty and his father? Johnnie untied the leather straps round the packs and Neill stacked them.

The air cooled as the sky darkened. A full moon glowed and stars twinkled in a midnight-blue sky. Johnnie sat on his haunches in front of Neill. 'Now, are you too tired to see to Pegasus? He needs grass, water and a rub down?'

Neill's face lit up. 'We'll do that, won't we Comrie?'

'Hungry.' Comrie's fingers sought Johnnie's hand.

'I've water here. He watched her gulp it down. 'There'll be food in a bit. Can you wait like a good lassie?'

Comrie sucked her thumb and nodded.

'Right. There's something I have to do.' Johnnie set off with Jeannie in his arms towards a weathered rock shaped like a seated child.

Sometime later Johnnie returned with armfuls of heather. 'Now we'll have comfortable beds.' A cold breeze combed the gorse and brought with it the scent of cooked meat. 'Comrie, we're going to eat now.'

The little girl ran to Johnnie. She slipped her hands into Neill's and they walked into the shadowy warmth of the cave.

Dand fingered his only ear, then speared and roasted chunks of venison over the fire.

'Mmm.' Comrie drooled and Neill couldn't take his eyes off the meat.

The Jacobite Affair

MacNair sat on a pile of plaids. 'Take the weight off your bones. He lifted a leather flask. 'Whisky, Mr. Stewart?'

'Aye, thank you and water for the bairns.'

'I hope you'll forgive me for that incident with the lad. We've had a rough time of it. Not slept. You understand, I hope? I wouldna like you to think I'm a cruel man.'

'As long as it doesna happen again. They've lost those… closest to them and have enough to contend with.'

'I'm sure the laddie knows it wasna meant.' MacNair ruffled Neill's hair.

Neill brushed his fringe back in place and smiled at MacNair.

'See, all's forgiven and for that you can have the biggest piece of meat.' MacNair's fingers danced over the cooking meat. 'Eeny, meeny, miny, mo.' His forefinger and thumb darted at one large chunk, like a heron's beak, and gave a piece to Comrie and then Neill. She nibbled at it and he wolfed it down.

'The lads were wonderin'- you won so many battles, why didn't you win the final one?' Hamish, picked at his yellow teeth and turned the venison over the flames.

'The prince chose the wrong ground, we were outnumbered and outgunned.' Johnnie handed horn tumblers to the children before he took his own drink. He downed it in one fiery gulp and the cave walls spun. Shouldn't drink on an empty stomach. He helped himself to a chunk of meat.

Steenie tut-tutted and Hamish sucked in his cheeks.

'And the horse,' said MacNair.

Johnnie glanced at the children. 'A kind redcoat loaned me him.'

MacNair's laughter started in his belly and rumbled up his throat.

Later, after the children had eaten as much of the venison as their stomachs could take, Johnnie made beds of heather and carried Comrie to one. 'Sleep little one.'

Comrie's eyes fluttered as she stuck her thumb in her mouth.

Lorna Windham

'Mr. Stewart, where's Jeannie?' whispered Neill as he looked around. 'You said you'd look after her.'

Johnnie put a hand on Neill's shoulder. This would be hard. 'Come with me laddie.'

MacNair looked up from his heaped plate, shrugged his shoulders and continued to shovel meat into his mouth.

Johnnie took Neill into the star-crusted night to a spot a 100 yards off, where a small mound of freshly dug earth lay in the shadow of a boulder.

Neill stared at it.

Johnnie put an arm round him. 'You did your best, laddie, you and Comrie, but Jeannie was too small and weak. She's in Heaven.'

Tears formed in the corner of Neill's eyes. 'No. I promised Mother.'

'It's time you heard about the battle and what I think happened to your Dadda.' Johnnie told him what he needed to know. 'Jeannie's with both your parents now.'

Neill swayed and Johnnie held him to his chest as the boy's shoulders heaved.

The Jacobite Affair

CHAPTER Forty-eight

The black cloak of night descended over the Lorne's farmhouse. Kirsty closed the spence's shutters. *That should keep out the gruff voices of Tolbain's men.* She slammed horn cups onto the dresser.

'Mind my letters.' Mother scooped them up. 'I like reading them again. Mrs. Balfour's are full of Edinburgh gossip. Hmph. Why you're in such a bad mood, I dinna ken.' With that she swept out of the room.

Didn't she? With those men watching and her on at me all the time about Tolbain. Why can't she accept I love Johnnie? He's the only person who really loves me. I won't throw him away for Tolbain, despite the duke's riches.

Ribald laughter flooded into the room with the smell of cooked meat. *Venison.* Kirsty made a face at the shutters. *They know we're starving, yet offer us nothing. If only we had the cattle money, hens or a cow.*

Kirsty blew out the candle and went into the kitchen. Mother sat by the fire, her thin figure lit by the cruisie lamp. Her needle darted in and out of a pink garter. She looked up.

'What a sullen face, if the wind changes…'

'Mother.'

'We're hungry and with no need to be. Just say yes to Tolbain, and our suffering ends.'

'No' again.'

'The battle took place weeks ago. Inverness will be crawling with redcoats. Johnnie Stewart's dead and his family will lose everything. Look what happened in the '15. Land and houses sequestered and heads rolled. What sort of life will you have, married to a hunted man?'

'I dinna want to hear this.' Kirsty clasped her hands over her ears.

Mother let her needle rest on her lap. 'We could be living in Toll House, no debt or hunger just feather beds, good food, best of everything. We'd be somebody. Wait much longer and he'll withdraw his offer. Where would we be then? You tell me, where would we be?'

'You badger and hector till my head aches. Will you give me no' peace? I'm going to bed.' Kirsty flung herself into her bed and drew the curtains. She lay in a foetal position and pulled the covers over her head. *Johnnie where are you?*

The Jacobite Affair

CHAPTER Forty-nine

A peach tinted sky heralded dawn. Neill sat upright and yawned.

'Take Comrie's hand, there's a good laddie,' Johnnie said. 'She needs to visit Jeannie.' He led them past two sentries to the boulder and a small mound.

'Is she in Heaven too?' asked Comrie.

'With Mother and Dadda.' Neill looked at Johnnie for reassurance.

'Aye, that's right. Why not pick some flowers for them?'

Comrie clapped her hands. 'Oh, yes.' She scampered off into the heather.

'No' sure she understands.' Neill looked downcast.

'She will, laddie, in time. And when she does, she'll need us both.'

'Look what I've got.' Comrie ran towards them with bunches of purple and white heather. 'That's better.' She covered the black soil with her treasures.

'Can I borrow your dirk?' asked Neill. 'I need to write Jeannie's name on the rock.'

'Stewart, what are those weens doing? There's plenty of chores here to keep them occupied,' shouted MacNair.

'I'll do them,' said Johnnie.

'Please yoursel'. My scouts say no one's on our trail. We leave tomorrow.'

'Very well.' Johnnie turned to Neill and gave him his dirk. 'You and your sister, spend as much time as you want with Jeannie.'

'Mr. Stewart…' Neill began.

'Aye, laddie.'

'Thank you, sir.' Neill held out his hand.

Johnnie took it, his insides churned for both children. Other than Duncan, he'd not dealt with bairns. Yet he'd told MacNair he'd look after them. How? The enormity of his decision hit him. He'd agreed to look after the orphans, to be

Lorna Windham

their father. He wasn't even married. What would Kirsty think?

Later that day as the sky darkened, Johnnie studied the cloudy skies and blanket of ground mist. He stood on a rocky shelf above the cave and had a view for miles around.

'Where do you journey now?' asked MacNair at his shoulder as he offered Johnnie a leather flask.

Typical of the man to sneak up on him. 'Home.' Johnnie drank.

'And that is…?

Johnnie's head cleared. Too many questions. 'North,' he lied.

'North? That's good, we're going that way too. You can travel with us.'

Damn. 'I thank you.'

MacNair sniffed the air. 'Let's eat. We've stew I believe.' He clasped a hand on Johnnie's shoulder and led him inside the cave. Neil and Comrie, their faces lit by the flames, sat cross-legged between Hamish and Dandy. Neill scrambled up and pulled Comrie with him. The children sat either side of Johnnie.

'Only a brave man would think of travellin' alone, with bairns in these times.' Hamish scratched his beard.

'They're comin' with us,' said MacNair. 'That's right isn't it Stewart?'

Johnnie shifted in his seat. 'Aye. Wish I'd got to Ruthven, though.' Aware of their inquisitive faces he added, 'I was held up.' He accepted a bowl of stew. 'Thank you.'

'We've just come from there,' said MacNair. 'Do you know it?'

Johnnie shook his head as he chewed a juicy morsel of meat.

MacNair raised his voice. 'Canna mistake Ruthven Barracks, it's built on a defensive mound, towers over the flood plain. Barracks form an inner square, stables slightly to the west. Guards a ford and ferry to Kingussie. One of the few places you can cross the middle reaches of the Spey. Courtesy

The Jacobite Affair

of General Wade, the roads from Inverness, Fort Augustus and Perth meet there.' MacNair tore at a chunk of meat and tossed it into his mouth. He chewed as he continued. 'Tried to capture it a year ago, but we were defeated by twelve bloody redcoats. Twelve. So, we went back with more men and artillery, then they surrendered.

Sheltered there after we heard about the battle with three thousand men and women who hadn't seen a proper roof for a long time. Expected the prince. Just saw discontented men. The majority determined to fight on. *The prince's safe*, they said, *so, The Cause isna' dead*.

Then General Murray arrived. You should have been there, man. Heard the roar of welcome and swords beat on targes. Murray mounted a cart to speak. I was so sure he'd tell us to put Culloden behind us, that we'd beaten the Redcoats before and the next time we'd be victorious.'

'What did he say?' Johnnie leaned forward.

'The prince sent his thanks and heartfelt appreciation for our loyalty, our bravery and all we'd been through. However, he felt he'd done all he could. Murray quoted his words, *Let each man seek his own safety in the best way he can.* Can you believe that?'

Johnnie blinked at him. All their sacrifices, all the deaths, for nothing?

'You can imagine the men's reaction. Pinned all their hopes and dreams on one man, Bonnie Prince Charlie. Bastard.'

'So the whore's son left us to it?' said Johnnie.

'Aye. Some men even grabbed at Murray's sleeve seekin' clarification, you ken? He shrugged them off, said, *This is not of my makin'. The prince wouldna' listen. Go back to your families, they'll need you now.* Then he rode off - Rode off.'

'Bloody hell. Johnnie tried to imagine the undefended crofts and people. Braedrumie. 'What are you going to do?'

MacNair looked at his men. 'Havena decided yet, have we?'

Hamish grinned and shook his head.

MacNair's smile seemed more like a sneer. 'More whisky?' He offered Johnnie a leather bottle.

'My thanks, but no.'

The conversation died as MacNair handed out meat on sharpened sticks.

Johnnie tore into his and every portion offered until his stomach groaned. Aware of Comrie who leant on one side of him and Neill's eyelid's which drooped, Johnnie excused himself. 'The bairns are tired. It's been a long day.' He carried Comrie to her heather-bed, tucked a plaid up to her chin and did the same for Neill. 'Good night to you both,' Johnnie said.

He struggled to sleep as his mind raced. He had responsibility for two bairns. How his brothers would laugh, but not Duncan, he'd never laugh again. He let his eyelids close. But the battle exploded into his mind with images of him as he dodged redcoat blades. Faces leered at him, severed limbs sprouted in all directions amongst blood and gore. He couldn't breathe, felt the press of bodies, he had to get out. He woke with a start to hear the low murmur of MacNair and his men, their faces lit by the fire. Johnnie lay in shadow.

'It's tomorrow then,' said MacNair. 'Once we've dealt with Stewart, we'll sell…'

The voices lowered. Johnnie strained to listen.

'…but the horse is mine.' MacNair's voice brooked no argument.

Damn. Johnnie waited. He hoped the children knew they could trust him. Neill slept on his back like an unkempt puppy and Comrie with her thumb in her mouth and arms above her head.

He waited several hours. Snores. Just before the grey light of dawn, Johnnie clasped his hand over Neill's mouth. The boy woke and struggled to come awake. A startled look appeared in his eyes. He stared at Johnnie. How to inform the laddie of their danger? Johnnie jerked his thumb at the men who slept all round them and shook his head. He pointed at himself, Neill and Comrie who still slept and indicated what he wanted Neill to do. The boy stared at him and then nodded his head.

The Jacobite Affair

Johnnie took his hand off Neill's mouth. 'Wake your sister,' he whispered as he glanced at the men close by. 'No noise.'

The lad slid out from under his plaid and mirrored what Johnnie had done to him.

Comrie woke, startled and then lay still. Neill withdrew his hand and warned her with a finger to his lips. She sat up and rubbed her eyes with her knuckles. Neill took Comrie's hand, followed Johnnie and they slipped out of the cave and into the shadows.

Johnnie signalled to the children to stay in the darkness. He had to deal with the sentries near the ponies. The children sank to the ground. He crept along the rock face. His heart pounded. He needed to put as many miles as possible between the MacNairs him and the children.

The sentries walked up and down, their breath like smoke. Johnnie came up behind them, one after another, clamped a hand over each mouth and drove his dirk between their ribs. The guards stiffened and slumped. Johnnie dragged the corpses behind some scrub. He covered the tracks with a large clump of heather. Then fought the sour taste in his throat as he saddled Pegasus and loaded a pony with provisions. He took the other mounts too and returned for the children.

The night hid Johnnie's group and allowed him to walk them through the ring of sentries, who stayed near their fires and didn't look into the dark. After a few miles, Johnnie put the children on the horse and mounted behind them.

Johnnie guided the horse and ponies round rocks, gorse and down into the glen. Behind him a band of gold shone in the east. Dawn would break soon. He headed west over a rise of ground towards Braedrumie. The murder of the sentries wouldn't be forgotten and he hoped MacNair would seek them in the north.

Lorna Windham

CHAPTER Fifty

Morning light filtered through the Lorne's farmhouse window and golden shards lit up the spence. Kirsty opened the lid of her trinket box. Johnnie's brooch lay nestled inside. She put it to her hollow cheek and tried to conjure his presence by her side. Would she see him again?

'No point mooning over him. Sell the brooch, we'd have money for food then.' Her mother's hand moved as if to snatch it.

'No.' Kirsty flung the brooch in its box and slammed the lid. 'I'd rather die of hunger.' She positioned herself between Mother's skeletal frame and the box.

Mother sank on a stool and spoke between clenched teeth. 'You'll soon get your wish.' One thin arm hugged her tiny waist. 'We ate the last of the oats this morning.'

Kirsty stared at her. *God help us.* She crossed herself aware of how her clothes hung to her skinny frame.

'Most daughters look after their mothers, why are you so cruel? Accept Tolbain. We could be waited on hand and foot. Looked up to. Safe. Imagine what we'd eat and drink. Best of everything when you're on the winning side.'

'No.' Kirsty turned away.

Mother hissed in Kirsty's ear. 'The redcoats will come, don't think they won't. They know Braedrumie's a nest of Jacobite vipers, not that I believed in their Cause.' She sniffed. 'If only poor Hughie had stayed behind. Now that Mary's had another wean, the bairns will need a strict hand.'

'She deserves our help, no' disdain, Mother. She's a good, honest woman.'

'Hmph. So you say. At least she chose a good man. Wish you had as much sense. You cannot put off this decision much longer, Kirsty. Accept he's dead, that life with him would have been hiding, evading redcoats, always looking over your shoulder, starving. I could be dead in a few months. Don't you love your own mother and want the best for her in her old age?'

The Jacobite Affair

'Of course, but...'

'There's always a 'but.' Mother stamped out and then stamped back in again. 'Have you looked outside this morning?'

'No.' Kirsty peered out of the window.

'Notice anything? It's quiet. Tolbain's men have gone. He's changed his mind. We'll be murdered in our beds.'

Kirsty let her mother's words flow over her like a waterfall and thought of Johnnie dead, hunted, wounded or dying. *I'll keep faith.* The trinket box held her only hope and she clasped it to her breast.

Lorna Windham

CHAPTER Fifty-one

No sign of MacNair and his men. Good. Johnnie released the ponies hours ago in the hope this would confuse his pursuers whilst he'd followed a trail of burnt out crofts through several glens. Redcoats. He'd guarded Comrie and Neill from the bodies. 'Keep those plaids on your heads until I tell you to remove them,' he'd ordered.

Best to take the least-travelled mountain passes. Comrie sat nestled in Johnnie's lap with Neill behind. Johnnie's heels encouraged his weary horse upward and west.

'Thirsty,' said Comrie. Johnnie stopped at a beck, then persuaded the children to mount again. If the MacNairs picked up their tracks, Johnnie would die and he didn't like to think what would happen to Neill and Comrie.

The sun played hide and seek behind gloomy clouds most of the afternoon until a thunderstorm threatened to burst over the group. He lifted Comrie and then Neill to the ground and joined them to shelter under an overhang in the cliff face. Rain pounded the ground and rivulets streamed down crags until the sun burst out once more.

The group re-mounted. This time Neill held Comrie. Jewelled beads of rainwater dripped down jade rock surfaces as Johnnie and the children climbed ever upward, along a trail which wound back on itself. He pulled Pegasus to a halt on the summit.

Below, glen after glen and loch after loch stretched out below like a sage and sapphire plaid. He expanded his lungs and smelt fresh mountain air. Good to be alive. The only sound, the wind's keen. Above, the dark silhouette of an eagle as it hunted its prey. Gold gorse burst forth again in contrast to the bloody world he'd inhabited. Duncan. He closed his eyes, lifted his face to the sun and enjoyed its warmth on his skin. His eyelids flickered. He'd sensed something, a familiar prickle of tension lifted the hair on his neck and the dark hair on his arms. The MacNairs?

The Jacobite Affair

Tell-tale traces of smoke in the east alerted him, followed by movement on the glen floor below. A river of blood streamed west along a drover's road. Too far away to make out any details. Redcoats.

Johnnie stood upright in his stirrups and scanned the next glen. He made out an isolated farmhouse with pinprick workers in the fields amongst the cattle.

'Mr. Stewart, why have we stopped?' Neill tugged Johnnie's plaid.

'We need to rest and enjoy the view.'

'There's redcoats down there.' Neill pointed.

'Aye.' Johnnie weighed the situation and then said, 'Neill, do you think you could look after Comrie here, whilst I try to warn that farmhouse?'

Neill looked at his sister. 'She's asleep.'

Johnnie dismounted, helped Neill lay Comrie on some plaids and placed his saddle bags beside the boy. 'If I dinna return you're to keep walking west till you come to Braedrumie, beside Loch Linnhe.' He put his hands on the boy's shoulders. 'Find the laird. Tell him Johnnie sent you and he'll look after you. Will you do that, Neill?'

Neill set his jaw. 'I will, Mr. Stewart, but you'll come back, I know you will.'

Johnnie wished he'd Neill's confidence. What could one man do against an army? But this time he'd arrive before the redcoats.

CHAPTER Fifty-two
27th April, 1746

Kirsty opened the farmhouse door. The hinges rattled in the cold wind and dark bands of cloud gathered overhead. Tolbain stood there. She clasped her shawl round her. 'There's no point…' she began.

'Take a walk with me.'

She sighed. *A walk? It's food we need.*

'I'll come with her, Your Grace.' Mother's voice came from behind Kirsty. 'It's not fitting for an unmarried lassie to walk alone with any man, begging your pardon, Your Grace.'

'Alexander. You keep a close eye on her, Gilly. Good. Can't be too careful these days. My arm, Miss Lorne.'

What's he up to? Kirsty paused, then put her arm in his.

He made no allowance for the hill, Kirsty's shorter strides nor Mother's knees. The couple left the older woman several yards behind as the wind beat into their faces under a thunderous sky. Tolbain took Kirsty up to the ridge.

'Well?' Kirsty's stomach cramped and her chest heaved. *Thank God he's stopped.*

'My apologies for the withdrawal of my men at such short notice.'

We didn't get any notice.

'Needed elsewhere.'

'We'll manage, we did before they came.' Kirsty knew she sounded ungracious. He used his forefinger and thumb and lifted her chin. She wrenched it out of his grasp as Mother stopped, flung her head back and gulped in lungfuls of air.

'You don't appear to understand the dangers you face.' A nerve twitched in Tolbain's cheek. 'Perhaps I have protected you too well. It pains me to say it, but yesterday a redcoat patrol fired a village a few miles from here; they assaulted women, murdered and hanged men, carrying arms or not.'

'No.' Kirsty stepped back and out of his grasp as Mother's ribs heaved.

The Jacobite Affair

His eyes blazed. 'Don't take my word for it.' He snapped his fingers and a woman stepped out from behind the gorse. She rubbed sooty fingers over her amber eyes and dirt-streaked face. Her torn bodice revealed the gap between her full breasts and her hips swayed under her skirt. A purple shawl hung from her shoulders.

My pattern, my shawl. The one Tolbain took at the market.

Thick, dark curls tumbled from the haystack on the woman's head. 'Meet Meg. Tell her your story, lass.'

Meg tried a parody of a curtsey and lifted her torn skirts to reveal bare legs. 'It's as His Grace says. Redcoats attacked Glaercowrie yesterday mornin'. It were bloody terrible. They killed the men, raped the women… Everyone's gone. Nought left but ashes.'

Kirsty's hand went to her mouth. 'That's dreadful news.'

'Terrible news. God help us.' Mother gripped Kirsty's arm.

'Thought if I travelled west I'd get away from them.' Meg wiped her nose on her ragged sleeve. 'His Grace has been so kind to give me food and shelter.'

Tolbain waved her into silence. 'Make your way back to Toll House, my dear.'

Meg bobbed a curtsey and set off over the moor.

'You see.' Tolbain turned to Kirsty. 'So far, I have managed to protect you and your mother from all this, but I risk my position. If we were betrothed, well that would be different.'

'Please accept our thanks for all you've done,' snapped Kirsty. 'We know the dangers.'

He spread his arms wide. 'Do you, do you really? And your mother, what about her?'

'Yes. What about me? Listen to him, Kirsty, you'll never get a better offer and he'll keep us safe until you're handfasted.'

'Say yes to my proposal.' Tolbain brushed a stray strand of Kirsty's hair behind her ear.

She stepped back.

He set his jaw. 'Place yourself under my protection and all will be well. I promise you will live in comfort all your days. In fact, you will wonder why you delayed.' He softened his voice. 'My family acted somewhat unkindly towards your mother in the past. Surely she deserves the comfort and luxury she enjoyed as a child?' Tolbain took hold of Kirsty's hand with its broken fingernails. 'You only have to say yes and it will be hers.'

'I canna.' Kirsty pulled away, but he kept her hand in his. *Johnnie, please come home.*

'I understand, you don't want me to think you're interested in my wealth. I admire that, I do, but I see how it is here with you and your mother. My influence has stayed the redcoats' hands so far, but I cannot do this for much longer.'

'Please, I canna.' Kirsty struggled in his grasp.

'Look, once you're mine, I'll do my best to protect Braedrumie and those you love.' His voice hardened. 'If you're still thinking of bonny Johnnie Stewart, well, if he's not dead, he soon will be as a traitor to the Crown. If he's alive, I'll be forced to hunt him down and have him hanged - unless we're handfasted.'

Kirsty gasped. 'No.'

He released her. 'I'll be back for my answer. The Stewarts will be beggared, no life for a woman with noble blood in her veins. On the other hand if you consent... You'll never do without again. Think on it.' He turned and strode away.

'I willna, do you hear me?' she shouted at his broad back. Tears formed in the corner of Kirsty's eyes. She wiped them away with her fingers. *Johnnie, I'm being torn in two. You promised you'd come home. Where are you?*

Thunder rolled overhead.

'You've riled him, now.' Mother hissed in her ear. 'Bet that poor lassie, Meg, will sleep with a full stomach tonight, more than you can say for us.' She pointed her bony finger at Kirsty. 'And it's all your fault.'

The first drops of rain fell as Kirsty watched Mother, thin shoulders bent, plod back down the hill. She followed at a slower pace. *I can't stand much more of this.* Like an animal in a trap her mind searched for a way out. *If only Johnnie would come home.*

CHAPTER Fifty-three

It took Johnnie longer than he thought to reach the glen as the sun blazed down. He peered at the far horizon. The redcoats would soon appear on the eastern skyline.

Johnnie worked his way down toward the farmhouse as he used the natural contours of the uneven ground to camouflage his movements. Two men worked with the cattle on the far, upper slopes and one, further down the hill, dug a ditch. A woman sat on the farmhouse doorstep, bowl on lap, hens at her feet whilst a young girl, at the back of the house, hung wet plaids over the heather to dry.

He scanned the rugged hills opposite. Nothing. He clambered down faster and prayed the redcoats would just take the cattle. Damn. The sun glinted off metal on top of the escarpment. It bristled with bayonets. He had to act. If he kept the farmhouse between him, the girl and the redcoats, he could sprint the last 100 yards. His breath came in short spurts as he skirted the thick, yellow gorse and grabbed a plaid from the heather. His hand clamped over the girl's mouth. She wriggled and kicked as he wrapped her beneath the wet wool and thrust her between the gorse and a stone wall.

He crawled into the prickly tunnel and pinned her to the wet earth. 'I'm a friend. It's redcoats. You're in danger.'

She beat at him with her fists.

'Be still. Promise me you willna scream and I'll take my hand away.'

She slipped her teeth around his thumb and bit down. He grunted, but his grip on her mouth tightened. She squirmed and his breath hissed in her ear, 'There's been a battle at Drumossie Moor. Charlie lost. Redcoats are killing everyone and burning everything. They're on the brow of yon hill. If you value your life, dinna' make a sound. Yes?'

She stilled, then jerked her head up and down like a puppet.

He pulled the plaid from her head to reveal a flushed face with damp wisps of fair hair over a high forehead. Her eyes darted black flecks of rage at him and her breasts rose at every

The Jacobite Affair

breath as if she fought down the fear which threatened to choke her. His wild hair, scratches from the cruel thorns and straggly beard must make him appear outlandish. He let her go.

She scrambled on all fours to the wall, turned and with her back against the stone, knelt in front of him. Her mouth moved, but no words came. She stared wide-eyed at him and tried again. Her hand went to her throat.

Has fear taken her speech?

The first musket shot came from the fields where the cattle grazed. She stared at him as if she begged an answer. He grabbed her and held her tight as a bow string. A second and third shot came to them. Her body jerked each time.

A woman's voice shrieked, 'No, oh no! Run, Alais, save yourself.' Another shot. The girl jerked again. Then silence.

After a time, he held her in a gentler grasp. She rested her head on his shoulder. Time meant nothing. He imagined her brain as it struggled to fathom it out: Four shots? Four shots. Unreality. Shock. Four shots, four lives, four deaths. My family? Not my family? Not all of them?

She lifted her eyes to his as they questioned what had happened. He shook his head as comprehension dawned and her mouth opened in a soundless shriek until he covered it with his hand again. She'd lost everyone she'd loved.

He held her for what seemed a lifetime. She tried to tear free. He knew she'd think one might still be alive and that she had to do something. He wouldn't let her go. He shook his head and held her tighter until the hens squawked, men cursed and the air rang with foreign voices and cruel laughter.

'Sergeant, take Hawkenshaw and search round the back.'

'Sir.'

Johnnie and the girl sat as if paralysed. Two pairs of boots rounded the farmhouse and with them came the pungent smell of tobacco. Jonnie peered through a tangle of thorns. He made out a baby-faced private who picked over the washing with his bayonet whilst a barrel-chested sergeant fingered wet plaids. His eyes searched the high grass.

'Alais, aint that what the old woman said?' Baby-Face smirked.

The sergeant studied the gorse, the wall and the moor beyond. A spume of brown liquid flew out of his mouth and landed with a splat on the earth. 'We'll search the gorse. Start either end and meet in the middle.' He raised his voice. 'Alais.'

'Alais,' yelled Baby-Face.

Thunk. Thunk. Thunk. Bayonets stabbed the earth and moved towards Johnnie until four grubby gaiters stood in front of the entwined thorny branches which concealed him and the girl. Johnnie tensed and the girl shrank against him. Thunk. Missed. Thunk. A 24 inch blade sliced down into the earth close to his shoulder. Johnnie sucked in a breath until Baby-Face jerked the steel out and up in a silver flash of light and moved on.

Johnnie's muscles relaxed, but the girl quivered.

''Ere 'awkinshaw and Edwards. Look out,' yelled a voice. A lit torch landed on the apex of the farmhouse's thatched roof. With a whoosh and a roar, flames flickered, flared and took hold. Men's voices roared.

The sergeant, brandished his musket in the air and howled his triumph. The private followed suit.

The girl buried her head in Johnnie's chest. He watched the soldiers' backs, one thin and the other burly as they jogged one behind the other, turned at the corner of the farmhouse and disappeared.

He listened to the voices and the tramp and mournful low of cattle until they faded into the distance. The fire crackled and turned tangerine then cinnabar as the roof timbers burnt and blackened.

The girl shook in Johnnie's arms as bright embers floated in the air. He waited until the last shouted order died away before he released her.

She scrambled to her knees and pushed past him as to escape their prison of thorns. He followed and stretched his cramped limbs before going after her.

The Jacobite Affair

The pungent stink of burnt wood and thatch surrounded them. Grey smoke swirled and indigo flames whooshed as the roof timbers crashed to the ground in a shower of sparks. An overturned bowl lay near the doorstep next to the body of the old woman. She'd a splash of crimson on her breast and her outstretched hand still held a bunch of kale. Damn. When would the killing stop?

He scanned the farmyard for the girl. Watched her race up the far slope, go from one body to another, kneel and then go on to the next. At the last her body sagged and then she struggled down the field towards him.

She mouthed the word, 'Mother.' Her legs collapsed under her as she sank beside the old woman's body as if in prayer. Then she gathered her up and rocked her. The girl's lips moved, but no sound came.

'I'll get the plaids and fetch the others so we can bury them together.' He tasted bile in his throat. Duncan.

She made no sign she'd heard, just rocked.

He laid the plaids by her and carried each body until they lay in a row at the girl's feet. 'Your father and brothers?'

She nodded.

He found a discarded leather bucket, filled it with water from the well and knelt beside her. 'Expect you'd like to wash them.' He tore a plaid into strips, thrust a piece of the coarse material into her hand and cleaned the blood and dirt from the old man's face and hands.

Silent tears streamed down her cheeks as she dipped the cloth into the water and cleansed her mother's palms.

'When you finish that, wrap the plaids round them.' He left her and searched the burnt timbers, found a half-charred shovel and walked a short distance away. Off came his jacket and he unrolled his shirt sleeves. Damn the redcoats, there'd been no need for this. He stuck the blade it into the ground and cut the first sod. The sun beat down on him and unused muscles ached as he laid the bodies to rest.

'What were their names?' Beads of sweat ran down his forehead and he wiped them away with his arm.

Lorna Windham

She worked her lips, moved her tongue, but no matter how hard she tried, no sound came. Tears formed and she swept them away with both hands.

'Their names?' he tried again in a softer voice.

She knelt in the dirt and wrote with her forefinger: MY FATHER CALUM MURRAY, MOTHER INA, BROTHERS, GEORGE AND WILLIAM. YOU TALK AS IF THEY'RE IN THE PAST, BUT THEY'RE STILL IN MY PRESENT.

He stared at the words and then her. Perhaps with time she'd regain her voice. He coughed and began, 'The Lord is my light and my salvation; whom should I fear?'

He finished the psalm, and dropped the first clods of earth on the bodies. The girl stood as if made of stone, her arms wrapped round herself. He imagined with each shovelful, pieces of her heart splintered and fell into that grave. They had for him when Duncan died.

'I'm Johnnie, Johnnie Stewart.'

She didn't look at him, but knelt in the earth and wrote with her forefinger: I WANT MY PARENTS AND BROTHERS. I NEED THEM.

'They've gone, lassie,' he said. 'I ken you know that. Come sit over here and share some food with me.' Not much, a handful of berries and burnt kale from her home. She didn't eat, but used her finger again in the dust and scrawled ALAIS MURRAY.

'Alais. 'A bonny name. I ken you canna speak for the moment. Dinna worry about it. This is a fine feast.' He wolfed down his portion. 'Please eat.'

She shook her head.

He put her portion in his saddlebags. 'For the bairns.'

Her brow creased.

'They're no' mine, they're orphans.' He pointed at a mountain with a shark-fin peak. 'Over there. Comrie and Neill.'

He offered her water in a cracked horn cup he'd found amongst the embers.

The Jacobite Affair

She went to the ashes of the croft and touched the broken remnants of a spinning wheel buried under the fallen roof beams.

'I have to go. You understand?'

She nodded.

'I must get to the bairns before dark and I've family in Braedrumie, they'll be worried. I must get back.'

She nodded again.

He turned and walked away as she knelt beside the mounds of earth. She wasn't kin, had nothing to do with him. He'd done all he could.

***

Damn his conscience. He returned as dark gathered and called out, 'It's Johnnie Stewart. I'm back with the bairns. You're no' safe here. I can offer you my protection, but you must leave this place.'

She fought him, but he threw her on his horse like a bale of wool behind the bairns. He took the reins and tramped westward into the last rays of the sun.

Lorna Windham

CHAPTER Fifty-four

Kirsty, bleary-eyed, hadn't slept well. There'd been a band of stationary riders on the ridge above the farm the previous afternoon and in the early hours of the night men's curses had woken the two women.

Torch flames danced through cracks in the kitchen shutters. Fists pounded on the door. Kirsty leapt out of bed and Mother shrieked and hid her head under her covers.

A guttural voice demanded, 'Open up.'

'Oh, God help us.' Mother crept to a dark corner and shrank down.

What to do? Father's musket above the fireplace. Kirsty took it and comforted by its weight, scrambled in the dresser drawer for paper cartridges.

'We ken you're in there,' yelled a surly voice.

A memory of Father as he poached flashed into her head. She cocked the firelock, tore off the end of the cartridge, primed and then loaded the weapon.

Knocks sounded on shutters.

She yelled, 'Get off our land or I'll fire.'

Howls of drunken laughter greeted this.

She stuck the musket barrel through a knot hole in the scullery shutter and kept the butt snug against her right shoulder. 'I mean it.'

Jeers.

A click. The musket mis-fired.

More jeers.

She cocked and reloaded the weapon again. A crack and puffs of smoke. Splinters of glass. A howl. Curses. The sound of hooves as they disappeared into the distance. Silence.

Kirsty half-carried Mother to a chair by the fire and rubbed her cold hands. 'Whisky?' Mother nodded.

Why had the men come? If only Johnnie was here.

Mother downed the glass in one swallow. Her back straightened and she lit a cruisie lamp. The two women

The Jacobite Affair

dressed and sat at the table until first light and they heard the sound of hooves outside. Mother's hand gripped Kirsty's.

Have the men returned? Kirsty put a nervous eye to the hole in the shutter. The sun cast a weak gleam as mist curled over the fields and encircled the lower slopes of the mountains to the south. 'It's Tolbain.'

Mother, locked her fingers as if in prayer. She wrapped a shawl round herself and cautioned Kirsty to stay back, whilst she opened the door. 'Thank God, you've come, cousin. A band of rogues came last night, frightened us out of our wits. We need your help.'

Her mother's words hung in the air for a few seconds above the jangle of reins and Tolbain's horse which champed at its bit. The cold air found Kirsty as she peered through the wooden slats which divided the kitchen from the byre.

'I warned you of lawless men. I've come for my answer.'

A shiver ran down Kirsty's spine and she found warmth in a plaid.

'But we're in danger, cousin.' Mother pleaded.

'My answer.'

'She needs time.'

'I've been very patient.' Tolbain sounded tetchy. His horse snorted in the early morning air. 'Persuade Kirsty that this handfasting is to her advantage, or by God, I'll have no more to do with her or you and Stewart's life is forfeit. Understand?'

No. Oh no. Kirsty's fingers, the knuckles white, gripped the laths.

'She's a good girl, she'll do as she's told.'

'She's got a day.' Tolbain raised his voice. 'One day, that's all.'

The roof and walls above and around Kirsty closed in. She'd visions of being locked in a barred cage with a huge bear. *Why hasn't Johnnie returned?*

The farmhouse door closed with a bang. Goosebumps formed on Kirsty's arms and she moved to the warmth of the kitchen fire.

'You heard him?' said Mother.

Lorna Windham

'Aye.' Kirsty cried out as Mother grabbed her wrist.

'He'll lose interest, find someone else who's wealthy. Forget Stewart, he's dead.'

'No. Dinna say that.' Kirsty wrested her wrist from Mother's grasp and put her hands over her ears.

Mother screamed at her. 'He's dead I say. Can you no' see Tolbain's our only way out? Look at you, getting scraggier by the day. Your looks won't last without food and who do you think will be interested in you then?' Mother's cruel words followed her into their parlour. 'You have to be handfasted to him. You must see that?'

Kirsty kicked a stool. It overturned with a crash onto the flagstones.

'Have you no sense or are you useless like your father?'

Kirsty turned, claws ready to rake Mother's face.

'So you'd attack your poor, old mother?'

Kirsty hung her head. 'I'm sorry, I'm so weary I don't know what I'm doing with Tolbain's threats and your voice in my head all the time. Like buzzing wasps.'

Mother put her mouth to her daughter's ear and softened her tone. 'I dinna want you to make the same mistake and marry for love. For God's sake, daughter, use your head. Dinna lose our future for the sake of a dead man.'

Kirsty brushed past her. 'I need to think.'

'Don't go out on your own. Those men could be skulking around.'

Kirsty ignored her. She needed fresh air. She followed the burn and rambled upstream through ferns and round bracken as the mist thinned and the liquid sun warmed the land. The earth smelt of peaty soil and new growth,

Will I end up an old maid who waits for a man who'll never return? I'd have no life, no bairns and live with Mother in poverty until I die. I want more than that. Images of Aunt Munro's house, servants, feather beds and food invaded her mind.

She stood on top of Ben Muraig, looked out to the hazy peaks and tried to send her thoughts over the wild moors and

The Jacobite Affair

lochs. *I've waited and waited for you, Johnnie. I love you so much. God forgive me for what I'm about to do.*

Lorna Windham

CHAPTER Fifty-five

Midnight black. Johnnie navigated by the stars and an innate awareness of the direction. Home. 'No' far now,' he said to his weary companions. He thought of Father, his grief for Duncan and how he'd hope his other sons would return.

Johnnie walked whilst he led Pegasus with its three riders along secret ways in the hills and hidden paths in the woods to Braedrumie House. The night covered them like a black shroud as the horse snorted and neighed. Had he scented sweet hay and a warm bed?

Ahead, a light moved and flickered through the trees. A latch rattled. The light went out. Redcoats? Johnnie stopped and signalled Alais. He dismounted, crawled forward and watched from behind a broken bough. The horse neighed again. Damn.

The stable door creaked opened. Murdo held a storm lantern, its weak shards of yellow light highlighted the new lines in his face and spluttered in the wind, 'Who's there?' he hissed and peered into the gloom.

Johnnie stepped out of the shelter of the trees. 'Me. You old rascal.'

'Johnnie man, is it really you?' Murdo crossed the cobbles and grasped Johnnie's hand as if afraid to let it go. 'Good to see you.' He blew out the light and the darkness closed in. 'Canna be too careful.'

'Aye.' All of Johnnie's body ached for rest and sleep. He'd travelled more miles than needed to evade redcoat patrols and lose the MacNairs. If they ever found him, he'd be a marked man. It would be a blood feud.

'My father and Kirsty?'

'Grievin'. Kirsty's back home.'

'So my poor aunt told me.'

Murdo raised his brow.

'The redcoats took her and imprisoned me. Nought I could do. I escaped.' He didn't mention Rob, the memory too bitter. 'Is Kirsty well?'

The Jacobite Affair

'Aye. Though their cattle were thieved, bastards picked them out. Nothin' I could do. And a couple of Tolbain's men are skulking round the farmhouse. Oh, and their cow died.'

'Damn, she never said.'

Johnnie jerked and Murdo turned at the clatter of hooves. Alais, sat astride Pegasus. Neill rested his head on her back. She held Comrie asleep in her arms.

Who's this you've brought with you? A woman and bairns?' Murdo motioned with his thumb.

'Aye. They've no one, I couldna leave them. This is Alais Murray, the bairns Comrie and Neill Douglas.'

Alais sagged in the saddle and nodded her head.

'Evenin'. A family.' Murdo stroked his beard then lowered his voice. 'Well, well. Your Kirsty will have somethin' to say.'

'They're no' my family,' Johnnie snapped. 'Sorry- I'm weary. I've offered them my protection and that's all. Is Euan back?'

'No' yet. Dougie and Morag have gone to Inverness to search for him.'

'Bloody hell. R.. Someone told me... Inverness crawls with redcoats. I just got out myself.' Guilt swept over him. He should have searched for Euan.

'Never seen such a determined woman as that Morag. Been gone a few days. Carts should be back soon,' said Murdo.

Johnnie gave him a blank look.

'They've taken provisions for the army to Inverness. Dougie's idea.'

'Bloody hell.' Johnnie lowered his voice. 'Murdo, the bairns are exhausted and we might have MacNairs on our tail.'

'MacNairs? Is Cumberland's army no' enough for you?'

Johnnie glared at him. 'It's a long story.'

'You're no' safe here. And after the news about Duncan... your father's... changed.' Murdo tugged his beard.

'I've a word or two to say to him about Duncan.'

'Poor wee laddie. I promised Dougie I'd look out for your father, but he'll no' accept any help. And there's regular redcoat patrols hunting down those of us who were at Culloden. That devil Tolbain gave them names.'

An owl hooted. Johnnie crouched and his hand went to his sword as Murdo's eyes searched the darkness.

'Best go to the den,' hissed Murdo.

'Take Alais and the bairns. I must see Father and Kirsty.' Johnnie swayed.

Murdo's arm held him up. 'You're bone weary, man. Sleep and wait till mornin'. I'll lead you. Wait a minute and I'll get what you need. Hold on to that saddle.'

Murdo returned a few minutes later with plaids and leather bags stuffed with provisions. 'Should keep you goin'. Here.' Murdo threw some cloths at Johnnie. 'We'll muffle the ponies' hooves.' Johnnie, too tired to resist, let Murdo lead his party through the woods and back into the hills. Alais made no sign of complaint, she held Comrie tighter and Neill's head lolled.

Murdo led them to the den a few miles away, with its cave, pool and waterfall roar close by.

Alais settled the children to sleep in the back of the cave under an assortment of plaids. Comrie didn't stir even when Alais kissed the girl's forehead.

Neill gripped Johnnie's hand. 'Tell me you'll stay with us, Mr. Stewart and we'll be safe.' His mouth relaxed into a yawn.

What will Kirsty think? 'I'm here, go to sleep laddie. You're safe.' Just like Duncan, poor bloody, Duncan. 'We've been remiss. Say your prayers laddie.'

'Must I?' Neill looked at Johnnie's face, knelt and put his palms together. 'Our Father which art in Heaven...' Neill's voice became thick and slow, his head drooped as he finished. He lay down and Johnnie covered him with a plaid. Neill's eyelids, fluttered then closed.

The sound of light footsteps caused Johnnie to twist round and see Alais head out of the cave towards Pegasus.

He caught up with her. 'Sleep,' he said. 'I'll see to him.'

She patted her breast with the fingertips of one hand and carried on.

The Jacobite Affair

Johnnie turned to find Murdo with a grin, beside him. 'Your woman doesna say much, Johnnie.'

'She's no' my woman,' Johnnie muttered. 'And she's just lost her family, she canna speak.'

Murdo hissed in a breath. 'I'm sorry to hear it. I'd best go back to the house.'

Johnnie watched him mount and leave. If he hadn't been so tired, he'd have said more about it. He joined Alais and rubbed down Pegasus. She fed the horse grain whilst he fetched water from the pool.

Later, Johnnie ensured his bed lay well away from Alais. She'd snuggled up to the children and from the curve of her lips enjoyed their warmth. His bed seemed particularly hard and cold. Johnnie gave a wry grin as the wind moaned around the cave entrance. At least home lay close. In the morning he'd visit his father and see Kirsty. He closed his eyes, his thoughts all of her.

Lorna Windham

CHAPTER Fifty-six

Johnnie woke before the others and braved the pool and the waterfall's icy water. He shivered. It had never seemed so cold. He dried himself with a plaid and dressed. Thank God, Murdo had thought of a clean shirt and hose. A tremor of impatience ran through Johnnie. It would be madness to visit his father or Kirsty during daylight.

He helped Alais make the cave more comfortable with plaids and rocks for a table and seats. She fetched buckets of water and he found wood. He watched the sun climb with impatience. At its zenith, he taught Neill to skim stones across the pool and encouraged Comrie to paddle.

The sun sank. Comrie, her woes forgotten for the moment, screamed as Neill splashed her.

'Time... to... come... out,' signed Alais. She beckoned with her fingers.

'Oh,' said Comrie.

Neill paddled towards where Johnnie sat beside Alais.

Johnnie looked at her. 'I must see my father. Will you come with me and bring the bairns? He's the laird, you ken and will want to meet you.'

Alais nodded and helped the children dress themselves as Comrie chatted away. 'It's been the bestest day, hasn't it, Neill? Can we play in the pool again?'

Johnnie tried to clear his head. How could he tell Father about Duncan or Rob's betrayal? Everything in Johnnie's being cried out to see Kirsty, but his duty as a loyal son came first.

A moonless night meant it took longer than usual to reach Braedrumie House, the dark full of rustles, flutters and screeches. Johnnie halted, listened and carried on. The group reached the walls of the house when a man's drunken song came from the bowels of the earth and broke the silence. Damn. Father. Johnnie found him in one of the cellars, propped against a barrel of whisky and wrapped in the clan's

The Jacobite Affair

bloody saltire. Duncan. Johnnie grimaced as wave of stale sweat and alcohol assailed him.

'So you're back?' Father growled.

'Aye. And Duncan's dead because of you.' Johnnie used two hands, grabbed his father's collar and snarled. 'We had a bargain.'

'A bargain?' His father shook his head. 'I canna remember.'

Johnnie closed his eyes and fought the tortured images in his head. He took a long breath and lowered his voice. 'You should have kept him close.' He pressed his forehead to his father's. 'Why didn't you keep him close?'

'I tried, but he wanted to be with you. You know that. My poor, wee Duncan.' A tear rolled down his Father's ruddy cheek. Johnnie stepped back. He's lost a son and me a brother. We share the same blood, feel the same agony. He's my father and he needs me.

'Look at the state of you.' Johnnie put an arm under the old man's shoulder, hauled him to his feet and dusted him down. 'You've visitors, Father, you need to make yourself presentable.' Johnnie reached for the saltire but froze when his father growled, 'Dinna, 'tis all I've left of him.'

His words acted like a dirk in Johnnie's chest. Duncan. Johnnie forced the memory back in its box. He half-carried his father up the cellar steps and led him to the small group of figures who stood and waited in the study. Johnnie breathed in a musty smell and saw desolation. Empty bottles stood on the laird's desk, lay scattered on the floor and decorated the mantelpiece.

Alais put her arms round Comrie who snuggled into her. Neill stared open-mouthed at the laird who sank into a chair.

Johnnie hissed to Alais, 'Please excuse him, we've lost my youngest brother and another's missing.' He turned to Father. 'Sir, I'd like to introduce Alais Murray. The bairns... Neill and Comrie Douglas.'

Alais curtsied and helped Comrie do the same. Neill attempted an inelegant bow. Johnnie spoke in his father's ear,

'Redcoats killed Alais' family. The bairns are orphans. The father died at Culloden. I couldna think of anywhere else to bring them.'

'You're a kind lad, always had a good heart. Damn the redcoats.' Father stared at Alais. 'Doesn't say much, does she?'

Alais pressed her lips together and shifted her feet.

'She hasn't spoken since it happened, but she can hear you and has her wits about her.'

'You're at the den, I hear?'

'Aye. You'll ensure we've regular provisions?'

'Of course, do you need to ask? So, you've a price on your heid.' His father lifted a whisky bottle in salute and drank from it.

'Aye.'

'They told me Duncan died... is it true?'

'Aye.' The saltire, he must know. Johnnie wet his lips. 'I... I was with him... at the end.'

His father struggled to his feet and placed his hand on Johnnie's shoulder. 'That's some comfort, Johnnie. He was with his brother who loved him.'

'Aye.' Johnnie couldn't meet his eyes, couldn't tell him that Duncan's death gnawed like a rat at his breast day and night and wouldn't let him sleep. Johnnie craved a priest.

'And Euan?'

'R.. someone told me Euan's wounded in Inverness, but he's no' a prisoner. You'll know Dougie and Morag have gone to seek him.'

'Aye. Damned woman, she'll just get in the way. Father looked Alais up and down. 'Join me in a wee dram, Johnnie?'

'Better not. I'd rather have a clear head. How's Kirsty and her mother?'

Alais' head jerked up. She looked at Johnnie, a question in her eyes.

'Alais? Something wrong?'

She shook her head and stroked Comrie's hair.

The Jacobite Affair

The laird stared at Alais and then Johnnie. 'Well. The lassie's been across once or twice to see me. Thinner.'

'Right,' said Johnnie. 'I'm off to see her.'

'Be careful. There's patrols about,' said Father.

'Will you ask Murdo to take Alais and the bairns back to the den?'

'I will,' said Father.

'I'm away then.'

The laird clutched Johnnie's arm. 'War changes people. Dinna forget that, Johnnie. War changes people.' He released Johnnie's arm and poured himself more whisky.

What the hell did his father mean by that? Johnnie stepped outside. The sky had cleared and become star-spangled. The moon a pale orb. His one thought: Kirsty. He raced across the meadow, checked the road, sped across it and mistimed his jump across the burn. He ignored the icy water which streamed into his shoes and over his hose. It had been too long since he'd seen her.

Kirsty's farm seemed little different, though he noted a broken fence post and empty fields. He hunkered down behind a string of heather. No sign of redcoats or Tolbain's men. He waited. Silence, except for the scuttle of field mice in the grass.

He crept up to the croft door and knocked. Would she be the same, feel the same about him? He sensed movement in the croft and heard the soft pad of footsteps coming towards the door and saw a light shine under it.

'Who is it? State your business or be off. My musket's loaded.' Kirsty's voice sounded gruff and muffled behind the oak door.

He drew his lips into a grin. 'It's Johnnie.'

The bolts clanked and the door opened. Kirsty had placed the cruisie lamp on the floor. Her night-gowned figure, shawl and golden hair appeared ethereal as he stared down the long barrel of her musket.

'Darling, it's me, Johnnie.'

She stood transfixed, her eyes wide and mouth open.

He swept his hand over his hair. His nose may have a little more character about it, but the rest of him hadn't changed. For months he'd thought only of her. Well, apart from the debacle with the drabs in Edinburgh. He dismissed the thought. That had been nought, but the whore's book had given him knowledge. Carnal, but knowledge all the same and Kirsty looked like an angel from some half-forgotten dream. He lowered her musket with his hand.

She bit her lip and looked at the ground. 'Dougie told us about Duncan. I'm so sorry.'

Duncan.

'And that Euan's missing. You should ken Mother hasna taken Uncle Hughie's death well.'

'What?' I've a price on my head. Risked my life to get home and all she can say is, *Mother hasna taken Uncle Hughie's death well.* She looks so damned beautiful in the lamplight and untouched by war. He swallowed. 'I'm sorry for her grief.' He reached out to play with a strand of Kirsty's hair. So soft. 'Darling, I got back late last night, couldna wait to see you. Took me a bit longer because of Alais and the bairns.'

She started and moved a step back. Her tresses fell out of his fingers. 'Alais? You've returned with a woman?' Her nose wrinkled and she looked at him as if he'd just crawled out of a midden. Her voice hardened. 'Perhaps it's for the best. Tolbain's asked for my hand.'

Johnnie's spine snapped upright. 'Tolbain? That thieving murderer.' His brain cleared. 'But you're my lassie. You've no' accepted? Alais is…'

'Alais is it?' she rolled her eyes. 'While you were with your Alais, we've been in danger.'

'Her name's Alais Murray and she's no' mine.'

'Tolbain sent men to protect us for a time. The night they left, raiders came. Mother was terrified. I think I wounded one. Our farm could have been burned or worse. We could have lost everything and you weren't here.'

'Why do you accept Tolbain's offer or speak well of him? He's one of the reasons we lost.'

The Jacobite Affair

A blush flooded across her face. 'He's... a distant relation.'

'So he is and a bloody Whig. Why set a guard and...? He wants you or the land or both.'

'You dinna understand, he's been kind to us.' Her eyes flashed at him as if he'd hit a raw nerve.

'Did he get what he wanted in return?' Johnnie couldn't stop the words. He heard her soft intake of breath.

She put the door between her and him. Her eyes flicked to either side of him as if she needed to escape. 'Uncle Hughie meant so much to us.'

Johnnie pulled himself together. 'Let me in so I can tell you how it was with Hughie?' He made to move, but to his surprise the door didn't budge an inch.

'You said you'd look after him.' Kirsty's voice sounded brittle and harsh.

'And I did. I tried to show him, kept him behind me in the battle. He wasna meant for war. Be comforted, he died for a cause he believed in.'

'And you returned.'

'I was damned lucky. What's wrong with you? Would you prefer I died beside Hughie? You keep me from your house as if I'm not wanted here. We're betrothed. I thought you'd be pleased to see I'd returned unscathed.'

'Pleased? Poor Uncle Hughie's dead.' Kirsty spat the words at him. 'Mother loved him. Now he's lying un-mourned in a lonely grave. It's broken her heart. I hate your stupid Cause and... I hate you.'

'Kirsty, you canna' mean it. It wasna my Cause. You're upset by Hughie's death. I understand it's a terrible shock. Let me...' He touched her hand.

'Dinna.' She moved out of reach. 'Go away.'

'What?'

She drew herself up. 'I canna bear the sight of you.'

'You dinna mean it.'

'Who is it?' Mother's voice came from behind the door.

'Mother...' Kirsty released her grip and the door swung back wide on its hinges.

Lorna Windham

A weathered sporran appeared on the step.

'Mother, it's only Mr. Stewart.'

Only. Johnnie bit down on his temper.

Mother's wrinkled hand went to her throat, whilst her voice rose to a shriek, 'Not... not you. They say poor Hughie's dead, but I dinna believe them. Tell me he's coming home,' she pleaded.

'I canna.' Johnnie stood nonplussed. 'He's dead.'

'No.' she shrieked. 'It's no true.'

Kirsty looked at him as if to say, *Now look what you've done.*

Mother beat at him with her hands.

He held her arms in a tight grip.'He died bravely in battle. Please be thankful for that.'

She stared out of the corners of her eyes. 'But you've returned.' She sounded calm.

'Aye.' Johnnie let her go.

'No wounds. Not dead. Not dead like poor Hughie who helped us in a time of need? Why aren't you dead?' She clawed at his face.

He grappled with her again. 'I see the way of it. We all lost someone.' He released Kirsty's mother into her daughter's care 'I'll leave you both to your grief and me to mine. I'll wish you good day. I'll return when you're more… yourselves. Your servant, ladies.' He imagined their white faces as the women watched him walk down the rutted track.

Then he heard Kirsty's voice, 'Wait.' She ran to him and shoved something hard and metallic into his palm.

Damnation. The brooch. He clasped his fingers round it and strode away from her.

She aimed words like musket balls at his back. 'Dinna come here again, Johnnie Stewart. You're no' wanted. I'm going to be handfasted to the Duke of Tolbain. At least he's on the winning side.'

He didn't give her the satisfaction of seeing him flinch at her barbed words. Aunt Munro was right Kirsty was, *a self-serving little madam.* He marched off down the hill with a

The Jacobite Affair

black-cloud face and wished Kirsty and her Mother would burn in Hell.

By the time he reached the den he realised Sophocles wasn't right when he said, *One word frees us of all the weight and pain. That word is love.* Johnnie loved her still.

***

Kirsty's mother trudged back to her truckle bed whilst Kirsty watched Johnnie until the darkness enveloped him. His broken nose had added a touch of devilment to his features. She closed the door and rested her wet cheek against the rough wood. *He'll be safe now. Safe. I'll be handfasted to Tolbain and Johnnie will be safe.*

God, the look of anguish in his eyes. Didn't think I could say such painful things to him and yet love him so. I wanted his arms around me, his lips crushed to mine and his body next to me. How could I explain Mother's debt and this handfasting? And Tolbain's threat to kill him tore me apart. So, Johnnie will hate me now and this torment will stay with me forever. Kirsty wiped her eyes with her sleeve as she entered the kitchen.

'You've done a wise thing, daughter, spurning Stewart.' Mother rocked in a chair by the fire. 'Tolbain answered our prayers. We'll live in comfort for the rest of our lives and I'll regain my place in society. Stewart could never offer this, not now.'

Realisation came like a thunderbolt. 'My God, you planned this all along. I was security for the loan. You sold me to him. You're as bad as Father. How could you, to your own daughter?'

'You'll see, it's for the best.'

Tears coursed down Kirsty's cheeks. *Tolbain and Mother. I've made a pact with two devils and now I've to live with the consequences.*

Lorna Windham

CHAPTER Fifty-seven

Night covered Johnnie like a black cloak. He spat out the bitter taste in his mouth. Head down and round-shouldered, he trudged to Braedrumie as a cool breeze ploughed silver waves across Loch Linnhe. How could Kirsty say such things to him? He turned her brooch over and over in his hand. They loved each other and that love had kept him alive throughout the campaign. What had happened to make her change and turn to Tolbain of all people? He shook his head.

He paused on the rise above Braedrumie and took in the scene below him. When he'd left in August 1745, the village bustled with activity. Tonight, only the odd glimmer appeared from cracks in shutters and round doors. Somewhere a child cried and smoke curled from rooves.

He arrived at Dougie's croft and knocked once.

'Who is it?' asked Isabel.

'A man who's been away too long,' he hissed.

Metal clinked, the door opened and a shard of light appeared. Isabel flung herself at him and whispered in his ear, 'It's good to see you, Johnnie, I prayed for you all. 'Tis a pity Dougie's… away. Did you ken Morag's with him?'

'Aye.' Johnnie still smarted from the Lorne's reception and enjoyed Isabel's warmth. His eyes searched the dark around him. 'I pray to God, they find … a certain someone.'

Her brow creased. 'Aye and I'm so sorry about Duncan. Come away in, there might be patrols.'

Duncan. His name, like a dirk, twisted in a wound. His jaw tightened. 'Thank you, but I've friends to see. I'll be careful.'

She nodded. 'You're a good lad.'

She's more lines round her eyes he thought. 'How are you?' he asked. He knew the answer. Hungry. He'd taken in her slighter frame.

Her hand brushed a grey strand of hair back in place. 'Well. All the better for seeing you. You've seen the laird and Kirsty I suppose?'

The Jacobite Affair

Kirsty. He bit back an angry retort. 'Aye, the laird's… taken Duncan's… you ken… hard.'

'The village is no' the same without our men.' Isabel looked at the ground.

'How's Mary McBean?' he asked.

'Recovering from the shock of her man's death **and** she's another mouth to feed. Kirsty's visited, but no' her mother. Odd, the old besom was fond of Hughie, you'd think she'd offer some help. But no. Nought as queer as folk.'

'I'll call on Mary, see if I can do anything.'

'She'll appreciate that, Johnnie.' She peered into the gloom. 'God bless you and watch out for redcoats.'

'God bless you, Isabel. I'm sure Dougie will be back soon.'

Isabel closed the door and he heard the click of her key.

Mary McBean's bairns' wails filled his ears long before he reached the croft. His knuckles rapped once on the door.

'Who is it at this time of night?' she asked, her voice soft and low through the wooden door.

'A friend.'

The door opened a tad. She held the stub of a candle in one hand and jiggled her red-faced baby in the crook of the other arm. 'Have you food to spare, Mr. Stewart? I wouldna ask for myself but, it's the bairns.' Cries sounded louder behind her and the baby opened its mouth and screamed.

'I'll ask Murdo to come with something tonight. I'm sorry about Hughie, we did our best to keep him safe, Mary.'

'Ay, I ken you did.' Mary rocked the baby to no avail. 'He was a good man, but no' meant for soldiering. You'll no' forget the food.'

'I willna. Consider it done, I've just to call on Granny Mac.'

'I was sorry to hear about Duncan.'

Duncan. Another twist of the blade.

'And I pray Euan comes home.' Mary gave him a slight smile and started to close her door.

'Lock your door, Mary. You canna be too careful in times like this.'

Lorna Windham

He didn't leave until the key clattered in the lock.

He tapped several times on Granny Mac's door. Several bolts and locks later she stood in front of him, dressed in her nightdress and a shawl. Her hair looked wild as she wielded a besom above her head. 'Who are you, you rascal, to bray on my door in the middle of the night?'

Johnnie took the besom off her and pecked her wizened cheek. 'Johnnie Stewart come to visit my sweetheart.'

'Johnnie Stewart? Johnnie Stewart?' Granny Mac peered at him. 'Why, the lad's a man. I heard about… Duncan, I'm so sorry. '

Johnnie shifted his feet. Would the ache never stop?

'No news of…'

'Euan?' suggested Johnnie. 'Ro… I was told he's alive in Inverness. '

Granny Mac's eyes bored into his. 'So, Dougie and Morag might find him?'

Johnnie shrugged his shoulders. 'Thought you were the one who saw into the future?'

'You're out of sorts? Been visiting Kirsty Lorne?'

Johnnie looked up. 'Now, what's it to you?'

'She's had visitors. Tolbain's been seen there and his men. They say he wants the land and is sweet on her.'

'I already ken that.' Johnnie made to leave.

'What are you going to do, laddie?'

'I've food to organise for Mary McBean's bairns.' He turned to go.

'Johnnie.' Granny Mac's veined hand grasped his. 'You're a good man and I'm glad you're home at last, but watch out for Tolbain. He has a double reason for killing you. You're a Jacobite and you love Kirsty.' She paused. 'What did I just say?'

The Jacobite Affair

CHAPTER Fifty-eight

Next evening Johnnie made his way down from the den to Braedrumie House. The cold air came in waves through the forest. It rustled through leaves and made boughs sway. No moon, just a restless movement all round him so he imagined a redcoat behind every tree. He huddled against a sturdy trunk and listened for any disquiet that hinted at patrols. In front of him lay the stables and beyond them the house.

His brain writhed with thoughts of Kirsty and Tolbain, their handfasting, the villain's mouth on hers - his hands - their bodies. Yet life continued and he had to go on and ache with an emptiness inside him.

A swift gleam of light appeared as Murdo swung his lantern by a stable door. Johnnie rose to his feet and raced forward. The flame died.

'Thanks.' Johnnie ground to a halt and patted Murdo's shoulder.

'I took the McBeans some food like you said.'

'Good.'

Murdo grunted and with his lantern in one hand and musket in the other, trudged away into the shadows.

The laird sat in his cold study, with his back to the door. He stared out of the window into the gloom. A row of empty brandy bottles stood like a line of soldiers on his desk. His fingers held a half-full glass.

Johnnie sniffed the air. Rank. He noted Duncan's bloody flag still wrapped round his father's bony shoulders. Unwanted images and sounds of the battle filled Johnnies' head. He forced them to retreat.

'Father.' Johnnie leant over him. 'It's good to see you.'

'So, you're back.' Father stared at him with bloodshot eyes, the whites tinged yellow. 'Ingrate, you returned without your brothers,'

Johnnie jerked back at Father's words and tone. 'Ingrate? What the hell is up with you? I didna send Duncan to war.'

266

'Nor did I. But he knew where his duty lay and ran away to join you. My bonny wee boy…my youngest… You should have protected him. It should be him standing here, no you… No you.'

An icy grip encased Johnnie's heart. First Kirsty and her mother and now this. Did his father know what he was saying? 'I tried to protect him, Father, Euan and I both did. He arrived late, the battle was about to begin… he fought well, you'd have been proud of him.'

'I expect no less of my sons. How did he…?

Oh, God. Johnnie gulped. 'A wound to his head, he knew nothing about it.' May God forgive me for the lie.

'My poor wee laddie. Had a look of your mother. Poor Duncan. And Euan?'

'I told you before, he's in Inverness and no' a prisoner either.'

'Who told you?'

'It's a long story.'

'And Rob, how's Rob?'

Johnnie's gut tightened. 'Rob? Why ask about him? He left Braedrumie before the Rising.' He couldn't speak of Rob's hand in his escape, too shameful to be helped by the enemy and it would be the death of Father.

'Did he?' His father put a hand to his forehead. 'I forget… forget lots of things now. Your mother will know. Who didna come home?'

'Mother? But mother's been…' Johnnie's gaze swept over his father's unkempt hair and beard, the crumbs on his dirty waistcoat and the frayed cuff of his un-ironed shirt. Why hadn't he realised before? 'Maggie, Maggie Sanderson,' he yelled at the top of his voice,

After a few minutes the woman stood at the door and wiped her hands on a filthy apron. 'Sir?'

'What the bloody hell do we pay you for? You're the housekeeper. Get my father cleaned up and in fresh clothes, the fire laid and this room fit for him to sit in.'

The Jacobite Affair

'Beggin' your pardon, sir, but I'm no nurse and he says he prefers it like this. We've had Morag McColl and Kirsty Lorne stickin' their noses in and demandin' the same as you, but he doesna want none of it.'

'He's no' right in the he… can you no see he's no' himself, woman?' Johnnie thumped his fist on the desk. 'You'll follow my orders until my brother returns, is that clear? Get a couple of men to help you. The laird should be in a fit state for visitors, if not you'll be out on your damned ear. And that goes for the rest of the servants as well.'

Johnnie slammed the front door. Hadn't Dougie or Murdo realised? Had Duncan's death harmed his father's mind? He'd tell Murdo to hide the drink from the old man.

Lorna Windham

CHAPTER Fifty-nine

The moon shone like a gold coin in a cloudless sky above the den. Johnnie checked that Jamie Moffat guarded the path below. The lad couldn't take his eyes off Alais. Johnnie would have to have a word.

Johnnie flung himself on his cold bed of plaids. Kirsty. He ached for her, Rob's wise advice, Euan's camaraderie and Duncan. He thought of Father who lived in the past and dredged up Duncan's name again and again. Johnnie yawned and his eyes drooped. Life, now, an agony of distorted images. Perhaps tonight he'd conquer his demons. The fire warmed him. If he could only sleep, but when he did he re-lived Duncan's death.

Johnnie dozed a few hours at the entrance to the den when a boot kicked him in the ribs. Redcoats. He tensed, ready to spring.

'Good thing I'm no' the enemy,' hissed a familiar voice. 'At least Jamie's no' asleep.'

Johnnie leapt up and stared at the figure in front of him. Euan's features peered at him through grime, matted hair and a beard. 'Is it you?' Johnnie grabbed his brother's hand and found himself locked in an embrace.

'Johnnie. My God, it's good to see you.' Euan's husky voice sounded in his ear.

'I thought the worst. Dougie and Morag?'

'Should be home soon. They had to go to Fort William with the carts. I… thought it safer for all of us, if I made my way here first. They told me about Duncan.'

Johnnie grimaced. 'Any news of the others?' he said.

Euan shook his head.

'At least Murdo made it back with Dougie.'

Euan stared into the distance. 'So Morag said.'

Silence. So many Stewarts missing and neither of them could voice it.

'Have you food?'

The Jacobite Affair

Johhnie noted the sharp angles of Euan's face and his thin frame. 'We've bread and cheese.'

'If it's spare.'

Johnnie nodded, rooted around in the cave and handed the food to Euan who grabbed a crust with both hands. He crammed it into his mouth and chewed. He didn't stop till the last crumb disappeared. Then he started on the cheese.

Johnnie stared at him.

'Sorry. Haven't eaten for days.'

Someone coughed in the den behind them. Euan whirled and lowered his knees ready to fight as his eyes tried to pierce the gloom.

Johnnie put his hand on Euan's shoulder. 'Relax. They're friends. Best whisper. Here, you'll be needing a dram.' Johnnie went to a keg and poured whisky into two horn tumblers.

'Who?' Euan jerked his head towards the blackness behind him.

'A wee young thing and two bairns, just waifs and strays.' Johnnie left one drink on the keg and handed the other to his brother, then threw some peat on the fire. The smoke curled up between them. 'I couldna' leave them. Their families...' Johnnie studied the ground and tried to erase the blood-soaked memories. Useless. He watched Euan tilt his head back, swallow the whisky in one gulp, close his eyes and use the tip of his tongue to savour the taste on his lips.

'My God, I'd almost forgotten. It's like liquid fire.' Euan held out the tumbler for more. This time he rolled the whisky round his mouth. 'Morag and Dougie got me away. Been lying senseless for days with the redcoat wounded in Inverness.'

Johnnie sucked in a breath. 'How...?'

Euan gripped Johnnie's shoulders and stared into his eyes. 'It's hard to believe... might have been me hallucinating... but I'm sure Rob's the redcoat who saved me and Dougie said he'd seen him as well and he didna betray him or Morag.'

'Rob.' Johnnie let the name hang in the air. 'Bastard helped me escape too. Damn him.'

270

Euan hung his head. 'No wonder we never heard from him. He never believed in The Cause. My God, it'll kill Father.'

'Dinna tell him. I havena. For the best.' Johnnie shifted the peat with his boot and released a crackle of flame from the centre of the fire. 'How did you know where I was?'

'Dougie.'

'Aye. Braedrumie's too dangerous. That bastard, Tolbain and redcoat patrols.'

'How's Father?' asked Euan.

'Changed. Duncan… you know.'

'Aye.' Euan eyed him. 'Must be hard.'

'Aye.'

Euan stretched and smelt his armpit, his nose wrinkled. 'Smell like game. Swim?'

'Wait.' Johnnie searched his saddlebags. 'Found it.' He brandished aloft a bar of Braedrumie's best lye soap.

'Canna wait,' said Euan.

With a look behind him, Johnnie left Alais and the children asleep in the cave and headed for the pool. Euan wrapped his arm round Johnnie's shoulders as they walked round the rock-face. The rush of water met them several yards away as it gushed down a fault in the rock, paused for a while in the pool, over-spilled and sped down the hillside.

Euan took one look at Johnnie and raced him to the edge. He gave a whoop and jumped in fully clothed. He disappeared in a huge splash which caught Johnnie in an icy shower. The ice-water streamed down him, chilled his veins and took his breath away. Bloody hell, even though Euan can barely swim he shows no fear of water. Johnnie, covered in goose-pimples, ripped off his plaid, shirt and hose and ball-shaped, leapt high into the air. He hit the water with a resounding thwack and hissed in a breath as his manhood shrunk. Waves crashed over Euan as he surfaced.

'Colder than I remember,' spluttered Euan.

'That's what living a soft life does for you.' Johnnie threw his brother the bar of lye soap. It landed with a splosh behind Euan and sank.

The Jacobite Affair

'I'll give you soft life.' Euan pushed Johnnie's head under the water.

Johnnie surfaced and beamed. Just like old times when Rob and Duncan... No. He pushed their images away.

Euan flung his sodden garments onto the bank. Johnnie dove under the water. Seconds later he surfaced and held the soap aloft. He rubbed the bar over his face, neck and dark chest hairs and created a lather. Once finished, he tossed the bar to Euan who kissed it, followed suit and handed the soap back to Johnnie. Euan's soapy head disappeared under the scummy water, then rose like a shaggy dog. He shook his hair and sent diamond water-bracelets round him.

Droplets pelted Johnnie as he rubbed the soap under one arm. Euan seemed even taller and leaner. His body covered in scars. At least he'd made it home, not like Duncan. Mustn't think about Duncan. The bloody wound - face creased in agony – blood - his ragged breaths- that last look in his eyes as they dimmed.

'Johnnie. Johnnie? You alright?' said Euan, a look of concern on his face.

'Aye.' Johnnie couldn't look at his brother. 'Just... find it difficult to think of Rob as a redcoat.' Johnnie applied the soap to his other armpit. 'He mentioned Mother. But he fought against us at Culloden.'

'He saved our lives at the risk of his own. I'll no' disown him. But I wonder why he left.'

'Dinna forget those that died in the rebellion.' Johnnie used the soap on his legs then lobbed it to Euan. His brother's right hand shot out and the bar landed in his palm with a slap.

'You canna' blame all their deaths on Rob. How's Father, really?' Euan worked the soap on his shoulders.

'He's no' as he was. His mind... Duncan's death... he's... no' right in the head. And he's drinking a lot. I dinna ken how to help him.'

'Do I detect a hint of love, of caring ...?'

'Soap.'

Euan flipped it across to Johnnie who lathered his hair.

'He's old and he's lost... so many he loved, of course I care.'

'Never thought I'd hear you say it,' Euan said. 'Always at loggerheads. Dinna suppose he sent Duncan to war?'

'He says Duncan ran off.' Johnnie turned and sank. Only the top of his head appeared above the soapy bubbles as an apparition appeared in front of them.

Euan's mouth hung open in shock then he turned saucer-eyed to Johnnie as if to beg a question.

Johnnie surfaced and gasped for breath.

Alais' mouth formed a wide 'O'. Her fair plait swung behind her as she jerked to a stop and dropped her buckets with a clatter on the ground.

Johnnie gaped. His spare white shirt covered her full bosom and his snug, brown breeches encased her slim waist, slender hips, long thighs and legs.

Bright pink with confusion she covered her eyes with her hands and ran in the opposite direction to the men. Johnnie watched her pert backside disappear from sight.

Euan said in a mock, serious tone, 'Think those breeches will catch on?'

Johnnie managed to grunt, 'That's Alais... she washed her clothes... I lent her mine...'

'The *wee young thing*?' Euan grinned at him. 'Thought you'd learned your lesson. Edinburgh...?'

'It's no' like that... she doesna' speak.'

'A woman who doesna' blether. Worth her weight in gold.' Euan elbowed his brother in the ribs.

'Ouch.' Johnnie rubbed his side and hoped his brother didn't notice how his face burned. 'Brought her home because it was either that or her starve. Nought else to it.'

'And Kirsty?'

Johnnie drew himself up, his voice sounded hard even to his ears. 'Agreed to a handfasting with that bastard, Tolbain.'

Euan froze. 'You're no' serious?'

Johnnie nodded.

The Jacobite Affair

Euan studied him for a moment. 'Sounds like they're well matched. At least she willna have to put up with your snores.'

Johnnie pushed him and Euan pushed him back. Within seconds they'd reverted to boys and carefree moments of their youth when they'd escaped the eagle-eyes of their parents and Dougie.

'I have to see Father.' Euan pulled himself out of the pool. 'See how he is. We need provisions.'

'We've some, courtesy of the MacNairs.' At Euan's mystified look Johnnie added, 'Long story. There's redcoat patrols about. Look, you're exhausted, sleep. We'll go, when it's dark.'

Later, as Johnnie helped Alais with the chores and she didn't look at him, he realised she'd seen him naked to the waist with soap suds for hair.

Lorna Windham

CHAPTER Sixty

Later that morning, Kirsty tramped the hills, head down, as her mind writhed. *I have to get away from our farm or I'll go mad.*

She stopped when she came to the dead oak which marked *Our Place,* the dilapidated croft of her childhood. *There's the trough, the roof has more holes and the walls seem lower. How strange I wandered here.* Her fingers brushed the tree's bark. *Full of memories.* She slid her hand inside the trunk and felt the smoothness of a stone.

A movement from the ruined croft above caught her eye. *Johnnie.* He stood beside the drunken door surrounded by long grass and lichen-pitted walls. She tripped over a rock hidden in the bracken and steadied herself. *The ribbon of our childhood still binds us.* Her world stopped and she stared at him. *Johnnie, older, wiser from the creases round his eyes.* 'How did you know?'

'You'd come here? Because you love me' Johnnie's voice sounded husky.

Dinna cry now, not now. She hardened her heart. 'It's dangerous, you shouldna and no' in daylight.' She searched the golden gorse which surrounded them. Emptiness.

'What did he promise? Wealth? Standing?'

The words pierced her like needles. 'Safety from the storm.'

'My role not his.'

'I...' She struggled to find the words. Her vocal chords tightened, seemed raw. 'I'm... sorry... so sorry.' A tremor racked her.

'My own one.' He stepped forward and wrapped his arms round her shoulders. She allowed herself to be gathered into the warmth of his embrace. A new wave of anguish scythed though her. Her head rested on his chest as it always had. *To hear the steady beat of his heart, smell his fresh male scent and feel his skin against mine again.*

'Tell me.' His voice sounded low and resonant in her ear.

The Jacobite Affair

Thought I could forget him, but he invades my days and nights. Tolbain or Johnnie? Johnnie. She said, 'The man's a devil. Once in his sights- you're lost. That's where I am… lost… and that's how you should think of me. Better forget.' She pulled away from him.

He reached out and caressed her cheek. 'I canna do it. You're in here.' He beat his fist against his chest.

A tear formed at the corner of her eye and she let it run unchecked. He swept it away with his thumb. 'Darling, I canna live without you.' He cradled her face in his hands. His lips brushed her forehead, swept across a cheekbone and seared her lips.

Branded.

'Tell me you dinna love me,' he whispered.

*His. I am **his**.* A tremor pulsed through her. 'I have to think of Mother.'

'Say it.' His lips nibbled her ear.

'She's no well. We were starving. Murdo must have told you we were robbed of the cattle, then the hens wouldna lay and the cow died. I tried to sell what we made, but a merchant didna abide by his word. I even stole milk from Old Grant…'

'Father didna offer you some?' said Johnnie aghast.

She hung her head. 'He didna know how it was with us, I couldna tell him. I thought he wouldna think me good enough for you.'

'Never think that, darling' He pulled her close. 'Dear God, you did what you had to do to survive. I've done things… terrible things…' He shuddered.

'But you were at war.'

'Aye and thought you'd wait for me.'

She blinked back a tear. 'Tolbain loaned Mother money and we couldna pay it back.'

He pushed her away. 'He bought you then with his fine title and lands.'

'I'm no whore.'

He turned from her.

She snapped at him. 'So easy for you to judge. You weren't here. The money was stolen. Mother had agreed if we couldna repay it, I'd be handfasted to him. She never said, you see. Sold me like a piece of meat. That's what hurts. She was on at me all the time and he wouldna leave me alone. You didna come and I'd no one to turn to.'

He faced her. 'My father.'

'I wouldna beg for scraps. Didna want him or anyone to know. The shame of it. Ever know hunger, Johnnie? It gnaws at you, fills every hour of every day.'

'I've known hunger,' said Johnnie.

'I prayed for you to come home and then you brought that woman.'

He grasped her shoulders. 'You and your damn pride. Redcoats shot Alais' parents and brothers, then fired her farm. She canna speak for the shock of it. If I'd left her, she'd have died. She deserves your pity no' your hate.'

Kirsty crumpled to the ground, clasped her hands round her knees and rocked to and fro. 'What have I done? What have I done?'

'I'll kill the bastard.'

'I'll no' have his death on your conscience and the redcoats would hunt you down, you and Euan.'

He knelt on one knee beside her and put his face next to hers. 'Must he have all of you?'

'Oh, Johnnie, dinna say this.'

'Do you love me?'

'You know I do.'

He held out his hand. 'My token.'

'Not the luckenbooth brooch. I'll treasure it.' She took it and pinned it to her bodice. 'I'm sorry for… everything.'

'Come.'

'Where are we going?'

He nodded towards the group of stones with half a roof. 'I want to show you what love is.'

She looked at him in wonderment and put out her fingers in his. They entered the croft and she leant her back against a

The Jacobite Affair

stone wall. She could see vast swathes of sky between the rotten timbers.

He gathered her to him. His lips searched. His fingers in her hair set her senses alight. She drew him on with kisses. So gentle, so slow, so playful. He paused. 'What have we here?' Butterfly wings explored the nape of her neck, each ear lobe, the length of her collar bones. Her mind took flight as want flooded every pore.

Her lips exalted at the roughness of his beard, his throat, Adam's apple and muscular chest. Every part of her willed him on as he used his teeth to draw her sleeves down and nibble each shoulder. 'I see I have peaks to climb.' He began on the half-moon of her breasts. He unlaced her, his lips nuzzled, aroused, drank her in as his fingers pulled her skirts up around her naked thighs and she felt the hardness of his manhood.

He shrugged off his plaid and shirt and she her skirt. *Naked.* 'You are so beautiful.'

'And you, a wonder.' She stroked his wide muscular shoulder, his deep chest, the taut skin over his ribs.

His breath caressed her neck. 'I'm going to explore.'

A tingle of excitement ran through her like an arrow. *Should I stop him? Could I? Do I want to?*

'A valley with a well. Let me drink you in.' His tongue circled her belly button, then nestled in it. Shivers ran down her spine. 'What have we here?' His lips crept downwards. 'A forest.' Her spine arched as the tip of his tongue searched her mound. 'And here's the cleft.' He buried his face in her and worked at her core. Her spine arched again as he transported her on waves. He lifted his head. 'Darling, I love all of you. Do you want this?'

'Aye.' She ran her hands through his hair. 'I dreamt that this is how it would be. I've never been so sure.' He lifted her and she clasped her legs round his waist so his manhood pressed against her sex.

He entered her and he took her with him, until she thought her heart would burst and they shuddered into a climax together.

'Dear God.' He lay beside her. 'I never realised it would be like this. I love you so. Did I hurt you?'

'A little. I didna think it would be so… wonderful. Skin next to skin.'

'It willna hurt again.'

She nodded and wiped off the smears of blood between her thighs with the hem of her skirt. 'Good.'

'You willna go through with the handfast now. You'll join us at the den. I'll find a priest somehow.'

Why was I so weak? She started to dress.

'Kirsty?'

'I canna do it. Mother's no' well it would kill her.' She re-plaited her hair.

'Stay at the farm then, but dinna bind yourself to that monster.'

'I've no choice, don't you see? If I refuse, he'll hunt you down and the rest of the Stewarts. You'd never be safe. He wouldn't stop till you're hanged.'

'You'll sacrifice yourself for us? Darling, I willna let you.'

'You canna stop me. My mind's made up.'

'So what was this all about? Didn't it mean anything to you?'

She clasped his face in her hands. 'Something to remember for the rest of our lives. I wanted you to be first.' *I can't tell him it means everything, everything, or he won't let me go.*

'So, we're to be just a memory to each other? I dinna think love works like that.'

'It'll have to, Johnnie.' She walked out into bright sunshine.

He didn't follow.

The Jacobite Affair

CHAPTER Sixty-one

June arrived with a flourish of white and pink wild roses.

'A fine affair,' Kirsty's mother said more than once. 'Your handfasting was the finest in the Highlands for years. Everybody said so. Chose the right side. The government's generous and so is Tolbain. Look at that wedding gown. French or was it Flemish? I forget. We'll never know want again.'

Kirsty bristled. *Trust Mother to remind me what Tolbain said: You're my bride and I expect you to reflect my position and wear the best not that… rag.*

She'd boiled with rage for she'd sewn *that rag* herself. Then she'd compared her dress to the gown and shoes of the finest gold silk, cream petticoats and floor-length French veil. *If only my groom had been Johnnie.*

Then Tolbain insisted the handfasting be held not in Braedrumie's church, but in Fort William. 'For the best. Don't want the natives to spoil our day.' Mother agreed with him and there'd been no unfortunate incidents from Jacobite sympathisers. The Earl of Morris and the Duke of Rothsay amongst others attended.

Kirsty, tight-lipped, stood in the barrack square which bristled with redcoats. *This has nothing to do with me. I just have to get through it and not shame me or Mother.*

'I will take you as my husband…' she forced the words out and winced as Tolbain smirked.

'And I will take you as my… wife…'
What have I done?

The ceremony over, he kissed her hand. 'You must excuse me my dear, I have business with the commanding officer. My tacksman, Campbell, and the Boids will escort you to the Duke of Rothsay's house, just outside Maryburgh for the reception. I'll join you later.'

Business? What's more important than celebrating our handfasting?

She noted Methuselah Boid rode with a grimace as if in pain. Finlay stayed close with a concerned look on his face.

'Are you alright?' she asked.

Methuselah flashed an odd look at her. 'Aye, Your Grace.' Both men spurred their horses forward.

Your Grace. Goodness I'm a duchess. But I don't know what to do.

The reception, a grand affair with long tables laden with food and decorated with cascades of crimson roses and garlands of wild flowers, almost overwhelmed her. She stood like a dove amongst hawks who examined her from afar. *They know I don't fit, I'm not meant for all this. How could Tolbain leave me on my own?*

'Most satisfying.' Mother pressed her hand on Kirsty's shoulder so she sat.

Tolbain arrived hours later.

He hasn't even apologised. So embarrassing, a bride without a groom and guests I don't even know. My head aches. I just want this to be over.

***

Several days later Kirsty and Mother inspected the first storey of Toll house.

'Can I get you anythin', Your Grace?' The maid with the lopsided jaw carried an armful of bedlinen along a gloomy passageway.

'What's your name?' asked Kirsty.

She bobbed a curtsey. 'Drewitt, Your Grace.'

'No thank you, Drewitt.'

The maid curtsied again and scurried away.

Will I ever be comfortable with servants? Will I get used to being called 'Your Grace' by inferiors or 'Duchess' or 'Madam' by my equals? Equals? How odd that sounds.

Mother interrupted her thoughts. 'I suppose Tolbain took pity on her misshapen face. At least his wealth spares us the

The Jacobite Affair

sight of beggars, so common place now. They make me feel quite faint.'

'Mother, they could have been us.'

Mother continued as if she hadn't heard. 'We have the finest carriage and four seen outside of Edinburgh. Tolbain promised I may ride in it when he sees fit. My, what it is to be wealthy.' She sniffed into a silk handkerchief. 'He's a fine figure of a man, don't you think? No' the breadth of shoulder or height of some, but his tailor makes up for what he lacks.' She blew her nose and coughed. 'Do you know, I think I'm getting a cold? All that standing about at the handfasting. I'm away to my bed. Tell that girl… Drewitt, I'd like hot chocolate in my chamber.' She swept out.

Kirsty sighed. *Thank God she's never asked about the wedding night or any other night for that matter.*

'Disrobe,' Tolbain had commanded as he'd shut the door.

Her face had burned as she'd fumbled with ties and knots. She'd shrugged off one fine garment after another until she stood in her shift in front of the fire's dancing flames.

His lips slid into a smirk as if he knew something she didn't. He moved his head from side to side as if he assessed her in some way, like a possession.

She looked down. He could see the outline of her body through the flimsy material. She put one hand on her bosom and one over her loins.

'Turn round.'

'But...'

'I don't want to see your face. What I want is obedience,' he snapped.

Surely he'll show some tenderness? She did as he asked.

'You'll do. Oh, yes, you'll do very well.'

She could have sworn he licked his lips.

'Husband?'

'Lie on the bed,' he commanded. 'Face down.'

Oh, the indignity of it. Worse when he lifted my shift.

'Now let's see if I can plough your furrow,' he said. 'You'd better pray you give me a son this night.'

No words of love, no tenderness. Just before he'd taken her like an animal, he'd whispered in her ear. 'You mind Drewitt's face? Broke her jaw. That's what happens when a woman tries to thwart me.' Then he plunged, thrust, and ripped. She'd cried out in pain. *Oh, yes there'd been pain. Johnnie had been wrong about that.* There'd have been more, if she hadn't been prepared and smuggled in the membrane of sheep's blood which she'd pierced and dripped on their sheets as he slept.

Next morning he ignored her protests about being tired and took her again. Then he went riding. Drewitt helped her bathe, but kept her thoughts to herself.

As night drew in and shadows approached the house, Tolbain returned with a woman and paraded her in silk and coarse makeup in front of a shocked Kirsty in the sitting room. 'Remember poor Meg? Burnt out, homeless? I believe it's our Christian duty to offer her a home.'

He looked straight at Kirsty and kissed Meg. 'Don't you think she has beautiful lips, riper than cherries and eyes as blue as Loch Linnhe? She's to be my guest and yours.'

Kirsty sprang from her seat, 'You've brought this... whore into my house and expect me to treat her as a guest? Are you out of your mind?'

'Well,' said Meg.

He grabbed Kirsty's wrist and pulled her to him as Meg watched. 'I've brought her to my bed. You sleep next door. Meg's our guest and you'll treat her as such or learn what it means to cross me.' Then he flung Kirsty away from him.

'It's bloody lovely here.' Meg sat on the settee, plumped up a cushion and smiled at them.

'You canna expect me to accept this?' Kirsty rose from the floor.

Tolbain smirked at her. 'I can and I do.'

Kirsty crossed her arms, unable to speak because of her anger. *How could he? Did he ever care for me? Is it Mother's land he wants after all?*

Tolbain paraded Meg in front of the servants and took Kirsty again and again in the privacy of her bedchamber.

The Jacobite Affair

'Please dinna,' she begged.

'It's your duty,' he replied.

Night after night she had to endure the same brutal treatment and during the day be humiliated by his whore.

Johnnie showed me how love should be and I've treated him abominably. Better if we'd never made love, then I'd have nothing to compare to Tolbain's... efforts. And if I'd married Johnnie? She knew it wouldn't have been a duty to share a bed with him.

She broached the subject with Mother. 'Do you ever get used to it?' she asked as she thought of Tolbain.

'*If?*' Mother looked down her long nose at Kirsty. 'Please dinna mention the subject again, you dinna want to upset... him.' She rose out of her chair and swept out of the room. Kirsty wondered how she'd been conceived.

As Meg became a constant in their lives, Kirsty found Tolbain bothered her less and less at night. Meg's high pitched giggles and Tolbain's deep throated laughs, informed the house of their delight in each other in his chamber.

Kirsty, brushed her hair at her dressing table, lost between shame and relief. She closed her ears to the intimate sounds of bed springs next door and tried to ignore the humiliation. *His whore mustn't mind Tolbain's cruelty and speedy withdrawal.*

Kirsty snuggled under her covers. *I need time- to be won-to love. Johnnie understood. But Tolbain's only interested in his own pleasures.*

Every evening Tolbain insisted he, Meg, Kirsty and Mother sat together and ate their evening meal in the vast dining room. Meg fluttered her eyelashes whilst Kirsty sat between them in silence. Mother perched opposite her with a cough which bent her double.

One night Tolbain pointed his forefinger at Mother. 'Must she splutter all over the table?' he hissed. 'Listen to her.'

'Sorry.' Beads of perspiration stood out on Mother's brow which she dabbed with her silk handkerchief. She looked pale with red-rimmed eyes.

Lorna Windham

'She has a fever and is aged,' Kirsty protested. 'She needs your protection not your disdain. I've sent for a healer from Braedrumie.'

Meg giggled.

Tolbain pounded his fist on the table and made the silver tableware do a jig. 'You sent for a healer without my say so and dare criticise **me**? His face contorted as he stood and overturned his chair with a clatter. 'I won't have it. Embarrassing me in front of Meg and the servants.'

A young footman shuffled his feet and another found something of interest in the floorboards. Meg stared at the ceiling and Mother covered her mouth with a handkerchief.

Tolbain dragged Kirsty from the room. 'You'll never do it again. By God you won't. I'm master here.'

***

The next morning Kirsty frowned and picked up her knitting. *Mother's never taken to her bed before. If he doesn't send for a healer, she could die.* She shifted in her seat in the sunlit sewing room, her back and buttocks lacerated by his whip. *My bruised flesh will mend, but the humiliation's hard to bear. The servants must have heard my screams.* She'd seen sympathy in several faces, particularly Drewitt's.

'Soon bloody mend.' Meg unpicked a crooked stitch. 'I'll send for some tea.'

'Ladies embroider.' Tolbain strode into the room.

Kirsty put her needles aside. *He thinks I'm common. Impossible to breathe or laugh in Toll House. Tolbain sucks all joy out of it. How to ask him for help for Mother?*

'Look at Meg,' Tolbain said. 'Such a fine figure. She behaves like a lady here and a whore in bed. You should try to be more like her. By the way, I've just turned away that hag, Granny Mac. It's to be hoped you're healthier than your mother. Look at you. No flesh, lank hair. Not like Meg. And the old bitch stays in her room until she's recovered or we

The Jacobite Affair

carry her out in a box. I don't want her to spread her contagion in my house.'

'Have you no pity?'

Tolbain took Kirsty by her hair.

Oh God, what have I done? She cried out.

'Pity? You dare question me? I'll show you pity.' He bundled her out of the room.

Later, she'd limped along the corridor to Mother's bedchamber. Flushed and restless, Mother lay with her eyes closed. *Vile man. I'll ensure Mother's comfortable, if he won't. Now, where's Drewitt?*

The maid stood in the linen cupboard and counted on her fingers. 'Four, five…' Her hand went to her jaw. 'Oh, you gave me a turn, Your Grace.'

'My Mother is no' well. Please ensure she has several pillows and some cold compresses for her head. She seems hot to me.'

'Your Grace.' Drewitt curtsied. 'And I'll find some witch hazel for that bruise on your cheek, shall I?'

Oh, God.

CHAPTER Sixty-two

That evening Johnnie and Euan picked their way through the undergrowth to Braedrumie House, the moon hidden by heavy cloud. As usual, Euan scouted round the back whilst Johnnie sank behind a pine tree and waited for him. The study had a light in it.

'Dougie says we're safe,' hissed Euan. 'A patrol went by hours ago. No one abroad except us. Come on.'

Johnnie followed Euan round prickly shrubs, over the gate and through the garden. Dougie bolted the back door behind them.

Father, eyes clear, shoulders back, slapped his sons on the back. 'Euan, Johnnie, what's kept you lads? Take a seat. Dougie, get the best whisky and have one yourself.'

Johnnie nudged his elbow in Euan's ribs. Father sober?

'I thank you.' Dougie gave Johnnie a wry glance as he followed the order and poured the amber liquid into four glasses. 'It's good to see you made it back, Johnnie.'

'And you,' said Johnnie as he accepted the tumbler.

'You look well, Father, doesn't he, Johnnie?' Euan savoured the drink with his tongue.

'Aye.' At least he'd discarded the bloody saltire. Johnnie swirled the potent liquid in his glass and inhaled the smoky fumes.

'I'm pleased you've come tonight. We need to plan, look to the future.' Father swigged his whisky. 'There's no' men to till the land or look after the cattle, same as after the '15. We need money to tide us over. Now, your Uncle John owes us from the last venture. I think a visit's called for. You should be back in a month.'

Johnnie's jaw dropped.

Euan grimaced. 'But, he's in Port Glasgow, we've a price on our heads and I promised Morag we'd marry soon.'

'She'll have to wait a little longer if she wants to eat,' said Father.

'She'll no' be happy.'

The Jacobite Affair

'After the '15, redcoats set fire to the fields and crofts and stole our cattle. That's why I've sent Murdo to the markets in the south with our best beasts. Lads, your Uncle John will be pleased to see you.'

Johnnie looked at Father and then Euan.

'You want us to ask for money?' Euan's eyes narrowed.

'That's right.' Father's eyes searched the room. 'Lost something. Important. Ah.' He pounced on the bloody saltire on a chair by the fire. 'Canna be without this.' He tugged it round his shoulders. 'Duncan will stay here.'

Johnnie almost choked on his whisky, Euan gaped and Dougie stared at the floor.

'Duncan's dead, Father.' Euan put down his half empty glass.

'They said that, but he'll be home soon. My youngest, you know. His mother and I have high hopes. Aye, high hopes.' He made to rise.

He's not sane. 'Do you no' want to sit till you feel better, Father?' asked Johnnie.

'Better? I'm no' an invalid. I'll see you off. Best you get to your beds before your mother comes.'

Dougie shook his head. 'Aye, best you do that, boys.' He ushered a stunned Euan and disconsolate Johnnie out of the study and closed the door behind them. 'The laird's no'... well, but he has a point. We're low on funds and Murdo will be lucky to make it out of Scotland with the cattle.'

Euan sighed. 'We'll go to Port Glasgow. God knows what I'm going to say to Morag.'

Johnnie grinned at Dougie, they'd both witnessed Morag's temper and it hadn't improved in adulthood.

'Have you heard about that hussy, Kirsty Lorne, Johnnie?' Dougie nudged him with his elbow. 'Suppose she thinks she's above the rest of us now. Isabel says Tolbain mistreats her and has his whore in the house. His whore. Serves her right. Don't you think, Johnnie?' Dougie looked at him, expectant. Euan shook his head.

Johnnie said nothing. A vision of Kirsty's tousled blonde hair thrown back, eyes only for him and her seductive lips filled his head. Her rapid breath and moans as she climaxed wormed into his ears. Something he couldn't share. 'No one deserves Tolbain,' he said at last.

'You've no' forgiven her?' Dougie's eyebrow rose. 'After what she's done to you.'

'I've no' forgiven her.' Johnnie couldn't. She'd brought heartbreak to both of them. She should have spurned Tolbain. They'd have sorted something out. But, no, she'd spurned him instead, lain with him and spurned him again. Damn her. He wouldn't defend her to the others and explain her sacrifice. At the moment he felt like the sacrificial lamb. Damn, Kirsty Lorne.

The Jacobite Affair

CHAPTER Sixty-three

Kirsty examined her face in Mother's dressing table mirror. *Too pale.* She pinched her cheeks and grimaced as two vivid blotches erupted on her tired skin. Today Mother's face stared back. Horrified, she adjusted the mirror to take in her length. *Too thin. And how to explain this listlessness? Of course I've nursed Mother with Drewitt's help, sometimes through the night. Perhaps I've caught the same fever?*

'Goin' to be a hot day, Your Grace.' Drewitt bustled in and opened a window.

Kirsty leant out and gulped in fresh air. *I have to get away from Mother's sick room, go somewhere I can breathe. And Tolbain stifles me with his insistence I'm accompanied, even to the stables.*

'She seems content, Your Grace.'

Kirsty turned to the four-poster bed and noted Mother's closed eyes and steady breath. *She's improving.* Kirsty pursed her lips and kissed the old woman's cheek. 'Thank you for looking after her, Drewitt.'

'Your Grace.'The girl tried to form the semblance of a smile thwarted by her lopsided jaw.

'I'm sorry he did that.'

Drewitt flushed and her hand went to the uneven lump. Flint flashed in her eyes.

'Why?' asked Kirsty

The girl shuffled her feet and looked at her shoes. 'I'm no' sure you want to know, Your Grace.'

'He forced himself on you?'

Drewitt nodded. 'Only the once. Said I wasna bonny enough… afterwards.'

Kirsty gritted her teeth. *God, what kind of man have I married?* She put her hand on Drewitt's arm. 'You and I know his true villainy. You've a friend here, if you're ever in need.'

'And you, Your Grace,' Drewitt curtsied. 'His whore will get her comeuppance. They never last long.'

Oh, God, *they. At least I've been free of his attentions most nights.* The thin figure in bed stirred. 'Mother?'

Mother turned away and Drewitt shook her head. 'Best let her rest, Your Grace. You're lookin' tired, if you dinna mind me sayin' so. Why don't you go for a walk in the sunshine?'

'He doesna like it.'

'Drewitt lowered her voice, 'There's a priest's hole in the end bedroom on the left, staircase goes all the way downstairs. Found it years ago. A bookcase conceals it, key's on the top. Opens into a cupboard with a false back. I'll say nothin', Your Grace.'

I'd be free of him and his men for a few hours. 'Thank you. If he asks…' began Kirsty.

'Heard him say he was goin' to look at some oak casks this afternoon. Mr. Campbell discovered them in the cellars. Made ale here once upon a time. If there's money in it, he'll be there for hours.'

Kirsty nodded, left the room and turned right towards her bedroom. She'd need her cloak. *So, Meg's one of many whores and as long as he parades her in Toll House, he dishonours me in front of the household. Villain.*

Kirsty passed Meg's bedchamber which stood ajar. 'Madam, a word.' Tolbain's command brought her back to reality

She steeled herself. *Will it be a word? Did he overhear my conversation with Drewitt?*

She entered the bedchamber. *Oh my.*

Tolbain sat on the bed with Meg on his lap. She gazed up at him in adoration, her scarlet garters and plump thighs on display. His eyes didn't waver from Kirsty's for a moment, as if he dared her to protest.

Kirsty curtsied. 'Your Grace?'

A bastard and his whore. Kirsty clenched her hands so the nails bit into her palms. *I thank God he only sleeps with me once a week and says he prefers someone, like her.*

'He loves me.' Meg and stroked his ear.

The Jacobite Affair

Has she no shame? Kirsty shifted her gaze to the window and the moors beyond.

'Didn't you hear what I said?' Meg nuzzled Tolbain's cheek.

'Aye.' *The air's stale like his harlot.*

'Don't you bloody care?'

Kirsty shrugged her shoulders and walked to the window. The loch rippled like a silver sheet.

'Meg, let her be,' said Tolbain. 'I've been hunting Stewarts.'

No. Kirsty whirled.

'I've heard rumours they're back.'

'But you said if we were handfasted….'

'But you said if we were handfasted... How naive.' He sprang up and Meg rolled onto the floor.

'Ow.' Meg screeched.

Tolbain ignored her and pinned Kirsty with his gaze. 'I'll no' be safe 'till they're all hanged from the nearest tree.'

Meg rubbed her backside. 'He'll bloody catch them you know.'

Waves of hopelessness enveloped Kirsty. Somehow she got out of the room and slammed the door behind her. *Oh, God. Johnnie. I have to warn him.* Gales of laughter followed her. She raced along the corridor and collected her cloak from her chamber. *The priest hole.* She turned left, willed herself to tiptoe past Meg's room and then rushed for the door at the end. A few sheets of parchment, ink and a blunt quill lay strewn on a dusty desk. She scratched a note, then found the rusty key on the shelf above a row of books. *How to get in?* She searched for a place in the carved wood to put her fingers, found nothing and started again. *There. At the end of a row of wooden slats, a hollow.* She tugged and a door the height of her waist sprang open to reveal an empty cupboard.

On her knees, she removed the back boards and discovered with a rush of cold air, a steep keystone staircase. She listened. Nothing stirred. She swirled the cloak round her shoulders, tugged the hood low over her face and pulled the door closed behind her. Her head spun as the stairs wound down to the ground floor and she came to a small, locked oak door. She inserted the key, the door swung open and she stepped outside.

No one in sight. She turned the key in the lock and looked up to marvel at how one of the turrets concealed the internal staircase. The sun warmed her face and she breathed in a lungful of fresh air. *What was that? The distant creak of a cart's wheels.* She studied the patch of green and pine trees in front of her. *No sign of Tolbain's men. He'll be furious I've ventured out without his say so. I don't care.*

She scanned the windows behind her. *No one.* The scent of pine needles tickled her nose as she climbed up onto the tousled moor and away from Toll House. She paused. No signs of pursuit. *Johnnie. Will he be there?*

Huge clouds like full sails followed her as they raced across the sapphire sea. The warm wind sang through the glen as her hood flew off and her hair streamed behind her. Spools of purple heather and clusters of yellow gorse swayed to and fro as if a giant hand raked through them. A stream of golden light appeared from behind a cloud. She ran, her heart raced and her lungs worked hard. Toll House seemed a black speck and Loch Linnhe like a silver band below. She continued to climb and breathed in the wild scent of the moors. An urge to walk barefoot and feel the grass cool and uneven beneath her feet, almost overtook her.

In the distance stood the dead tree and beyond that, *Our Place*. The ground strewn with stones. *A hard life up here.* She ran towards the tree and reached inside its hollow, no pebble. Her heart sank. *Of course, he'll never forgive me.*

Kirsty placed a pebble and the note in the tree and turned to go.

'I love your hair unbound like that. They say the bastard hurts you- is it true?' Johnnie stood beside her.

Oh, God, he knows. 'You shouldna be here.'

'Every day, only for you. Patrol passed an hour ago. Well?'

'No.' She cringed inside.

'You're lying.'

The Jacobite Affair

'No.'

'Just as you lied after we lay together. I'm no' just a memory or you wouldna be here.' His eyes held hers.

'I came to warn you. He lied, he's hunting Stewarts now.'

His arms drew her close. 'You love me.'

Thought I could forget him. Close a door on that part of my life. But he invades my days and nights and always will.

'Kirsty?'

'Aye. I love you, but it's too late.' She sagged in his arms.

'Can you no' see this is killing both of us?'

She closed her eyes.

'Darling, give up this mad handfasting. I'll ask Father if you and your mother can live at Braedrumie House.'

She stepped back and forced him to loosen his grip. 'Tolbain willna let one of his possessions go as easily as that and Mother's no' well.'

'For God's sake she as good as sold you to him.'

'She's still my mother.'

'You canna expect me to bear this and do nought. I should have gone to Fort William, stopped it.'

She put a finger over his lips. 'No. They'd have hanged you.' She pulled her hood over her head. 'I must leave and you must too. If we're seen…' She set off down the hill.

'Kirsty.'

'I dinna want you caught.'

'Caught? Are you no' caught by his money and fancy ways? Is it true he brought his whore to the house the day after you wed?'

She whirled, her anger fuelled by humiliation and strode towards him. 'How dare you judge me by his actions, Johnnie Stewart.'

'You're only handfasted, leave him.' His face cold, implacable.

'He willna let me go. Whilst he's got me, he has Mother and her land.'

He stared at her.

'Now you can gloat and enjoy my situation.'

'Why would you think I'd enjoy your pain?' He stared at her. 'Because he does? I'll love you, Kirsty Lorne, until my heart ceases to beat.' He waved a folded piece of parchment at her. 'I came to leave this for you. Euan and I have to visit a relative in Port Glasgow. You willna see me for three or four weeks, no' that you care.'

She flung herself at him and breathed him in. 'Never think I dinna care. Everything I've done, am, will be, all for you, Johnnie. I'll love you 'til the day the sun doesna rise.' She stood on tiptoe and her lips brushed and caressed his.

His body responded in kind. His mouth rampaged over hers. He kissed her throat, then traced the line of her slender shoulder blade with his finger until she flinched.

He paused and studied the purple marks.'The bastard,' he said, then his lips brushed her bruised skin.

Kirsty trembled. 'Let me know what love is again,' she whispered in his ear.

He swept her off her feet and carried her inside the croft.

***

Later that afternoon Tolbain slammed Toll House's front door. He strode into the sitting room.

Kirsty turned to face him. *Did he know?* 'Were the cellars interesting?' she asked.

'They will be once I start brewing ale. Where's Meg?'

'In your room.' Kirsty's shoulders relaxed. 'Where else?'

He paused. 'You're glowing.'

Her heart skipped a beat. 'Am I?' She widened her eyes.

'Something- Send a flagon of wine up. I don't want to be disturbed.'

Thank God

'And take off that brooch. You're mine now.'

She made a face as his back disappeared up the flight of stairs. Johnnie's brooch lay wrapped inside her clenched fingers. The rubies glinted at her and spoke of the promises

The Jacobite Affair

they'd made to each other. *I have to get out of this farce of a handfasting, but how?*

Lorna Windham

CHAPTER Sixty-four

By the time Johnnie and Euan left for Port Glasgow, clouds chased the silver moon. Alais, silent as ever, said nothing, but her eyes made Johnnie uncomfortable.

'She cares for you.' Euan nudged his pony nearer Johnnie's. 'Anyone can see that.'

'You're wrong. We're just friends. I helped her and she's grateful.'

'You're like a blind man.' Euan tightened his reins. 'Dinna say I didn't warn you.'

Warn him? He'd never thought about Alais in that way. How could he tell her about Kirsty? How tell the bairns? They'd never understand. He didn't even understand. As soon as he got back from Uncle John's, he'd sort things out.

Johnnie and Euan travelled at night and hid from redcoat patrols during the day. Both carried dirks which they could hide, aware of the penalty if caught with weapons. Johnnie struggled to sleep, Duncan's face haunted him.

The brothers stabled their ponies in Port Glasgow. Uncle John grimaced when he opened his door and saw his nephews on his doorstep. His brow creased as he peered through his spectacles at the dark, fashionable street behind them. He set his lips in a firm line and hauled his nephews, one after another into his hallway. Then he turned the key in the door.

'Evening, uncle. How's Aunt Jane?' Euan asked.

'Keep your voice down,' Uncle John snapped. 'So, your father backed the Jacobites in the '15 and he's done it again.' He ran his fingers through his grey hair.

Johnnie rolled his eyes.

'Sir...' Euan began.

'Dinna defend him, I ken him of old. He's led you to ruin.'

'Uncle, Father's not as you knew him, he's no' well.' Johnnie explained.

'Not well?' Uncle John's eyes stared at him like cannon ports.

'His memory comes and goes like the tide.' Euan added.

297

The Jacobite Affair

'How convenient for him. Has he any idea of the danger he places me in? Made sure I kept my nose clean and family safe. Neighbours know me as a Whig and loyal to the crown. Any idea how Glasgow feels about you all? **They** havena forgotten the prince's demands when you stopped off on your retreat north, you ken?'

Damn. Johnnie remembered the grim faces when the prince demanded food, clothes and shoes.

'I take it you were at Culloden and have a price on your heads?'

'Aye and Duncan died there.' Euan's face became stone.

Johnnie closed his eyes. Duncan, his head so heavy. His blood.

His uncle put a hand to his forehead. 'Duncan? Dear God what were you all thinking?'

A crash which sounded like broken crockery came from the inner depths of the house followed by their aunt's voice raised in anger.

Uncle John put a finger to his lips. 'Too dangerous here. At least you had the sense to call at night. Go to *The Gentleman*, you mind the inn, Euan?'

Euan nodded. 'Aye, sir.'

Their uncle bundled them out, glanced up and down the empty street and closed the door in their faces.

'Made the inn's acquaintance at university. Follow me.' Euan led Johnnie through a labyrinth of dank, narrow streets; over dunes and along a deserted part of the waterfront which smelt of rancid fish and seaweed. Gulls waded near wooden hulks and men slunk back into wynds. In the distance, chinks of light came from a building which stood on its own, hunched against the elements.

In the gloom, Johnnie made out the inn's top floor which overhung as if about to tip into the sea. At first floor level, the weathered sign of a drunken gentleman with a bottle, swung to and fro. The stout shutters and door stood closed against the cold wind. A scent of sour ale seeped from the building and invaded Johnnie's nostrils.

Lorna Windham

Euan entered first and Johnnie followed to be greeted by a blast of stale, warm air. Lit tallow candles and cruisie lamps littered window sills. A grizzled gentleman at one table lifted his tankard at them. Johnnie sat and stretched his long legs in front of the fire whilst Euan ordered fish soup and hot toddies from the landlord who tap-tapped in on a wooden leg. He asked no questions and they didn't offer any conversation.

They gulped down the last spoonful as a gust of cold night air announced Uncle John.

'Damn these spectacles.' He plumped himself beside Euan and cleaned the glass with his silk handkerchief. He replaced the spectacles on his nose and called out, 'Pegleg, a whisky, if you please.'

'Sir.' The landlord limped across the room and put the drink on the table. Uncle John downed it in one. 'Another, if you please.'

'Uncle...' Johnnie began

'Keep your voices down,' he whispered. 'This place is safer than most for business like ours, but there's some, like Peadar there, who'd sell their own mother for a crust.' He indicated the grizzled man who placed his tankard on his table, sighed and rose to go. The door closed behind the man and Uncle John leaned forwards. 'You'll want passage to France I suppose? Only sensible. Your father hasna charted a wise course, no' wise at all.'

'Sir, if you can find no kind words for your brother, our father, we'd rather you kept them to yourself,' said Euan. 'We havena come to explain his actions.'

'Ah, my apologies. I've offended you. It wasna my intention. I'm an old man and I speak as I find. I'll say no more about your father, it's you that needs help and I'll give it. *Valiant's* in France, but *Reliant's* here in the harbour. She's already got one extra passenger, she may as well have others.'

'You dinna mean the prince?' Euan leant forward.

'No, no laddie. A priest, has to leave or the authorities will hang him.'

'A priest?' Johnnie jerked upright.

The Jacobite Affair

'Aye.' Uncle John scratched under his wig. 'This time tomorrow you could be safely on your way.'

'I thought all our business, at the moment, was in the Americas in furs and tobacco?' Queried Johnnie.

'Aye, well we do the odd run to France.' Their uncle stared out of the window. 'Money to be made in brandy and lace. Dangerous.' He turned his gaze on his nephews. 'The English Navy stops and searches every vessel for the prince, you see?'

'We're involved in smuggling contraband?' Euan came alert.

'Aye.'

'Does Father know?' asked Johnnie.

'Not exactly.' Uncle John pursed his lips. 'Well, with the way things have been recently in the Highlands... Difficult to get a message. Now, about you leaving Scotland...'

'Uncle, it's no' passage to France we want. We've come to claim payments owed to our family from the legal side of our business, if you please. And now I've discovered there's a priest, to persuade him to come to Braedrumie and marry me and Morag.'

'Are you mad?' You'll be wanted men. And the priest won't do it, it's too dangerous.'

'Would you arrange a meeting?' Euan raised his brows.

Their uncle sighed and stared at both of them. 'Against my better judgement.'

'When does *Reliant* sail?' asked Johnnie.

'On tomorrow's tide, in the evening about ten.'

'We'll meet him early morning,' said Euan. 'And we expect the transfer of money to us, half in cash and half as a banker's note if you please.'

'As soon as the bank opens tomorrow, though it may take some days, weeks even.'

'We can wait.' Johnnie ignored the voice in his head that said no he couldn't. He'd a vision of Kirsty naked and in his arms.

'I'll make sure you have a note for the captain of *Reliant*. He'll ensure there's no gossip about your visit or the priest.'

Lorna Windham

Uncle John tapped his nose. 'I'll buy you a berth for the night here, should be safe enough. When you leave ask Pegleg to show you the stairs, he'll ken what I mean. He can be trusted, I know too much about him.' He swallowed the last of his whisky and put on his hat and cape. 'Stay close lads. I'll be back before nine tomorrow evening.'

***

As soon as Euan's head touched the pillow his breath settled into a slow rhythm.

Johnnie closed his eyes. Easier when you have a clear conscience. He wrestled with sleep and woke with a start, sure Duncan's hand lay on his shoulder.

Euan stood over him. 'Time to rise. Looks like you had a restless night.' He pointed at the pillow and counterpane on the floor.

'I've known more comfortable beds.' Johnnie sprang up to meet the early morning light. Once they'd washed, dressed and eaten Johnnie asked Pegleg about *the stairs.*

The man's eyes narrowed and he beckoned the brothers to follow him. As he raised the cellar trapdoor a musty smell rose to meet them. Johnnie made out a set of rickety, wooden steps. The landlord levered himself down first, then Euan and then Johnnie. An iron cage, with bars from floor to ceiling, stood in one dark corner. The landlord unlocked the door and limped towards a crate. He lifted it to one side and revealed another trapdoor which he heaved open. Below, just ebony darkness and a faraway sound of slurp and slap.

Pegleg turned to Euan and Johnnie. 'Here's the note from your uncle. Dinna ask questions, just follow your ears and noses lads. You've got three hours before the tide turns. Remember, three hours. Make sure no one sees you leave or enter when you get to the beach.'

Johnnie took the note, looked at Euan and without a word, both men grasped their dirks. Euan led the way down the worn, stone stairs. The boom of the sea became louder as the

The Jacobite Affair

twists and turns in the tunnel led the brothers closer to the exit. The salt tang of the sea invaded Johnnie's nose as Euan pointed out a pinprick of light ahead. Euan's boots crunched underfoot. Sand. Johnnie trod in Euan's footsteps as the men approached the cave mouth where daylight shimmered and seaweed glistened.

Ahead, lay a sheltered cove. Gulls soared in the grey sky and white waves crashed on the desolate shingle beach. Johnnie imagined this would be a perfect place to land contraband. They walked a couple of hundred yards and rounded the headland to see the harbour and a forest of masts. Ships and boats of every size bobbed up and down in the breeze. In the distance, on the far side of the River Clyde, lay a blue mountain horizon.

The brothers threaded their way through stashes of goods, handcarts and neat piles of rope until Johnnie spotted *Reliant,* a two masted brigantine built for speed. It lay amongst several vessels. Euan showed their uncle's letter to a bearded seaman who sat on deck and stabbed a needle into a yellowed sail.

''E's down below on the left of the captain's cabin.' He grinned and showed a broken black tooth.

Johnnie and Euan headed below decks. Euan knocked on the cabin's wooden door.

It opened and a pale face peered at them through the small gap. 'Who... is it?' The man's brown eyes shifted from Johnnie to Euan and back again.

Scared, thought Johnnie.

'Good morning to you Father.' My name is Euan Stewart and this my brother Johnnie. We're sorry to disturb you, but have a wee favour to ask.'

'Ask my son, and if it's in my power, I'll help.' The priest's bony fingers came together as if in prayer.

'We come from a little village in the north called Braedrumie, Father, where there's a lot of good catholics needing your services. We havena a priest since the last one ten years ago. I'm to be married and want to do it properly.'

The priest licked his thin lips. 'You're asking me to go with you to this Braedrumie? No, no. I won't. If I'm caught... I have to go to France, tonight, now.'

'Father.' Euan leant over him. 'We're of your faith and understand your concerns. Once you've performed my wedding ceremony and perhaps confessions we'll ensure you're put aboard a ship and taken straight to France.'

'The authorities, they've threatened to... they'll kill me if I get off this ship.'

Euan's lips tightened. 'But if you don't go with us, **we'll** kill you and you willna see France or anywhere else ever again. Do I make myself clear?'

The colour flooded from the priest's face. He couldn't take his eyes off Johnnie who'd carved his initials into a wooden beam with his dirk and winked at him.

'Yes.' The priest gulped.

The brothers bundled the terrified priest back to the inn via the cave.

Pegleg paled. 'Thought I'd seen the last of 'im,' he growled. 'Want him off my premises sharpish.'

The priest turned to run, but Euan grabbed him. 'Dinna try that again, Father, or I'll be forced to take strong measures.' Euan put a hand on his dirk.

The priest shrank back.

That night Euan and Johnnie enveloped the priest in a cloak. They blindfolded and gagged him, then pulled the hood low over his face. Once satisfied, the brothers walked on either side and led him to their uncle's house.

Euan thrust the priest inside his uncle's hallway. Johnnie followed and closed the door.

'This isn't what we agreed. Were you followed?' hissed their uncle.

'No. We were careful.' Johnnie kept one hand on the priest's collar.

'It's a good thing I sent your aunt to her sister's. Sorry, Father, but you sleep one night here and one night only,' muttered Uncle John. 'Too risky to have you longer, any of

The Jacobite Affair

you. Be away before the servants rise. Lads, give up this foolish notion. Euan's wedding will be food enough for the gossips, but if news of a priest gets around, there'll be a price on all our heads.' He lowered his bushy brows.

'We'll bring him back.' A tic of annoyance flicked between Euan's brows.

'So, you're not to be persuaded. Stubborn, like your father.' Euan glared at him.

'Alright, alright. Just make sure you're in good time for *Valiant* to take him to France,' said Uncle John. We've a ship comes once a month, but they don't hang around. They'll wait an hour, no more. Once the cargo's off and loaded up again, they'll sail. I have what you wanted from the bank, by the way. As an old customer, they did what I asked.'

The brothers left before dawn with the cash, a bankers draft and the priest. The two men poked and prodded him onwards through the dark and gathered their ponies from the stable. At dusk, weary from their ride, the group camped in a gorse-covered glen, beside a brae and several stone graves.

The priest's eyes spat fire at them as he settled down on the bank.

'Euan, let me have a little time with him,' begged Johnnie as he unbuckled a girth. 'I'm in sore need of confession.'

'Confession?' Euan's brow creased. He threw his saddle to the ground. 'It's no' the battle is it? You don't have any of Cumberland's butchers on your conscience do you?'

'Euan...'

'I'll get us some water. When you're finished it's my turn.' Johnnie paused. 'No' Rory Graham?'

'Aye.'

'You had to do it.'

'Did I?' Euan looked away.

'This is a heathenish place. The priest crossed himself.

'Father, will you hear my confession?' said Johnnie.

The priest's face became inscrutable. 'Of course, my son. Let us walk to a more Godly spot.' He led Johnnie further along the brae into a deep gorge with a pebbled shore. The priest sat on a flat stone.

Johnnie knelt beside him and said, 'I've committed heinous crimes...'

'Go on, my son.'

'I can't, Father... I...'

'You must, for it is only through God hearing your repentance for your sin, that you will receive absolution.'

All Johnnie's anguish broke like a sea around him. He hung his head and started again. The priest sat and listened in silence. After a time Johnnie finished. 'And Duncan's death has made my father an old man. What am I to do?'

'Dominus Noster Jesus Christus te absolvat...' the priest murmured. 'You must do serious penance for this sin my son. You will take responsibility for your father for the rest of your life. He needs your strength as do your brothers.'

The priest sighed and pursed his lips. 'In nomine Patris et Filii et Spiritus Sancti.'

'Amen.'

'I will pray for you, my son. Go in peace.'

The Jacobite Affair

CHAPTER Sixty-five

Kirsty eased herself into her seat and picked up her knitting. Pinpricks of pain danced along her spine and hate spun over the web of her being. *Tolbain. Johnnie's been away for ever, at least he showed me tenderness, unlike that creature.*

The previous night Tolbain had entered their bedchamber. He'd held her to his chest whilst she squirmed to get away. She'd begun to loathe lemon-scented cologne. 'I wanted the land, but I also wanted you.' She smelt his fetid breath as his poisonous words snaked into her ear. 'So innocent, so naïve, such young flesh. I do enjoy our encounters, my dear.' He squeezed her breast.

Pain zig-zagged through her. 'No. I dinna want this, use your whore.' She caught him off guard and pushed him away.

He lunged at her and his backhanded slap made her eyes water as he knocked her to the floor. 'You'll do it.' He grabbed her by her wrists and jerked her upright as his spittle flecked her face. 'Or I'll throw the old bitch out on her fine arse.'

'No. You wouldna. She's old and frail. Family.'

'She wouldn't last a week in that farmhouse on her own. You'll not make a fool of me. Don't think Johnnie Stewart can save you either.'

She blanched. *Johnnie. But he's in Glasgow.*

'My spies say he's been seen.'

Oh God. 'He died at Culloden.'

'No. He's gone to ground, but I'll see him hang.'

Oh, God. Johnnie. 'You disgust me.' The words came without thought.

He rose to his knees and towered above her. 'Do I now? Seems to me you've forgotten who's master here.' He reached for his whip.

'No.' She shrank back, but he held her wrists and ensured she'd never forget.

Lorna Windham

***

Next morning Drewitt had sucked in her breath. 'It... your wounds need someone with more knowledge. I'll ask the master.'

Before Kirsty could stop her Drewitt had called out to Tolbain in the doorway. 'Your Grace, may I send for a healer?'

'What for? Nought but a scratch. Tell her to get on with it.' He walked away.

Drewitt's lopsided mouth and jaw became even more obvious as she clenched her teeth. 'Your Grace.'

Kirsty bit back tears. *How can I warn Johnnie?*

'This may hurt.' Drewitt dabbed her fingers into a small earthenware pot.

Kirsty smelt camomile and mint as Drewitt's hand rubbed the salve over her spine. 'Agh.' Kirsty arched in pain.

'Sorry, Your Grace. Best humour him next time.'

***

Kirsty struggled for days to leave her home. No matter which direction she took, a guard turned her back. *How can I warn Johnnie?*

A week later, Kirsty looked in on Mother whose closed eyes lay sunken in her face. *Oh, God. She's failing.*

Tolbain stopped at the open door. 'I'm going out. Nought beats hunting a man unless of course, it's a wench.' He strode off.

'Johnnie.'

Why call his name? 'Hush, Mother.'

Mother's tongue wet her cracked lips. 'Made... mistake. Johnnie... one... for... you. Danger.'

Oh, God. 'He's safe for the moment. Dinna worry, save your strength.' A pang of anguish lanced through Kirsty. She kissed Mother's withered cheek and put a hand to her fevered brow. *Red hot.* She dipped a cloth into a bowl of cold water on

The Jacobite Affair

the bedside table, wrung it and dabbed at the old woman's face. Beside the bowl lay an unopened letter, sprinkled by water droplets and addressed to Mrs. Lorne.

'Arrived today, Your Grace.' Drewitt entered with a pile of clean, white linen in her arms.

'I'll read it to her later. Make sure you keep her cool and moisten her lips.' She broke the letter's seal and unfolded the parchment. *Peggie Balfour.* What she read made Kirsty raise her eyebrows. *Who would have guessed it of Morag McColl?* Kirsty looked out of the window. Horses galloped into the distance. *Tolbain and his men.* An idea sprang into her mind. 'I'll look in on her later.' She sped to her bedchamber and flung open the window. 'Saddle my horse,' she yelled.

A startled, thin-faced groom looked up at her from the yard below. 'Master's orders, I'm to accompany you.'

Drat. Kirsty bit her lip. 'Very well.' She pulled at her stays and changed into her riding habit. *Revenge.* The word seeped into her bones, swirled in her bloodstream and made her heart beat faster. *Tolbain. Morag understands herbs. I'll ask for a potion. She'd understand, surely? And if not, I've this letter.* She tapped it against her lips. *Morag won't be fond of a Whig who'd fought at Culloden against her precious Euan.*

***

Kirsty seethed after her visit to Morag. *She didn't understand, even questioned why I'm handfasted to Tolbain. Not that I told her, she wouldn't have believed it. Took the wind out of her though, when I threatened to tell what I knew. Fancy being unaccompanied in Edinburgh and not expecting vile gossip. But, Morag being Morag said my request* was a sin. *A sin to rid the devil from the Earth? Couldn't tell her about Tolbain's sins. She's only ever known love, how could she understand?*

Kirsty thought of her loveless childhood, drunken father and spiteful mother. *What did I do to deserve them? There's only been Johnnie, strong and steadfast who worked on our farm, not for the land, but because he loves me. God, there has to be another way out of this loveless handfasting and Morag McColl needs a lesson. I just have to think.*

***

Johnnie wanted to get home with the priest and see Kirsty. The journey to and from Port Glasgow had taken longer than he'd thought. Four weeks. Only a few miles from Braedrumie and lost in his thoughts, his pony almost bolted when Kirsty, with wild hair and eyes stepped out of the undergrowth. She mouthed *Our Place* to him then demanded to speak to Euan alone. Johnnie went to say something then tightened his lips. Why am I caught between her and my family? I love them all, but I can't betray our affair. The Stewarts would never forgive me.

His brother returned with tight lips and stormy eyes.

'Kirsty said what?'

'I warned Morag, Johnnie. Told her it was unseemly to join our baggage train. Did she listen? Oh, no. As usual she knew better. Now look. Her reputation's in tatters and I've her father and mine breathing down my neck, blaming me. They'll force me to marry her. Why are you grinning?'

'Well, isn't that what you both want?'

'No' like this. I have to talk to her. Hear what she has to say.' Euan galloped off with a scowl on his face.

Damn, thought Johnnie. Why had Kirsty done it?

The Jacobite Affair

CHAPTER Sixty-six

Kirsty woke in her bedchamber. *Dawn, by the light which streamed through the shutters and onto the floor.* Men's gruff voices and horses' hooves sounded outside. *What now?* She scrambled out of bed and peered at the courtyard below.

'Let's hunt Stewarts again.' Tolbain raised his arm as a signal to move off.

Villain. She watched him and his men spur into the distance. *At least I warned Euan and now Johnnie's back, I'll go to Our Place. Tell him about Tolbain.* Her heart lightened.

***

The ruined croft stood against a backcloth of grey clouds which careered across the cerulean sky. She scanned the rolling hills, the gorse and heather. *Of course Johnnie isn't here. Why should he be? I gave him no time..* Her mind seethed. *Surely he wants me as much as I want him*?

Kirsty put her hand inside the oak's trunk. Her fingers scrabbled, then found the smooth surface of a pebble. *Johnnie.* She whirled. *The croft.* She scrambled up the overgrown path and paused at the drunken doorway. He leaned against the back wall in deep shadow.

'Johnnie, darling. Where have you been?' She opened her arms to him. 'Mother's still no' well.'

He made no move to welcome her. 'Why did you do it? Morag's done nought to you. Euan could have refused to marry her. You've humiliated them in front of the village and the priest we brought back. Do you know Euan has to sit in the sinners' pew? No' that I'd believe Peggie Balfour's malicious tongue.'

'Dinna be cross.' Kirsty laid her head on his chest. 'I canna bear it.'

'You shouldna have done it.' Johnnie lifted her chin with his forefinger. 'Was it spite? I know you and Morag have never got on.'

Lorna Windham

'Not spite.' Kirsty looked at the ground. 'I asked Morag for help and she refused.'

'What help?'

'I canna say.' She turned from him.

'Kirsty.' He stood behind her, put his arms round her waist and nestled his cheek against hers.

'It's a sin.'

'Tell me.' His lips brushed her neck.

Oh God, I love it when he does that. 'I asked for a potion for Tolbain.'

'A potion?' He pulled her round to face him. His eyes narrowed. 'To murder him?'

'Aye.' She bit her lip.

'Your life must be hell with that fiend.' He crushed her to him. 'Darling, dinna do it. Leave it to me.'

She closed her eyes. 'He kens you're back. He'll kill you.'

'He can try- You shouldna have done that to Euan and Morag.'

She stared at him. 'But, Euan's marrying her and they've a priest.'

'You've made them unhappy when they should be full of joy. We'd have been married by the priest if you'd just waited.'

Her shoulders slumped. *Oh, God.* 'I'm sorry.'

His lips scorched hers. 'My own one, leave Tolbain.'

'I canna, I've Mother to think of. He treats her shamefully.' She rested her body against his and ran one hand down his chest whilst the other undid his buttons. 'I think we're wasting time don't you?'

He cradled her face in his hands. 'You drive me insane Kirsty Lorne.' His lips ravished hers.

The Jacobite Affair

CHAPTER Sixty-seven

The sky darkened and distant thunder rumbled. Dusk fell on the garlanded tables which sat on Braedrumie House's front lawn. Candles winked at wedding guests and torches lit the scene.

Johnnie downed his whisky amongst the remnants of the feast. At least the cellar's well stocked. His head swam.

Euan thumped Johnnie between his shoulder blades.'Now's your chance, brother.'

'What do you mean?' Johnnie searched Euan's face. Did he know about Kirsty? Euan wouldn't approve, not after Kirsty upset Morag. And he'd be concerned Tolbain would find out.

'Ask Alais for her hand, whilst I'm away.'

Johnnie's glass slammed on the table. 'What the devil makes you think I want to do that?'

'The way she looks at you, man. She loves you. Then there's the bairns. They treat you both like parents. It would work out well for all.'

Johnnie managed to say, 'Would it now?' His insides twisted as he recognised some truth in Euan's words. Alais visited the laird most mornings, made sure he ate and kept him company. The children played in the grounds whilst she mended and altered clothes. Safer that Johnnie and Euan spent daylight hours at the den. Her lack of speech didn't matter. She made herself understood with signs and he understood more and more every day.

Kirsty. Her breasts and long limbs even invaded his sleep. He didn't hate Alais and he loved the children. In different circumstances, well. No one would dream he and Kirsty slept together. Their secret would be safe. 'Thought you had more on your mind than me and Alais.' Johnnie jerked a thumb at Morag.

'I have, I have.' Euan gave Johnnie a rueful grin. 'Just promise me you'll think about what I said.'

'Aye, I'll do that.' Johnnie downed another whisky, 'Get away with you, I'll see to Father.'

Lorna Windham

Euan slapped him on the back. 'My thanks, brother.'

Johnnie glanced across at the laird. He swayed in his chair as he sang drunken songs. Euan and Morag, their backs stiff, rode off into the mountains. Johnnie envied them, certain the couple's differences would be forgotten on their days alone together.

He wrapped his father's arm round his shoulder and signalled to Jamie Moffat to help get his father to bed. Alais, Jamie and the children trooped behind and waved at the young guards. Thank goodness the wedding passed without incident. Euan had ensured a wider cordon of Stewarts at every pass. Johnnie pondered the redcoat raids on villages. There'd been none at Braedrumie. Why?

The group's footsteps rang out in the hallway. Months fell away. Johnnie could see Mother as she sewed. Rob stride into the sitting room. Worse: Duncan hurtle down the bannister, backside first. He closed his eyes to make Duncan vanish. Poor, Duncan.

Books and papers lay strewn on every surface of the laird's bedroom. It's as if Father sought an answer in one of the manuscripts. Johnnie and Jamie laid him on his four-poster bed and covered him with plaids. A wasted shell, with fewer servants every day, apart from Dougie.

Alais pointed at Duncan's saltire draped over a chair. She signed. 'Never... out... of... his... sight.'

Good he could understand her better now. 'Gives him comfort.' Johnnie shook his head. Comrie stopped her jig when Alais put a hand on the little girl's shoulder. Neill stood silent beside the laird.

The music and singing became more raucous outside. Johnnie closed the shutters and Jamie banked up the laird's fire with the last of the peat.

Alais signed again. 'Tidy... tomorrow.' Her mouth curved into a smile and she squeezed Johnnie's hand.

Damn. Euan's right, Alais does care for me.

The Jacobite Affair

'A grand wedding.' Dougie stomped into the room with a stack of peat in his hands. 'Reminds me of the old days. My Isabel says your mother would be proud of you all.'

'Aye.' Johnnie grimaced. Mother. Rob had something to answer for there.

'Perhaps we'll have another wedding to look forward to soon?' Dougie winked at Johnnie and then looked at Alais who flushed and stared at her feet.

Jamie scowled.

Damn Dougie. 'You'll sit with Father a wee while?' asked Johnnie.

'As I do every evening.' Dougie replied. 'Best you get back to the den in case word of this wedding's got out.'

Night had fallen when Johnnie and Alais swung Comrie by her arms as they walked. Neill and Jamie marched ahead. He had to let Alais know, unfair to let her think he loved her or even hope. Nearer the den he carried Comrie whose feet dragged. Her head slumped on his shoulder. A jangle of reins? Redcoats. The group hid in the heather. A flutter of wings sent them to crouch behind gorse and at the screech of an animal Johnnie signalled them to freeze. He let out a sigh of relief when he set Jamie on guard outside the den.

He tucked Comrie underneath some rugs whilst Alais put Neill to bed. Johnnie kissed Comrie whose eyes never opened and ensured Neill said his prayers. 'God bless.' Johnnie pressed the boy's shoulder.

'Night, Dada.' Neill closed his eyes. A faraway rumble sounded and he sat up. 'What's that?'

'Thunder. Nought to worry about. Sleep.'

Johnnie strode to the cave mouth. Behind him he imagined Alais as she signed her *Good... nights* and wondered what her voice would sound like if she could speak.

He looked up at the night sky studded with stars. Across to the south, in the direction Euan and Morag had gone, thunder rolled. Sheet and forked lightning illuminated the distant mountains and turned them into crouched monsters.

Alais stood beside him.

She signed. 'They're… tired.'

He nodded. She made a good mother and the children loved her.

She signed. 'Worried?'

'It's nothing.' Coward.

Her warm fingers brushed his arm. 'Me… help?'

He shook his head. How could he tell her about Kirsty?

'The… bairns?'

'I promise I'll always be there for you and the bairns.'

'They… think… you… Father.'

'I ken that. I'm honoured and will do my best for them… and you.'

She held his gaze and signed. 'I… love… you.'

Johnnie started to protest, but she put a slender finger on his lips.

'I… not… child…'

Bloody hell. His head swam and his insides churned. He couldn't reveal he loved Kirsty. If Tolbain found out, all hell would break loose.

Alais left him. He listened to the wind as it soughed through the trees. The first drops of rain fell and a storm broke overhead.

The Jacobite Affair

CHAPTER Sixty-eight

The following morning, Johnnie followed the well-trodden path to the dead oak at *Our Place*. He drank in the azure sky streaked with white clouds and thought of Kirsty. His hand groped for the feel of a soft, round pebble. Got it. They really should meet at night.

Kirsty stood in the dark of the croft's doorway. 'So, how was the wedding?' She walked into the light towards a grassy bank. The sunlight played on her hair.

He shrugged his shoulders. How could he tell her about Alais?

She sat and patted the area beside her.

'Everyone heard about it, except Tolbain of course. You'd no trouble from redcoats?'

He hunkered beside her. 'No, but thanks to you, the bride and groom weren't in the best of moods.'

She put a hand on his arm. 'Oh Johnnie, I said I'm sorry. I hate it when you're out of sorts with me. This time's so precious and it's more and more difficult to leave the house.'

He drew her to him and smothered her face with kisses which drifted to her neck and breasts. He paused. 'You're wearing my brooch, darling. It's too dangerous. Oh God, let me drink you in.' He lifted her and carried into the croft.

Afterwards she lay back, semi-naked, in the hay and studied a patch of blue sky through the hole in the croft's roof.

Johnnie tickled her ear with a grass stalk. 'He doesna suspect, does he?'

'If he did, you wouldna be sitting here.'

'Where is he?'

'Searching for you and your brother in the west. Said he had it on good authority, you'd be there. He'll be gone a few days.'

'We didna want Tolbain sniffing around at the wedding. How's your mother?'

Kirsty shook her head. 'No better. He willna let healers near.'

Lorna Windham

'I'm sorry to hear it. I asked Granny Mac for a tonic, she didna know it was for your mother and asked if I was ailing.' He handed the bottle to Kirsty. 'Hope it helps.'

Kirsty kissed his cheek and took the potion. 'You're a good man, Johnnie Stewart.'

'Aye, I am that. And good men deserve a reward.'

'What do you mean?'

'Well, I'm sure Euan and Morag are enjoying their honeymoon.' He tickled her bare leg with a grass stalk. 'And I feel my brother's stolen a march on me.'

'Bur we've only just- you're insatiable.'

'And that makes us a very fortunate couple, don't you think?' His lips caressed the soft inside of her knee, then stilled. Hooves, the stamp of feet and the low sound of men's voices filtered towards the croft.

He grabbed his sgian-dubh from his hose. Its sharp blade glinted. Kirsty's eyes filled with terror. He signalled her to be quiet. She reached for her stays, stockings and garters. He crept to a tumble of stone, once part of the walls, and looked between one of the chinks. What he saw chilled his blood.

He crawled back to where she struggled into her clothes and helped her. He whispered in her ear, 'Tolbain, his men and redcoats are heading this way.'

She gave a sudden intake of breath and stared at him open-mouthed.

'You've a chance. Use the ditch on the other side of those brambles. Go now and stay low.'

'What about you? Johnnie, you need to leave with me.'

He held her white face in his hands and his lips held hers for a moment. 'Hush, darling. I'll be alright. Just do as I say.' He pushed her towards the back door as he returned to the ruined wall. She turned on the threshold and looked at him.

'Go.' Johnnie motioned her away. The croft lay between her and the interlopers. She had to leave.

She mouthed, 'I love you.' Then sped off and disappeared into the maze of brambles.

Now he could think about himself.

The Jacobite Affair

Outside, a ruddy-faced major held up his hand. 'Detail, halt. Stand at ease.'

Tolbain and his men stopped beside the redcoats. The horses drank from the stone trough in the weed-covered yard. 'Good thing we came across you, Major. No point in my searching west if they've been seen nearby.'

'It's Lord Kinross you need to thank, Your Grace.'

'Ah, yes.' Tolbain smirked

Johnnie jerked upright. Kinross, that cur.

'You know each other, Your Grace?' asked the major.

'In a manner of speaking.'

The major raised his voice to his men. 'Fall out.'

Kinross? In league with redcoats? Johnnie watched two privates sprawl backwards into the heather whilst the rest sat on the ground.

A barrel-chested sergeant barked, 'Don't make yourselves too comfortable you 'orrible little men. Carter, Partridge- let's be havin' you, stand guard. No moans Partridge or you'll feel the point of my bayonet. Brown, Werridge to me.' The sergeant and his men headed for the croft.

Time to leave. Johnnie retreated towards the open back door. Kirsty should be well away now.

Tolbain's voice. 'Derelict for years. No point.'

'Odd.' The major pointed at the ground. 'The grass is flat here. Sergeant.'

The soldier's boots stopped.

Your Grace?' The major raised an eyebrow at Tolbain.

Johnnie's heart hammered in his chest.

'Search it if you must.'

Damn the bastard. Johnnie's hand crept towards the far door post.

'Carry on, sergeant.' The major eased himself in his saddle.

'Perhaps you and your men would like to take refreshment at Toll House, Major? You obviously know more of the whereabouts of these treacherous rebels, than I do.'

'My thanks, sir.'

318

Lorna Windham

Johnnie plunged into sunlight, then stopped, his back to the wall. Had something glinted in the hay?

'Lots of footprints, sir. A man and a woman by the size. Could be someone's hidin' here.' One of the privates. His voice close, too close.

Johnnie flung himself over the brambles, rolled and landed in the ditch. Dry - thank God. A hundred yards below him he spied Kirsty's back and wished her to hurry. He let out a breath as she disappeared into a tunnel of heather. He turned and clambered upwards and off at an angle. He had to get as much gorse between himself and his enemies as possible.

The sergeant's voice wafted to him on the breeze. 'Fresh hay. Look out the back Werridge. See anythin', Brown?'

Johnnie ducked.

A scrawny private took a few steps out of the croft. 'No serg.'

A corporal, scanned the heather and gorse. 'No serg.'

The sergeant blocked the doorway. 'Use your bleedin' bayonet in those brambles, Werridge. Not like that, man, like this. You're not at a tea party. Don't want one of those nice Jacobites getting' the jump on you.'

Tolbain's voice drifted across to where Johnnie hid twenty yards away. 'What have you found?'

Another voice. 'A brooch, sir... there.'

Kirsty's. Johnnie watched Tolbain come out of the back of the croft and hold the object to the light. The rubies flashed as he snapped his hand round it.

'Bit of hanky-panky, sir.' The sergeant sent a flume of spit onto the ground. 'Perfect spot for lovers to meet, that's a luckenbooth brooch that is.'

'Shut your filthy mouth.' The major looked out over the gorse where Johnnie hid.

Johnnie hugged the ground and prayed.

The major and Tolbain turned to the croft. The next thing Johnnie heard: hooves. He watched as Tolbain galloped downhill towards Toll House.

The Jacobite Affair

Had he recognised the brooch? But it could belong to anyone. A cold sweat broke out on his forehead. He prayed Kirsty would get home before Tolbain.

Lorna Windham

CHAPTER Sixty-nine

Kirsty scanned the open ground in front of the side entrance to Toll House. A guard turned the corner and disappeared. *No one.* She flung herself through the secret door and locked it behind her. *No cries of alarm.* Her heart thudded against her ribs as she sped up the priest hole stairs. She concealed the entrance and raced into her bedchamber. Her breath came in gasps. She stripped off her muddy clothes, balled them up, threw them in the back of the wardrobe and took fresh ones. Her reflection in the mirror told her she looked dishevelled. *Drat.* She scrubbed at her face and hands with a damp cloth from her washstand. Then ran her fingers through her hair and removed a twig. Hooves pounded outside. She peeked out of the window. Tolbain galloped along the drive towards the house.

Back at the washstand, her hands shook as she used a comb and tidied stray strands of hair. *Did he see me or suspect something? Did Johnnie get away? Please God he hasn't been caught.* The hooves stopped. She raced back to the window as Tolbain's gruff voice shouted orders at a groom. Meg stood on the steps, he brushed her aside as servants scurried in several directions. A trickle of red dots on the skyline behind Tolbain caught Kirsty's eye. *Skirmishers.* She steadied herself and walked at her normal pace into Mother's bedchamber. 'How is she, Drewitt?'

Drewitt stood. 'No better, Your Grace.' She curtsied.

A door banged open below. 'Kirsty? Kirsty?' Tolbain's voice rang up the stairs.

Kirsty's heart skipped a beat. Then she took a wet cloth and dabbed at Mother's forehead.

'It's… it's the master, Your Grace.'

Kirsty let herself imagine his face, lobster-red from frustration because she hadn't answered at once, his large feet as they sped upstairs and his eyes as they sparked with anger. She kept her voice low and steady. 'Fetch fresh water, would

The Jacobite Affair

you Drewitt? Oh, and if the Master asks, I was resting this afternoon.'

Drewitt's eyelids flickered. She paused. 'Your Grace.'

'Kirsty?'

Tolbain at the top of the stairs?

Drewitt pursed her thin lips into a lopsided look of determination. She took up the basin, curtsied and closed the door behind her.

'Kirsty? Damn it, where is the bitch? You, where is she?' Tolbain's voice came through the wall.

A trickle of fear ran down Kirsty's spine.

'Why, with her mother as usual, Your Grace.'

'All afternoon? Answer me?'

'Aggh, my wrist.'

Kirsty flinched at Drewitt's squeal of pain. *Does he have to be so cruel?*

'She… she's no been well, only left to rest in her chamber, I swear.'

Let him come to me. Kirsty sat beside Mother and held her cold hand. She sensed the tiniest pressure from Mother's fingers. Her eyes remained closed.

The door swung open. 'Didn't you hear me?' Tolbain, his hair matted in sweat, jiggled something in his right hand.

'I was praying. What have you there?'

'A luckenbooth brooch.'

Oh God. She stopped her hand going to her breast. *I shouldn't have worn it.* She forced her voice to be steady. 'A sweethearts' brooch. Really?'

'Where have you been all day?' His eyes bored into her.

'Tending mother, resting. Ask Drewitt. Why these questions?'

He snapped. 'Someone's been on my land using old Soutar's croft.' He turned the brooch over and over in the palm of his hand. 'Lovers.' He stared at her. 'Don't you have a brooch like it?'

Her throat went dry. She forced a laugh. 'Lovers? A redcoat will have bribed a starving lass to give herself for the sake of it. Happens all the time, so they say. Shocking.'

His eyes popped again. 'Trespassing, f………. on my land?'

'Husband, you forget yourself.' Kirsty brushed imaginary fluff from her sleeve. 'Let me see.' She took the brooch and pretended to examine it. 'This gee-gaw is no' at all like mine. Fool's gold and glass. Really, husband, I'd expect you to ken the difference.'

His cheeks reddened as he snatched it back and his fingers curled over it.

Drat. Please God, don't ask to see my brooch.

'They won't do it again, I'll complain to the military. I've guests arriving, a redcoat major and his men. They'll need refreshment. I expect you to join us.'

She steadied her breath. 'Will he be here long?'

'As long as it takes. Bring your brooch.' He slammed the door.

Oh God. She sagged against Mother's window. Outside grey smoke from a garden bonfire curled into the air. Kirsty came to a decision and sped to her bedchamber. She stuffed the muddy clothes inside her dress and rushed downstairs just as Dunbar, the butler, opened the front door. A ruddy-face major stood on the doorstep.

Oh, no. 'Good afternoon, Major.' She sank into a curtsey.

'Major Curtis, at your service, Your Grace. His Grace was kind enough to invite us to accept his hospitality. Met him looking for rebels west of here? Saved him a wasted journey. Told him we'd reliable information they're closer to home.'

'By home…?' began Kirsty.

The study door opened. 'Major, you do me great honour. Come.' Tolbain ushered him in. 'Tell me more of Kinross.'

Kinross? 'If you'll excuse me for a moment, gentlemen. I'll join you after I've ensured we've refreshment for the major and his men.'

Tolbain's study door closed behind them.

The Jacobite Affair

Kirsty raced into the scullery. The boot boy's eyes rolled and. Reid, the plump cook, nudged a squint-eyed maid. Mrs Mills, the housekeeper, quirked an eyebrow. *Their territory, not mine.*

Kirsty clapped her hands. 'Mrs. Mills, a bottle of our best claret for His Grace in the study and ale to be served to the major's men at the front of the house.'

No one moved.

'Now.' Kirsty raised her voice. 'His Grace's orders.'

'Mr. Dunbar's job.' Reid sneered. 'I'll tell him.'

'**Your Grace.**'

Reid's face turned sullen. 'Your Grace.'

'See to it.' 'I'm taking some air.' *Drat these servants and their lack of respect.* Kirsty left by the back door and kept an eye on the gardeners who worked in the walled garden. Flames crackled as she approached. She checked all round her. No one near, just the gardeners who raked the beds. She reached inside her skirts, pulled out her muddy garments and threw them into the flames. When no sign of them remained, she hurried back to the house and almost bumped into Dunbar.

'Have the refreshments been served?' she asked.

'Yes… Your Grace.' Dunbar wet his thin lips. 'It's not done…you… in the scullery. His Grace willna be happy.'

'No? Oh, dear.' Kirsty left and wound her way through passageways, into the hall and to the study door. *The brooch- what am I going to do?*

Drewitt ventured from the shadows and whispered, 'I listened at the door.' She pressed something hard and shiny into Kirsty's hand. 'It's no' quite the same, but maybe it'll do?'

Kirsty's fingers closed round it. 'Bless you.' Drewitt scurried off. Kirsty reached for the doorknob when she heard the major say, 'We've a raid planned in this area, sir. I'm told there's rebels in Braedrumie…'

The door opened and Tolbain stood there.

'Oh dear, I've dropped my handkerchief,' Kirsty pointed at the square of white lace on the floor.

Lorna Windham

'Tolbain picked it up and sniffed the air as he passed it to her. 'Smells of wood smoke as do you.'

'Yes... well, I went to the scullery...'

'What?' Tolbain glared at her.

'I willna do it again. I just wanted to ensure the major and his men received refreshment immediately, and felt the need for fresh air. The gardeners lit a bonfire. The smoke is quite dreadful.'

'Hmm. Do sit, my dear.' Tolbain used his hand to press her into a seat. 'Did you find your brooch?'

'Yes. See.' She held up Drewitt's brooch and hid the garnets behind her finger tips.

Tolbain's lips snapped shut. 'By the way, the major tells me they've increased patrols in the area. I'd prefer it, for your own safety, if you remain inside the house from today.'

Kirsty forced a smile. 'As you wish.' She put the brooch in her pocket. Her mind ticked like a clock. *He knows. Johnnie must be safe, but for how much longer? I must warn him about Kinross and Braedrumie, but how? The raid's imminent. Maybe tonight or tomorrow.* 'Please excuse me gentlemen. I need to see to my mother and retire.'

'I'd rather you kept to your room.'

'Very well.' As she climbed the stairs she turned and watched Tolbain issue orders to Dunbar. She stopped on the landing. *Shouts?* She looked out of the window where a number of armed men ran to new positions around the house. *He's increased the guard. One's in front of the priest's hole door. Drat.*

'Is everything alright... Your Grace?' Dunbar stood at the foot of the stairs.

'Yes... Yes. Thank you.'

She mounted the stairs, turned the corner and dashed to Mother's room. The scent of lavender wafted towards her from where Mother lay asleep. *No Drewitt. Where is she? Every minute counts. The linen cupboard.* The clean smell of starch made Kirsty's nose twitch as she walked in, past the shelves

The Jacobite Affair

piled high with white sheets and pillowcases. Drewitt turned towards her.

Kirsty put a finger to her lips and spoke in a hushed whisper. 'There's going to be a redcoat raid. I'm watched and he's doubled the guard. I can't use the priest's stairs. Would you warn the Stewarts and Braedrumie?'

'More than my life's worth, Your Grace,' hissed Drewitt. 'Master's suspicious and I've done too much already.' She made to go.

Kirsty grasped Drewitt's hands in hers. 'I'm begging you. Please.'

'I canna do it.' Drewitt pulled herself free. 'He'll find out.'

'I'll say it was me.'

'How? If there's more guards. Let me go.' Drewitt pushed past her and left.

Oh, God. The poor village and what about Johnnie and his family? I have to do something. But, what?

Kirsty left the linen room and sped along the empty corridor. She opened the door of the room which held the priest's stairs. *What about the guard?* A board creaked and someone coughed behind her. *Dunbar.*

'His Grace gave orders you were to stay in your bedchamber, Your Grace.'

Drat the man. 'Such a little room.' She closed the door, retreated to her chamber and ran from window to window. *If I could only leap to freedom and Johnnie.*

The sun, dipped below the horizon in a gold blaze. *Perhaps I can use the ivy to climb down unseen in the darkness?* Flames flared in the grounds, then another and another. *Campfires round the house. I can't get out. What will happen to Braedrumie and Johnnie?*

Lorna Windham

CHAPTER Seventy

Days went by and Johnnie still found it impossible to remain still or sleep for long. His mind twisted with thoughts of Kirsty and her safety. He could get no news of her and didn't dare go to the croft again. Frustrated, he gathered peat, fished and hunted for hares.

One morning the crimson-tipped sun rose in the east and the first fingers of light crept towards the entrance of the den. Dust motes floated in the warm air and Johnnie went to check some snares he'd set near Inver Beck. The gurgle of water muffled the sound of horses and tramp of boots.

'Halt.' An educated English voice cut through the air. A stag bounded across the moor and Johnnie dived into the heather. He sneaked a look. About a 100 yards away, a redcoat column. Damn. Had they seen him?

A gruff voice bawled, 'Right, form line.'

The redcoats faced him across the floor of the glen. Skirmishers. If he didn't get away, they'd be on him. He sacrificed his snare, squirmed through the undergrowth at a diagonal and kept well in front of the soldiers. An outcrop of granite snaked over the hillside to his right. If he could reach it before the redcoats, he'd use the rocks as cover until he reached the crest.

He mounted the summit at the same time as a shout rang out from below. A private knelt on the ground. He held up a snare. Johnnie ducked. He knew all eyes would turn and search the glen and ridge for sight of him.

When he returned to the den by a circuitous route, he heard the children's raised voices.

'It's mine.' Comrie held her clenched fist behind her back.

'I found it.' Neill put his hands on his hips. 'Give it back.'

Alais stepped forward and signed. 'Let… me… see.'

Comrie put a small object in Alais' palm.

Alais dropped it as if scalded and held Comrie close to her.

The Jacobite Affair

'What's this?' Johnnie stepped forward and picked up a shiny, brass button. His brow furrowed. 'Where did you find it, Comrie?'

Comrie sucked her thumb.

'Over there.' Neill pointed in the opposite direction to which Johnnie had come. 'It's a redcoat's isn't it?'

'Aye.' Johnnie stared at the rugged skyline around them. 'I want you and Comrie to stay nearer the den in future.'

'But… ' Neill began.

'It's an order.'

Neill kicked his foot in the dust and reminded Johnnie of Duncan. His heart ached and his gut twisted. Mustn't think of Duncan.

'You're almost a man now.' He put his hands on Neill's bony shoulders. 'I need you to keep Alais and your sister safe. Understand?'

Neill's shoulders straightened and he lifted his dark head. 'Aye.'

Johnnie forced his voice to sound as it usually did. He didn't want to frighten Alais or Comrie, but two redcoat patrols close by made him uneasy. 'Were you thinking of visiting my father this morning?' he asked.

Alais stared at him with huge, fearful eyes. She nodded.

His father looked forward to her visits. And Alais always returned with gossip about Braedrumie and Dougie's assurance that the old man was as well as could be expected. He put an arm round her shoulders and felt the tension leave her. 'I'll come with you.'

She took his hand, drew him to one side and shook her head. 'You… danger…' she signed.

'There's another patrol in the next glen,' he whispered. He caught her arm as fear flashed in her eyes. 'Dinna worry, we'll be safe as long as we're careful. The den's well- hidden, no fires, but if they caught you alone with the bairns… you know what they can do. Safer if I'm with you.'

The muscles in her arm relaxed and she dipped her head.

Lorna Windham

He led her and the children by little used trails to Braedrumie House. Neill brushed out their tracks in the dusty earth with a clump of heather. Johnnie stopped them several times, before he waved them forward and through the garden gate at the back of the house.

'Red sky last night.' The laird shook his head as if at a bad omen.

Neill put an empty bottle to his eye as Comrie collected the others. Alais tidied papers. Then she sat by the fireplace and chose a sock from a basket. She threaded a needle, inserted a wooden mushroom in a hole and began to darn.

'You're always making or mending something Alais.' The laird's lips curled into a smile. 'Elizabeth sat at her spinning wheel every night. Said it gave her peace.'

'Mother.' Johnnie remembered her slim, upright figure as she spun.

A look of pain flashed across Alais' face.

Johnnie had an image of bodies and the charred spinning wheel at Alais' home. He moved towards the door. 'I'll get cook to make breakfast for everyone.'

***

Una, wafted a hand over her flushed face as she stirred the porridge in the pot over the fire. Johnnie breathed in the fresh dewdrop scent of morning and home at the open window. The splash of water made him turn and look out of the scullery door. Dougie had just doused his face in a wooden bucket full of icy water in the cobbled yard. Murdo stood, bare chested, by his side and dried himself with a coarse cloth.

'You're back,' Johnnie shouted to Murdo. 'How was the cattle drive?'

'It didna go well. No' much to show for it.' Murdo pulled on his shirt. 'Had to bribe my way past the border and do the same comin' back.'

'Breakfast,' Johnnie beckoned the men indoors.

The Jacobite Affair

Murdo's face brightened and Dougie strode towards the house.

Cows lowed, their udders heavy with milk and their tails lashed the fence posts. Ponies stamped and champed in the stables. Then a stray dog barked and more joined in. Puzzled, Johnnie walked out of the scullery and round to the front of the house. He increased his speed as he heard the sound of voices raised in fear.

He stopped to see a tide of Braedrumie crofters who headed towards him. A white- haired man led all the rest. He held farm implements. His daughter, Catrina carried two bundles and his middle-aged wife, Jean hugged a cooking pot.

'What's wrong, Gordon?' yelled Johnnie.

'Redcoats,' Gordon shouted and looked behind him.

Damn.

'Run,' shrieked Jean as she shoved Catrina ahead of her.

Johnnie looked past the line of villagers to Braedrumie. On a ridge to the east, a redcoat officer sat on horseback whilst his soldiers, red smudges in the trees, encircled the dwellings.

Johnnie froze. Retribution. He'd hoped Braedrumie was too isolated and too far from Fort William or had been forgotten. He should have known. The few men who'd survived Culloden, hid in the mountains. But the most vulnerable: the old men, women and children lived in Braedrumie.

Johnnie sprinted. He used the front door, took the stairs two at a time and raced into his bedroom which faced north. From its window he spied the far end of the glen where a red carpet of soldiers gathered cattle. Worse, a red file of troops marched towards Braedrumie House. They'd arrive in minutes.

Johnnie leapt down the stairs three at a time. 'Redcoats,' he yelled.

Dougie barred the front door with a wooden bench as Alais backed away, her mouth set in a silent scream. Neill took Alais' hand as Comrie clung to her. Johnnie grabbed Alais.

'We'll look after the laird.' Dougie handed Murdo a musket. 'Johnnie. Best you take Alais and the bairns out the back. There's no' a minute to lose.'

330

Lorna Windham

'Father?' Johnnie tugged at his sleeve.

'I'll no' leave my own home.' Father, his face set in stubborn lines, took a claymore from over the fireplace.

'We'll delay them, then use the cellar.' Dougie winked at Johnnie and motioned with his head that he should go.

Why did Euan have to be away now? Johnnie gathered Alais, Neill and Comrie as Dougie and Murdo took their places either side of the entrance.

Johnnie ran. He pulled Alais and the children behind him.

'Redcoats,' he shouted at Una. Her mouth formed a large O as the group raced out of the back door and into bright sunlight. He guided Alais and the children through the rose garden along a little used path, away from the gate, towards the wall a hundred yards away.

'Aagh.' Comrie tripped over a root, so he carried her between the gnarled apple trees. Light, shadow, light shadow. Branches whipped his face and lashed his arms as he tried to shield the small girl from the worst of it.

Alais' breath came in ragged gasps.

Were her thoughts of the raid on her farm? Of the shots that rang out and the knowledge she'd never see her family again? Images he wanted to forget flared and came to life in front of him. Culloden. Duncan. Behind, came shots followed by harsh commands and the splinter of wood as the soldiers forced their way into Braedrumie House. Father? Dougie? Murdo? Una? Fear for Alais and the children drove him to the wooden door. No sound of pursuit. Alais' hands shook as she struggled with the ancient iron latch. She thumped the warped wood with her fist in frustration at the rusted hinge and low bolt which refused to budge.

No time to twist the heavy bolt free. 'Stand back.' Johnnie ran at the gate and used his right foot. The wood groaned and exploded into the undergrowth some feet in front of them.

He led Alais and Neill down a wooded path towards the gurgle of water, then balanced on stones to cross the beck. Johnnie jumped onto dry land with Comrie's fingers dug into his shoulders and her face buried in his neck.

The Jacobite Affair

He turned to help Alais and then Neill cross. His heart steadied, when they joined him on the far bank. 'Go to the den. I must go back and help.'

'What have we here?' A voice with a Lowland Scots accent rang out.

Johnnie tensed. A figure rose from behind a pine and he'd just enough time to register MacNair's fist as it smashed into his jaw. The force drove Johnnie and Comrie backwards into a clump of nettles.

Comrie screamed as Johnnie's head reeled. He heard a thwack and then MacNair's cry, 'You little bastard.' MacNair had back-handed Neill into the beck where he landed with a splash and his head hit a rock. He lay still.

MacNair pushed Alais to the ground. He knelt over her and forced her legs apart with his knees. 'If you're a good lassie, I might let you live.' He collapsed on top of her, Johnnie's dirk in his back.

'Prickles sting,' cried Comrie as Johnnie picked her up. She rubbed at the livid, raised lumps on her legs.

'You alright lass?' Johnnie asked Alais as she struggled to her feet.

She bit her lip and nodded. Her eyes grew wide. She pointed at Neill.

'Take Comrie.' Johnnie knelt in the cold water beside the boy. 'He's breathing.' He wiped his hand over Neill's face and the boy's eyelids fluttered.

'What happened?' said Neill.

'You... kicked... him.' Alais stared at MacNair.

I dinna think he liked it.' Johnnie's eyes scanned the undergrowth for danger. 'Here, lad.' He stretched out his hand, Neill grabbed it and allowed himself to be hauled out. Johnnie lowered his voice, 'Next time aim for his balls.'

Alais put a finger to her lips. Too late. Redcoats poured out of the bushes. A bull-faced sergeant yelled, 'Seize 'em.'

Damn. 'Arrest me. Leave them alone.' Johnnie growled.

A private, with a filthy bandage over one ear, held Johnnie's arm behind his back, whilst another, grinned through tobacco-stained teeth. He pushed Neill aside and grabbed at Alais as Comrie whimpered.

'Bastard's killed Steenie MacNair.' A wiry private examined the body on the ground.

'Let the major deal with 'em.' The sergeant signalled to his men. 'Shoot, if they try to escape. This way, lads.'

The redcoats dragged the forlorn group down to Braedrumie. Father? Johnnie searched for him in the crowd of villagers. Dougie? Beside Isabel. Dougie nodded at Johnnie. Safe. Murdo? And Una? He looked behind him. Nowhere to be seen.

A roar made Johnnie turn. He watched with horror as a lantern-jawed officer unleashed his men on the village below. One soldier after another let out a howl that froze the blood. A corporal kicked in a door, privates tore at shutters whilst another scrambled on a thatch and dug into it with his bayonet. Furniture and cooking pots lay on the ground, their contents trampled into the mud. Where the hell was Euan?

At the curt directions of Lantern-Jaw, a group of redcoats herded Johnnie's group towards the village centre whilst several privates plundered black-faced cattle, hens and geese. The soldiers shouted and beat at the beasts' tough hides with broken branches. Moos, clucks and hisses blended together in a cacophony of sound. The crofters shouted and surged forward as starvation stared at them, but surly guards pushed back the unruly crowd.

Johnnie heard Granny Mac ask, 'Who are they?' She pointed at Johnnie's group and sucked her gums.

'Hush now.' Isabel held her. 'You ken that's poor Johnnie, Alais and the bairns.'

Johnnie knew the soldiers would search for weapons. Thank God they'd been hidden.

'Halooo.' A whisky cache. The soldiers hooted and hollered like demented devils as they drank their fill.

Johnnie struggled to be free when the troops lit torches from the fires in the crofts and threw brands which hissed and spat onto the rooves, into doorways and open windows. The

The Jacobite Affair

multi-coloured tongues of flame took hold and licked round eaves, shutters and doors. The crackle and heavy scent of wood aflame filled the air.

A low animal moan came from the villagers. Old men sagged and women wept and dropped to their knees. Children, their world gone mad, and terrified about what might happen next, clung to hands and skirts. Plumes of black smoke swirled above the village.

The cattle, made restless by the smoke, flames and dreadful clamour moved out in clouds of dust, with the soldiers.

Lantern-Jaw sat on his chestnut thoroughbred, one hand on his hip and a smirk on his face. He didn't bother to conceal the brutality of his expression or that he enjoyed his work. A dog bared its teeth and snarled.

'Quiet Romsey.' Lantern-Jaw clicked his fingers.

The dog whined and sat.

'Please sir, I beg you.' A woman slipped between the soldiers and hung onto the Lantern-Jaw's boot as she pleaded with him. 'Stop this. My man's dead. I'm five months gone and have five bairns. We need a roof over our heads.'

Johnnie's heart sank. Betty Bissett. Her man had died in the retreat to Culloden.

Lantern-Jaw raised his boot and kicked her so she lay sprawled on the ground. Johnnie struggled again with his captors, but stopped when threatened with bayonets. At the officer's signal one of the redcoats used the butt of his rifle on Betty's belly.

'Aagh!' she shrieked.

Crofters raced towards her, but redcoats stood in their way.

Dougie shouted, 'Stop. In the name of God, this is wickedness you do here.'

'Dougie.' yelled Johnnie. A private slammed his rifle butt into Johnnie's stomach and he doubled over in pain.

'Sergeant.' Lantern-Jaw snarled. The soldier's bayonet sank into Dougie's chest and he collapsed in Isabel's arms.

Roof timbers groaned, split and cracked with a great whoosh and roar into the flames below as families wailed and shrieked.

Three strangers, their hands tied behind their backs stumbled to the front of the ranks of soldiers. Blood dripped from one man's lip, another had a bruised, half-closed eye and the third had a broken nose covered with congealed blood.

'Well.' Lantern-Jaw looked pleased. 'It's time to teach these rebel scum a lesson.'

The Jacobite Affair

CHAPTER Seventy-one

Kirsty nursed Mother through the night with Drewitt and then slept until late morning. She yawned as she wiped porridge from Mother's chin. *I've been a prisoner for days. How can I find out if Braedrumie's been raided?*

Tolbain opened the door. 'I want you ready, we're leaving.'

'Leaving? Where are we going?' asked Kirsty.

Tolbain grinned at her. 'Just make sure you're ready.'

'But you've given me no warning and Mother shouldn't be moved?'

'Leave the old bitch.'

Vile man. 'I'll do no such thing. What about the packing?'

'You won't need much.' Tolbain preened. 'I've risen in the world.'

I despise you.

Dunbar organised manservants to carry Mother, unconscious and swaddled in blankets, to the carriage. 'This could kill her.' Kirsty pleaded with Tolbain.

'You chose to bring her.'

Has he no compassion? Kirsty clenched her fists. 'Do we really need dragoons as escort as well as your own men?' She stared at the column of redcoats.

'Leave me to look after our personal safety.' Tolbain gave a wave of his hand. A footman assisted her into the coach. 'Your duties lie with the household.'

Kirsty put an arm round Mother who rested her head on Kirsty's shoulder. Tolbain sat opposite Kirsty who tried to avoid his gaze and looked out of the window. *Better to have lived with Johnnie and be hunted. Though with Mother, in such delicate health- impossible now.*

The carriage turned east and they followed the rutted track along Loch Linnhe. After several miles she noted a curl of grey above the trees. She leant forward- *Braedrumie.* The smoke blackened and crimson flames leapt.

I haven't been able to warn them. Oh God, oh God. Johnnie.

336

Lorna Windham

Tolbain stared at her with snake eyes.

She stared back at him. 'You knew. That's why we have dragoons guarding us. You helped plan it.'

'For the best. Nest of traitors.'

She could hear guttural orders, shouts and screams now. She turned to Tolbain. 'How could you? These people are our neighbours, friends...'

'No friends of mine.'

The coach turned inland and whipped past pine trees, like sentinels. 'Where are we going?' Kirsty asked. The track narrowed and the coach rattled and rolled as its passengers swayed. The stink of burnt thatch and timbers made her nose wrinkle. A roar split the air. A space appeared between trees. *What?* Villagers appeared surrounded by a sea of red being driven towards the old dool tree. *No.*

She could see the gates and drive of Braedrumie House in the distance. *Tolbain won't be welcome here and nor will I. Why come here?* Realisation struck her like a thunderbolt. She turned to him. 'Dear God, the Stewart's house and land, it's yours isn't it?'

'They're traitors. It's been sequestered.'

The coach came to a halt. Kirsty gripped Mother as they both jerked forward and almost clashed heads with Tolbain.

He rose to step out of the coach.

Kirsty held his arm. 'Please dinna do this. The laird's an old man, he's lost his youngest son. They say he's... no' himself.'

Tolbain shrugged her off. 'Traitors deserve all they get.' He leapt out and addressed one of the privates on guard at the door. 'Is all secure?'

The private snapped to attention. 'Sir.'

She watched as Tolbain and soldiers ran up the steps and through the splintered door. It leaned on its hinges.

'Mother,' she whispered. 'Mother. What are we going to do?'

Mother's eyelids fluttered and closed.

The Jacobite Affair

Kirsty's stomach churned. *This is a nightmare. Braedrumie and the Stewarts will never forgive this.*

'Well?' Tolbain stood at the carriage window, a smug expression on his face. 'What are you waiting for? Do you no' want to explore our new home? Better than that hovel of a farmhouse I took you from.' He opened the door.

'But what about the Stewarts?'

He shrugged his shoulders. 'They can beg, but it'll do no good.'

Foul man.

'My mother needs help.' A red-faced private carried Mother into the house. Kirsty followed. She forced back a tear in the entrance hall so full of memories. An overturned bench lay on the floor; glass crunched under her feet and a shutter hung like a broken arm. Only the grandfather clock stood upright. The Stewarts hadn't given up without a fight. *Johnnie.* The hairs on her neck stood upright. *Too many Stewart ghosts here: Johnnie's mother and Duncan.*

Kirsty made her way upstairs.

'Which bedchamber, Your Grace?' asked the red-faced private.

Kirsty looked along the square balcony at the numerous doors. 'A minute.' She opened and shut doors until she came to a central bedchamber which overlooked the garden. 'Here. Bring her here.'

'Put her in one of the smaller bedrooms.' Tolbain called behind her. 'She won't know the difference.'

But I do.

Kirsty tutted at the dust, but that could be remedied. She folded back the bed clothes and tucked in her mother. *Pity I can't warm the bed. Such niceties will come when servants arrive. God, what about Braedrumie and Johnnie?* She paced the floor all afternoon.

***

Later that night in the dining room as darkness descended and candles flickered, Tolbain thrust out his chest. 'I've plans for the new wings. It will be grand, probably the grandest property in Scotland.' He drew himself up. 'I'm certainly the wealthiest landowner on the west coast.'

The Stewarts won't let you rest here. Surely you can see that? Kirsty shook her head at his arrogance. She let the thin soup drip from her spoon into the bowl.

Tolbain continued, 'There's a large scullery, but the fire doesn't draw properly. I'll have the chimney swept. The dining room's dark, the drawing room too feminine, the library far too big and the study too small. There are changes to be made. I'll start by getting rid of the books.'

Johnnie will hate that. 'Perhaps we could settle in first.'

'Perhaps. A pity the troops had to withdraw.' He used a napkin with the Stewart monogram to wipe his mouth.

A throb began behind her brow. 'I wish to retire.'

'Do you now? Let me light the way.' He swept candelabrum from the table and she followed his huge shadow as it crept up stairs.

'**This** is the master bedchamber.' Tolbain flung open the door.

Kirsty sniffed the air. A hint of rose-scented perfume. *Elizabeth.* She looked around the wood-panelled room. Saw the dressing table, a scent bottle and a hairbrush where its owner had left them. Kirsty walked to where moonlight flooded in the window and gazed at the garden and orchard. *Does he mean this for me?*

'Well?'

'It's beautiful.' *The only drawback your proximity.*

'It's mine and Meg's. She'll be along when all the excitement's over. Find yourself another room.' He thrust the candelabrum at her. 'I'm away to my bed.' He flung himself full length on the counterpane.

Meg. Kirsty's anger surged, but she managed to control it. 'As you wish.' She left the room, closed the door and used the

The Jacobite Affair

candles' flames to look in on each bedchamber until she paused in one which faced Braedrumie.

In the distance, through the sash window, she saw a glow above the village. *Is Johnnie safe? And his father and all the Stewarts?* She turned away, her heart like lead.

Several bedchambers faced the garden and she stopped in one with deep blue curtains, dark floorboards and blue bed covers. A stack of dusty books sat on a bedside table. *Johnnie's room?* She took a deep breath and tried to scent him out, feel his presence. She opened a wardrobe, found a man's cloak and a couple of jackets. One, black velvet. *Did Johnnie wear this at our betrothal?* It seemed so long ago. She took it out and inhaled him, then returned the garment to the back of the wardrobe. She brushed a touch of wig powder from a sleeve and put down the candelabrum. *This will be my bedchamber.* Fear for Johnnie squeezed her heart.

CHAPTER Seventy-two

On the night of the raid, ribbons of stars twinkled above Loch Linnhe. But in Braedrumie, bright embers swirled round the bedraggled survivors as smoke billowed and flames gushed from blackened crofts.

'Are you and the bairns alright?' asked Johnnie. Even his bones ached.

Alais nodded and pointed at two sleeping bundles. She put her hands together as if in prayer.

'Dougie?' he asked.

She shook her head.

Johnnie grimaced. 'What a waste.' The man had been with the Stewarts since before Rob had been born. He'd taught them all and would be missed. Poor Isabel. He'd speak to her.

'Una?'

She smiled and nodded.

'Good.'

'I... thought... you... killed...' she signed.

'Nine lives. Bairns asleep?' asked Johnnie.

She nodded and signed, 'Tell... me.'

'Let me tuck them in first.' He knelt beside Comrie and Neill, kissed their cheeks and pulled the plaids round their ears.

Alais handed him a bowl of broth and he sat by her side at the fire. 'Eat...' she signed.

He took several mouthfuls and warmth crept into his limbs.

She signed, 'Tell... me.'

'Morag's fine, but the man who took her...' He yawned. 'Oh and Euan's got a wee wound.'

She raised her shoulders and spread her hands.

Johnnie shrugged. 'Oh, and Rob's back, he's my older brother. The one who saved me again. No' that I consider him family anymore.'

Alais' brow wrinkled.

The Jacobite Affair

'Too long a story,' said Johnnie. 'He's a redcoat, but family and honour always come first with him. Let's hope Lantern-Jaw doesn't know he's been duped.'

She clasped her palms together by her cheek.

He nodded and his eyelids drooped. Duncan.

***

The next morning the cold shuffled under Johnnie's covers and the smell of charred timber pervaded the air. He realised someone, probably Alais, had put plaids over him whilst he'd slept beside the fire, and he'd kicked some off. He sprang up. The redcoats had left Braedrumie a wasteland. What about his father and Braedrumie House?

'You didna sleep well either.' Euan sat beside Johnnie and motioned at the rumpled plaids.

'You've set guards?'

'Of course.'

'Your wound?' asked Johnnie, concerned at Euan's white face.

Euan gave a wry grin. 'Morag gave it her full attention.'

Johnnie laughed. 'Hurt's like hell fire then. Father?'

'Escaped through the cellar thanks to Murdo and Dougie. Jamie Moffat took him to the den. Pity about Dougie. A fine man.'

'Aye. A fine man. And the house?' Johnnie threw half burnt timbers on the fire so it sparked and spat.

Euan warmed his hands. 'Sequestered, Dougie said. Nought we can do. Tolbain's moved in with his whore and that bitch, Kirsty.'

Johnnie raised his head. 'Dinna call her that.'

'You still carry a torch for her?' Euan sat back.

Johnnie snarled, 'Just dinna call her that.' He couldn't share his feelings for Kirsty. So near and yet... Johnnie closed his eyes. Euan would never understand. To think of Tolbain in Braedrumie House made him want to vomit. As hunted

Lorna Windham

outlaws no one would listen to the Stewarts' pleas, not when three sons had fought for Charlie. God curse Tolbain.

'Thanks for offering to take the priest back last night.'

'I'll do it after the…' Johnnie indicated the bodies which lay still under plaids. Perhaps if he talked to the priest he could lay Duncan to rest.

'Aye.'

Euan coughed. 'Good Rob's back. I think he's shocked Father's no' in a good way. He wants to make his peace with you, Johnnie.'

'Pity he canna do it with Mother and Duncan.' He mustn't think of Duncan. And what about Kirsty?

The Jacobite Affair

CHAPTER Seventy-three

That evening, Johnnie let the smoke and dark shroud him as he crept towards a canopy of oaks. He froze. Damn. A Stewart sentry, a young boy, strolled past. Johnnie slunk behind him and sped through the trees towards Braedrumie House and Kirsty. He stopped in the shadows at the edge of the wood.

The building loomed ahead, not home any more. No lights. Wise to be cautious. Two of Tolbain's men, muskets in hands stood in front of the stone entrance and iron gates. Johnnie took his time. He crawled through the undergrowth and circled the house. The skitter of tiny paws and rustle of leaves made him cautious, though the dank mud, sweet grass and familiar patches of nettles brought back his boyhood.

He slipped into the grounds in a hollow under the gnarled roots of an oak. Bit of a squeeze now. The bark grazed his back. He ignored the pain and sped on. A light flared at his bedchamber window. He listened. A tall guard sneezed to his left. Johnnie caught his breath. Damn.

'Noisy bugger, want to get us killed?' snarled another guard with a paunch on the right.

Johnnie's hand slid to his hose and sgian-dubh. He clenched his teeth on the metal blade, sank on his haunches and slithered on his belly between the guards, through the orchard and into the rose garden below his bedchamber. What had Kirsty said when he left with Charlie's army? '*I'll always keep a lamp lit for you. So you'll know I'm there, waiting for you to come home.*'

Was she in his bedchamber? What about Tolbain? The thought of that animal in bed next to Kirsty made Johnnie white-hot with fury. He forced himself to suck in breaths and slow the beat of his heart. He'd come because he thirsted for her and she needed to know he was alive and would be away for weeks. When he returned he'd deal with Tolbain and make her his again. He kept to the shadows of the house. How to get in and not alert the household?

He pondered a moment. He'd use his father's escape route-the cellar. The trap doors lay to the left near the scullery. Set in the ground with a ramp down which barrels had been rolled, they'd often been left unbolted. Dougie and his escape party wouldn't have thought of anything, but getting the laird away, surely?

Johnnie stepped towards the two iron doors. He grasped one, put his fingers in the iron ring and tugged. It squeaked as it opened. Damn. A shout came from the orchard. He sat at the top of the ramp held onto the door's internal ring, pulled it over his crouched back, then slid into the blackness below. He landed on his feet. His heart raced as he listened and the muffled voices from the garden faded away.

He groped along the walls, found the cellar steps, turned right, then left along passages at the top and entered the scullery. Tolbain's scullion lay asleep by the embers of the fire which gave the room an eerie glow. Johnnie tip-toed past him, the huge table and the pots and pans on the dresser.

A noise? No. He left through the door which led to a long corridor, another door and into the hall. The central staircase lay to his left surrounded by the balcony above and closed bedchamber doors. He cocked his ears. Heard the familiar tick from the grandfather clock in the hall, the groan of timber as it contracted and the rise and fall of a distant snore.

He sped up the stairs, smelled lavender and roses. Mother. How well he knew this house and its secrets, more than any of these interlopers. He leant over the bannister and checked the shadows below. Nothing. His bedchamber lay before him. The snore came from his mother's bedchamber to his left.

Johnnie turned the handle of his door. It rattled. Damn. Father had promised to fix it. Johnnie peered in. Nothing stirred. The lamp's flame danced in front of the open shutters. He parted the bed's curtains. Kirsty lay on her back like a child in sleep. Her arms at angles, her hands open. Alone.

He stuck the sgian-dubh back in his hose, leant over her and put a hand over mouth. Her eyes opened, fear flared in them as she struggled to sit. Her breast rose and fell, then

The Jacobite Affair

stilled. He took his hand away and his lips sought hers, nibbled, teased and devoured until she pulled away. Her hair tumbled in golden disarray over her shoulders. He'd never seen her more desirable.

'Tolbain's down the corridor,' she hissed.

'So, I hear,' whispered Johnnie as Tolbain's snore filled the air. He put his hand on his sgian-dubh.

'No. You'll be caught, there's guards everywhere.'

A muscle worked in his cheek. 'Does he suspect?'

'He found my brooch, but can't prove anything.'

'Thank God.' Johnnie stroked her cheek with his thumb.

'He's kept a closer watch on me and willna let me out of my bedchamber.' She cupped his face in her hands. 'It's so good to see you, Johnnie. I've been so worried. He's furious he hasn't caught you and your brother. I've been desperate to see you, know you're alright. I'm so sorry about the raid, about being here, everything. I couldna warn you. He's been meeting redcoats and knows a traitor, Kinross.'

'**He'll** no be troubling anyone again.'

'The laird?' Kirsty clutched his hand.

'Safe.'

'Good. The rest of your family?'

'Dougie…' He shook his head.

She sighed. 'Oh, dear God. I'm so sorry. Poor Isabel.'

'Rob's back. Bit of a shock. Couldna shake his hand at first.'

Kirsty leant her head on his chest. 'Dearest, dinna blame him for leaving. Elizabeth, your mother… I know you couldna see it, but she'd been ailing for some time.'

He pulled away as words came out like a flood. 'And Duncan? Does he deserve forgiveness for him too? You've no idea of his agony, the blood. So young and so cold. I couldna help him, Kirsty. You can see that, can't you? I couldna help. It would have taken hours for him to die on that moor. I couldna bear to see him suffer.' He took a deep breath. 'I drew my dirk across his neck and held him till the life blood drained from his body.'

Lorna Windham

She gasped, her eyes like small moons. 'You… killed him?'

'Aye.' He couldn't look at her.

'Holy Mother of God.' She crossed herself.

Tears streamed down Johnnie's face. 'Thought you'd understand. Canna rid myself of the deed. Canna sleep because of it. I havena said anything, to my father or brothers. I confessed, to the priest, but it didna help. My dirk eased Duncan's passing, so why do I feel so guilty?' He held his head in his hands.

She used her palms and drew his face up, her forehead to his. 'We all have to do things… Hush. Hush, darling.' She cradled him in her arms, then tensed. 'Did you hear something?'

Johnnie's hand went back to his sgian-dubh. He didn't breathe, just listened for the faintest sound that meant he'd been detected. A windowpane rattled, a branch tapped on glass, and timbers creaked. He breathed again.

She held his hands. 'You loved your brother, Johnnie. Everyone knows that. Duncan knew that. You eased his passing. He'd have wanted you to do it.' Her lips brushed his cheek. 'My poor, darling. You should have told me. It's too much of a burden for you to carry alone. But this isna why you've come, is it?'

'No. I'm taking the priest back to Port Glasgow after the funerals. Shouldn't be gone more than three weeks at most.'

She rested her head on his chest. 'Again. Does it have to be you? I dinna want you to go. I need you so. Tolbain's a brute.'

He put a finger under her chin and raised it. 'I'll deal with him when I return.'

'I'll do it.'

He kissed her forehead. 'Sweetheart, dinna. Let it be me.'

She flung herself at him. 'No. The redcoats would hunt you down. They'll never rest till you hang. I couldna bear it.'

'Darling, **we** willna stand for him living here for long.'

'Oh, Johnnie.'

The Jacobite Affair

He squeezed her hand. 'Promise me you won't do anything.'

She bowed her head. 'I promise. Come back soon, Johnnie.'

The sky lightened and a blade of light lifted the gloom.

'I will. I'd better go, dawn's not far off. I need to leave with the priest.' Her lips sought his and his senses reeled.

Kirsty broke from him. 'I'll wait for you, this time I'll wait for ever.'

'My own one.' He wanted her now.

On the way out, Johnnie went into the pantry. He used lard to grease the rusty hinges of the cellar trapdoor and then left Braedrumie House and its grounds.

Lorna Windham

CHAPTER Seventy-four

The early morning sunshine did nothing to dispel the gloom in the den. Johnnie's father lay with a saddle for a headrest and with several rugs tucked round him.

'Morning, Father.' Johnnie hunkered beside him.

'Have you a drink?'

Johnnie clenched his jaw. 'Water.' He offered him a deerskin water bag.

The old man curled his mouth in disdain.

'Good to see Rob yesterday.' Johnnie drank and savoured the cold water in his mouth.

'Who?' His father's eyes searched the den for answers.

Wide-eyed, Johnnie swallowed. He doesn't remember his eldest son?

'Is this where I live?'

'Aye, for the moment.' Johnnie gave him an odd look. 'We thought it safer. I'm taking the priest to the west coast today. Euan and Morag will look after you, Alais and the bairns.'

'You're to blame for Duncan's death.' His father pointed a gnarled forefinger at him. 'I blame it all on you.'

Johnnie reeled as if struck. He tried to explain Father's words, make excuses, pretend they'd never been said. But Johnnie's guilt doubled in size. He stumbled out into the light. He'd come to say goodbye to Father and received condemnation in exchange.

'And what about me? When do we leave?' The priest hectored him.

Johnnie bit back a surly reply and ignored him. The priest could wait. But Comrie's use of 'Dada' and Neill's upright stance and bit lip, almost undid Johnnie. He took Alais to one side. 'Look after the bairns for me and... yourself.' He hugged her, kissed her soft cheek and sensed she wanted more from him than he could give. Coward.

He mounted his pony and led the priest west. Risky to travel through the day, but he wanted to deliver the priest and get home to Kirsty. With a bit of luck, if he journeyed most of

The Jacobite Affair

the miles at night, he wouldn't bump into any redcoat patrols on his way to Port Glasgow. He'd use the same little known tracks Euan and he had followed before.

***

A couple of weeks later Johnnie and the priest huddled behind a dune with a small band of smugglers. The soft ripple of surf sang in his ears. Apart from the ponies which champed at their bits, the land lay dark and silent behind them.

Uncle John had organised this, though at great risk to himself. He'd adjusted his spectacles as his wrinkled brow betrayed his concerns and mumbled something about and exchange of tobacco, furs and whisky for French wine and brandy. Then he mentioned *a special cargo* he expected delivered by the *Valiant*.

Johnnie rolled his eyes. More contraband.

'Once you've delivered the priest and goods to the ship, we go to *The Gentleman's* cave.' Uncle John lowered his voice. 'The chests are a different matter. You're to take them to this loch and bury them, here.' He pointed to a spot on a map. 'Will you do it?'

Johnnie sighed. 'Uncle, you've increased the danger twofold and I need to get home.'

'It's that or you're stuck with the priest.'

Damn. 'What's in these chests?' asked Johnnie.

'Nothing for you to worry about.'

Johnnie stared at him.

His uncle lowered his voice even further. 'Alright, it's for The Cause.'

A prickle of alarm started on the back of Johnnie's neck. 'I thought you had no time for The Cause. Didn't you tell Euan and me off, call Father, for being part of it?' He paused. 'How much were you offered?'

'Johnnie, nephew, how could you think that?' His uncle leant towards him. 'Will you do it? You're the only one I trust.'

Lorna Windham

'Bloody hell.' Johnnie's chest heaved, the risk enormous. But they were marked men anyway. Then Johnnie thought of all those who'd died for The Cause. He shook his uncle's hand, but inwardly cursed him.

'She's here,' a bandy-legged smuggler hissed in Johnnie's ear and brought him back to the present. 'Follow me.'

The Atlantic Ocean glittered as Johnnie crawled behind Bandy Legs to the top of the dune. In front of him lay a cove shaped like a horseshoe. A schooner rounded the headland rigged with sail fore and aft. A ghost ship, thought Johnnie as it followed the moon's silver trail.

Bandy Legs handed him a telescope. Moonlight glinted on the schooner's prow and Johnnie made out the gold letters *Valiant*. The smuggler lit a lantern, let it flare three times and then doused the flame. The ship repeated the signal and anchored off shore.

Johnnie put the telescope to his eye again. Men rowed towards them, slowed by the weight of their illicit cargo. As the boat ground onto the shingle, sailors leapt thigh deep into the sea, oblivious of its icy grip. The hull grated as the men hauled the boat up the beach, out of the ocean's greedy grasp.

Bandy Legs beckoned the ponies forward to receive kegs, boxes and several chests in return for barrels, packages and bundles. A pony neighed as a breeze ruffled the marram grass.

Johnnie pushed the priest onto the beach as they launched a laden rowing boat. The frightened man clambered aboard and squeezed into a small space behind some barrels.

'Thank you, Father,' Johnnie whispered and held out his hand.

'Bless you, my son.' The priest made the sign of the cross. 'May you find peace.'

Johnnie grimaced as he put both hands on the wooden planks, bent his back and helped steer the boat through the waves. He waded back to the beach, wet to his knees then watched the sailors fight the surf and, with a splash of oars, pull towards the *Valiant*.

The Jacobite Affair

It wasn't until the priest disappeared over the rail of the ship that Johnnie's muscles relaxed. Bandy Legs tapped Johnnie's shoulder as the ponies disappeared inland along a slow trickle of a burn.

'Tidal.' Bandy Legs lowered an eyelid. 'No tracks.'

Johnnie looked back, the schooner had slipped anchor and he could see no sign of it. After several miles along a trail which wound, undulated and paralleled the coast, the smugglers unloaded the contraband in *The Gentleman's* cave. Then they urged the ponies north and inland as the clouds released their burden.

The smugglers travelled all night as rain fell in sheets. One of the ponies' packs slipped and a leather strap snapped. Chests crashed to the ground, rolled down the hillside and smashed into rocks as they went.

'My God, that'll waken the dead.' Bandy Legs peered into the darkness. The wind buffeted them and the odd shriek of an animal pierced the night. Nothing moved as a silver moon stepped out from behind a cloud and lit the scene.

'You two.' Johnnie jerked his head at a youngster and a man with a pigeon chest. 'Come with me.' Johnnie slipped and slithered to where he thought the chest must be. The splintered lid lay to one side and hundreds of gold coins glittered at Johnnie's feet.

'Bloody hell, it's a fortune.' Pigeon Chest's eyes never left the coins.

'Havena' seen so much money in all my life.' Youngster rubbed his hands together.

Johnnie picked up a coin and felt its weight. Solid gold. He turned it over in his hand. French. No mistaking Louis' head in profile on one side and the French royal coat of arms on the reverse. A Louis d'or.

'Get a move on down there,' yelled a voice from above.

'We could hide some of it, no' tell the others, split it three ways?' Pigeon Chest spoke in a hushed voice. His eyes gleamed at the pile of coins in his hands.

'Make that suggestion again and I'll kill you where you stand,' Johnnie snarled. 'This is French gold for The Cause. Men died for want of this. Now put them back. Back I say.'

Youngster glared at him and Pigeon Chest spat on the ground. To Johnnie's relief they bent to the task. When they'd finished Johnnie raised his chin. 'Make a blood oath, say you'll never reveal...'

'Stand where you are. You're surrounded.' The voice came from the hillside opposite.

'What the...?' Johnnie spun as his hand went to his dirk.

Pigeon Chest and Youngster ran. The air exploded and whined with the sound of musket balls. An unseen force struck Johnnie's shoulder and spun him backwards into space. He landed with a thump.

His brain clouded. Pain clawed at his being. He fought to stay alert and watched those of his group, on higher ground, flee over the crest. As his sight dimmed, he saw that Pigeon Chest and Youngster lay still.

The Jacobite Affair

CHAPTER Seventy-five

At Braedrumie House, grey light streamed through the window and onto Mother's face.

'I'm sorry, Your Grace. I tried to wake her, but she's cold.' Drewitt stood blank-faced in front of Kirsty.

Cold? Dead? Kirsty felt for a pulse in Mother's neck. *She can't be?* She wrung her hands as terror washed over her. *Alone and married to a monster. Oh, God. And Johnnie no' here to offer any comfort.*

'Your Grace?' asked Drewitt. 'Shall I cover her face and close the curtains?'

'Aye.' Kirsty gathered her wits as Drewitt lifted the snowy-white sheet and let it fall over Mother's stiff features. She then moved to the window and tugged at the heavy material. Darkness smothered the room.

'I'll inform His Grace when he returns.' Kirsty struggled to keep her voice emotionless. 'I want the servants gathered in the hall at three o'clock.'

'Your Grace.' Drewitt, bobbed a curtsey and withdrew.

There'd be no show of regret from Tolbain. He's got Mother's farm and land now through this travesty of a handfasting. Kirsty flung herself over the still form on the bed. 'I shouldna have bound myself to him. You kenned it and loved me a little in the end, I know you did. I just wish... but it's all in the past now.'

Hours later she braced herself to tell the servants and paused on the balcony as she heard their chatter. She peered down at the heads in the hall. Dunbar caught sight of her and nudged a footman. A hush washed over the group as she descended the stairs.

Kirsty stopped in front of them and ignored Mrs. Mill's rolled eyes, Reid's smirk and the squint-eyed maid's folded arms. 'My mother... passed away this morning. I expect you... to respect her memory and that His Grace and I are grieving.'

Someone muffled a laugh.

Oh, God. I'm so alone. 'That's all.' She mounted the stairs.

Reid's voice rang out. 'Old besom took her time about it. Perhaps it's a blessin'.'

Kirsty turned.

Reid's rolling pin clattered to the floor and rested against a chair leg. Dunbar glared at her, Drewitt examined her sleeve and a footman stared at his feet.

Kirsty drew herself up. *I won't let them see my misery.* She raised her voice and pointed her words at Reid. 'Pack your bags. Apart from your lack of respect, the meals you serve when His Grace is away, turn my stomach.'

Reid blanched. 'Sorry, Your Grace. It willna happen again.' She bobbed a curtsey.

'You'll be gone within the hour. And that goes for anyone who feels the same way. There's no shortage of those wanting to be servants, especially in times like this.' Kirsty swept up the staircase to the sound of Reid's shrieks and consternation below.

***

Days passed, until under a leaden sky Kirsty and Tolbain, dressed in crow-black, trudged up the muddy track to the churchyard. They followed behind the coffin carried on a cart. Kirsty held a bunch of white heather and rain fell like tears. The carter sat grim-faced. He used his tongue and teeth to click the horses on, whilst four menservants sat upright on either side of the oak box. The only mourners: Kirsty and her husband.

'Trust the old bitch to be buried on a bloody, miserable day.' Tolbain examined his mud-splattered hose and muddy boots. 'You'd better hope we've a good meal waiting for us. Cooks are not easy to find.'

Kirsty's lips tightened. *I just want to lie down and close all this out.* A strange lethargy fell on her and she struggled to fight against it as she tramped behind the cart. *Mother's death seems unreal. As a child I longed for love, at least we came to some sort of mutual understanding and now... now I'll miss*

355

The Jacobite Affair

her. Not that she ever supported me against Tolbain. But I'll miss her tetchy voice. Kirsty bit back a howl of anguish which formed a ragged gasp in her throat. She gulped. *Can an adult be an orphan?* Her vocal chords strained with emotion. *It was like this when they buried Father. A fall into an abyss, a black hole, which spun, swirled and nose-dived into a pit of memories. And me desperate to be held, hugged and loved. If Johnnie was here I could bear this.* She glanced across at Tolbain. *Here because it's expected, not because he feels anything. I just want this day to be over.*

She dragged her legs up the bank. She needed to lie down and rest, but first she had to bury Mother.

'Woah.' The cart creaked to a halt. The four menservants leapt out and slipped the coffin onto their shoulders.

Will this day never end?

Kirsty and Tolbain followed the servants and their burden through the churchyard's wooden gate and down to where a pile of earth and the sextant stood, cap in hand.

No priest. No relatives and only a note from Aunt Lizzie who sent her condolences and said she and Michael had been advised to stay in Inverness in case of contagion. *So much for sisterly love and duty.*

The procession stopped at the graveside. The surly sextant gave a stout servant two thick ropes to slide under the coffin.

'Well.' Tolbain's voice rang out. 'May our dear Mother, rest in peace.' He leant over Kirsty and she recoiled at his foul breath. 'Wood cost me a small fortune.'

Kirsty's vision misted and her head swam. Tolbain's hand grasped her elbow. She shrugged him off.

'Careful, don't want to end up in the same grave as your mother, do you?' He guffawed and when no one joined in, he waved a hand at the servants. 'Get on with it.'

The sextant's hands clenched his shovel as the servants lowered Mother into the black earth. Kirsty looked down at the oak lid. Her throat raw from emotion she threw the bunch of white heather onto it. *Johnnie. I need your strong arm round me. And a priest, Mother needs a priest.*

Lorna Windham

'Right,' said Tolbain. 'I suggest we get home, before we're soaked to the skin.'

'But...'

He gripped her arm and drew her away. She heard the dribble of soil as it streamed onto the coffin, but not before she spotted Murdo. He stood in the undergrowth with his head bowed. *Was Mother wrong, had Murdo loved her after all?*

***

Later, Kirsty changed into dry clothes with Drewitt's help. Rain pattered on her bedchamber window.

'You're lookin' a little pale, will you rest now, Your Grace?'

'I think I may. Thank you, Drewitt.'

'It's been a tryin' day for you, Your Grace.' Drewitt left and closed the door behind her.

Kirsty lay on the white cotton counterpane and her head sank of its own accord onto the pillow. Her muscles relaxed and her eyelids fluttered as her thoughts took her back through the last few difficult months. She paused. Used her fingers to count. *No.* Thought again. She sifted pieces of a puzzle until they came together. *No.* She jerked upright. Her heart fluttered against her ribcage. *Johnnie. He won't be back for days. What about Tolbain?- I can make this news work in my favour.*

She tidied her hair, went downstairs to the study and paused at the open door. Meg lounged on Tolbain's desk with one arm draped round his neck.

Kirsty strode in. 'Tolbain, I must talk with you.'

'Must? Must? Mind your tongue, bitch, you're not master here. The poorest beast in my fields has more worth.' He laughed at that and his whore let a giggle escape.

'Oh, but I have worth.' Kirsty sank into a chair. 'I am your greatest pearl, a fruitful prize, a treasure chest which brims with your hopes and dreams.'

'What's this, a riddle?' Tolbain's brow wrinkled. 'Have you lost your senses? Off the desk, Meg.'

357

The Jacobite Affair

'But, Alexander.'

He shoved her as he stood. Meg sprawled at Kirsty's feet. *Her rightful place.*

'Ow. That bloody hurt, Alexander.' Meg rubbed her backside.

'She calls you, Alexander.' Kirsty arched a brow. 'Tut-tut.'

Tolbain shrugged. 'What is it to you?'

'Alexander,' Meg whispered in soft voice. 'Tell her I'm yours for ever. Tell her she's no use to a man such as you. Tell her. Tell her.' Her voice rose to a shriek.

'Poor little Meg, did he say you were the only one?' Kirsty forced a smile. 'He lied. Now go away. I have something I must share with my husband.'

'Alexander?' Meg tugged at his breeches.

'Go to our room, Meg.' He helped her to her feet.

'But Alexander…'

'Later, Meg,' He patted her backside as he pushed her out of the door. He closed it and turned to Kirsty. 'This better be good, Madam.'

Oh, it is. Kirsty rose and circled the room. She lifted a porcelain bowl here and a silver candlestick there as if she assessed their value.

'Well, well, what are you waiting for? Spit it out, then leave. Your sour face makes me sick to the stomach.'

She turned to him. 'I'm with child.'

Shocked silence. Then his eyes gleamed. 'What? You're carrying my son? Are you sure? How far gone?'

''Tis three months since my courses.'

'Three months?' He spread possessive fingers over the slight rise of her belly.

She did her best not to show repugnance.

'In six I'll have a son and heir, in seven perhaps another on the way. So, I planted my seed in fertile ground.'

***Your** seed? This babe's Johnnie's. It has to be Johnnie's.*

'Sit, take the weight off your feet.' He pulled out a chair for her and opened a desk drawer. He balanced a leather pouch in his hand, let the coins inside chink and handed it to her. 'A gift, for you.'

She weighed the pouch on her palm. *Generous. The first kindness since our marriage.* She made to give it back, but a warning sounded in her head. *You may need it.*

'Look after yourself, my dear, eat nought but the best. I'll tell cook. My son must be healthy, he's the heir to vast estates. I have great plans. This house will be the grandest in the Highlands. And you my dear, will reign over all.' He pinched her cheek so it hurt. 'As long as you give birth to a healthy son.' He placed his hand on her womb. 'Perhaps you're a proper wife after all.'

Kirsty's head spun. *Will this nightmare ever end? Only Johnnie really loves me. First deal with Meg.* 'The whore goes.'

'But…'

Kirsty raised an eyebrow. 'Do you want your son contaminated by her presence before he's born?'

'No- I- very well.'

***

Kirsty led Tolbain to his bedchamber. The curtains had been drawn and Meg lay sprawled on her belly across the bed.

'Get out,' Kirsty stood over her.

Meg's tear-stained face screeched at her, 'Dinna talk to me like that. Tell her, Alexander.'

Tolbain leant against the bed post. Meg scrambled towards him. She showered kisses on his face and neck.

'She loves me.' He looked across at Kirsty and his mouth widened in a smirk. 'What can I do?'

'As I say.' Kirsty returned his smirk.

'Oh, Alexander.' Meg put her arms round his neck and turned a cat's smile on Kirsty. See, it said, I've won.

He unclasped her arms. 'You're very beautiful and willing, Meg, but you're not carrying my son and heir.'

The Jacobite Affair

Meg, bewildered, stared at the slight rise below Kirsty's waist.

'She's lyin' to get you into her bed again.'

'Get dressed.' He threw Meg's clothes at her. 'You'll leave now and dinna return or I'll have you whipped from the door.'

At last.

Meg's eyes grew large. 'You dinna mean it?'

'I'll throw you out as you are. Kirsty, give her five minutes. If she hasna left, send for me.' He strode out of the room and slammed the door.

Tears rolled down Meg's cheeks as she struggled into her garments.

Oh God, she'll be destitute. I can't let her go with nothing.

'Here, take this.' She thrust Tolbain's pouch at her.

Meg's fingers curled round the leather. 'Why, when I've lain with your husband?'

'Because I ken what it's like to be poor.' *And you kept his mind and foul body off me most of the time.*

Meg stared at her in wonder and placed the pouch in her pocket. 'I'm sorry.'

'You saw an opportunity and took it. But I never want to see you again.'

Meg sniffed. 'There's plenty will want my wares in Auld Reekie.' She picked up her skirts and left without a backward glance.

CHAPTER Seventy-Six

The next day the wind rattled the doors as Drewitt burst into Kirsty's bedchamber. 'Your Grace, somethin'... awful's... happened.' The maid put a hand to her small bosom which heaved up and down.

'What on earth? Please catch your breath, Drewitt.'

'Sorry... to disturb you... Your Grace, you with child... and all, but His... Grace has... had a fall.'

Kirsty stared at her. 'Is he badly hurt?' *Say yes.*

'I dinna ken, Your Grace. Mr. Campbell said, you're to come at once.'

'Take me to him.' Kirsty gathered up her skirts.

'Your Grace, he's in the cellar.'

'What happened?' Scream after scream filtered towards them as Drewitt led her downstairs.

'Tripped at the top of the steps, Your Grace.'

'What was he doing there?'

'Seein' to the ale, so I was told.' Drewitt pointed to a door. 'It's this way, Your Grace.'

Kirsty followed her through the narrow, corridor which led to the scullery. Servants chattered at the top of the stone steps. One nudged another as she approached. Silence. The new cook, Ogle, fiddled with her apron, the scullion couldn't keep still and the squint-eyed maid shook.

'Aaagh.' Dreadful groans came from the darkness below.

'Get some light down there,' ordered Kirsty. A manservant raced to do as Kirsty bid. Shadowy figures moved below. 'Mr. Campbell is that you?'

'Aye. Best stay where you are Your Grace.' The tacksman sounded business-like.

'Aaagh.'

Kirsty called into the darkness. 'He sounds badly hurt.'

'Dinna worry, Your Grace, we're bringing him up now.' Campbell shouted.

Drewitt held up a lit candelabrum as the tacksman, like a wizened dog, led the way up to the ground floor. Four footmen

The Jacobite Affair

carried Tolbain between them. As they passed Kirsty, she saw Tolbain's face set into a grimace. One of his lower leg bones stuck out of his skin like a mast.

'Could have broken his neck.' The new cook, Ogle, muttered to the scullery maid and they both stared at Kirsty. 'Wonder how he did it?'

'Get back to your duties,' snapped Kirsty. *My God- they blame me, but I've been upstairs. Not that the thought of murder hasn't crossed my mind.* 'Drewitt, give me the light.'

'You need to rest, Your Grace, think of your bairn.' Two fine lines appeared between Drewitt's brows.

'In a minute.' Kirsty lifted her skirts and went down the steps. She avoided a puddle of blood, picked up a mop and Tolbain's keys from the floor and went back to the scullery. Ogle, her fat backside on a stool, faced the open door whilst the scullery maid fanned her with a towel.

'No one warned me about her. We're no' safe in our beds.'

'There, there, cook.' The scullery maid patted Ogle's hand. 'You've had a terrible shock.'

'You're quite safe.' Kirsty held out the mop

Ogle leapt up and the maid shrunk behind her.

'I suggest someone cleans up the blood in the cellar?' said Kirsty.

***

Kirsty stood with Campbell and Drewitt in Tolbain's bedchamber. His ashen face looked up at them between blood-smeared fingers which clutched Campbell's hand. Blood pumped from his leg and streamed from a gash on the back of his head.

'Drewitt, I need towels to staunch his wounds and hot water,' ordered Kirsty.

Drewitt curtsied and withdrew.

'Aargh.' Tolbain groaned between gritted teeth, his gaze malevolent.

Kirsty's hopes soared. *Not many survive a break like this. Do I want him to linger, have a painful death? No. I just wish to be free of him.*

Tolbain's spoke between gritted teeth. 'Help me.'

'Of course, Your Grace.' Campbell unwrapped the Duke's fingers and rubbed his bruised hand.

'Tripped on... something, foot ... rolled away... from me.' Tolbain turned a malicious eye on Kirsty. 'Can't be... too careful, there's many... would like... me dead.'

'Your Grace.' Campbell gave him a startled look.

Tolbain made to say more, but moved his leg. 'Aargh.'

'My husband is in great pain as you can see.' Kirsty drew Campbell from the bed. 'Please send for the nearest bone setter.'

Campbell looked downcast.'Didna come back from Culloden, Your Grace.'

'There must be someone.'

'Fort William has an army surgeon. Should I fetch him?'

'A... surgeon,' said Tolbain. 'Aargh.'

'What a good idea, Mr. Campbell, please do that.' She led him out of the room and closed the door behind them. 'If you but wait a few minutes, Mr. Campbell. Captain Scott is in charge at Fort William, I think. I'll pen a letter to him on my husband's behalf and reinforce the urgency of my poor husband's injury and the haste required.'

'I'll ensure a pony's saddled at once, Your Grace.'

His footsteps faded down the stairs and the front door slammed as Kirsty returned to Tolbain's bedchamber.

A knock. Drewitt opened the door and bent down to pick up a bowl and jug she'd placed on the floor. Strips of crisp white linen hung over her left arm. 'Mr. Campbell's in a hurry.'

'He's going to fetch an army surgeon.' Fresh blood spurted from Tolbain's wound. 'I'll staunch this.' Kirsty re-tied the twisted linen at the top of his thigh.

'Aargh.' Tolbain groaned.

She bound his head. *So difficult to show him sympathy.*

The Jacobite Affair

Drewitt looked at her out of the corners of her eyes.

Did she think-? No. She fetched me from my room. 'Drewitt, fetch fresh linen for the bed. I would have him comfortable.'

'Your Grace.' Drewitt left.

Kirsty squeezed Tolbain's hand. 'I'll write to Captain Scott for you and implore him to send a surgeon, post haste.'

'You will? Aargh. The estate accounts.'

Kirsty nodded. 'I'll tell Mr. Campbell to consult with me. I'll be back soon.'

'But… argh.'

She took his keys from the bedside table and almost bumped into Drewitt who'd returned with an armful of linen. 'See to him whilst I write to the surgeon.'

'Your Grace.'

Tolbain's moans rolled down the stairs behind Kirsty. She tried three keys before one unlocked the study. A fire burned in the fireplace. This, her first chance to admire the walls lined with Stewart books. She sat in Tolbain's leather chair at his desk, and revelled in her unfettered access to, ink, sand, seal and parchment.

Footsteps in the hall? She stared at the door and held her breath. *Tolbain? But I've every right to be here.* The steps faded. *Where's my brooch?* She lifted ledgers, then parchment on his desk- nothing. Slid open two drawers, nought but papers. Closed them, but the last refused to open. *I can't break the lock, he'd know.* A key lay by his quill. She used it. and it turned. The brooch glinted at her. She put her lips to it and though tempted to take it, put it back. *He must have no suspicions.* She sat back in the chair. *So, this is power.*

A tentative knock sounded on the study door.

'Aye?'

Campbell's worried face peered at her as Tolbain's groans and curses came from upstairs. 'I'm sorry, Your Grace, but time is of the essence.'

Lorna Windham

'Indeed. I've almost finished, Mr. Campbell. Bear with me a moment, please.' She closed the door, sat, bent over the desk and wrote the letter:

Braedrumie House,
Dear Captain Scott,
  I would be most grateful if you would send us your surgeon. My husband, the Duke, has broken his leg in an accident and urgently needs medical help.
  I remain your most esteemed servant,
  She paused, quill in mouth. *How to sign it?* Her pen scratched on the parchment as she wrote *Her Grace, the Duchess of Tolbain.* She read the letter aloud. *That should do.*

She sprinkled sand over the parchment and sealed it. Satisfied with herself, she summoned Campbell from the hall and gave him the letter. 'I'm so sorry it took longer than I thought. Please make all haste. Oh, and Mr. Campbell, until my husband recovers, refer all estate matters to me.'

'Your Grace. And the Stewart rents? The villagers say the redcoats burnt them out and they've nothing, but I've heard different.' He rubbed his hands together. 'There's a rumour they've already paid the money to Euan Stewart.' Screams sounded above their heads. Campbell winced.

Perhaps Drewitt wasn't being as gentle as she should? 'I never listen to rumours, Mr. Campbell. Leave the rents, those poor people have lost enough. If you'll excuse me. I think my dear… husband needs me.'

'Your Grace.' Campbell left and Kirsty watched him through the window as he spurred his pony in the direction of Fort William.

She settled back in Tolbain's chair, put her hands over the lions' heads on the arms and surveyed his study. The day couldn't have been better.

The Jacobite Affair

CHAPTER Seventy-seven

Kirsty lay in her bedchamber and woke in darkness from a dream about Johnnie. He'd been so close, but when her arms reached out to him he disappeared. *I miss him.* She spread her fingers over her womb. *This babe's, not Tolbain's, but Johnnie's, created out of love. Safe.*

Johnnie's been away more than three weeks. Surely he should be home soon? But how will I know? I need to tell him about the bairn. How will we contact each other? Tolbain won't let me out of sight. My pregnancy and new status mean the servants act with the correct amount of subservience, though they're still surly.

A loud pig-like snort made her turn away and Tolbain's arm flopped off her shoulder. His bandaged leg shifted and he grunted with pain. She shuddered and retreated to her side of the bed. *Why did I order Meg away?* He lay flat on his back, his mouth open. Her hand went to her womb again. *The thought it might be his makes me want to vomit. He asks, How do you feel? And I want to reply*: *Stifled. Drewitt walks me down the stairs, I rest every afternoon and eat what he chooses. At night he sucks my breasts, strokes my belly and talks to the babe. When I mentioned the possibility of a daughter, he'd said, I only sire sons. A daughter's no use to me nor will you be if you don't present me with a son. After all I now own the farmhouse and land.*

Kirsty searched Tolbain's character for some vestige of humanity. Perhaps when the scullion burnt his hand on the stock pot and Tolbain pulled the lad on his knee, bellowed for goose fat and applied the grease with gentle fingers. He'd said the boy reminded him of himself when young.

She turned, leant on an elbow and examined the cruel lines of his face. *How I long to suffocate you with your own pillow or kill you with your own dirk.* It glinted on a chair near the bed.

Lorna Windham

***

Late next morning, Kirsty thought the earth had opened up and she'd die. The corridor outside Tolbain's bedchamber had swirled around her and everything turned black. She woke, confused, on the poster bed in her room. Her hand went to her womb. 'Is the bairn alright?'

Drewitt sat beside her. 'Yes, Your Grace. You fainted. It's usual for women in your condition, so they say.'

Kirsty dredged her memory to recall what she'd overheard. She remembered a mud splattered messenger in Tolbain's bedchamber. The door had been open. Tolbain's voice had said, 'Give... Lord... Posenby... my regards... aagh. Curse this leg. Aaag. No. Deserves... a... note. AAAGH. Damn it. Johnnie Stewart's... in Carlisle Castle... and has to be... executed without delay. Aaaagh. Give me that pen... ink... and writing desk. AAAAGH. I'll... write... it... later. AAAAAgh. Get out!'

Kirsty's heart had thudded to a stop. *God help Johnnie.* Drewitt's voice brought her back to the present.

'This room is airless, Your Grace. Why not walk in the garden? You like that.'

Kirsty tried to still the thoughts which seethed in her mind. *Johnnie. What can I do? It's hopeless. Carlisle's so far away.* She breathed in the autumn scents of damp soil and smoky bonfires. Russet and gold leaves littered the ground as Drewitt accompanied her through the orchard. Boughs swayed, heavy with succulent apples.

'Do you feel better, Your Grace?' asked Drewitt.

Not with Johnnie in prison. 'Mmm. I've never thanked you, for the brooch.'

'That's alright, Your Grace. It's done you more good than it did me.' She pointed at her jaw. 'When my man saw this, he never came near me again.'

'I'm sorry.'

The Jacobite Affair

'Don't be. Better off without him, Your Grace.' Drewitt waved away an errant bee.

She's right, we women need steadfast men. Wasps crawled over bruised apples on the ground.

Ahead, a flash of movement by an oak tree made Kirsty pause. A small hand beckoned and she glimpsed a slim ankle. *What woman, in her right senses, would risk capture by Tolbains guards?*

A bough quivered as an apple dropped into Drewitt's hand. 'Fruit's ripe, Your Grace, shall I pick some for cook?'

'Yes, you do that.'

Drewitt gave a crimson apple a twist, let it fall into her palm and stored it in her apron. She stood on tiptoe as her hand went to the next ripe fruit. Kirsty picked up a large, green apple and threw it into the undergrowth to her left.

'What was that?' A guard stepped forward in a crouch, bayonet at the ready.

'Came from over there.' Kirsty pointed to her left.

'Best go back to the house, Your Grace, be on the safe side,' he said.

She watched him lumber off and disappear behind a tangle of overgrown blackberries.

'Silly man, frightened of his own shadow. Drewitt, would you fetch me some water? It's so hot out here. Cook will be so pleased with those apples.'

Drewitt bobbed a curtsey. 'Are you sure, Your Grace?'

'Aye. Who would harm us here? '

Drewitt disappeared down the track behind the trees.

Kirsty rushed to the fence and whispered, 'Who are you and what do you want?'

A young girl, her fair hair in a plait over one shoulder, stepped out from behind a tree and thrust a note into Kirsty's hand.

'What's this?'

The girl motioned her to open it.

'Cat got your tongue?' Kirsty watched a pink hue cover the girl's face.

Kirsty frowned as she opened the parchment and read.

Johnnie Stewart's been arrested and is in Carlisle Castle. You're the only one who might be able to help as you care for him.

Please send a letter testifying to Johnnie's good character and ask for clemency as we're feared for his life.

Alais

Kirsty's brain raced. *And you must be Alais, the girl Johnnie rescued from the redcoats. How he must loathe imprisonment and long to escape. There'll be a trial, surely? But he'll be convicted. I'll never see him again. Alais is thin, drawn and there's dark shadows under her eyes. And I thought this, silent lassie, a rival. Yet there's beauty in her high cheekbones and heart-shaped face. And her eyes have a strange, luminous quality and change from a light brown to gold with the light.*

A *letter pleading for clemency? Tolbain will never allow it. And even if he did, no one in authority would take much notice of me, a mere woman.*

'Did you pen this?' asked Kirsty.

Alais dipped her head. Her eyes begged Kirsty to answer in a positive fashion. *What had Johnnie said? Redcoats killed her family and she couldn't speak. Poor lassie.*

Kirsty folded the note and gave it back. 'I'll do what I can.' *But how? Her mind whirled.*

A smile lit up Alais' face.

An idea came to Kirsty. *Perhaps I can help.* 'I'll need money for a bribe. About £50 should be enough.'

Alais' eyes opened wider and she shrugged.

'Did Euan send you?' asked Kirsty,

The girl shook her head and patted her breast with one hand.

She loves him. Johnnie. Why else would she do this?

The thrash of undergrowth and the sound of footsteps in the orchard, reminded Kirsty of the dangers. She pushed Alais towards the shelter of the treeline. 'Go.' *What did Alais mean, you care for him? How does she know?*

The Jacobite Affair

The guard grumbled as he returned to his position and Drewitt arrived full of the new cook's praises. 'There's to be apple pie for dinner tonight. Here's your water, Your Grace.'

As she sipped the cold liquid Kirsty went over her idea. *So simple. Strange to think this girl, this Alais instigated it. But I can't do it without the bribe. Pity I gave Tolbain's pouch to Meg.*

***

The following day, Kirsty paced the sitting room, her eyes heavy with lack of sleep. Three questions circled in her head. *Has Tolbain written Posenby's note? How can I stop it being delivered? Will the Stewarts get the bribe to me in time?*

Dunbar entered. 'Sorry to bother you, Your Grace, but cook says there's a woman, Morag, at the back door, said you'd know her. She's selling a salmon. Cook offered to buy it, but the woman said she wanted a better price and demanded to see you. Shall I call His Grace?'

Kirsty's heart raced. 'No. No. I'll deal with her.'

***

Guards stood either side of Morag as she curtsied. 'I've a salmon to sell, are you interested, **Your Grace**?' She raised her eyes which sparked flint at Kirsty.

'It's good to see you again.' Kirsty turned to the men. 'She's an old friend, you can leave us.' She watched the guards' backs as they returned to their posts.

'We're no friends, Kirsty Lorne,' spat Morag. 'I haven't forgotten the foul gossip you told Euan.'

'Are you mad? Keep your voice down,' hissed Kirsty. 'I'm you're only hope of saving Johnnie, remember? As to the salmon, let me examine it where there's more light and no one can overhear.' *She'll never understand.*

Morag made a face at her, took the fish out of her basket and handed it to Kirsty.

370

'Walk with me, beyond those shrubs.' Kirsty stopped and lifted the salmon to inspect it. The silvery scales glinted in the morning light. She raised her voice. 'A fine specimen. You're right. It's worth more money. Cook will pay what you've asked.'

'Thank you, Your Grace.' Morag's eyes scanned the trees before she handed a leather bag to Kirsty.

'I'll do what I can,' whispered Kirsty. 'Tell Euan I'm sorry…'

'Sorry?' Morag's face filled with venom. 'You're a Whig and we regret the day Johnnie met you. Bet you havena even thought about your Aunty Mary and her bairns? With Hughie dead, they're starving and she's just had the babe.'

Kirsty took a step back. *Oh, God. So much had happened. I should have visited more often.* Guilt swept over her. Words wouldn't come.

'If you ever cared a fig for Johnnie…' Morag stabbed a finger at Kirsty's breast. '…do what we want and write the letter that might just save him.'

Kirsty steadied herself. *Morag will never understand about Johnnie and me. And the Stewarts neither forget nor forgive.* She raised her shoulders and her voice. 'Please tell cook I've agreed the price you asked. I bid you good day.' Kirsty concealed the pouch in her pocket and strode away. *Johnnie has so little time.*

The Jacobite Affair

CHAPTER Seventy-eight

Kirsty sped into the house. *I'll show Morag McColl.* She collected Mrs. Mills on her way to Tolbain's bedchamber. 'Tell cook I want food sent every day to my aunt, Mary McBean in Braedrumie. She's three bairns and a baby. Make sure there's milk. Oh, and send warm clothing.'

The housekeeper's brow wrinkled. 'I heard the Stewards send provisions. Is this His Grace's orders?'

'No, mine and as he is seriously ill, I suggest you do as I say.' *Had Morag lied?*

'-Your Grace.' Mrs. Mills turned towards the scullery.

Kirsty raced to Tolbain's bedchamber and closed the door behind her. He lay eyes closed as his chest rose and fell. *Asleep.* The empty glass of potion the surgeon had left, beside him. *Where's that note to Posenby?* She lifted his pillow. *Nothing.* Checked the bedside table. *Nothing.* Lifted leaves of parchment. *Nothing.* Then looked under a small bronze statue of Apollo. *Sealed parchment scrawled in his shaky hand. The address: Lord B. Posenby, Posenby Hall, Cumberland, England. Yes.* She slid it into her pocket. *Now, the study.*

Campbell bumped into her in the hall.

Drat.

He gave a deep bow. 'Begging your pardon, Your Grace, but His Grace mentioned an urgent note for me to post?'

Oh, God. 'Thank you, Mr. Campbell, I'll look for it. Give me a few moments.'

'Your Grace.' The tacksman bowed as she sped into the study and closed the door.

Her fingers trembled as they broke Tolbain's seal and unfolded the parchment.

Braedrumie House.
September 1746
  My dear Posenby,
  I hope you and your family are in good health?

I write because Johnnie Stewart is incarcerated in Carlisle Castle and about to be tried by you. I know the man as a foul traitor, cattle thief and rabble rouser.

I would be grateful if you would ensure he experiences the full weight of the law.

Your servant,

Tolbain.

Viper. How could he do this to Johnnie? Another day and these lies would have been on their way south. She screwed up the parchment and threw it in the fire. It twisted and turned, but wouldn't burn. She rescued it with the poker and stuffed it in her pocket. *I'll bury it.* She dipped a quill in the black ink. A tremor ran through her hand and ink spluttered over the page before her. She screwed it up. *Calm.* She took a deep breath and wrote:

Braedrumie House,
September 1746

My dear Posenby,

I hope you are and your family are in good health?

It has come to our knowledge that Mr. Johnnie Stewart of Braedrumie is a prisoner of His Majesty's Government in Carlisle Castle and about to be tried by you.

He is but twenty years of age and is known to me as a gentleman of honour, substance and standing.

Despite his previous good character, he was pressed to join the rebels by his father, so that his brother of fourteen years stayed at home. I would therefore ask you, as a token of your regard for me, to show clemency.

I will, of course, be deeply indebted to you.

Your esteemed servant,

Tolbain

She dusted the letter, stamped Tolbain's seal on it and took Morag's leather bag of coins from her pocket. *Campbell can*

The Jacobite Affair

deliver the note. I'll ask Murdo to take the coins to Lord Posenby. I just hope the ruse works and the bribe's enough.

CHAPTER Seventy-nine

Fingers of snow covered the mountains and the air had a cold bite as Kirsty walked up to Braedrumie's churchyard. *Is it really a month since I heard about Johnnie's capture? Dear God, look after him and keep him safe.* She'd buried Tolbain's malicious note at *Our Place* and prayed her version and the bribe would reach Posenby in time.

Tolbain remained in bed with a high fever.

'His leg will mend.' The bone-setter declared.

More's the pity.

'But he'll always have a limp.'

The wind moaned and played with the multi-coloured carpet of leaves. The church sat like a sentry amongst the graves. Kirsty stood in front of Mother's headstone, the piled earth a reminder of her miserable burial. *Better out of this world.*

Her father's overgrown grave lay a distance away. She thought back to the day when he'd gambled her away. *Nothing will make me do that to my bairn.* She spread her fingers over the rise of her womb. She turned and walked by lines of tilted headstones. Then bolted the churchyard gate behind her and strolled past fields of Tolbain's cattle. *Fine beasts. Pity about our cattle.* She took a breath and paused. *It can't be. A bull trundled by with the Lorne's double L brand on its rump. How? - Did Tolbain thieve them to beggar us, so he got our farm and land? And what about when he called his men away? I shot one of them. Didn't Angus favour his arm at the handfasting? -My God, Tolbain has played us for a couple of fools. Viper.*

A breeze swept across the pasture and lifted Kirsty's cloak like a cloud around her. A feather-like touch on her shoulder made her jump.

Waif-like Alais stood behind her.

'What do you want?'

Alais' fingers moved at speed.

'I dinna understand.'

The Jacobite Affair

Alais' forehead creased and showed Kirsty a note with the words: *Johnnies's safe, he's been transported.*

Kirsty stared at her open- mouthed. 'You're sure?' Relief flooded over her in waves. *Thank God.*

Alais nodded.

Kirsty grasped Alais' hands. 'Where to, where's he been transported?' *Johnnie's alive.* Alais signed.

Kirsty couldn't make it out. 'Africa?'

Alais shook her head.

'The West Indies? *No. Where have they sent him?* 'The Americas?'

Alais' eyes sparkled.

'Yes? The Americas. So far away.' Kirsty's heart sank. *We'll never see each other again, he'll never know about his bairn.*

'Did Morag send you?'

Alais shook her head and mouthed, *Thank you.* With a sweet smile she turned back the way she'd come.

Kirsty watched Alais' slight figure walk away. *What is Alais to Johnnie? She obviously cares for him. And Johnnie cares about her and those two bairns. But what about our child? Johnnie's and mine?* Kirsty's forehead creased. *What if he believes Tolbain's the father?*

***

Kirsty fed Tolbain beef broth and washed and dressed his wound. Hard, when she thought of his deception, but whilst he lived, she needed to show she cared. She ignored the servants who grew quiet when she approached and whispered as she left.

Tolbain said something rolled under his feet. The mop? On the cellar steps? Odd. If he ever discovers I've written to Posenby, God knows what he'll do. I could have been Johnnie's wife. We'd have been so happy. Now, he's being taken to a strange land. Despair seeped into her bones. *I want to kill Tolbain, but there can't be any more accidents and what if the bairn's a daughter? Dear God, let it be a son, for both our sakes.*

The Jacobite Affair

CHAPTER Eighty
1746

In mid-October Tolbain tried to get up and fell.

'You've put back your recovery several weeks, Your Grace,' the bald-headed surgeon told him. 'You must rest and let your good wife cosset you.'

Tolbain growled, 'I would, if I'd a good wife. We're handfasted. I raised her up and can pull her down. But now she's in pup... and I only breed sons.'

The surgeon pressed his thick lips together.

Kirsty blanched. She led the surgeon from the room.

He gave her a wry grin. 'A pity illness doesna improve His Grace's temper.'

Kirsty gave him a rueful smile. 'I'm afraid my husband has never been the most mild-tempered, but of course the pain makes it worse. Have you anything that might help?'

'I'll prepare a tincture of poppy. It's strong, so only give him a few drops when the pain is unbearable.'

Whose pain? Only a few drops. Should I give him more?

***

By December Tolbain took back the reins of his estates. He summoned Kirsty to his bedchamber. 'You look as plump as a peach. My heir grows apace, I see. Drewitt, make sure she rests, and sort this out behind me.' He gestured to his pillows.

He leant forward as Drewitt pounded them into submission.

He turned to Kirsty. 'I see you sent my note to Posenby.'

She tensed. 'Of course, you ordered it, didn't you?'

He smirked. 'Checked with Campbell. Says you told him not to collect the rents. 'Tis hoped you've not bankrupted me.'

'I'm a woman, I've no head for business.'

'And yet the household accounts are in order?'

She looked at him from below lowered lashes. 'Just. Your estates need a man's acumen.'

378

Lorna Windham

'Quite so. My tenants will soon find I'm in the saddle again. Campbell tells me Johnnie Stewart's been transported.' Tolbain gave her a speculative look.

She held her breath and then released it. 'Has he?'

'Posenby was ever weak-livered.' He pounded a clenched fist in his palm. 'Johnnie Stewart's as good as dead.'

The Jacobite Affair

CHAPTER Eighty-one
1747

Kirsty stood at the sitting room window of Braedrumie House. March hares gambolled on the lawn and a breeze rippled over the moors as the sun played with light and shade on the mountains beyond. Closer, in the glen, she could make out the ruins of Braedrumie village.

Her womb made it more difficult to see her feet as each week passed. In fact her shoes pinched as her flesh hung over the tops. *I must rest or I'll have boats, not feet.*

She lay on the settee as a knock sounded on the door.

'It's good you're havin' a rest. I've just the thing, Your Grace.' Drewitt took a mauve plaid from a chair and covered Kirsty with it. She lowered her voice. 'They say Prince Charlie left Scotland some weeks ago.'

All those Jacobite dead and the suffering, all for the dreams of one man. Madness. Johnnie should have gone to university; Duncan should have grown into a fine young man and the Stewarts should be living in Braedrumie House.

She glanced up as Tolbain limped into the room with the aid of a silver-mounted walking stick. 'I need to go over our accounts for my heir.' He patted Kirsty's rounded womb and turned away from him. 'I don't wish to be disturbed.' He left her.

She heard the key turn in the study's lock as inky clouds gathered outside and the sky darkened.

Some hours later, when raindrops beat against the window, Mr. Campbell arrived and Dunbar ushered him into the sitting room.

'Good afternoon, Your Grace. I've news for His Grace.'

Kirsty said, 'Will you no' have a whisky, Mr. Campbell? It's a dreich day.'

'My thanks, Your Grace, but I really need to see...'

'He's in his study, Mr. Campbell, and gave orders not to be disturbed. Your news must be important.'

Lorna Windham

'It is, I've heard those damn Stewarts are in an inn on the north side of the loch. If we're quick, we'll catch them. There's a fine reward.'

A chill raced through Kirsty, but she managed to appear calm. 'You're right, His Grace will want to know at once.'

She rose with an effort. The babe low and heavy now. She took Campbell to the study door, then mounted the stairs. *Would Drewitt help? She wouldn't before.* Kirsty found her in the sewing room. She beckoned the maid into her bedchamber, then closed the door. 'You're loyal to me are you no'?'

'Your Grace.' Drewitt curtsied.

'This is very important. I need your help. Can you warn Euan Stewart that His Grace knows where the Stewarts will be tonight?'

Drewitt stared at her, seemed as if she would say something and then her gaze shifted to her feet. 'I canna, Your Grace, the duke would kill me if he found out.'

'But you must.' Kirsty's hand went to her clenched womb and a dull ache radiated from her back.

'Are you alright, Your Grace?'

'I... I think it's the babe.' As Drewitt helped Kirsty upstairs, doors slammed below, Tolbain shouted, horses neighed and then hooves pounded away into the distance. 'Is it my husband? Has he left?' Kirsty sank on to her bed.

Drewitt looked out of the window. 'Yes, Your Grace.'

Pity he can ride.

'Shall I send for Granny Mac?'

'She's too old and His Grace willna have her in the house. He's made arrangements for Goody Grant to attend me and please, you must get a message to Euan Stewart.'

'Let's see to you first, Your Grace.'

Kirsty's womb cramped, went taut and pain's fingers stretched round her back. *Let it be a son. Johnnie's son.* She clutched at Drewitt's hands. 'It's important my message gets to Euan Stewart.'

The Jacobite Affair

***

As night fell, Kirsty, drenched in sweat, her womb on fire, her back as if broken, shrieked like a banshee as she pushed. Her babe slipped out between her thighs in a bloody rush of amniotic fluid.

'It's a wee boy.' Goody Grant's voice sounded calm and authoritative.

Thank God. Kirsty brushed a tired hand over her forehead.

'Here, Your Grace,' said Drewitt and offered Kirsty a drink of ale.

Goody pursed her thin lips and put a hand on her lower back. 'I'm sure His Grace, like all good fathers will dote on him and you. Your first bairn and a son. Didn't you do well, givin' him an heir?' She cut the cord and swaddled the babe in fine linen. 'Here.' She bundled up the afterbirth and some bloody rags. 'Burn these.'

Drewitt took them away and left the two women alone.

'Let me hold him.' Kirsty put out her hands. She marvelled at her son's scrunched-up face, the length of his body and his fingers which curled around her thumb. *I'm safe from Tolbain now, unless he takes the boy and throws me out.* She pushed the thought to one side and whispered into her babe's crumpled ear, 'Johnnie would love you so.'

'Did you say somethin', Your Grace?' Goody washed her hands in a china bowl.

'Just that his father will love him.' *Oh, Johnnie, why aren't you here?*

'He's a fine wee boy, a six footer if I've ever seen one. That's it, put him to your breast, let him suck. He'll sleep and so will you.' She wrung out a cloth and wiped Kirsty's face. 'You'll be a good mother.'

'Will I?' Kirsty clutched the woman's wrist. *Or will I be like Mother? Unloving, unkind.*

'Course.' Goody removed Kirsty's hand. 'You're no' worried about that. I saw it in you, when you held him. He's asleep. Let me put him in his fine cradle. There. Your bairn's

Lorna Windham

done a lot of work and he's tired. Let's get you clean and tidy ready for His Grace's return. He's got a lovely surprise waitin' for him.'

Kirsty's stomach churned. *I don't want that monster near my bairn.*

Goody Grant hummed as she washed Kirsty, slipped a clean nightdress over her head and brushed her hair. 'And have you a name for the wee mite?'

'I canna think.'

'You're tired. Best rest. Plenty of time to name your wee laddie.'

'There's payment for you.' Kirsty waved a hand at some coins on the bedside table.

'Thank you, Your Grace. Do you need ought else before I go?'

'No. Tell one of the grooms I said he should see you safe home and thank you. Thank you for my son.'

Goody Grant's lips creased into a smile. 'That's kind of you, Your Grace. You sleep, best for both of you.' She nodded towards the baby's pink-flushed cheeks and outstretched hands.

Drewitt tapped on the door and entered.

'I've left a sleepin' draught for your mistress.' Goody waved a hand at a glass of cloudy liquid on the bedside table. 'Make sure she takes it.'

Drewitt nodded as Goody gathered her belongings inside her blue plaid and tied the ends together.

'Thank you.' Kirsty gave Goody a grateful smile.

Goody dipped her head. 'Good night, Your Grace.' The door closed behind her.

Cold air slithered round Kirsty's shoulders. 'Make sure the Bairn's warm, Drewitt. The house seems silent. Did you warn the Stewarts?'

'Aye.'

'That's good.'

'Your sleeping draught, Your Grace. Drink up.' Drewitt raised the glass to Kirsty's lips and ensured she finished it all.

The Jacobite Affair

'Tastes horrible.' Kirsty let her head rest on the pillow. 'Tell the servants they can see the bairn tomorrow.'

'The servants have left, Your Grace.'

'Left?' Kirsty jerked upright. 'What, all of them?'

'Aye. And I have to leave too.'

Kirsty fought to keep her eyelids open. 'But, why?'

'You'll find out soon enough. You know it was me, don't you? Left the mop on the stairs. Payback for this.' She touched her jaw. 'I prayed I'd watch the devil die in agony, but it didna do any good.'

'But… everyone…. thinks… it… was… me.' Kirsty's tongue seemed thick from the draught.

'I'm sorry about that, but I stayed to see you through the birth. I hope Tolbain never finds out whose bairn it is.'

Drewitt's face faded as Kirsty's eyes closed. She dreamt of Johnnie, the derelict croft, of making love and their bairn. She woke as a hand clamped over her mouth and terror seized her brain.

***

Hours later Kirsty sat with icy limbs and shivered in the Stewart's den. She clutched Johnnie's brooch, grateful Euan had allowed her to retrieve it from Tolbain's desk. She cuddled her son to her breast beneath several plaids. *I should be grateful the Stewarts let us live.* She searched the baby's face for some sign of Tolbain's brutal features. Innocence stared back at her. Milky-blue eyes, a snub nose and rosebud lips gave nothing away.

What's that? She jerked upright as a huge explosion sounded from the direction of Braedrumie House. The baby screwed up his face and screamed.

'Hush. Hush.' She rocked the baby. 'Close your eyes, little one. I'll see no' harm comes to you. Hush.' He closed his eyes. She got up. The den's entrance swayed in front of her. *I won't faint.* She held her son close and walked to the cave's mouth, past the dark outlines of rocks and undergrowth until she faced north towards Braedrumie. In the black distance below her, a crimson sky lit up the land, smoke plumed and flames danced. Realisation came like a sleep walker. *Johnnie was right, the Stewarts couldn't tolerate Tolbain in their house.*

The Jacobite Affair

CHAPTER Eighty- two
1750

Dark clouds gathered outside the window of Lorne House. Kirsty sat in the sitting room surrounded by trunks full of clothes.

'Mother, look at me.'

Her three year old son, waved a wooden sword at her. He sat astride a chair as if he rode a horse.

'Be careful, little man.' *Don't mollycoddle him even though he's so precious and had one illness after another.* She gazed at his healthy features and sturdy body. *He needs to know his father and I need to find him. It's as if the earth has swallowed him. Johnnie, where are you?*

She tried not to think of Tolbain. At first some said he'd fallen in a loch or bog and couldn't get out, others that he'd been murdered. The redcoats had found his body some months later, could have been anyone, except for the fine clothes. She thought she'd recognised the remnants.

A wealthy widow, she didn't stint on her son, now heir to the Duke of Tolbain's estates, and dressed him in silks and velvets. She could have lived in Toll House or had Braedrumie House rebuilt, but the two buildings held too many bad memories for her.

No one lived in Braedrumie. When the Stewarts left, the glen had remained deserted except for ghosts and the odd redcoat patrol.

Kirsty had built a fine house close to *Our Place* and hired new servants. She sensed Johnnie's presence in the fields they'd walked together and often took her son to the Lorne's farmhouse which she rented out to a young family.

Johnnie's situation gnawed at her. He could be anywhere in the Americas and in a desperate state. She'd written to the Munro's in Inverness and to Johnnie's Uncle John in Port Glasgow about Johnnie's whereabouts. A formal, though noncommittal reply arrived from the former and nothing from the latter. She spread her net wider and wrote to ship's captains who sailed to the Americas and offered a reward for information.

She'd received a water-stained letter from a Captain Blandford.

Blandford House,
Wilmington,
North Carolina
1750

To the Duchess of Tolbain,

Madam, a friend of mine, Captain Freeman, says you are searching for a Jacobite prisoner called Johnnie Stewart. Such a man, sailed with me from Newgate and the Thames to Wilmington in the Americas aboard the Revenge.

Stewart was sold with others aboard ship and taken to the local slave market. That is all I know. I must warn you the prisoner might not be your Johnnie Stewart and he may have been sold-on several times.

Please send my reward to the address above,

Your esteemed servant,

Captain Blandford

The thought of proud, clever Johnnie as someone's slave sent her into despair. Months later, a second captain, Watson, wrote and professed to have seen a Johnnie Stewart, similar to her description, sold at the same slave market to a plantation owner, but didn't know any more. *Poor Johnnie.*

Kirsty sent the captains their rewards and wrote to several more as well as merchants and plantation owners. She'd received no reply. Frustration welled up inside her. *If Duncan's health had been better I'd have gone to the Americas long before this.*

An idea leapt into her head and grew. *I won't wait for news. My son's been well for some months. I'll take him to the Americas, search for Johnnie myself and buy his freedom. Please God he's well and alive.*

The Jacobite Affair

Her heart lightened after years of inaction, though difficult questions leapt into her brain. *Will Johnnie recognise me and accept the boy as his? What if he's forgotten me? Married Alais? Had bairns of his own? I'll drive myself mad if I don't calm down. What if he's dead?*

A light tap sounded on the sitting room door.

'Come in.'

'Your Grace, there's a merchant, at the door, a Mr. Dalhousie.' Her butler, Jameson, pulled in his paunch and dabbed his nose with a handkerchief.

'Did he say what he wanted?'

'Said he'd a letter he must deliver into your hands.'

'Show Mr. Dalhousie in and bring some refreshment.'

'Your Grace.'

'And Jameson…'

'Your Grace?'

'Get cook to give you some whisky for that cold.'

'Your Grace. Thank you, Your Grace.' He bowed himself out.

Her son scrambled down from the toy horse as if to run after the butler. Kirsty scooped him up and kissed his cheek.

'Pretty.' He stroked her luckenbooth brooch.

'Mr. Dalhousie, Your Grace,' boomed Jameson.

A tall, broad-shouldered man stood in the doorway, hat in hand. His face tanned, nose broken and he'd a jagged scar from his left eyebrow to his chin.

Jameson left and shut the door behind him. The little boy put out his hands as he played with a shaft of light from the window.

'Kirsty?'

A tremor ran through her. *I know that voice. Know this man. It can't be.*

'Down,' commanded her son.

She lowered him to the floor, then couldn't make her limbs move.

Lorna Windham

'I know it's been a long time. I understand if you've a new life, but I needed to see you again. So you knew I hadn't forgotten, I'd never forget.'

'Oh, God, Johnnie it is you.' She ran to him and held his face in her hands. Her eyes took in the scar and her heart twisted for him. *What he must have suffered.* 'Where have you been?'

'Euan found me working as an indentured servant on a farm in North Carolina. Looked for me for over two years. Anyway, he bought me, brought me back to health and that's how I'm here.'

'As Mr. Dalhousie.'

'Aye. I dinna think the authorities will be too happy.'

'And Alais Murray?'

'Why do you ask?'

'She loved you.'

'I promised I'd always look after her and the bairns, a matter of honour, you ken? She accepts that.'

'Oh, Johnnie, you and your generous heart.'

'And Jamie Moffat's got his eye on her. -You're wearing my brooch.' His arms went round her waist.

'Every day.' She let him draw her to him.

'It's you I love.' His lips ravished hers as she clung to him. 'My own one, you look how I saw you in my dreams. Euan told me about your mother. I'm sorry for your loss, though I ken she never liked me. And Tolbain, I'll no' waste words on that devil. I've money from the Stewart's ships and I've such plans. I must tell you about the Americas. The land's fertile with mountains and rivers and lochs, lakes they call them. Will you, can you leave all this and come to the Americas with me as my wife?'

Her heart raced. 'I sent letters, searched for you. Please believe me, I never gave up.'

'Darling, I missed you so.' She leant her head against his chest and heard the steady beat of his heart.

'Mama, crying.' Her son pulled at her skirt. She lifted him.

'Your son.' A shadow crossed Johnnie's face. 'Euan mentioned him.'

'**Our** son.' Kirsty squeezed Johnnie's hand. 'Duncan, this is your daddy.'

Johnnie started and his head went up.

She put the boy in Johnnie's arms.

Duncan stared at Johnnie and Johnnie stared at the little boy with bracken hair and grey eyes.

'Daddy.' Duncan explored Johnnie's face with his fingers.

Johnnie's mouth opened, shut, then opened again. 'I have something you might like.' He put a carved wooden salmon in Duncan's palm. The little boy examined it, then wrapped his chubby arms round Johnnie's neck. A single tear glistened and ran down Johnnie's cheek.

The End.

Lorna Windham

The Jacobite Affair

Bibliography

Allison, Hugh (2007). Culloden Tales, Edinburgh and London, Mainstream Publishing.

Ashley, Mike (2002). British Kings, London, Robinson.

Craig, Maggie (1997). Damn' Rebel Bitches, Edinburgh, Mainstream Publishing.

Devine, T.M. (2004). Scotland's Empire 1600-1815, London, Penguin Books Ltd.

Donaldson, James (1697). James Donaldson's Husbandry anatomized, overture for establishing a society to improve the kingdom 1698.

Duffy, Christopher (2003). The '45, Bonnie Prince Charlie and the Untold Story of the Jacobite Rising, London, Cassell.

Forbes, Robert (1747-1775). The Lyon in Mourning edited by Henry Paton, (1895). Scottish History Society.

Herman, Arthur (2001). The Scottish Enlightenment, The Scot's Invention of the Modern World, London, Fourth Estate a Division of Harper Collins Publishers.

Hunter, James (2001). Culloden and the Last Clansman, Edinburgh, Mainstream Publishing Company Ltd.

Lanman, Bruce (1980). The Jacobite Risings in Britain 1689-1746, Edinburgh, Scottish Cultural Press.

Magnusson, Magnus (2001). The Story of a Nation, Edinburgh and London, Scotland, Harper Collins.

Maxwell, Robert (1743). Secret transactions of the Honourable the Society of Improvers.

Millot, Michel (1680)The School of Venus, or the Ladies Delight, Reduced into Rules of Practice.

Tull, Jethro (1733). Horse-hoeing husbandry in 1733.

Printed in Dunstable, United Kingdom

66046482R00231